F. Coineau

***Chesapeake Shores
†The Rose Cottage Sisters

SHERRYL WOODS

Moonlight Cove

**Doubleday Large Print
Home Library Edition**

MIRA®

ISBN 978-1-61129-584-9

resemblance to actual persons, living or dead, business establishments, events or locales is entirely coincidental.

Dear Friends,

Ever since Jess O'Brien first appeared in *The Inn at Eagle Point,* you've been asking me to tell the story of this complicated woman. Here it is at last in *Moonlight Cove.*

As a woman who has struggled since early childhood against the feelings of abandonment caused when her mother, Megan, walked out on the family, as well as with her long-undiagnosed attention deficit disorder, Jess has had a tough time getting her life together. Now, at long last, she has a career she loves as the owner of the Inn at Eagle Point, but so far love has eluded her.

No longer. Will Lincoln has been in love with Jess most of their lives. As a psychologist, he understands her flaws better than most and loves her unconditionally despite them. But it's the fact that he understands her so well that scares Jess. She fears he views her only as some sort of psychological case study.

It's going to take a lot for Will to convince Jess that he's the man of her dreams, and on a romantic night at Moonlight Cove, he finally does just that. I hope the moment will make you sigh, just as it took Jess's breath away.

And next month, I hope you'll be eagerly awaiting Susie and Mack's story in *Beach Lane.* This romance has been a very long time coming, but I think this touching story of the healing power of love is well worth the wait. I hope you'll agree.

All the best,

Sherryl

1

"We have an idea," Laila Riley announced when she and Connie Collins turned up in Jess O'Brien's office at The Inn at Eagle Point on a Saturday night.

There was a twinkle in her eye that immediately made Jess nervous about what her friends had in mind. "Is it going to get us arrested?" she inquired suspiciously. Not that she was unwilling to take the risk, but she would like to know about the possibility in advance, calculate the odds and have a backup plan.

Laila grinned. "If there were anyone interesting working for the sheriff's department, we'd consider it, but no. This is just doing something outside the box, something none of us would ever consider unless we all decided to do it together."

"Do I dare ask?" Jess wondered.

"Online dating," Connie revealed. The lack of enthusiasm in her voice suggested that this had been Laila's idea and that Connie had only agreed because of the same boredom that had been affecting Jess's mood recently.

Jess, however, wasn't quite that desperate. "You can't be serious."

"Oh, but we are," Laila confirmed.

Jess studied the two women who'd invaded her office on a night of the week when most attractive, intelligent women should have been out on dates. Connie and Laila were related to her indirectly by the marriages of their siblings to hers. They were friends by choice despite the differences in their ages.

Connie was the forty-one-year-old single mother of a teen who'd recently left for college. Her younger brother, Jake, was married to Jess's sister, Bree. Laila was the thirty-six-year-old manager of the local bank and younger sister of Trace, who was married to Abby, Jess's oldest sister. Jess, at thirty, was the youngest. At times it seemed as if everyone in Chesapeake Shores was related to an O'Brien one way or another.

"Okay, now, let's think about this," Laila said, making herself at home by pouring a glass of tea from the ever-present pitcher on Jess's desk. "What are you doing tonight? I mean, seriously, here you are in your office when you should be out on the town, right?"

Jess glanced at the ever-present mound of paperwork on her desk. It was the worst part of her job. She was beginning to see Laila's point.

"And does that make one bit of sense to you?" Laila pressed. "What is wrong with the men in this town that the three of us are alone on a Saturday night? We obviously need to broaden our horizons. Put ourselves out there. Stir things up."

"And find some geographically unsuitable men who'll never be around?" Jess replied. "Seems counterproductive to me."

"I thought the same thing at first," Connie said, beckoning for her own glass of tea. Laila poured it and handed it to her. "But the sad truth is that boredom has made me more open-minded. For the longest time I couldn't wait until my daughter was grown and off to college, but now that Jenny's actually gone, the house feels so empty I can hardly stand it."

"And I've been mind-numbingly bored ever since Dave and I broke up three years ago, which is saying something, since dating him was about as stimulating as watching grass grow," Laila said. She sat up straighter. "Online dating is the perfect way to change the status quo. It's trendy. It'll be fun."

Jess remained unconvinced. She turned to Connie, who was known for being sensible. "Are you really in favor of this?"

Connie shrugged. "I can see some advantages."

"Geographically undesirable," Jess repeated with emphasis.

"Not a problem," Laila insisted. "It's a new local service. These men are all right around here."

Jess couldn't quite wrap her mind around either the idea or the fact that Connie was willing, if not eager, to try online dating. Looking her in the eye, Jess began, "But I thought . . ." Her voice trailed off. She wasn't supposed to know that sparks had been flying between Connie and Jess's uncle, Thomas O'Brien. Her brothers Connor and Kevin both had sworn her to secrecy. She sighed. "Never mind."

Connie studied her with suspicion, but since it was a kettle of fish she clearly didn't want to dive into, she remained silent.

Laila, seemingly unaware of the under-currents, jumped back in. "It's perfect, don't you think?" she asked excitedly.

"Are there any single men around here we don't already know?" Jess asked, still skeptical. "Isn't that precisely why we're sitting here on a weekend without dates?"

"The region does extend beyond the town limits," Connie conceded.

"It includes Annapolis," Laila explained, pulling a brochure from her pocket and handing it to Jess. "See, Lunch by the Bay. Doesn't that sound lovely? And that's all we'd be committing to, an occasional lunch with someone new. It has to beat waiting around to be noticed in the bar at Brady's. If I spend any more time in there, Dillon's threatened to name a barstool after me."

"At least you'd have a lasting legacy of your life in Chesapeake Shores," Jess teased. "Much better than having your picture on the wall of that stodgy old bank your family owns and that you're so attached to."

"Make fun of me all you want, but I really think we should do this," Laila insisted. "We're intelligent, attractive women. We deserve to spend time with exciting, successful men who aren't related to us."

"And I for one am tired of the Saturday night pity dinners at Jake and Bree's," Connie added with a shudder. "Ever since Jenny left, they expect me to come there and coo over the new baby. She's a cutie, but that is not how I see myself spending Saturday nights for the next who-knows-how-many years."

"I've had my share of those dinners," Jess agreed, "but at least I get passed off from Bree to Abby to Kevin and now even Connor."

"I don't even get the pity dinners," Laila said. "Trace and Abby just count on me to babysit the twins. If I'm not married soon, they'll probably move me in and make me a full-time nanny."

"You have a career," Jess reminded her. "I'm pretty sure you can maintain an independent lifestyle."

"Independence sucks," Laila declared.

"Amen," Connie added. "Not that I want some man controlling what I do with my life," she said emphatically, "but it would be nice to cuddle with someone in front of the fire at night."

"Say what you really mean," Jess said. "You want sex."

Connie sighed. "Don't we all?"

"So, are we going to do this?" Laila asked, tapping the brochure.

Though she was hardly known for her caution, Jess couldn't seem to keep herself from asking, "But what do we know about this company?"

"Only what it says in the brochure," Laila replied, glancing at the back page. "It promises discreet matches, handled by a psychologist who's been working with single clients for years. He's developed criteria for making sure that people have the same goals and values." She set down the brochure and regarded them earnestly. "Come on, you guys. What do we have to lose? If the dates are awful, we can laugh about them later over drinks at Brady's."

"I'm in," Connie said at once. "Jess?"

Jess glanced at the paperwork on her

desk. It wasn't going anywhere. "What the heck! I'm in."

She turned and flipped on her computer, checked the link to the company's website and found it. "Nice design," she said approvingly.

"See, it looks perfectly respectable," Connie noted.

"And I love the picture," Laila said. "I'm pretty sure it was taken right on Shore Road. See, there's the town fishing pier off to the left."

"Aren't you worried that we could wind up being paired off with someone we already know, even someone we used to date?" Jess asked. "That could be humiliating."

"Or it could make us take another look at him," Connie responded, her expression thoughtful. "After all, if an expert thought we'd be a match, maybe we were selling the other person short."

"Or maybe the expert isn't all that smart," Jess countered.

Still, when the form for signing up appeared on the screen, she was the first one to fill it out. She considered the temptation to fake her replies just to see what might happen, but Connie and Laila forestalled her.

"You have to take this seriously," Connie scolded.

"We're expecting a computer and some so-called expert to do what we haven't been able to do on our own," Jess replied. "And you want me to take it seriously?"

"*I* do," Connie said. "Because this could be my last chance."

"It is not going to be your last chance," Laila said fiercely. "If you're going to look at it like that, Connie, then maybe you shouldn't do it. Desperation is never smart when it comes to meeting men. We're doing this for laughs and a few free lunches, that's it. We need to keep our expectations low and just concentrate on having fun."

Jess nodded. Connie didn't look entirely convinced, but when Jess's form was complete, Connie immediately nudged her aside and took her place in front of the computer. Laila followed.

When the last form had been sent in, they exchanged a look.

"I need a drink," Jess said.

"I'm in," Laila said.

Connie nodded agreement. "I think I'd better make mine a double."

* * *

One of the few things that hadn't changed since Jake had married Bree was that he, Mack Franklin and Will Lincoln continued to have lunch every day at Sally's. The lunches had started when Jake needed support after he and Bree had split up a few years ago. Now that they were together again and happily married, the lunch tradition had become an occasion for the three men to keep their friendship grounded. Will counted on these two men more than either of them probably realized.

As a psychologist, Will spent his days listening to other people's problems, but he didn't really have anyone other than Jake and Mack to listen to his. Even though the three of them knew just about everything concerning each other's lives, there was one thing Will had been keeping from them for a while now: his new business, Lunch by the Bay.

The dating service had been born out of frustration. He spent way too much of his time counseling singles on the relationships in their lives and way too little of his time nurturing any kind of relationship of his own. The name of the company, which had come to him in the middle of a lonely night, was meant to be ironic, if only to him. As much as he loved getting together with his buddies, he thought it was past time to start having lunch with people who wore dresses and perfume. Jake might occasionally smell like roses, but it was only after he'd spent a morning planting rose bushes for one of his many landscaping clients. It was hardly the same.

It was also, Will thought, way past time to stop carrying the torch for Jess O'Brien, youngest sister of his friends Kevin and Connor O'Brien. Over the years Jess had had ample opportunities to indicate even a whiff of interest in Will, but she mostly treated him like an especially annoying big brother.

Worse, since he'd become a psychologist, she regularly accused him of analyzing her because she had ADD. She didn't trust his slightest bit of attention, fully expecting him to turn her into some professional case study. None of his denials had gotten her off that ridiculous tangent. Since they were thrown together a lot, her suspicion made most of their encounters awkward and testy.

Which meant it was time to move on once and for all, no easy task in a town with a population under five thousand except when tourists and weekenders filled it during the spring and summer. Lunch by the Bay had been created not only to fill a gap in the Chesapeake Shores social scene, but also to save him from growing old alone.

He explained all of this to Jake and Mack, who stared at him as if he'd suddenly sprouted antlers.

"You're starting a dating website?" Mack repeated, as if checking the accuracy of his hearing.

"Exactly," Will said. "If you weren't so busy *not* dating Susie, I'd encourage you to sign up. You're one of the town's most eligible bachelors."

"You intend to use this site yourself?" Jake said, looking puzzled. "I thought you were seeing some psychologist who bought a summer house here."

"I was," Will said. "Two years ago. It didn't work out, which you would know if you ever paid attention to a thing I tell you."

"But you've been dating," Jake persisted. "I'm not imagining that. You've blown us off to go on dates."

"What can I say?" Will said with a shrug. "None of them have amounted to anything."

"I suppose it makes sense," Mack said eventually. "Susie is always grumbling about the dearth of available men in town."

Jake barely managed to swallow a chuckle.

Mack scowled at him. "What?"

"I thought she had you," Jake responded.

"We're not dating," Mack repeated for the umpteenth unbelievable time.

"And yet neither of you seems to be looking for anyone else," Will pointed out. "If I'm wrong and you are open to other possibilities, I can sign you right up on the new website. You're an ex-jock and a semi-famous sports columnist. I'll have you matched up with someone new by the end of the week."

Jake regarded him incredulously. "You already have clients?"

"About thirty so far," Will confirmed.

"Anyone we know?" Mack asked, then frowned. "Susie, for instance?" There was a discernible hitch in his voice when he asked, proving that there was more to that relationship than he wanted to acknowledge.

"I'm not at liberty to say," Will told him.

"When did you start this company?" Jake asked.

"Three weeks ago officially, though I'd

been working out the criteria for matching people for a while. I finally incorporated, then put out a few brochures around town. I had no idea what to expect, but when the clients started signing up, I figured I ought to tell you all about it before you heard about it from another source. Someone's bound to figure out I'm the professional psychologist behind it. After all, there aren't that many of us in the area."

"So you're doing this to make money?" Mack said, clearly still trying to grasp his motivation. Before Susie, Mack had had absolutely no difficulty attracting single women, so he didn't understand Will's frustration.

"It could be a gold mine, yes, but that wasn't really my motivation," Will insisted. "I think of it more as a community service."

"Nice spin," Jake commented wryly. "You've already admitted that you're doing this so you can meet women. Couldn't you just have hung out at Brady's more often?"

Will shook his head. "That wasn't really working for me."

"What about church? I hear a lot of men meet women at church," Mack said. "Come to think of it, if I'd known you were this desperate, I could have asked Susie to fix you up. She has a bunch of girlfriends."

"I'm not desperate," Will said, offended by the characterization. "I'm being proactive."

Jake and Mack exchanged a glance. It was Jake who dared to ask, "What about Jess?"

Will stilled. "What about her?"

"You've always been crazy about her," Jake said.

"But she's not crazy about me," Will said, not denying his feelings since he'd never been all that good at hiding them. "Leave her out of this. She has nothing to do with it."

Neither of his friends looked convinced, but they backed off.

Mack regarded him with amusement. "So, are you going to hold mixers like they had in college? Have everyone wear cute little nametags? Or what about those sixty-second dating things? You know, the ones like musical chairs? I hear those can be lively."

Will scowled at his flip tone. "Bite me." He stood up. "Now, if you'll excuse me, I'm going back to my office to play matchmaker."

"You and Dolly Levi," Mack said with an unrepentant grin.

Will stared at him blankly. "Who?"

"*Hello, Dolly.* It's a musical. Susie and I saw the revival recently. She's a matchmaker."

Jake groaned. "Please do not tell a lot of people that you, once a Chesapeake Shores and college gridiron star, are going to girly musicals these days. It'll destroy your fine reputation as one of the town's all-time great bachelors. You'll no longer be considered a player on the dating scene. In fact, it's entirely likely you'll never have another date."

"He doesn't need another date," Will said. "He already has Susie."

"Who is obviously a very bad influence," Jake said.

Mack frowned at him. "Do I need to point out that your wife produces plays at her fancy new Chesapeake Shores Theater, including, I might add, the occasional musical? You planning to attend?"

Jake winced. "That's spousal obligation, not choice. There's a difference."

"Will, do you buy that? Is it different?"

"I'm not mediating this one, guys," Will declared emphatically. "You're on your own."

He was going back to his office to see

if he could find the woman of his dreams. Maybe she was right around the corner, though if she was, he ought to have stumbled across her long before now.

For the first time since the previous Friday, Will opened his email Monday afternoon to check the new applications for membership in the Lunch by the Bay online dating service. There were a half dozen that had come in over the weekend. He'd input the data from three of them, when he spotted those submitted by Laila, Connie and Jess. His eyes widened. Laila and Connie were one thing, but *Jess?* What was he supposed to do about her?

Since she'd submitted her credit card payment with her application, professional integrity absolutely required that he put the data into the system and see if his criteria matched her with anyone. The churning in his gut, however, told him to delete the application as if he'd never seen it. He didn't want to be the man who helped Jess walk off into the sunset with someone else. She might ultimately do that anyway, but he didn't want to be the one who'd facilitated it.

He wrestled with his conscience for a full

ten minutes before he reluctantly fed the data into his system. He deliberately left his own information out of the equation. When the computer came back with no immediate matches, he breathed a sigh of relief.

He told himself to send back her money and tell her to reapply at a later date, but when it came time to push the send key, he couldn't do it. He knew it was because he was a little too eager to reject her for his own reasons. For anyone else, he'd take a fresh look at the data in a few days. Much as he might not like it, he owed that to Jess, too.

As for Laila and Connie, he had an easier time with their applications. Three potential matches turned up almost immediately for Connie. He sent all of them mutual contact information. There were four possibilities for Laila. Astonishingly, one of the best matches, the man with whom she had the most in common, seemed to be him.

"No way," he muttered. He'd never once thought of dating Trace's younger sister . . . and yet, why not? Maybe this would be the best possible test of the criteria he was using. It was the first match that had come back for him with so many connections.

He'd almost convinced himself to call

Laila, when it occurred to him that it was no coincidence that the applications from her, Connie and Jess had come in within minutes of each other on Saturday night. Had they sent them in as some kind of dare? And how would Jess react if he went out with Laila? Would she be offended that her friends had gotten dates and she hadn't? Would it bother her in the slightest if Laila's first date was him? And why should he care, anyway, if he was truly moving on as he'd sworn to himself he was doing?

Before he could change his mind, he picked up the phone and called Laila at the bank.

"Hey, Will, what's up?" she said, her tone friendly.

"You're probably not going to believe this, but we've been matched up by an on-line dating service," he told her, not explaining that it was *his* business. She'd learn that soon enough.

"Lunch by the Bay?" she said. "You're kidding! I didn't expect anything to happen this quickly."

"I'm as surprised as you are, but I thought maybe we should give it a try. Would you like to have lunch tomorrow?"

"Why not?" she said, then hesitated. "Are you sure this is a good idea?"

"Why wouldn't it be?" he asked. "Obviously we're both looking for new ways to meet people, and if a computer says we're compatible, I think we should at least check it out."

"At least we'll have a few laughs, right?"

"Exactly. What do you say?"

"What time and where?" she asked.

"Panini Bistro at noon? Or is there somewhere else you'd rather go?"

"I thought you always ate with Mack and Jake at noon," she said, proving that his rut had been widely noted.

"I decided it was past time to shake up my routine," he told her.

"Then count me in, and Panini Bistro is fine. I'll see you there. Should I wear a red carnation behind my ear so you can spot me?" she asked with a laugh.

"Unless you've changed dramatically since dinner at the O'Briens a couple of Sundays ago, I think I'll recognize you," he said. He hesitated, then added, "Maybe we should keep this just between us for now. What do you think?"

"Are you ashamed to be seen in public

with me, Will Lincoln?" she asked, a teasing note in her voice.

"If I were, we wouldn't be going to lunch on Shore Road," he assured her. "I just thought maybe low-key might be best till we see how this goes. Our friends might have quite a lot to say if they hear about it."

"You wouldn't be thinking about one friend in particular, would you?" Laila asked knowingly. "Is it Jess you'd prefer to keep in the dark?"

"Of course not!" Will said emphatically. "Why would she care one way or the other?"

"I'm glad you feel that way, because I'm not all that great at keeping secrets, especially not from friends."

"Okay, then," Will said, resigned to the possibility that his lunch with Laila could stir up a commotion. "See you tomorrow."

"Looking forward to it," Laila said.

Will wished he could say the same. Instead, a feeling of dread had settled in his stomach. Any shrink worth his salt could have told him it was because he was playing with fire.

2

A few days after signing up for Lunch by the Bay, Jess checked her inbox online. "I don't get this," she muttered in frustration to Laila, who'd just dropped by the inn. "You and Connie both had responses almost immediately. I've had nothing, not even an acknowledgment that I'm signed up."

"I'm sure that's just an oversight," Laila said, though Jess thought she looked oddly guilty when she said it.

"Do you know something I don't?" Jess asked, studying her friend with a narrowed gaze.

"Of course not," Laila responded a little too quickly. "Maybe the interests you wrote down were too narrow. The company promises someone with similar interests. It may be taking a little longer to find the right match. I'm sure not everyone hears right away. The important thing is that the person you're eventually matched with is the right one."

Jess shrugged it off. "It doesn't really matter. I wasn't counting on this anyway. How about running over to Sally's and grabbing a bite to eat?"

Laila winced. "Sorry, I can't. I have my first date."

Jess stared at her, trying to judge the odd expression on her friend's face. Laila looked more worried than excited. It wasn't the reaction Jess had expected.

"Why didn't you say something when you first walked in here?" she asked. "Who is he? Do you have a name? Where are you meeting him?"

"We're meeting at Panini Bistro," Laila said.

Again, Jess studied her intently. "It still feels as if you're hiding something. Who is this man? Do I know him?"

Laila nodded, her expression sheepish. "Actually, you do. That's the reason I came by, so I could run it past you in case you had objections."

"Why on earth would I object to your date?" Jess asked. "There's no one in this town with whom I've ever been serious, unless you count Stuart Charles in third grade. I went to a lot of Little League games to watch that boy play."

Laila lost her train of thought. "I thought you went to those games to see Connor."

"Do you think I wanted anyone to know about my crush on an older man?" Jess responded with a grin. "I believe Stuart was twelve. We were doomed from the start." Her grin faded. "We've gotten off track. We were talking about this date of yours, and I was trying to make it clear there was nothing for you to worry about where I'm concerned."

"I'm not so sure about that," Laila said. Not quite meeting Jess's eyes, she admitted, "It's Will."

Jess went perfectly still. She could have sworn her heart even took an unexpected lurch. "You're having lunch with Will?" she asked slowly. "You're telling me the computer actually matched you with him?"

Laila nodded, then asked worriedly, "You're not upset, are you? I wanted you to hear this from me in case someone spots the two of us out together. If it bothers you, I can still call it off."

"Don't be ridiculous. Why would I be upset?" Jess asked, managing to keep a carefree note in her voice, even though the news had been oddly disconcerting. "I've never dated Will." She hesitated. "You don't suppose . . . ?"

"Suppose what?"

"That brochure said this company was being run by a psychologist. Do you think that could be Will?"

Laila shrugged. "Could be, but I don't see why it matters."

"You don't think it'll be weird dating a shrink?" Jess had certainly had enough difficulty just being in the same room with him. She'd never been able to stop feeling self-conscious, as if Will was seeing right through her, analyzing every word she uttered. Maybe under other circumstances that attentiveness would have been flattering, but it made her feel exposed. She'd had enough of those feelings when doctors had been trying to determine whether she had attention deficit disorder years ago. All that psychological probing and testing had made her feel like a lab specimen.

"Why would it be weird?" Laila asked with a shrug. "Hopefully, he'll be more insightful than most of the men I've run across. It's funny, but somehow I never even thought about dating Will before. We're actually the same age, but we never hung around with the same crowd in school."

"Because you were with the in crowd and he was a nerd."

"Will was most definitely not a nerd," Laila said, jumping to his defense in a way that took Jess aback. "Jake and Mack are his two best friends, and they were both jocks. He was always hanging out at your house with Kevin and Connor, too. If I remember correctly, Will even played varsity basketball." Her expression brightened. "That's another good thing. He's taller than I am. I'm tired of having to wear flats when I go out so I don't intimidate some guy who's barely five-eight."

Jess couldn't explain why the idea of Laila going out with Will bothered her so much. Was it because she was more interested in him than she'd ever admitted to herself? Or was it because that stupid computer had confirmed what she'd always said, that they'd be a terrible match? Because she didn't want her friend worrying about any of that, she forced a smile.

"I hope you have a great time," she told Laila. "It really would be something if this whole matchmaking thing turns out to work."

Laila grinned, clearly relieved to have Jess's blessing, lukewarm though it might have been. "Fingers crossed. I'll call later and let you know how it went."

The minute she'd gone, Jess grabbed her keys and headed for Sally's. She knew she'd find Jake and Mack there. Maybe they could fill her in on whether Will was behind Lunch by the Bay. If he was, once she got over the shock, she was never going to let him hear the end of it.

Will stood on the sidewalk in front of Panini Bistro waiting for Laila Riley. He'd felt a little odd matching himself up with someone he'd known for most of his life, but they'd exchanged a few emails since his phone call the day before and discovered several additional things they had in common, aside from all the people they both knew and the interests they'd both mentioned on their applications. At least they'd be able to spend the next hour catching up, with no real pressure on either of them. It made her the ideal Lunch by the Bay first date.

He saw her exit her car just up the road, then walk purposefully toward him with a stride that could easily keep up with his. She smiled when she saw him, started to hold out a hand, then shrugged and hugged him.

"This is weird, huh?" she said.

"I was just thinking how easy it should be," he countered. "It's not as if we haven't known each other forever."

"But not like this," she said. "Not as a potential spouse."

Will gave her a startled look that made her laugh.

"Sorry," she said at once. "Computer compatibility notwithstanding, I'm not suggesting we call a minister quite yet. I just meant that this isn't bumping into each other at a party or at Brady's. It's a real date, even if it is only lunch."

Will grinned as the awkward moment passed. "Then I should be pulling out a chair and asking you to have a seat," he said, doing just that before seating himself at the outside table. "Would you like a glass of wine with lunch?"

She shook her head. "One thing I've learned about banking is that I can't stare at all those numbers without a clear head. You go ahead, if you want to."

"Not me. My clients expect me to be giving them sober, thoughtful advice."

They glanced at their menus, placed their orders, then sat back. Will couldn't think of one single thing to say that hadn't already been covered in their emails.

"I saw Jess before I came over here," Laila said eventually.

To his annoyance, Will's heart skipped a couple of beats. "Oh? How is she?"

"She seemed a little taken aback to hear that I was meeting you," Laila told him. "I felt like I had to tell her."

"Why?"

"You know, I'm not sure," she admitted.

"I suppose it's because I've always thought the two of you had some kind of connection of your own. And, of course, she and I are friends. I warned you I was no good at keeping secrets from my friends."

Will told himself that what she was saying about Jess's reaction didn't have to mean anything. It was probably no more of a shock to Jess than hearing, say, that he and Laila had crossed paths at the grocery store.

When he said nothing, Laila added, "Jess wondered if maybe this whole Lunch by the Bay thing isn't your idea. Is it?"

Will hesitated, but saw no point in an evasive answer. "It is." He explained his reasons for launching the company, then added, "So far, I've actually matched up about ten couples for first dates, though this is the first time I've gone out with anyone myself."

"Really?" she said, looking impressed. "And you chose me? Why?"

"Truthfully?"

"Of course."

"I wanted to check out my criteria for myself, and you seemed like the least threatening opportunity to do that," he admitted.

"Worst case scenario, if it turned out to be a total bust, I figured we could laugh about it."

"I'm not sure if there's a compliment buried in there somewhere or not," she said.

"Probably pretty deeply," Will said, chuckling.

"So, how about the other couples? Anything look as if it's working out?"

"The early feedback has been very positive," he said. "My criteria seem to be working, at least for strangers. Several people have told me they're on their third—and, in one case, a fourth—date with the first person they were matched with."

"So what was the criteria that made you match yourself up with me?" Laila asked, then studied him intently. "Instead of Jess, for instance? She applied the same day I did."

Will couldn't deny that he'd considered exactly that. After all, it was the perfect opportunity to nudge Jess into thinking of him in a different way. He just hadn't been quite ready for the humiliation of having her laugh hysterically at the suggestion that they go on a date.

"Jess and I don't really click," he said carefully.

"According to these criteria of yours?" Laila pressed.

Will squirmed. "Not exactly. I left myself out of the mix when I ran her data through the computer."

Laila looked surprised. "Why?"

"Like I said, I already knew we didn't click."

"But *we* do, according to the computer?" Laila repeated.

He nodded. "You and I had at least a half dozen or more things in common, similar interests, ambitions and so on."

She gave him an amused look. "Sounds as if we're a match made in heaven."

"Who knows? We could be." He held her gaze, hoping he'd feel something, even a hint of the chemistry he felt when he was in a room with Jess. There was nothing. It didn't mean his criteria were off. It just meant he had no quantifiable way to measure attraction, and even he knew that was a key ingredient in any relationship.

After an awkward moment, he changed the subject, asking her opinion of a variety of economic and banking issues. Laila, he discovered, could hold her own when it came to such a debate. She was informed, opinionated and direct, all good traits to his way of thinking. They'd finished dessert before he realized that the time was late and he was due back at his office for his next appointment.

"This was fun," he said, meaning it. "I'd love to have lunch again sometime."

"So would I," she said, "but next time it's on me."

Will saw the declaration for what it was, an offer of friendship. Since he'd been thinking along the same lines, he was relieved. "It's a deal."

"But not a date," she responded. "Forget your stupid computer, Will. Ask Jess out. You know she's the one you want. She always has been."

He frowned at the statement. "We're not suited."

Laila waved off the comment. "Says who?"

"Mostly Jess," he confessed.

"You've actually asked her out and she's blown you off?"

"Well, no, but she's made it abundantly clear that I make her uncomfortable."

"That's exactly what Jess needs, some-one who can shake her up," Laila said. "Stop wasting your time trying to find a re-placement who'll never measure up. Go for the real thing." She gave him a hug. "That's my advice to you." She grinned. "And lucky for you, I don't charge your hourly rates for it."

She strode off down the street, leaving Will to stare after her and wonder why she couldn't have been the one. Candid, no-nonsense Laila Riley was a whole lot less complicated than Jess O'Brien would ever be.

He sighed. That, of course, was the problem. He apparently liked complica-tions. Unfortunately, that was probably go-ing to be his downfall.

Connie's first official blind date was with an accountant in Annapolis, a single father whose children, like Jenny, were away at college. On paper, he'd sounded great. Their email exchanges had revealed several other things they had in common, including a love of the water. She'd anticipated an en-joyable lunch, maybe some stimulating conversation, even if it didn't go any further than that.

Since she'd agreed to drive to Annapolis, she'd decided to go early and stop by Thomas O'Brien's foundation offices to touch base on their fundraising efforts to protect the Chesapeake Bay. Even though it was a Saturday morning, she knew she'd find Jess's uncle at work. His workaholic reputation was widely recognized. When she tapped on his office door, he glanced up from the papers on his desk and beamed at her.

"Now, if you aren't exactly what I needed on this dreary morning," he said, removing his reading glasses and putting aside his pen. "What brings you to Annapolis?"

Connie's pulse leapt at the enthusiasm in his voice, even though she'd told herself a thousand times that it was his gratitude for her efforts for the foundation and nothing more.

"I have a date," she admitted, wrinkling her nose. "A blind date, at that."

He sat back, a look of astonishment on his face. "Now tell me why a lovely woman like you would be going on a blind date?"

"I signed up for an online dating service," she said sheepishly. "Jess and Laila did, too."

"All three of you?" He gave a sad shake of his head. "I can't imagine what the men of Chesapeake Shores are thinking if you're resorting to an online dating service." Still, he looked vaguely intrigued. "And is this your first date?"

Connie nodded. "To be honest, I'm a little nervous."

"In this day and age, that's perfectly understandable. Maybe you should reconsider."

"I can't just not show up," she protested. "That would be rude."

"Then I'll come with you," he said decisively. "Not on the date, of course, but just to be nearby in case there's a problem."

She studied him oddly. "You'd do that?"

"I feel obligated to, as a matter of fact. Someone needs to look out for you, and we're practically family."

She laughed at the serious note in his voice. "Do you know how old I am?"

"I have some idea. What's your point?"

"That I'm old enough to look out for myself."

"Not if this man turns out to be some kind of smooth-talking predator," he insisted, his jaw set determinedly.

"Why am I starting to think that stopping by here was a bad idea?" she said, amused despite herself at his overly protective attitude. And maybe a little touched, if she were to be totally honest.

He smiled at her, the smile that always made her toes curl. "Since you obviously aren't here for my protection, why did you stop by?"

To see that smile, for one thing, she thought but didn't dare say. Her conflicted feelings for Thomas O'Brien were a constant source of dismay to her. She couldn't imagine them ever going anywhere. At the same time, she couldn't seem to stay away. She was drawn to his passion for his work, his caring personality, his wicked sense of humor . . . to *him,* for that matter.

"I haven't seen you since the last of the summer events," she said. "I wanted to catch up on how fundraising is going and see what I can do to help over the winter."

"Now I've had a few ideas about that," he said at once. "Why don't we go a bit early to this lunch of yours and have coffee while we wait for your date to arrive? Once I've met him and seen for myself that he means no harm, I'll fade into the woodwork," he promised.

Connie could see all sorts of things potentially disastrous about that plan, but she couldn't seem to tell him to forget it. Coffee with Thomas sounded a whole lot better, frankly, than lunch with a total stranger.

"That would be great," she said.

They walked to the restaurant her date had suggested, chose a table overlooking the nearby Severn River and ordered coffee. Connie was so engrossed in what Thomas had to say, she barely noticed when another man approached the table and stood looking down at them with an irritated expression on his face.

"You're Connie Collins?" he asked.

She jumped guiltily. "I am. Steve Lorton?"

He nodded, then scowled at Thomas. "Am I interrupting?"

"Of course not," Connie said before Thomas could reply. He had an oddly territorial look on his face that she didn't quite trust. She introduced the two men. "Thomas and I were just discussing the latest progress in his foundation's efforts to protect the bay. I've been doing some volunteer work for him."

Steve looked somewhat mollified by the explanation, but when Thomas made no move to leave, he was forced to drag a chair over from a nearby table. He sat down next to Connie, as if to claim her for his own. Connie couldn't recall the last time she'd been caught in a turf war between two men, if ever, but she discovered she didn't like it nearly as much as she'd always imagined she might.

"Thomas was just leaving," she announced pointedly, though, to her dismay, he didn't seem to be budging.

"I'm sure Steve won't mind if I stick around a little longer," Thomas said.

His jaw was set in a way Connie recognized. She'd seen it on other O'Brien men often enough.

She was about to push him to leave, anyway, when he added, "There are several more things we need to discuss, Connie."

Connie stared at him in confusion. "What things?"

"Our plans for next weekend, in fact."

Now she really was confused. "We have plans?"

"We *do,*" he said emphatically, staring down Steve as he said it.

Steve stood up so suddenly his chair fell over. "Look, I had no idea you were already involved with someone," he said to Connie, his gaze accusing. "You should have told me."

Before she could defend herself, he turned and left without another word.

She stared after him, then whirled on Thomas. "Why would you do that? Why would you deliberately chase him off?"

"I didn't like him," he said, without even a hint of remorse.

She stared at him incredulously. "I think the point of going on this date was to find out if *I'd* like him."

"You wouldn't have," Thomas predicted. "He's too self-absorbed."

"You could tell that from the two minutes he was sitting here?"

"I could tell that when there wasn't the slightest spark of interest in his eyes when you mentioned protecting the bay."

She couldn't deny that. Still, she felt compelled to say, "I think you might be a bit biased when it comes to the bay. Not everyone is as passionate about what you do as you are."

He held her gaze. "You are," he said quietly. "Can you honestly tell me you'd be seriously interested in a man who doesn't care about his surroundings?"

"Probably not, but you don't get to decide that," she replied.

"I did you a favor," he said stubbornly.

She sighed. She could tell she wasn't going to win this argument. To be honest, she wasn't all that unhappy about what he'd done, not if it gave the two of them more time together. She wasn't sure she liked what that said about her state of mind, but there it was, the honest-to-God truth.

"Let's say I accept that you *thought* you were doing me a favor," she said. "I drove all this way to have lunch. Does that mean you're treating me now?"

His expression brightened and his booming laugh drew smiles from those at nearby tables. "I think it's the least I can do," he agreed readily.

"And what about those plans we supposedly have for next weekend?" she asked, suddenly feeling daring in a way she hadn't in a very long time.

"Dinner at Brady's on Saturday night?" he suggested.

Despite the little *zing* of anticipation that rushed through her at the suggestion, Connie hesitated. "Brady's? Are you sure about that?"

"O'Brien turf?" he asked, proving he understood exactly what her concerns were.

"Pretty much."

"Well, I can't very well ask you to drive back to Annapolis, can I? We'll just have to find someplace down there that my family hasn't discovered. Chesapeake Shores isn't the only town with restaurants. Leave it to me."

"Okay," she said, her hands suddenly shaking so badly she had to set her menu back on the table. Just to be sure she wasn't misinterpreting what was going on here, she forced herself to meet his gaze.

"Is this a date, Thomas? Or a business meeting? I want to be clear."

He didn't answer immediately. In fact, it looked as if he was struggling to decide.

"The smart answer would be to call it a business meeting, wouldn't it?" he said, regret in his voice.

"It would probably be wise," she agreed, not even trying to disguise her own disappointment. Then she reminded herself that she was over forty, not some shy little teenage wallflower. Thomas O'Brien was the first man in years who'd captured her attention. Why shouldn't she throw caution to the wind? She looked him directly in the eyes then, and added, "But I'd really hoped it was a date."

His expression immediately lit up in a thoroughly gratifying way. "Then a date it is!" He hesitated, then said, "But—"

"You don't have to say it, Thomas. The family doesn't need to know about any of this."

"Not that I think there's anything wrong with the two of us going on a date," he was quick to say.

Connie laughed. "Believe me, I get it. Once unleashed, the meddling O'Briens are hard to contain."

"Exactly." He picked up his menu. "Suddenly I'm starving. I think I'll have the seafood platter. How about you?"

Connie was pretty sure she wasn't going to be able to eat a single bite. "A small house salad for me."

"Nonsense. You need some protein before you have to drive home. At least have the crabcakes. They're excellent here."

She gave in because it made no sense to fight him. She knew she'd be regretting that salad halfway home when her stomach started growling. Still, she couldn't let him have his way about it entirely. It would set a bad precedent with a man as strong-willed as he obviously was.

"A crabcake sandwich, then," she compromised.

"Excellent!"

She looked into his blue, blue eyes, sparkling with mirth, and thought she hadn't been captivated by anyone like this as far back as she could remember, not even Jenny's father. As much as she'd thought she loved Sam, he'd lacked strength, maturity, passion and compassion, all qualities Thomas personified.

She was smitten, all right. If only the situation didn't have the potential for heartbreak written all over it.

3

Ever since she'd found out that Lunch by the Bay was, indeed, Will's new enterprise, Jess had been feeling more restless and out of sorts than usual. She'd been avoiding Laila's calls as well, not sure she wanted to hear about how wonderful the date with Will had been. Jess knew, though, that she couldn't put her friend off forever. In fact, it was childish that she'd done it this long.

She walked into the inn's kitchen, where Gail was preparing food for the picnic baskets that several of the guests had requested.

"I'm going to take off for an hour or so," Jess told her chef. "Call me on my cell phone if you need me."

"Who's working out front?"

"Ronnie's got it."

Gail regarded her with surprise. "Boy, you must be anxious to get out of here. I thought you didn't trust Ronnie to handle the desk."

Ronnie Forrest was in his early twenties, but he had the maturity of a preteen. His father, a friend of Mick's, had despaired of Ronnie ever getting a responsible job and holding on to it. Jess had been willing to take a chance on him, but so far the only task he handled without bungling was carrying bags for the guests. More often than not, he could be found in the main lounge watching TV, rather than doing any of the other chores assigned to him.

As frustrating as his malingering was, on some level Jess could identify with him. She'd wondered more than once if he didn't have an undiagnosed case of the same ADD that had plagued her life.

Jess beamed at Gail. "Which is why you're going to supervise him while I'm gone. You're much tougher than I am.

Maybe you can get him to take this job seriously."

Gail didn't deny her toughness. However, with a lifted brow, she inquired, "And just how am I supposed to keep an eye on him from here in the kitchen?"

"Transfer the calls to your line, if you want to, and bring him in here and assign him to peel onions," Jess suggested. "Maybe he'll start to figure out that my threats to fire him if he doesn't shape up aren't idle ones."

Gail regarded her with surprise. "You've actually told him his job's on the line?"

Jess nodded. "Last week. I had no choice after three people complained that no one had answered when they called to make reservations and I found him watching reruns of *Law and Order*."

"What's your father going to say?"

"I'll tell him if he wants to give the guy a break, then *he* should hire him," Jess said. "It might be best all around. Dad doesn't tolerate anyone who doesn't pull their weight on a job. Maybe he'll even tell Ronnie's father to get him tested for ADD, which is what I suspect is going on."

Gail studied her with surprise. "Seriously?"

Jess nodded.

"And that's why you keep cutting him slack, despite the tough talk?"

"More than likely," Jess conceded with a sigh. "Meantime, he's all yours. I'll send him in here on my way out."

Of course, she didn't find Ronnie in the lobby where he was supposed to be. Nor was he in the lounge. He was on the porch, an Orioles baseball cap pulled low over his eyes, sound asleep. The sight so ticked her off that she grabbed the back of the rocker in which he was seated and came close to upending him right off the porch and onto the lawn.

"What the . . . !" he muttered as he grabbed a post to keep himself from falling. He scowled at her. "Are you crazy?"

"Not half as crazy as you are, if you think this is an acceptable on-the-job performance," she said, facing him down and suddenly realizing why Abby spent so much time annoyed with her.

"Did you not understand it when I told you last week that you were getting on my very last nerve?" she asked.

"Chill," he said. "There's nothing going on around here."

"How could you possibly know that when the phone you're supposed to be answering is inside? I've transferred the reservation line into the kitchen. Get in there and help Gail. If I don't get a rave review from her when I get back, you're fired. Is that clear enough?" This time, she simply had to stick to her guns. She wasn't doing him any favors by letting him get away with this kind of lackadaisical behavior on the job.

He finally looked at least moderately shaken. "Come on, Jess."

"That's Ms. O'Brien to you," she snapped.

He grinned as if she'd said something hysterically funny. "Come on, *Ms. O'Brien,* you know my old man's going to have a conniption fit if I lose another job."

"Then don't lose it," she said and walked away before she said a few more things about his work ethic that he probably wouldn't understand anyway. If Devlin Forrest complained to Mick about Ronnie being fired, she'd deal with her father. Insolence and laziness were two traits Mick would never tolerate either. She was confident of that.

Concluding that she needed the fresh air and a long walk to improve her mood, she hiked the mile or so into town, then headed for the bank. At the front desk, she greeted Mariah, then nodded toward the executive offices.

"Is Laila back there? Is she free?"

Mariah nodded. "Go on back. Maybe a friendly face will improve her mood."

"She's having a bad day?"

"Days," Mariah confided, "but don't you dare tell her I said so."

"Any idea why?"

"None."

Jess walked back to the office that had once belonged to Trace before he'd convinced his father that Laila was the one who belonged in it. Trace had done nothing during his brief stint there to make it his own, but Laila had painted the walls a warmer shade of cream, then added bright splashes of modern art to the walls. The paintings had horrified her father, who thought they weren't nearly sedate enough for a community bank, but Laila had stuck to her guns. It was the most cheerful room in an otherwise dreary old building.

Laila, however, looked anything but cheerful, at least until she looked up and

saw Jess standing hesitantly in the doorway.

"I hear the mood is dark back here," Jess
said. "Is it safe to come in?"

Laila smiled wearily. "Come on in. I
promise not to bite your head off."

Jess took a seat and studied her friend.
"You look worn out. What's going on?"

"I'm trying to figure out how to keep
some of our oldest customers from losing
their homes to foreclosure," Laila said. "I
thought the economy was turning around,
but we've still got people around here who
are struggling. The board doesn't want to
hear their excuses. I'm arguing for compassion and a little ingenuity. I'm afraid I'm
going to lose the battle."

"I'm sorry. Having been on the other side
of a foreclosure notice, I know how awful
that is. If it hadn't been for Abby coming
down here to fight for me and straighten
out the inn's finances, who knows what
would have happened?"

"But it worked out for you," Laila said.
"The bank knew you were good for the
loan, just like I know these people will make
good on theirs if we can just cut them a
little slack. Putting families out on the

street should be a last resort." She waved off the topic. "Let's talk about something else. Do you have time for lunch? It's been ages since we've talked."

Jess grinned, relieved that the tension she'd been feeling had evaporated once she was actually in a room with her friend. "I was hoping you'd suggest that. Shall we have Connie meet us?"

"Absolutely," Laila said, placing the call and getting Connie's immediate agreement to meet them at a new soup and salad restaurant that had opened a few weeks earlier. When she'd hung up, she said, "I would have suggested Sally's, but Will's bound to be there, so I figured you'd rather go someplace else."

"That's why you're my friend," Jess said. "You know me so well. I do want to hear about your date with him, though."

Laila regarded her doubtfully. "Really? I thought maybe that was why you weren't taking my calls."

Jess winced. She should have known Laila would recognize exactly what she'd been thinking. "It was," she admitted, "but I was being stupid. I want to know everything."

"And I want to hear about Connie's date in Annapolis the other day," Laila said, as she grabbed her purse and they left for the restaurant. "She mentioned he was an accountant. I could have warned her about that. We're not that interesting, but I didn't want to scare her off."

Jess laughed. "I can't speak for all accountants, but you are the least boring person I know," she told her. "Maybe she got lucky."

A few minutes later, though, when they were all seated at an outdoor table facing the bay, Connie squirmed when Laila brought up her date.

Laila regarded her knowingly. "It was a bust, right?"

"Totally," Connie said, though her cheeks were bright pink. She hesitated, then said, "I wound up having lunch with Thomas, instead."

Jess stared at her. "Thomas? My uncle?"

Connie nodded. "It just sort of happened. We got to talking about fundraising and stuff, and ended up having lunch. No big deal."

But Jess could see it *was* a big deal. Laila, however, seemed to accept Connie's explanation at face value. There were a hundred questions on the tip of Jess's tongue, but she bit them back.

Connie quickly turned to Laila. "And your lunch with Will? How did that go?" She flushed guiltily, faced Jess and asked, "Are you okay with her talking about this?"

"I wish everyone would stop acting as if Will and I shared some big romance," Jess complained. "We didn't. We've never even been on a date."

"Only because he thinks you don't want to go out with him," Laila said. "That's what he told me."

Jess frowned. "The two of you were talking about me on your date? No wonder your social life sucks."

"We were talking about you, because you were like this huge elephant in the room. We couldn't ignore the obvious. He has feelings for you, and contrary to all your claims, I think *you* have feelings for *him*."

"I think he's annoying," Jess said. "Is that what you mean?"

Laila rolled her eyes and Connie chuckled.

"The denials aren't working for me," Laila

said, then grinned at Connie. "How about you?"

"Nope," Connie said.

Jess was within a second of blowing that smug expression off Connie's face by blabbing what she knew about Connie's feelings for Uncle Thomas, but when push came to shove, she couldn't do it. If there was something going on between those two, she didn't want to be the one to ruin it by getting the whole family in an uproar. Kevin and Connor had obviously felt the same way when they'd sworn her to secrecy.

"Look, you two, think whatever you want," Jess said. "Will and I would never work as a couple. We barely tolerate each other as friends. And if he were as interested in me as you two seem to think and we were at all suited, wouldn't that fancy computer program of his have spit us out as a match?"

"He didn't put his name in when he ran yours through," Laila revealed.

"See what I mean?" Jess said, seizing on that. "He doesn't want anything to do with me. That proves it. Let's just drop this, okay? I don't want to talk about Will or about the fact that this stupid company of his is a fraud."

Both of her friends regarded her with dismay. "That's a little harsh," Laila said. "Just because Connie's first date and mine didn't work doesn't mean the next ones won't."

"You're going to accept more dates?" Jess asked incredulously.

"Why not?" Laila said. "Nothing's changed about the reasons we all signed up, right, Connie?"

Connie nodded, though Jess thought her expression looked doubtful.

"I'm game," Connie said with lackluster enthusiasm.

Laila focused her attention on Jess. "You paid your money. You can't back out now."

"Since I haven't had a single email or phone call, I'm thinking I should demand my money back," Jess said. "In fact, the next time I see Will, I intend to tell him what I think of this whole ridiculous online dating scheme of his."

"You have to give it a chance," Laila insisted. "You don't want just any old match. It has to be the right one. Give it time."

"Like you and Will were such a great match," Jess said sarcastically. "Or Connie and her accountant. Come on, guys, admit this was a mistake. When it comes to this matchmaking stuff, Will is an amateur."

"I'm not throwing in the towel yet," Laila replied determinedly. "Neither is Connie, and you promised you were in, too, Jess. Are you going back on your word to us?"

"It's not as if we're double- or triple-dating, for goodness' sakes," Jess protested. "You two can do whatever you want to do. I'm out."

"A promise is a promise," Laila persisted.

Jess sighed and caved. "Okay, fine. I'll give it a little longer."

But despite Laila's optimism and Connie's reluctant agreement, no one was going to persuade Jess that it wasn't a big old waste of time and energy.

Will's client, a single woman who'd despaired of ever finding the right man, arrived for her appointment with a man in tow.

"This is Carl Mason," Kathy Pierson told Will, her eyes sparkling with excitement. "I hope you don't mind, but I asked him to sit in on our session today. We met through Lunch by the Bay, and we're getting married."

Will saw the blush on her cheeks and the adoration in Carl Mason's eyes and realized this was exactly what he'd hoped for when he launched the company. Unfortunately, though, he also knew that Kathy had a way of rushing into things without giving them sufficient thought. What if this was one of those occasions? They couldn't possibly have had more than a handful of dates. He was pretty sure he'd arranged the match less than two weeks ago.

"When something's right, it's right," Carl told him, obviously picking up on Will's lack of enthusiasm for the news. "I know it must seem fast to you, but the minute I met Kathy, something clicked."

"I'm happy for you both. I truly am," Will assured them. "But marriage is a huge step. Shouldn't you spend a little more time together before you make that kind of commitment?"

Kathy frowned at him. "I'm forty-six years old. I've waited my whole life to meet a man like Carl. I've already lost my chance to have children, but that doesn't mean it's too late for love. You're the one who's been telling me that for months now. I've finally found it, and I don't want to wait. *We* don't want to wait."

"You're both telling me how right this is," Will said, treading cautiously. "Won't it be just as right a few weeks from now, or even a few months from now? Then you'll know for certain."

"And we'll have wasted weeks or months of our lives," Kathy said.

"They won't be wasted," Will insisted. "I'm not suggesting you can't be together during that time, just that you not jump into marriage. You'll be getting to know each other, making sure that you're as compatible as you think you are."

"I don't understand why you can't just be happy for us," Kathy said. "I mean, we're practically the poster couple for Lunch by the Bay. We're a success story! You should be gloating about the fact that your computer program made a successful match, not trying to bring us down."

"I'm not trying to bring you down," Will

assured her. "In fact, if this works out, I'll be the first to stand up and offer a toast at your wedding. I'm just worried that you've put a little too much faith in a computer program and not trusted your own judgment. It takes time to get to know another person. The computer is a tool that can cut that process down somewhat, but it's not infallible."

Kathy stood up. "Well, aren't you Mr. Doom and Gloom all of a sudden. I'd hoped you'd come to the wedding, but I can see that's a terrible idea. I don't want any bad vibes ruining the happiest day of my life. Let's go, Carl."

Carl followed her to the door. "To be honest, I thought the whole computer thing was a crazy idea, but once I met Kathy, I became a believer. This is going to be okay, Doc. You don't have to worry about us."

Will appreciated the effort to reassure him, but he stared after them with a feeling of dread in his stomach. Client confidentiality required that he not tell Carl that Kathy had a long history of lightning-quick enthusiasms that faded all too rapidly. It was one thing to embrace a hobby and drop it practically overnight. It was quite another to do that with a husband.

He was trying to figure out if there was anything else he could do to slow down this impulsive wedding they were planning when his cell phone rang. Relieved by the distraction, he answered on the second ring.

"Is this Will Lincoln?" a woman asked hesitantly.

"It is."

"Your name turned up as a prospective match from Lunch by the Bay," she said. "I was wondering if you might be available for lunch one day this week. I probably should have waited for you to call, but I was afraid if I did, I'd lose my nerve altogether. I've never done anything like this before."

Will bit back a sigh. How could he turn her down? He was the one who'd founded the company in part so he could meet people himself. It would pretty much destroy the company's reputation if its own founder started rejecting the matches it kicked out.

"I'd love to have lunch with you," he said, trying to inject a note of enthusiasm into his voice. "How about Friday?"

He chatted a little longer, then hung up.

Merry Landry had sounded sweet. And from the information he'd managed to pull from the computer, on the surface it seemed they had at least a few interests in common. She was well-educated, had her own business and had the kind of large family he'd always envied. A family like the O'Briens.

Of course, there was only one huge drawback over which Merry obviously had no control. She wasn't Jess.

On Friday at noon, Jess got a call from Heather, Connor's wife. Heather owned a quilt shop on Shore Road, right next door to the art gallery Jess's mother had opened.

"You busy?" Heather asked.

"It's Friday, so we're expecting a packed house for the weekend, but most of them won't be showing up for a couple of hours. Why?"

Jess thought she heard a whispered exchange in the background, but it might have been customers talking.

Eventually Heather said, "I was hoping you could meet me for a quick bite. Connor, too. We've missed you."

Something in her voice sounded off to

Jess, but she couldn't put her finger on it. "Is Connor there now?"

"Nope," Heather said hurriedly. "He just left to claim a table for us at Panini Bistro. Can you get there?"

"Do you two have news?" Jess asked, wondering if Heather was pregnant. They already had a son who'd been born before they'd married.

Heather laughed. "If you stopped asking questions and drove over here, you'd have your answers in less time."

Jess sighed. "Fine. Give me ten minutes. Order a ham and cheese panini with lettuce and tomato for me."

"Will do," Heather promised.

Jess checked in with Gail, assured herself that Ronnie was at work in the kitchen again with the reservation line forwarded in there, then drove into town. It took several minutes to find a parking spot, then a few more to walk back to the restaurant. She immediately spotted her brother and his wife. Then, at another table way too nearby to be a coincidence, she saw Will and some attractive blonde woman who seemed to be regarding him with an adoring expression.

Though the chair Connor and Heather had left for Jess had a clear view of Will and his date, Jess grabbed the chair and shoved it between the happy newlyweds so her back was to Will.

"Please tell me *that* is not why you got me down here," she said under her breath, shrugging a shoulder in Will's direction.

Connor regarded her innocently. "Are you talking about Will? I think he's on one of those Lunch by the Bay dates of his. Pretty woman, don't you think?"

Jess's temper flared. "I do not give two hoots if she's more gorgeous than Marilyn Monroe. Why would you do this? Just to make me crazy?"

Heather started to laugh, then covered her mouth, but there was no hiding the merriment in her eyes. "Then seeing Will with another woman does make you crazy?" she inquired. Though she went for an innocent tone, there was too much amusement threading through her voice to pull it off. "Why is that?"

Jess wanted to kill them both. She really did, but she wasn't going to give Will the satisfaction of witnessing her losing her cool in public. She plastered a smile on her face and caught the attention of the waitress.

"Could you make my order to go, please? I have to get back to work."

"Jess!" Heather protested, looking dismayed. "Please stay."

"Running isn't the answer," Connor scolded. "Don't you see how silly it is for the two of you to go on wasting time by denying your feelings?"

"The only feeling I have for Will right this second is contempt, and, frankly, my feelings for you, dear brother, aren't much better." She frowned at Heather. "Why would you go along with this? I know it was Connor's idea."

Heather flushed. "I thought it was a good one," she admitted, then added earnestly, "Connor's right. You should at least give Will a chance."

Jess decided she needed to point out the obvious. "Will doesn't seem to want a chance. He's right here with someone else. I'm not going to turn around and look now, but he seemed happy enough to be with her when I arrived. And not that long ago, he was here with Laila."

Connor looked startled. "Laila? Will had a date with Trace's sister?"

"He did," Jess said. "Obviously he's enjoying playing the field. Now will you please stay out of my business?" She grabbed her to-go order when the waitress came, then gave her brother a sour look. "Thanks for lunch, by the way. It's been lovely."

She stewed all the way back to the inn, stormed into the kitchen and tossed her food onto one of the stainless steel countertops. Gail took one look at her face and turned to Ronnie.

"Transfer the calls back to the front desk," she ordered. "And stay there to take them."

"Sure thing," Ronnie said willingly.

Jess stared after him. "Did you hypnotize that man?"

"It's amazing what you can accomplish when a guy sees you wielding a carving knife," Gail said with a laugh. "Haven't had a bit of trouble with him."

Jess shook her head. "I'm not sure that's a strategy many employers could get away with, but I'm grateful."

"Okay, so tell me why you're tied up in

knots and looking mad enough to chew nails," Gail said. "And split that panini with me. It smells fabulous and I'm starved."

"Need I point out that you're a chef with an entire pantry and a freezer at your disposal?" Jess said even as she put half of the sandwich on a plate, added a few of the French-fried sweet potatoes and handed it over.

"I'm much too busy to cook for myself," Gail claimed. "My boss—that's you, by the way—insisted on very labor-intensive hors d'oeuvres to welcome the guests on Friday nights. I had Ronnie helping out, but you sent him on his way, so I'm on my own. Now tell me what happened. I'm pretty sure you intended to eat lunch at the restaurant."

Jess told Gail what she'd found when she arrived. "I don't know what they were thinking," she said of her brother and Heather.

"That you need to wake up and smell the roses before it's too late," Gail suggested.

Jess scowled at her. "Why does everyone keep saying that?"

"Because you're the only one who hasn't seemed to notice that Will is perfect for you."

Jess still wasn't buying it. "The most obnoxious, infuriating, patronizing man in Chesapeake Shores is perfect for me? What does that say about me?"

"At the moment, it says that you're blind and stubborn," Gail said cheerfully. She slid a knife in Jess's direction. "Now chop those mushrooms or send Ronnie back in here. I have work to do."

Jess started chopping, then glanced sideways at Gail. "I need to remember that when it comes to sympathy, you are definitely not my go-to girl."

Gail laughed. "Not in my job description, that's for sure. Now, chop."

At least the effort to avoid cutting off her own fingers kept Jess from spending too much time thinking about Will and the pretty blonde who'd been hanging on his every word. She'd have plenty of time to relive that sight when she was lying all alone in her bed tonight.

4

Megan looked up from the canvas she was framing in preparation for an upcoming show at the gallery to see Mick heading her way, a scowl on his face.

"What's wrong with you?" she asked her husband when he'd settled on a nearby stool in the workroom behind the gallery.

"I just spotted our daughter—"

"Which one?" Megan interrupted to ask.

"Jess. She was storming off from that sandwich shop up the street looking as if she was itching for a fight. She didn't even turn around when I called out to her."

"I'm surprised you didn't follow her," Megan said dryly.

"Did you not hear me?" Mick asked impatiently. "I said she looked like she wanted a fight. Even I know better than to try to deal with her before she's calmed down."

Megan smiled. "So, you have learned a few new tricks since we remarried," she teased.

Mick scowled. "Will you stop worrying about me and my tricks? We need to focus on our youngest daughter. Something's up with her, Meggie. She's not happy. I tried to get some information out of Connor and Heather, but they clammed up on me."

Megan regarded him with confusion. "What do Connor and Heather have to do with this?"

"That's who Jess couldn't get away from fast enough, at least that's how it looked to me." He frowned. "Or maybe it had something to do with Will."

Now he had Megan's full attention. "Will? He was there?"

"At the next table, with some woman I've never seen before. A pretty little thing." His expression turned thoughtful. "Jess wouldn't be upset by that, would she?"

Megan didn't know how to respond. She'd thought for some time now that Will and Jess had unacknowledged feelings for each other, but she'd kept her suspicions from Mick. He wasn't the kind of man who could sit back and let things happen at their own pace. He'd been fretting about Jess's lack of a social life for some time now. He'd be meddling the instant he saw any reason for it.

"I have no idea," she said eventually, which was true enough. Jess had never once mentioned to her that she felt any attraction to Will.

Mick studied her skeptically. "Why do I get the feeling that was an evasive answer? Did you leave some kind of loophole in there?"

"Why would I do that?" she asked, hoping her tone sounded innocent enough to fool him.

"Because you don't want me interfering," he said at once. "You think I lack tact."

She chuckled despite herself. "I know you lack tact."

"So you *are* deliberately hiding something from me," he concluded. "Are those two involved? Will and Jess, I mean."

"Not that I know of," Megan insisted with total honesty.

Mick's gaze narrowed suspiciously. "But you suspect something, don't you?"

She regarded him with impatience. "Mick, have you learned nothing from our other children? Meddling only makes things worse."

"Which means there's something going on you don't want me meddling in," he said triumphantly. "I knew it! Jess ran off because Will was there with another woman. Seeing him there upset her."

His momentary delight in having figured that out faded almost instantly. "If that man hurt Jess, he'll answer to me, by God!"

He started to rise, but Megan put her hand on his arm and locked her gaze with his. "Unless Jess comes to you and asks for your help, you will stay out of this, Mick O'Brien. Neither of us has any idea what's going on with those two, if anything. If you go after Will, you could be making matters worse. You might even be humiliating your daughter."

Mick sat back down, though he didn't look happy about it. "Then maybe I should stop by the inn and have a talk with Jess," he said. "Find out the score for myself."

Megan cringed at the thought, but rather than telling him flat-out not to go—a waste of breath, if ever there was one—she settled for warning, "If you want to go and visit with Jess, that's one thing. If you want to cross-examine her about Will or about what happened today, forget it. It's a bad idea. Jess is her own woman."

"She's our baby," he corrected. "And she always felt that neither of us paid enough attention to her. It may be late, but she has to know we're here for her now."

Megan sighed. "No one is more aware that I abandoned Jess when she was barely seven than I am. I think she's finally come to understand all the reasons behind our divorce. I even think she's starting to believe that I never stopped loving her. That doesn't mean she's ready for me to jump in and start parenting her at this late date. The same goes for you, Mick. We have to let Jess come to us."

Mick heaved an unhappy sigh. "I don't like sitting on the sidelines when one of my kids is miserable."

"I know that," she said more sympathetically. "But maybe she's not miserable. Maybe she and Connor had one of their usual spats. That's possible."

"I suppose."

"Why don't you just drop in at the inn to see if she needs any help?" Megan suggested. "Fridays are always crazy over there once the weekend guests start pouring in. She'll appreciate the gesture, and you'll be there if she decides she wants to open up. How about that?"

Mick's expression brightened. "I can do that. I'll get the lay of the land and report to you over dinner. Are we still going to Brady's tonight?"

"Unless you'd like to invite Jess to join us at the house," she said.

"And have you cooking at the end of a long day?" Mick chided. "I'll invite her to join us at Brady's. I'll call and let you know what she says." He walked around the counter and kissed her. "Marrying a sensible woman was the smartest thing I've ever done."

Megan laughed. "Then isn't it nice that I gave you the chance to do it twice?"

She watched him leave, then shook her

head, wondering if sending him over to the inn had been the smart thing to do. She knew all about Mick's good intentions. They lasted just as long as he wanted them to, then got lost the minute he concluded he knew what was best for everyone.

She could trust him to stick to the plan or she could call and give Jess a heads-up that her father was on his way. Either path had its risks.

In the end, she opted to do nothing. After all, she was the one who'd said her daughter was her own woman now. She had to trust that Jess could handle Mick and his well-meant interference.

Then again, she also knew better than anyone that handling Mick required a delicate balancing act between staunch self-confidence and the quick footwork and blocking skills of an offensive lineman. Otherwise Mick could bulldoze right over you.

Jess had a crowd of new arrivals at the desk trying to check in. Ronnie had vanished twenty minutes ago. She was about two seconds from a nervous breakdown when she glanced up and caught sight of her father.

"What can I do to help?" he asked. "Need me to carry some of these bags for you?"

"Would you?" she asked, not questioning why he'd appeared just when she needed him. She was too grateful to have an extra pair of hands.

"Not a problem," Mick told her. "Where's that Forrest kid? I thought this was his job."

"Don't get me started," she muttered, then smiled at the couple who'd just finished registering. "Mr. And Mrs. Longwell, you have a room on the second floor with a view of the bay. Dad, can you help them with their luggage?"

"Of course," Mick said, grabbing the two small suitcases and heading for the stairs.

He was back by the time she'd finished registering the next guests, two women who'd come from New Jersey. Within an hour, all of the guests had been checked in, and several were already relaxing in the lounge with the inn's complimentary wine and hors d'oeuvres. Jess had just taken her first deep breath of the afternoon when her father reappeared.

"Everyone's settled," he assured her. "Looks like business is good."

"It should be like this at least through

the end of October," Jess told him. "We're almost full for Thanksgiving, too."

"Good for you," he said, beaming at her. "You should be proud, Jess. This place is every bit the success you thought it could be. Your mother and I are so happy for you. You've done a terrific job."

"Thanks, Dad," she said, genuinely appreciative of his praise. "What brings you by, anyway? I'm sure you didn't come over here to carry suitcases for me, though you were certainly a godsend this afternoon."

"Happy to pitch in," he said.

"Would you like a glass of wine or some of Gail's hors d'oeuvres?"

"Not for me. I wanted to see if you'd like to join your mother and me for dinner at Brady's tonight, if you're not busy."

Jess stilled. "Why?"

"Why not?" he countered. "You deserve a night out, don't you? Unless you already have plans, of course."

"Dad, you and Mom are practically still in the honeymoon phase. I know these dinners at Brady's are your official date nights. Why would you suddenly want me along?"

He flushed guiltily. "We haven't seen much of you lately, that's all."

"I was at the house for dinner last Sunday," she reminded him. "And I stopped by the gallery for coffee with Mom earlier this week."

He shrugged. "She didn't mention that."

Jess studied her father with a narrowed gaze. "This doesn't have anything to do with the fact that you saw me take off from Panini Bistro earlier, does it?"

Mick frowned. "You heard me calling you?"

"They could have heard you in Ocean City, Dad."

"Well, why didn't you stop? You looked upset. I just wanted to make sure everything was all right."

"I'm sure Connor and Heather filled you in."

"They didn't tell me a blasted thing," he grumbled. "I think I figured out a few things for myself. You want to tell me if I got it right? Did it have anything to do with Will being there with that woman?"

Jess tried not to let it show that his question had thrown her. "Why on earth would you think that?" she asked, hoping to keep a tremor out of her voice.

She had no idea why seeing Will with

another woman had shaken her so badly. In fact, she'd told herself initially that her annoyance had been aimed solely at Connor and Heather. Only after she was well away from the restaurant had she conceded to herself that seeing Will on a date, especially one likely arranged by that online dating service of his, had infuriated her.

She forced herself to meet her father's gaze. "You do know there's nothing going on between Will and me, right?"

"Is that so?" he said, sounding skeptical. "I'll admit it was guesswork on my part, but when I ran the theory past your mother, she didn't deny it was a possibility."

"So you and Mom have been speculating about this already?" Jess said, having no problem at all making her tone icy. Just the thought of it chilled her. It was a little late in life for the two of them to suddenly start caring about her feelings.

"I'm worried about you," Mick said unrepentantly. "That's what fathers do."

"You didn't worry all that much when I was seven, did you?" she said accusingly. "Mom had just left, and you were running all over the country on various jobs.

Neither of you spent a lot of time taking my feelings into account back then."

Mick frowned. "Different time," he said, not even trying to defend the indefensible. "I'm right here now, and I care about what's going on in your life."

Jess knew the only way to get him to back off was to tell him some kind of tale that would reassure him. "Look, Connor and I had words earlier, that's all. It was no big deal. We've been fighting since we were toddlers. We always get over it."

Mick didn't look entirely convinced. "And that's all it was, just a spat with your brother? It had nothing to do with Will?"

"Nothing at all," she insisted. "Everything's fine with me. I promise I'll even be speaking to Connor by the time Sunday dinner rolls around."

"Okay, then," Mick said, accepting the explanation with obvious reluctance. "And you're not interested in dinner tonight?"

"I wish I could, but I don't like to leave here when we're swamped. One of the guests might need something."

He pulled her into an embrace, then kissed the top of her head. "Call me if you need anything, okay?"

She let go of her irritation, glad to have the matter settled for now. "I will, Dad. I promise. Thanks for helping out this afternoon."

"Anytime, kiddo."

She watched him leave, then breathed a sigh of relief, only to jump when she heard Gail's chuckle right beside her.

"You fibbed to your daddy," Gail taunted.

"I did what I had to do to throw him off the scent," Jess told her. "If he had any idea I was annoyed about Will, neither one of us would be safe from Dad's meddling."

"Are you scared he'd meddle, or are you terrified he might be good at it?" Gail asked.

"Meaning?"

"The way I hear it, once Mick O'Brien sets his mind to something, things usually work out the way he intended."

"My father can meddle from now till doomsday, and it wouldn't make a bit of difference when it comes to Will and me," Jess retorted.

Unfortunately, there wasn't half as much conviction behind her declaration as there probably should have been.

* * *

When another week passed without even one date being arranged by Lunch by the Bay, Jess became even more infuriated. It was worse now that she knew it was Will's company. It proved just how little he thought of her.

She could practically hear his recitation of all the reasons why he didn't want to match her with any of the men paying for his service. He thought she was flighty. He thought her dating history was too erratic. He knew her too darned well—or thought he did—and didn't want to risk his stupid company's reputation by pairing her up with some poor sap.

Just thinking about the way he'd dismissed her made her see red. Add in the fact that he'd never even acknowledged her enrollment in the service and that he didn't have the courage to return her money, and she was ready to tear into him if they ever crossed paths.

Not that she intended to go looking for him, of course. In fact, it might be best if they didn't cross paths for months, maybe even years.

And then, long before she'd had a chance to work off her full head of steam, she spotted him in the bar at Brady's on a rare Friday night away from the inn.

"There he is, the worm," she grumbled to Connie and Laila as she got to her feet. The two glasses of wine she'd consumed on an empty stomach made her a little unsteady.

"Sit back down," Connie pleaded. "Dillon Brady may adore you, but he will not be happy if you cause a scene in his restaurant. It's the classiest place in town. He doesn't condone bar brawls."

Jess turned her attention to Connie. "Then Will should leave," she declared. "He's scum. He's impossible. He's annoyingly judgmental. And he's a coward to boot."

"Talking about me, I assume," Will said, pulling out a chair to join them.

Connie gave him a warning look. "This may not be the best time," she murmured.

"Oh, I'm used to having Jess take potshots at me," he responded easily. "It's what she does whenever she thinks I'm getting the best of her in a discussion. Instead of offering rational arguments, she resorts to personal attacks."

Jess's temper kicked up another notch

at his thoroughly condescending tone. "We don't argue," she retorted. "You're just plain stuffy and pompous. You utter decrees as if they're the gospel truth and we mere mortals shouldn't dare to question you."

Will stared at her incredulously. "When have I ever done that?"

"All the time," she said.

"Name once," he challenged.

Jess faltered and took a sip of her wine. Unfortunately, specific instances seemed to be lost in the depths of her faintly inebriated brain. "I don't have to. You know I'm right," she said, proud of her evasive maneuver.

Will, blast him, merely smiled in that superior way he had that always set her teeth on edge.

"Oh, go away," she said irritably.

"Not five minutes ago I thought you had things you wanted to say to me. Now's your chance. Go for it."

"I changed my mind. It would be a waste of breath. You never listen to a word I say, or at least you never take anything I say seriously."

"No, go ahead," he urged. "Bring it on. I can take it."

Connie sighed. "I think I'll go up to the bar and get another drink. Laila, you want anything?"

"Are you kidding?" Laila said, standing up. "I'm coming with you."

"I'll have more wine," Jess said.

"Not a chance," Connie replied.

Her two friends left her sitting there with Will, who seemed to be waiting patiently for her to say something.

"Well?" he urged. "Does this have anything to do with you seeing me at Panini Bistro with a woman last week? You seemed upset."

"I was not upset," she said. "Why would I be upset? You mean nothing to me. Less than nothing."

He didn't look as if he bought her denial. "Then what's going on in that head of yours? You're obviously ticked off at me about something. More than usual, in fact. Just get it out in the open, so we can deal with it."

"That's your solution for everything, isn't it? Talk it to death."

"I find communication to be helpful, yes," he said, fighting a smile. "Try it, why don't you?"

She wanted really badly to wipe the smug expression from his face. "Okay, fine," she said. "Why haven't you matched me up with anyone on that stupid computer system of yours? I have half a mind to charge you with fraud or something."

He lifted a brow. "Fraud?"

"You promise to find dates for people. I paid my money, and I haven't had a single date! You haven't even had the gumption just to tell me you're never going to match me with anyone."

"Right now there's no one in the system who'd be a good match," he said. "I'm adding new clients every day, though. The perfect guy could come along tomorrow."

"Nice spin," she said. "We both know it's because you don't think I'm good enough. You think I'm a messed-up scatterbrain, and you're not willing to put your precious reputation on the line to recommend me to one single client."

To his credit, Will looked genuinely stunned by the accusation. "That's what you think?"

"It's what I know," she said stubbornly, unable to keep a hurt note out of her voice. "You're supposed to be my friend, even though you know about the ADD. That doesn't make me a bad person, Will Lincoln. You, of all people, should get that. It doesn't mean I can't have a decent relationship. Maybe I haven't had one up to now, but if this system of yours were any good, you could find the right man for me."

Will shook his head as her tirade wound down. "You are without a doubt the most exasperating, infuriating, mixed-up woman I have ever known."

"See?" she said, seizing on his words. "That's exactly what I mean. You have a very low opinion of me."

"Hush," he said, sliding his chair closer.

"Why?"

"Just hush," he repeated, reaching out a hand to cup the back of her neck.

Jess was so startled, she simply stared at him. "Will?"

He gave her an exasperated look. "Do you not know how to be quiet for just ten seconds?"

He leaned forward and sealed his mouth over hers. The kiss did what nothing else had done. It silenced her. In fact, it pretty much knocked her senseless. Will's mouth was firm, persuasive, tender.

When he released her, she blinked. "Will?" This time when she murmured his name, she sounded breathless. She *was* breathless. Talk about an unexpected turn of events! Who knew the man could kiss like that, with barely leashed passion simmering just below the surface?

Dazed, she asked, "What just happened here?"

"There you go again, talking," he said, once again covering her mouth.

This kiss went on and on until her heart was pounding and she was just about two seconds from ripping the man's clothes off right where they were. Will's clothes! That thought had her breaking free and regarding him with shock.

"You kissed me!" she announced, as if he might not be aware of what he'd done.

"I did," he said calmly, looking disgustingly unruffled by the encounter.

Her gaze narrowed. "Are you going to do it again?"

He smiled, most likely at the disgustingly wistful note in her voice. "I might."

"When?"

"That remains to be seen." He stood up.

She stared at him in shock. "You're leaving? Now?"

"I think it's best."

"Why?"

"I'll let you figure that out on your own. See you, Jess."

She stared after him as he walked out of Brady's, then blinked when Connie and Laila sat back down beside her.

"That was interesting," Connie said, looking amused.

"That was hot!" Laila declared, fanning herself.

When Jess remained silent, Connie gave her arm a tug. "Hey, are you okay?"

"I'm not sure," she said, shaking off the stupor she'd been in since the kiss. She couldn't keep the surprise out of her voice when she told them, "Will kissed me. I mean, he *really* kissed me."

Laila laughed. "We noticed. Everyone in here noticed. Kate even ran and dragged Dillon out of the kitchen to watch. I'm surprised there weren't cheers. It was quite the show. If Chesapeake Shores had a TV station, that kiss would be on the eleven o'clock news."

Still dazed, Jess said, "He said it might happen again."

"Well, hallelujah!" Laila responded with enthusiasm.

Jess wasn't entirely sure what *had* just happened here tonight, but she was pretty sure a few choruses of hallelujahs were definitely in order.

What she didn't know was what on earth could possibly happen next. Whatever it was, it couldn't be any more surprising than that kiss.

5

Kissing Jess had been everything Will had expected it to be and then some. Not even in his very vivid imagination had he expected such an immediate and total sensation of something being right, something finally, at long last, being exactly as it should be. And that scared him to death.

He was smart enough to know that he'd caught Jess completely off guard. Her emotions had been running high. She'd been a little drunk as well, and he'd taken advantage of the situation. It was a simple matter to turn one kind of passion into another. Any psychology textbook could have told him that. It didn't mean Jess's opinion of him had suddenly shifted. It certainly didn't guarantee she'd turn her back on years of dismissing him and suddenly see him as boyfriend material.

But despite his very stern reminders to remain cautious, he couldn't help thinking that just maybe the dazed look in her eyes had told another story. He hoped it meant she'd suddenly seen him in a new light. Maybe the kiss had been the start of something, after all.

Or not. As he waffled back and forth, he wasn't sure he wanted to know which way things were truly leaning. Not just yet, anyway.

Stop with the analyzing, he told himself. Right now he wanted to bask in the sensations that kiss had aroused in him. He didn't want to do what was instinctive to him and analyze it to death, or to risk running into Jess and having her shatter his fragile hope that their relationship might be on a whole new footing.

In a move clearly designed to avoid any chance encounters, he hunkered down in his office during the day and in his condo at night. Despite the obvious reasons for his behavior, he managed to convince himself that he was behind on his case notes, that he needed to catch up on the business of running Lunch by the Bay. Deep in denial, he even made a case for telling himself that he wasn't hiding out, not from his own emotions and certainly not from Jess.

Still, after several days of not following his usual routine or answering phone calls from his friends, he wasn't all that surprised to answer his door one night and find Mack on his doorstep.

"You've skipped lunch for three days running," Mack said, looking him up and down. "You haven't called me or Jake back."

"You can't have been too worried, given how long it took you to come and check on me," Will noted.

Mack merely frowned at the comment. "You don't look sick, so what's going on?"

"I got behind on my paperwork," Will told him.

Mack didn't look as if he believed him, but he was already wandering around the apartment with a distracted expression that told Will something else entirely had brought him over here tonight.

"Is something on your mind?" Will asked him.

"Not really," Mack said. "You have any beer in this place?"

"Always," Will responded, barely concealing his amusement. Since they'd been of legal age and he'd had his own place, he'd always kept beer on hand for Jake and Mack. "Help yourself."

"You want one?"

Will shook his head. "I'm good."

Mack returned with his beer, but he still didn't sit. He continued to pace, pausing only to stare out the window at the sliver of a view Will had of the bay. When he sighed heavily, Will couldn't stand it any longer.

"How's Susie?" Will asked, feeling his way.

Mack shrugged. "Okay, I guess."

"What do you mean, you guess? Haven't you seen her?"

"Yesterday," Mack said. "She was fine, then. I haven't spoken to her today."

Will knew all about being patient when one of his clients was dancing around a tough issue, but in his personal life he tended to be more direct. He hated watching Mack working so hard *not* to say whatever was on his mind.

"You know," he began, "we could play twenty questions for a while and eventually I'd hit on whatever's bugging you, but it would be easier if you'd just tell me."

Mack stood across the room, his back to Will, still staring out the window. "Susie asked me something yesterday that I haven't been able to get out of my head."

"Something about your relationship?"

"No, we were talking about newspapers, you know, the way they're struggling, that kind of thing."

"Okay," Will said slowly, still not following. "And?"

"She asked me what I'd do if I ever lost my job as a columnist for the paper in Baltimore."

Will stared at him. "You think your job's on the line?" he asked, startled. No wonder Mack looked shaken.

Mack's column was one of the most popular in the paper, as far as Will knew. The guy's picture was plastered all over bus benches in Baltimore, for heaven's sake.

Mack had gone from being a celebrated local athlete to writing about sports in a town that loved its teams. He was as much of a celebrity now as he had been on the gridiron during his all-too-brief professional career. It was one of the reasons he was such an eligible bachelor and why Will and Jake both thought it was so astounding that he'd given up all those fawning women in exchange for a relationship with Susie that he refused to define.

"My job's secure," Mack said, though he still looked troubled. "At least for now. But I can't deny that the business is changing." He turned and faced Will. "What the hell would I do if I lost it?"

"You'd find something else," Will said confidently. "Remember when you blew out your knee and ended your football career? You were convinced your life was over. Then you wrote a couple of pieces on spec-ulation for the paper, and the next thing you knew, they'd hired you. That's the way life is. When one door closes, another one opens."

Mack gave him a disgruntled look. "Could you save the clichés? Besides, it's not as if there's another newspaper around I could jump to. They're all cutting back."

"There are TV stations," Will reminded

him. "You're a good-looking guy. You could work on the air. Besides, aren't you getting way ahead of yourself? There's nothing to indicate that you're about to be fired. That is what you said, right?"

Mack nodded but then gave him a bleak look. "But the paper let half a dozen reporters go today. It happened out of the blue. It almost felt as if Susie had been tapped into some sort of ESP gossip mill."

Will lifted a brow. "Really? You believe that?"

"Well, come on. She's the one who brought it up yesterday, and then, *boom,* today things started happening. At the paper we hadn't even heard any rumors that there was a possibility of cuts. More people were eliminated from the production side, too. They didn't even offer buyouts. They just fired those with the least seniority. What if this is the start of the belt-tightening?"

"Then you'll deal with it," Will assured him. "Baltimore's not the only city in the country. There are a couple of papers in Washington. That's not far away."

"There have been massive buyouts over there, too," Mack said, still not consoled. "The long-term future for the whole industry is on shaky ground. Everybody's scrambling to see if they can stem these tides of red ink."

Will studied him. "What are you really worried about, Mack? Is it your job? You must know you'd have options outside of newspapers or TV. You could come back here and coach, if you really wanted to. I know the high school principal has talked to you about that."

Mack didn't look relieved, so Will took another stab at what he thought was really behind his friend's mood. "Mack, is this really about having to move away at some point and leave Susie behind?"

For a moment, Mack looked startled. Then he grinned, almost looking relieved to have Will cut to the chase. "Damn, you're good."

Will laughed. "That's why they pay me the big bucks. As for Susie, despite your failure to admit that the two of you actually have a relationship, you're the only ones who don't seem to know that you do. I'm not saying I want you to lose your job, but maybe it would be the wake-up call you both need to face how much you mean to each other."

He met Mack's still-troubled gaze. "Or

you could just face it now and get on with having the kind of relationship you both really want. Then if something changes with your career, you'd be facing that together."

Mack shook his head. "Susie's made it clear she'd never date a guy like me."

"A player?" Will assessed.

Mack nodded. "She doesn't want to get lumped in with all the other women I've dated and dumped."

Will rolled his eyes. "Haven't either of you noticed that you haven't been a player for quite a while now? Unless I've missed something, you haven't been on a date with another woman since you and Susie started spending so much time together."

"I'm pretty sure she thinks it's a fluke," Mack said.

"Okay, it's just you and me right now and I swear I will not repeat this or throw it back in your face later, but for once just say it. Do you love her?"

To Will's astonishment, Mack looked genuinely startled by the question. "Everybody knows I don't do love," he said a little too quickly. "Or commitment."

"And yet for three years or so, you've been not-dating Susie. In my book, that shows an amazing level of commitment, especially since you haven't even slept together." His gaze narrowed. "Or have you?"

"How many times do I have to say that we don't have that kind of relationship?" Mack said in frustration.

"Then if you ask me, it's all the more remarkable that you haven't once cheated on her," Will said. "Not that it would be cheating, if you aren't actually dating." He frowned. "Do you know how muddy and ridiculous all of this is, if not for you, then for the rest of us?"

"You're not my problem," Mack said testily.

"Okay, here's how I see it. I know it would be easy enough to look at your past, at all the ways your family was messed up, and figure out exactly why you don't believe in love and commitment, but the truth is, you're better at both than you give yourself credit for. I'm not just talking about Susie, either. You're one of the best friends I have. I think Jake would say the same thing. We count on you. You've never once let either of us down."

Mack looked embarrassed by the praise.

"Come on. You guys would do the same for me."

"Of course, because we both care about you. You've got what it takes to be in a relationship for the long haul, Mack. I hope you wake up and accept that before it's too late. Don't lose Susie because you're scared."

Mack scowled at his choice of words. "I'm not scared," he insisted.

"Then you're crazy," Will said. "When it comes down to it, we're all a little scared of love and making a lifelong commitment. It's a big deal."

Mack leveled a knowing look right back at him. "Is that why you haven't pushed harder to win Jess?"

Will wasn't used to having the tables turned on him, certainly not by Mack, who tended to avoid talk about emotional issues. In fact, this whole conversation had been a rarity.

"Maybe," Will admitted, since Mack had opened the door. "Or maybe I've been terrified that if I pushed hard and still lost her, I'd never get over it."

"Then I should tell you what my grandmama once told me before she took off to dance in Vegas or wherever the hell she went," Mack said. "Nothing beats a try but a failure. That advice was what kept me on a playing field when I was a kid and everyone said I was too small to play football. I figured if I kept trying, I might fail, but if I gave up, I'd fail for sure."

Will laughed. "Words to live by," he confirmed. "We should both take them to heart."

But he wondered if either one of them was quite ready to try wholeheartedly for the women they wanted in their lives . . . and risk losing them forever.

Sunday dinners at home had always been an O'Brien family obligation, but they were changing. For one thing, Gram had given up the reins. Oh, Nell O'Brien still contributed the main dish more often than not, but she'd been training the rest of them to cook their favorite side dishes and desserts. Each week her grandchildren were assigned to bring a new dish, made according to Gram's carefully handwritten recipes.

This week Jess was supposed to be bringing homemade Irish soda bread. She wondered if Gram would figure out that she'd enlisted Gail's help in making it. Jess, like her mother, was hopeless in the kitchen. Before she'd left them all, Megan had kept them from starving, but no one could claim that her meals were anything more than barely edible.

Jess walked into the kitchen on Sunday, found Gram at the stove and kissed her cheek before setting two perfectly baked loaves of bread on the counter. Her grandmother eyed them suspiciously.

"You baked those yourself?" she asked.

"What's wrong with them?" Jess asked, bristling. They'd looked perfect to her.

"Usually the first time someone bakes bread, it doesn't turn out so well," Gram said, gazing directly into Jess's eyes.

She waited, and Jess flinched. "Okay, you caught me. Gail baked the bread."

Gram shook her head. "I thought as much. How do you expect to master my recipes if you don't do it yourself?"

"I'm counting on everyone else in the family to master them," Jess told her, grinning as Abby came in and deposited a bowl of rice pudding on the table. She peered under the lid of the plastic bowl. "Looks edible."

"I should hope so," Abby said. "It's my third batch. Trace made me throw out the first two attempts. Even the twins turned their noses up at it, and those two little garbage disposals will eat anything."

"How on earth can you mess up rice pudding?" Gram asked. "Did I teach you girls nothing?"

"You only had a year after Mom left to influence me," Abby said. "I seem to recall you throwing me out of the kitchen in disgust on more than one occasion. I was no better at cooking than I was at needlework."

Nell chuckled. "That's true enough. Let's hope Bree has a knack for this, or you'll all starve after I'm gone."

"First of all, you're not going anywhere for a very long time," Abby said, slipping an arm around Nell's waist. "And second, for every failure that Bree, Jess and I have, you can count on Kevin to get it right. Our brother inherited the cooking genes in the family. You wait and see. He'll come in here in a few minutes with something that will have our mouths watering. What was his assignment this week, anyway?"

"He's making my chicken and dumplings," Nell told them. "I spoke to him a half hour ago, and he said his dumplings are lighter than air." She looked doubtful. "We'll see. It takes years of practice to get dumplings just right."

"Oh, I think you can count on Kevin," Abby said, seemingly oblivious to the fact that Gram might not be quite ready to yield her place as the family's best cook. She seemed almost happier about their failures than about Kevin's possible success.

Jess stepped in. "Gram, no matter how good Kevin's dumplings are, they won't be half as good as yours," she assured her grandmother.

Nell looked pleased by the compliment. "I know you're saying that just to spare my feelings, but I do appreciate it."

Abby flushed guiltily when she realized she'd inadvertently upset Gram, but she wisely didn't prolong the conversation. Instead, she turned her attention to Jess. "You look tired. Everything okay?"

"It's been a wild couple of weeks at the inn," Jess said, not about to reveal that she'd slept hardly a wink since that infamous kiss Will had placed on her at Brady's. She hadn't been able to get it out of her head. Always restless, she'd been even more so than usual since that night.

Worse, Will had been making himself scarce. She'd even tried dropping into Sally's at lunchtime, to no avail. Jake and Mack had been there without him. Since she didn't want anyone to guess that she was practically chasing after him, she'd stopped going there or anywhere else she might bump into him.

"Then it doesn't have anything to do with your social life?" Abby said, a wicked sparkle in her eyes.

"I have no social life," Jess declared. "None."

"Really?" Abby said. "Then Will didn't—"

Jess cut her off. "I haven't seen Will in ages."

Gram listened to all this without a word, but Jess couldn't help noticing the smile that was tugging at her lips. She frowned at her grandmother. "What?"

"I was just thinking that it's a good thing Will's coming for dinner today," Nell said innocently. "The two of you will be able to catch up. Maybe get your stories straight."

"Will is coming for dinner?" Jess repeated. "Who invited him?" If it was her father or Connor, she was going to kill them. "And what do you mean about getting our stories straight? There's no story."

"That's not the way I hear it," Gram said, then gave her a defiant look. "And I'm the one who invited him."

"But—" She was about to protest, but Gram cut her off with a chiding look.

"You know he doesn't have any family left in the area," Gram said. "He should spend Sundays with people who care about him. Will has always been welcome here. That is not about to change just because it might make you uncomfortable."

"Who said anything about being uncomfortable?" Jess said. "I guess I'm just surprised that he accepted." She'd have thought the O'Brien Sunday dinner would be the last place he'd want to be at the moment. Not only would he have to face her, but he'd have to deal with the prying eyes of her entire family.

"Of course he accepted," Gram said. "Why wouldn't he?"

"I just thought he might find it awkward," Jess said before she'd considered the ramifications of such a remark.

"Why would Will feel awkward around

us?" Abby asked, seizing on the comment. "Like Gram said, he's practically family. He's been hanging around with Kevin and Connor since grade school. I can't even count the number of holidays he's spent over here."

"I just meant . . ." Jess began, then realized she had no reasonable explanation. "Oh, never mind. I'll go see if Mom needs help setting the table."

Before she could leave, though, her grandmother pinned her with a look. "You wouldn't be trying to avoid talking about Will kissing you at Brady's recently, would you?"

Jess regarded her with shock. "How do you know about that?"

Gram chuckled. "Word about a thing like that gets around."

"Indeed, it does," Abby agreed. Her broad grin proved she'd known about it, too. "Who knew Dillon Brady could be such a gossip?"

"I heard about it from his wife," Gram added.

"Well, I have nothing to say about it," Jess said, all but running from the kitchen.

"I imagine Will might be more forthcoming," Gram called after her. "He's awfully fond of my chicken and dumplings. I suspect that'll loosen his tongue."

Jess bit back a groan and kept going. If she could have, she would have bolted from the house and not looked back, but the commotion that would cause wasn't worth it. Nope, she just had to stay here and do her best to steer clear of Will so that none of the too-eager observers in her family would get any wild ideas that something had changed between the two of them. If it had. She honestly couldn't be sure.

When she found the dining room table set and no sign of her mother, she wandered outside. No sooner was she seated in a rocker on the porch than Will himself appeared, carrying a large bouquet of flowers.

She blinked at the lavish arrangement. "Will, that's a really bad idea. You shouldn't have brought me flowers. It will stir up a hornet's nest."

He laughed. "Then it's a good thing they're not for you. I brought them for your grandmother to thank her for including me today."

Jess sat back, not sure whether she felt

more embarrassed or deflated. "Oh, of course. She'll love them. But you probably ought to know that she's more interested in information."

"Oh?" he said, immediately looking troubled.

"She's heard about the kiss. So has Abby. I imagine everyone else knows about it by now as well. The way I hear it, Dillon and Kate are bigger blabbermouths than the O'Briens."

He sat down hard in the chair next to hers. "I see."

"Gram seems to think we should get our stories straight."

He stared at her blankly. "What stories?"

"The ones where we deny it meant anything or try to convince them that our lips locked by accident," she said with a shrug. "Anything to keep them from jumping on this and starting some kind of matchmaking frenzy."

"Why do I think it's probably too late for that?" he asked bleakly.

"Because you know the O'Briens. We're nothing if not eager to meddle."

"So what's our story?" he asked. "Any thoughts?"

"I'm all for trying out the accidental lip-lock theory," she said.

Will had the audacity to laugh. "No one who saw us that night is going to buy that. The first kiss, maybe, but there were two."

Jess shivered. "I remember." The second had been even more potent than the first. "Maybe they don't know that."

"Maybe instead of worrying about them, we should be focusing on what the kisses really meant," he suggested, looking directly into her eyes in a way that disconcerted her.

Jess shook her head.

"Why not?"

"I'm not ready to start analyzing what happened," she said.

"You'd rather pretend that nothing did?"

"I'd like to try," she admitted wistfully. "But I'm pretty sure that's going to be impossible."

Will tried to conceal a smile but didn't quite pull it off.

Jess scowled at him. "Don't let that go to your head. I'm just saying it's not so easy to un-ring that bell."

"I wouldn't dream of trying," he said quickly.

She gave him a plaintive look. "Why did you come here today?"

He held her gaze for a long time before he said, "For your grandmother's chicken and dumplings, of course."

"You know Kevin cooked, right? It might not be the same as Gram's."

He laughed. "It'll be close enough, I imagine. And it's bound to be better than anything in my freezer."

Jess felt guilty at even hinting that he shouldn't have come. "Sorry. I'm being selfish. I'm just not ready to deal with any of this, I guess. Whatever *this* is."

Instead of trying to define it for her, he plucked a white rose from the arrangement of hydrangeas and roses and held it out to her. "I don't think Nell will miss it."

She frowned, ignoring the flower. Maybe it was a sweet gesture, but suddenly she wasn't in the mood for sweet gestures. "Thanks, but even that's likely to arouse questions, Will. Just take the flowers inside and get them into water."

He studied her quietly. "Jess, do we need to talk? We could leave and go somewhere else, if you want to."

"What could we possibly need to discuss?" she said, not entirely sure why she was so annoyed. Nothing about this encounter had gone the way she'd expected it to. Truthfully, she wasn't even sure what her expectations had been.

Will looked justifiably confused. "I'm not sure exactly what we need to talk about. I just know that you seem angry all of a sudden."

"I'm not angry," she said. Hurt, maybe. Confused, for sure. But not angry. Had that blasted kiss meant nothing, after all? Will was all about honesty and being direct, but he hadn't said a single word to indicate that the kiss had affected him at all. She'd opened herself up—well, a little, anyway—but all he'd done was make light of what had happened.

Though he didn't look as if he believed her denial about being angry, he simply nodded and stood up. "Then I'll see you inside."

After he'd gone, Jess sighed. This was going to be a whole lot harder than she'd anticipated. It was as if the kiss had unleashed all sorts of unexpected emotions, and now she was supposed to stuff them back inside and pretend they didn't exist, not just in front of her family, but in front of Will, too.

A part of her wanted to march inside and throw caution to the wind, but she knew better, at least in this setting. Because if she did what she wanted to do and kissed Will in front of her entire family just to see if the experience was still magical, there would be no turning back.

And though she might not know much these days, she knew with every fiber of her being that she wasn't ready for that.

6

Will didn't have too much time to worry about Jess's odd mood once dinner was over. They'd barely finished dessert when Susie appeared at his side.

"We need to talk," she announced, her usually animated expression dejected. "Outside."

Will glanced across the room, saw that Jess was slipping out through the kitchen and knew that she wasn't likely to welcome him chasing after her. He forced a smile for Susie. "Sure," he said. "Want to go for a walk on the beach?"

Though the fall day was surprisingly hot,

there was a good breeze off the water. They fell into step and walked along the narrow strip of sand in silence.

He glanced over at her eventually. "You going to tell me why you wanted to talk to me?"

She sighed. "It's Mack," she said, then added in frustration, "It's always Mack. The man is going to drive me insane."

Will couldn't keep himself from chuckling. "I think the effect is mutual."

Susie waved off the comment. "Come on. Mack's oblivious, and lately it's been even worse than usual."

"What do you mean?"

She paused and faced Will. "Can I be honest with you?"

"Of course."

"And you won't go running to Mack?"

"Absolutely not."

"Okay, then," she said, and drew in a deep breath. "I'm crazy about him. I have been for years."

"Now there's a news flash," Will said before he could stop himself. He met her gaze and smiled. "I'm sorry. You're not telling me anything I haven't known before."

She sighed. "I figured. I guess I knew it wasn't a secret, but I kind of hoped I could pretend seeing him was no big deal. That way, if he walked away, which he's eventually bound to do, my pride would still be intact."

"Why are you so certain he'd leave you?"

"Because that's what Mack does," she said pragmatically. "He leaves. He thinks he's just like his father, the sleaze who left before he was born. He's spent his whole life proving it to himself by dating one woman after another and dumping every one of them. I think there were even a few along the way that he actually liked, but he didn't stick around long enough to see if the relationship would work. I watched him do it all through high school and college. Even though I had feelings for him, I vowed it wasn't going to happen to me."

"So you decided to be his friend," Will concluded.

Susie nodded. "Men might leave women, but they usually keep their friends. Just look at you, Jake and Mack. You're like the three musketeers or something. I wanted that kind of relationship with Mack, one that would last. I figured if it was easy, with no demands or expectations, maybe he'd relax."

"And finally notice you?" Will suggested gently.

Susie nodded, her expression miserable. "A while back, when Shanna first came to town and got involved with Kevin, she told me she thought Mack was crazy about me. I actually started to get my hopes up. I figured, hey, if an objective observer noticed something, then maybe it was true." She sighed. "But nothing changed. Now I don't know if it ever will. It's like we're locked in this pattern and we're both too scared to risk changing it."

She gave him a hopeful look. "Do you think it's possible to ever break out of the friend mold? Or have I doomed myself by making such a big deal of the fact that I'd never date Mack?"

Will thought about her question. "In some ways, I do think it's harder to go from being friends to being something more. If the friendship matters, no one wants to take the risk of changing things."

"Tell me about it," she said gloomily.

"But here's the thing," Will told her. "If

you don't ask for more or expect more from Mack—if you just stick with the status quo—will you ever be truly happy? Sometimes you have to take the risk of losing it all to get what you really want."

Susie blinked at the question, then grinned. "That sounds a lot like the pot calling the kettle black," she said. "Have you ever asked yourself the same thing about Jess?"

Will frowned. He'd asked himself that very thing just days earlier. He wasn't about to discuss it with Susie, though. "I thought we were talking about you and Mack."

"We can spend a couple of minutes on you, while we're at it," she said. "It'll make me feel better to focus on someone else's mixed-up love life."

"Not necessary," Will said adamantly. "You've told me why you and Mack got stuck in this nonrelationship thing, and I get it. Up until now you've been content to leave things alone. What's changed?"

To his dismay, tears welled up in her eyes. "I don't know," she said. "The last couple of weeks, it's as if he's been backing away, and I have no idea why." She met Will's gaze. "If I lose him as a friend, it'll be pretty ironic, don't you think? Especially after all I've done to make sure that's enough for me. I mean, I've been lying to myself for years now that being friends is better than nothing. Other guys have asked me out, but I wasn't interested. Mack was always around, so who had time for someone else, anyway?" She shook her head. "I am such an idiot."

"You're not an idiot," Will soothed. "You made a choice that seemed right at the time."

"Well, obviously it was a lousy choice."

Will resisted the urge to smile. "Really? You and Mack have been pretty tight for years now. You're so close, you practically complete each other's sentences, just the way a married couple does. Surely that's worth something." He met her gaze. "Have you tried to talk to him about this?"

"Not really," she admitted. "I didn't want to make too big a deal out of it."

Will saw the trap she'd created for herself. Friends gave each other space. They didn't crowd each other or sit down and have deep relationship talks.

"It's quite a dilemma, isn't it, trying to

maintain the illusion that Mack doesn't really matter to you?" Will said, regarding her with sympathy.

"It sucks," she said candidly.

"Maybe it's time to stop pretending," Will suggested.

"I don't know if I can. I don't want to lose him, Will."

"But you don't have him now," he pointed out.

"He's my friend now," she corrected.

"Then you should be able to go to him and ask what's going on," Will told her.

"I thought maybe you could just tell me, and then I'd know what he needs from me."

Will laughed. "If I promised to keep your confidence, what makes you think I'd violate his?"

Her expression brightened. "Then something is going on and you do know what it is," she said triumphantly.

"Talk to Mack," he advised.

"You won't even give me a hint?"

"Not a chance."

"I guess I knew you wouldn't tell me," she said, looking resigned. "Do you want to talk about Jess now?"

"I do not," he said emphatically.

For the first time since they'd begun their walk, Susie laughed. "I figured as much. We're quite a pair, aren't we?"

Will sighed. "We are, indeed."

Jess had watched Will head off to the beach with Susie, and an unfamiliar feeling had stirred inside her, one she'd never felt before, at least in connection with Will. It was flat-out jealousy. She knew it was ridiculous on a whole lot of levels, especially since everyone knew Susie had eyes only for Mack, but there it was. Jess didn't like staying behind while Will was off with another woman, especially Susie. She'd had some kind of crazy rivalry going with her too-perfect cousin for years now. That's probably all it was, not wanting to share Will with the cousin who already had everything Jess had always wanted: respect, academic success, popularity.

This cannot happen, she told herself adamantly. She was not going to turn into that kind of woman. She already had enough insecurities without allowing Will to turn her into some kind of jealous freak. Nothing good came out of that dark emotion.

She probably ought to leave, just go back to the inn and dig into the pile of paperwork on her desk. It hadn't gone away, and there was certainly enough there to keep her distracted for hours. Or there would have been, if she'd been able to concentrate on anything for hours. Her ADD precluded that.

She'd been cleaning out the attic recently, hoping to eventually convert it into another guestroom and bath. She could do that, she thought, her gaze still straying toward the bay as she watched for some sign of Will and Susie returning.

"Looking for someone?" Abby inquired, coming outside to perch on the porch railing in front of her.

"No," she lied. "Just relaxing."

"You could always go down to the beach and catch up with Will and Susie," Abby said.

Jess scowled at her. "Why would I want to do that?"

"Because sitting here waiting for them to come back is making you crazy," Abby said. "You do know you have nothing to worry about with those two, don't you?"

"Of course I know," she said.

"Then why the glum expression?"

"Because apparently I've lost my grip on reality recently," Jess admitted reluctantly.

Abby chuckled. "You mean because you liked kissing Will?"

Jess nodded. "Who knew the man could kiss like that? It caught me off guard. I mean, that's probably all it was, right?"

"Is that what you think?" Abby said.

Jess nodded, eager to seize on the explanation. "I'm sure that's it." She cast a plaintive look at her big sister. "Remember how you tried to fix Heather up with some guy from your office just to get Connor all worked up?"

"I remember," Abby said.

"Why haven't you ever tried to fix me up? Is it because you don't think I'm capable of settling down?"

"Don't be ridiculous," Abby said. "I think when the right man comes along, you're going to be a wonderful wife and mother. And if you'd ever asked me to fix you up, I'd have done it happily."

Jess wasn't entirely sure she believed her. "Really? Despite the whole ADD thing?"

"Sweetie, you've been managing that

really well. Look at the inn. It's a huge success. You've figured out what you need to
do to handle all the demands of the job.
You've learned how to ask for help when
you need it. You'll do the same when it
comes to having a family."

Jess sighed. "I want to believe that. But
even you have to admit, when it comes to
men, my attention span has been pretty
short."

"Maybe that's the ADD, or maybe it's
because none of them were right for you,"
Abby said. "Remember all those jobs you
had before you opened the inn? They just
weren't what you needed. The inn was.
The same will hold true for a man."

"I hope you're right. If I ever do get married, I want it to last," Jess said wistfully. "I
want to have what you and Bree have
found with Trace and Jake, what Kevin has
with Shanna and Connor has with Heather."

"You're a gorgeous, smart, exciting, unpredictable woman, and I mean that in the
best way. You'll find everything you deserve. I promise you that." Abby grinned.
"And if you don't find it on your own, you
know Dad will stick his nose into it sooner
or later."

"Heaven forbid!" Jess said with feeling. She stood up, then cast one last look toward the steps up from the beach. Still no sign of Will and Susie, but she didn't feel quite so crazed about it. "Thanks, Abby. As always, you've grounded me. I think I'll head back to the inn."

"If you need any help with the bills, let me know," Abby said casually.

Jess bristled. "Between the accountant and me, everything's under control," she said.

"It was just an offer," Abby chided. "Just a reminder that I'm here if you need me."

Jess sighed. "I know. Sorry. Actually, though, I think I'm going to do something physical. I need to burn off some energy. I bought a bunch of boxes the other day, so I thought I'd pack up some of the stuff in the attic and get it ready to give away. When I can free up some money, I'd like to get that area converted into another guest-room and bath, maybe even make it a honeymoon suite. There's a glorious view from up there."

She waited for Abby to scold her about spending money she didn't have, but surprisingly, her sister, the family financial wizard, nodded.

"Sounds like a smart idea," Abby said approvingly. "Why don't you have Dad take a look and give you an estimate?"

Jess stared at her. "Seriously?"

Abby held up a cautioning hand. "It depends on the numbers, but yes, it's worth checking out. We'll see if we can figure out a way to make it happen."

Jess threw her arms around her sister and gave her a fierce hug. "Thanks, Abby."

"Don't thank me. You're the one who's made the inn into a business worth expanding."

Jess felt herself standing a little taller at the praise. "I have, haven't I?"

All thoughts of Will forgotten for the moment, she headed back to the inn with her step considerably lighter than it had been just a half-hour earlier.

Jess had changed into old shorts and a tanktop before heading up to the dusty attic. Over the past few years, she'd spent a few scattered hours up here, getting lost in some of the old books she'd found in the trunks that had been stored here for years before she'd bought the place. Today, though, she was determined to stay focused.

Armed with boxes and garbage bags, she intended to sort things into three batches—items to be given away, those she might be able to use in the inn, and trash that wasn't worth keeping. Unfortunately, all of it came with a heavy layer of dust, so she spent almost as much time sneezing and wiping things off as she did making decisions.

She'd been at it for an hour when she heard footsteps approaching. When Will appeared at the top of the stairs, a grin broke across his face.

"You're quite a picture," he commented.

"Thanks," she said wryly. "You might want to reconsider coming up here in your good clothes."

"Everything I'm wearing is washable," he said of his neatly pressed chinos and the dress shirt with its sleeves rolled up. Still, he stood hesitantly. "Want some help? Abby mentioned you were over here trying to sort through all this stuff." He glanced at the trash bags she'd already filled. "I could at least haul those downstairs for you."

"That would be fantastic," she said gratefully, "if you're sure you don't mind."

"I wouldn't have come if I didn't want to help. Let me run those down. Do you want them in your Dumpster out back or where?"

"The Dumpster's great. Trash pickup's tomorrow."

He picked up the four bags she'd filled so far and took them as if they weighed next to nothing. When he came back, he brought bottles of water from the fridge she kept in her office. He handed one to her.

"I thought you might be thirsty," he said,

"You're a godsend," she told him, taking a long swallow, aware that his gaze seemed to be glued to her chest, which was glistening with perspiration. Her tank top seemed to be clinging to her curves. "Um, Will . . ." Her voice hitched as she tried to snag his attention.

He blinked and stared at her, this time at her face. "Sorry," he said, an actual blush climbing into his cheeks. "What would you like me to do now?"

Throw me down on this floor and make

love to me. The outrageous thought popped into her head, bringing a flood of heat into her own cheeks.

"Trunk," she said, gesturing across the attic. "Over there." As far from her as it was possible to get.

His lips quirked. "You want me to sort through the things in the trunk," he said.

"Yes."

"How will I know what's worth keeping?"

She drew in a breath and tried to steady her nerves and her voice. "You'll know. If you have any questions, just ask." She gave him a hopeful look. "Unless you'd rather go. You don't have to help."

"I've never known anyone so eager to turn down a willing volunteer," he said, as he opened the trunk and began to sort through it. "Why is that, Jess? Do I make you nervous all of a sudden?"

"You scare me to death," she blurted before she could censor herself. She immediately groaned. "I can't believe I said that."

Will laughed. "In my business, honesty's considered a good thing. So, why do I scare you?"

She frowned at him. "There you go again,

getting all shrinklike on me. Do you really want to dissect this?"

He nodded, his expression serious. "I believe I do."

"Well, I don't. It makes me feel like one of your case studies. I've told you before, I hate that feeling."

"Has it occurred to you that friends actually talk about their emotions to one another? I know for a fact you talk to Abby and Connor about stuff. Why is it different talking to me?"

"You're a shrink," she said as if that explained everything. In fact, she thought it did.

"But I'm not *your* shrink," he said.

"It just feels weird."

He backed off at once. "Okay, then we won't talk about anything you're feeling, about me or anything else," he said readily. "What are you planning to do with this space, once you have it cleaned out?"

"I'm hoping to turn it into a suite," she said at once, eager to change the subject. "A honeymoon suite, in fact." In her enthusiasm for the project, she described every detail she'd envisioned. "And look out the window, Will. There's the most amazing view from up here. I'd like to open up that wall with more windows, if Dad says the structure can take it. It would be so incredible to wake up in this room with the bay and practically the whole town bathed in sunlight at daybreak."

Will smiled at her enthusiasm. He moved to look out the window, then nodded. "It would be fantastic, Jess. Instead of a honeymoon suite, though, you could make this area into your rooms. There's enough space for a living room, even a little kitchenette. It would be incredibly cozy up here. In fact, the chimney's right over there. I'll bet you could even put in a fireplace."

She glanced around, suddenly seeing the space as he'd described it. "Oh, my gosh, I never even thought of that. What a great idea!" She sobered at once. "Of course, I shouldn't keep the best space for myself. Guests would pay a fortune for a self-contained suite like that."

"Up to you, but it seems to me the inn's owner should be comfortable."

"My rooms downstairs are fine," she insisted. Besides, she had a feeling that the room she was envisioning and that Will was describing would be far too romantic for one. It would be meant for a couple, two people in love. Still, the thought of it charmed her.

Will's gaze caught hers. "What happens when you have a family, Jess? Will you live somewhere else or stay here?"

"I've never thought that far ahead," she admitted. "I mean, if it was just me and a husband, I suppose we'd stay here, but if there were kids . . ." Her voice trailed off and she shrugged.

"You have plenty of property," he reminded her. "You could always build a home right here. That way you'd have your privacy, but you'd be close enough to keep an eye on things."

She couldn't deny the idea made sense, but such a thing was a long way down the road. She didn't even have a man, much less a family.

Even as she told herself that, though, she couldn't help envisioning Will up here in this very space, by her side, sitting in front of a cozy fire, the view of Chesapeake Shores spread out before them. The image was so clear, so captivating, it stunned her. She blinked and forced her attention back to the trunk of old books in front of her.

"I'm never going to be able to do anything up here if I don't stop daydreaming," she said.

"But daydreaming serves a purpose, don't you think?" Will said. "It allows us to play out all the scenarios of our future so we can sort through them and see which ones seem to fit."

"Do you do a lot of daydreaming?"

"All the time."

"What do you think about?"

Will's cheeks colored again. "Oh, this and that. Nothing worth talking about."

Jess chuckled. "This and that, huh? Is there somebody special in these daydreams of yours?"

He pinned her with a look. "What fun is a daydream if there's no one in it with you?"

She had to bite her tongue to keep from asking what woman he saw. She wasn't sure she wanted to know. If he said it was her, what then? No, better to leave it alone.

"For the longest time, in mine it was Brad Pitt," she said to lighten the moment. "And then he had to go and dump Jennifer Anniston and get together with Angelina Jolie. That ruined it for me."

Will laughed. "And nobody's been able to replace Brad?"

"If I tell you, will you promise not to blab to a single soul?"

"I am the very soul of discretion," he assured her.

"Tim McGraw," she said. "But then, I gather Faith Hill has a wicked temper when anyone gets too close to her man." She sighed dramatically. "Who can blame her, though?"

"Who, indeed?" Will said with a chuckle.

Suddenly being in a confined space with all this talk of daydreams was too much. Jess stood up. "We've done enough for today. Let's go down to the kitchen and raid the fridge," she suggested. "We can have a picnic on one of the tables overlooking the beach. All of the guests have checked out, so we have the whole place to ourselves."

Will stood up and followed her downstairs to the inn's large gourmet kitchen. "Um, Jess," he began hesitantly as he stood in the doorway.

She held the door of the refrigerator open and looked back at him. "What?"

"Last I heard, you couldn't cook. Maybe

we should go out and grab a burger or pizza or something."

"We're both a mess, and I don't want to take the time to clean up," she said, then grinned. "Never fear, Gail always leaves a few things tucked in here for me. Next to Dillon, she's the best chef in town."

His expression brightened. "In that case, let's see what the possibilities are," he said, stepping up behind her.

He was so close, she could smell the lingering scent of his aftershave. Suddenly it took everything in her not to turn around and bury her face in the curve of his shoulder. She straightened so suddenly, she bumped her head on his chin.

"Sorry," she said, regarding him with a wince. "Are you okay?"

"Nothing an ice pack won't cure," he said, then stopped her when she would have reached into the freezer for one. "I'm kidding. I'm fine." His eyes lit up. "And I see roasted chicken in there. Can we have that?"

"We had chicken for lunch."

"Doesn't matter. There's nothing better than cold chicken with a glass of wine. I'm assuming you can come up with a bottle of pinot grigio or a sauvignon blanc. I've heard the wine cellar here is second to none."

"Cold chicken and wine, it is," she said. "I'll grab the chicken. You check out the wines." She gestured toward the oversize wine cooler they'd had installed just a few weeks earlier. It was stocked with some excellent California labels, as well as several local wines and even a few more expensive French vintages. Will whistled as he scanned the labels. "Excellent selection."

"Gail knows what she's doing. I don't," Jess said, digging through a drawer for a corkscrew. "Pick whatever you want."

She found a few more things for their meal—some cut veggies, a wedge of cheese, a cluster of chilled red grapes and a loaf of French bread baked earlier in the day. The tray was loaded down when she'd finished.

Will shook his head at the sight of it. "I thought we were having a simple snack."

"This was simple," Jess said. "Did you see me turn on a single burner on the stove? You take the tray. I'll take the wine and glasses."

The sun was starting to dip in the west when they sat down at one of the picnic tables scattered around the inn's sweeping lawn. Will poured the wine, then held up his glass.

"To simple meals with good friends," he said quietly.

There wasn't anything even remotely suggestive in his words, no hint of innuendo that he wanted something more. And yet Jess thought she could read the desire in his eyes and couldn't help wondering if it was reflected in her own.

The thought of it was so terrifying, she felt she had to say something. "Will?"

He nodded, his gaze never leaving her face.

"You know this . . ." She gestured to their meal, which had yet to be touched. "It's not a date. We should probably be clear on that."

He frowned slightly. "How would you describe it?"

"Just a snack, you know, to thank you for helping out earlier."

"Okay," he said slowly. "But since we're being clear, let me tell you that I do not intend to get caught up in one of those ridiculous not-dating situations that Susie and Mack have found themselves in. Since this was your idea, you can call this whatever you want tonight." He leveled a look into her eyes. "But the next time you and I share a meal—if we ever share another meal—it *will* be a date."

Jess trembled at the intensity in his voice and in his eyes. She was even more shaken when he stood up, dropped a quick kiss on her forehead and announced he had to go.

"But—"

"You stay out here and enjoy watching the moon come up," he said, cutting off her protest. "It's going to be a full one tonight."

He was gone before she could ask him to stay. She told herself it was just as well. With the conflicted feelings she was suddenly having about him, sitting here with him watching the rise of a full moon might be a little too romantic. Who knew what crazy things she might be tempted to do.

7

Connie had been on three blind dates so far, each one more depressing than the one before. It wasn't that the men weren't nice. They just weren't Thomas O'Brien. They lacked his maturity, his passion for his work preserving the Chesapeake Bay, his blue eyes that sparkled with laughter when they shared a joke.

The way she was pining for the man was pitiful. And it had only gotten worse since they'd gone to dinner a couple of weeks ago.

As innocent as that dinner had been— they hadn't even shared a hug, much less a kiss—she'd been replaying every second of it in her head ever since. Those three intellectually stimulating hours had spoiled her for everyone else. Nor had she laughed that hard in years. Thomas had a wonderfully self-deprecating way of telling stories on himself and everyone in the O'Brien family.

She was sitting in her office at her brother's nursery, trying to work up some enthusiasm for calling a customer to explain that it wasn't possible to plant palm trees on the Maryland shore and expect them to live through the winter, when Jess wandered in.

"You look as down as I'm feeling," Jess commented, lifting a chair over piles of seed catalogues in the cramped room and sitting down. "What's on your mind?"

Since just the thought of discussing her feelings for Thomas with an O'Brien made her cringe, Connie opted for an evasion. "I'm just overloaded with work."

Jess gave her a knowing look. "You sure it doesn't have anything to do with my uncle?"

Connie feigned shock, hoping she sounded convincing. "You mean Thomas?

Why would my mood have anything to do with him?"

"I could have meant Jeff," Jess teased. "That you jumped to the conclusion I was talking about Thomas is very telling."

"Oh, please," Connie said. "What kind of issues could Jeff and I possibly have?"

"Landscaping issues," Jess improvised. "He does manage a lot of properties around town."

Connie wished she'd seized on that possibility a lot sooner. "I don't have issues with Jeff, or Thomas, for that matter. I don't know where you got such a crazy idea."

"Because from all the reports I've been hearing, sparks fly whenever the two of you are in the same space," Jess said.

Connie sighed. "You've been talking to Connor."

Jess grinned. "And Kevin. I believe Heather's also mentioned a time or two the way your face lights up when you see him. I've seen it for myself, my friend. And then there's the rumor that the two of you were spotted in Easton having dinner a couple of weeks ago."

Connie groaned. "That is so humiliating.

I could have sworn nobody in the family saw us."

"They didn't," Jess said. "My chef Gail and her husband had a rare night out. She wanted to try a new restaurant. She'd heard the place has a great chef, and you know how competitive she is."

"I never saw her," Connie said, chagrined by the realization that she'd had eyes for no one in the room except Thomas.

"I don't think you were paying much attention to your surroundings," Jess teased. "Of course, I already had an inkling about what was going on from my brothers and my own observations. This just confirmed it."

"I might have to kill them," Connie said with a groan. "I knew they'd figured out how I felt, but I didn't think they'd blab."

"They're O'Briens," Jess said. "None of us can keep a secret worth a damn. Surely you've seen that." She leaned forward. "So, what are you going to do about it? Are you two actually dating finally? I think it would be great if you did, by the way. Uncle Thomas needs a strong, wonderful woman who shares his interests."

"We had dinner," Connie said, then added, in the interest of full disclosure, "And a couple of lunches, plus coffee a few times."

Jess chuckled at the recitation.

"Oh, stop it," Connie muttered. "It's not like it's turned into some big romance or anything."

"What do you plan to do to change that?" Jess pressed.

"Me?" Connie asked, looking horrified. "Nothing."

"You're not going to wait around for him to do something, are you? Because I can practically hear the wheels in my uncle's head grinding while he assesses how the whole family, especially your brother, would react if he seriously started dating you. I imagine he's sensitive to the age issue, too. It's up to you to show him that the feeling's mutual."

"I don't know that it is," Connie said. "I mean, I know *I'm* attracted to *him,* but for all I know he's just being nice to me. He's probably just grateful for the help I've given to him with all those events to raise money for the foundation. Dinner the other night was friendly, nothing more."

She uttered the words without allowing her frustration to show. She'd actually braved humiliation by telling Thomas in advance that she wanted it to be a date, but once they'd met at the restaurant, he'd behaved like a total gentleman, nothing more than a casual friend. She could hardly criticize his manners, only his astounding self-control. The relationship was beginning to take on the same bizarre hands-off style that defined Susie and Mack's and even Will and Jess's. She found that worrisome, to say nothing of frustrating.

Jess rolled her eyes. "Friendly? You can't be that naive. If he invited you to dinner, that's huge. Every woman can tell the difference between gratitude and attraction. I know you practically lived like a nun while Jenny was at an impressionable age, but you haven't been away from the dating scene that long."

Connie frowned at her certainty. "Some women I know can't seem to tell the difference between attraction and professional interest. Want to talk about that kiss between you and Will at Brady's?"

"I do not," Jess said, her cheeks pink with embarrassment.

"Then I guess there's nothing more to say. Why'd you come over here, anyway?"

"I was looking for a distraction, to be honest. My next stop's the bank. Maybe Laila will be more forthcoming about what's going on in her life. She seems to be the only one of us who's been actively dating since she signed up for Will's online match-making."

"I've gone out on a bunch of dates," Connie protested.

"Have you seen any of the men twice?"

"No, but neither has Laila. What's your point?"

"She's still accepting dates. You're not."

"How on earth do you know that?" Connie asked indignantly. "Did Will tell you?"

Jess grinned. "Nope. It was a lucky guess, which you just confirmed." She stood up, then kissed Connie's cheek. "Talk to Thomas. Ask him out, if you're really interested. I'm telling you, you're going to have to take the lead with him, at least in the beginning."

She was gone before Connie could respond. Jess was probably right, Connie thought. Maybe she did need to be the one to make the next overture, but doing so was way too far out of her comfort zone. Besides, it was only a couple of weeks before they'd be thrown together at a last-minute fundraiser they'd arranged to hold at a nearby fall festival. With luck, the decision might be taken out of her hands. Otherwise she'd have a long, lonely winter to survive without even the chance encounters she'd come to count on.

En route to the bank, Jess dropped by Sally's and picked up a couple of raspberry croissants along with two cups of coffee to take with her. Before she could leave, though, she turned too quickly and nearly walked straight into Will. He put a steadying hand on her arm, which she immediately shrugged off.

"What are you doing here?" she asked, frowning. "It's not even close to noon."

He smiled. "I usually pick up coffee to take to my office first thing in the morning," he said. "What about you?" He gestured toward her take-out order. "Don't you usually grab something at the inn in the morning?"

"I felt like a change of pace this morning. I'm on my way over to the bank to visit with Laila."

"Then I won't keep you," he said. "Enjoy your day."

The dismissal grated. Jess had half a mind to stay right where she was, but since she had no idea what she'd do next, she sighed and left, grumbling under her breath about men in general, and one man in particular.

When she bumped directly into someone just outside the café, she looked up to find Connor regarding her with amusement.

"You seem distracted, sis. First you run into Will inside Sally's, and now you practically mow me down. Is something wrong?"

"Not a thing," she assured him, as he fell into step beside her.

"It wouldn't have anything to do with your encounter with Will back there, would it?"

She stopped in her tracks and scowled at him. "Does this family have spies everywhere? Do I need to tie bells around your necks, so I'll know when an O'Brien is in the vicinity?"

He had the audacity to laugh. "I was sitting at the counter, minding my own business, when you came in. It is not my fault if you and Will started dancing around each other like a couple of boxers waiting for the first punch to be thrown."

"A lovely analogy," she commented. "And it wasn't like that."

"Then what was it like? You left there muttering about Will. You weren't even looking where you were going, which explains our close encounter on the sidewalk out front. What did he say to get under your skin this time?"

"Not a thing," she insisted, then couldn't stop herself from adding, "He dismissed me. Do you believe that? He actually dismissed me, like some teacher graciously letting class go even though the bell's already rung anyway."

Connor looked confused. "Meaning?"

"What right does he have to send me on my way with a pat on the head?"

"I never saw him pat you on the head."

"Figuratively," she said impatiently. "He was condescending. And all because I told him last night wasn't a date."

Connor stared at her. "Last night? You were with Will last night? You didn't leave Mom and Dad's with him."

"No, he came by the inn to help me

clean the attic. Without an invitation, in case you were wondering."

Connor, who was used to dealing with reluctant witnesses in a courtroom, nodded as if what she was saying made perfect sense, even though he was clearly confused. "Okay, so the two of you cleaning the attic together wasn't a date. Did he think it was?"

"No, he thought dinner was," she said. "Well, actually he didn't say he did, but I told him it wasn't, just so there'd be no misunderstanding about it, and he got all huffy and left."

Connor laughed. He didn't even have the courtesy to try to hide it. "You know, I always thought Mack and Susie lived in some crazy state of denial, but you and Will may have taken up residence right next to them."

"Will said almost the same thing, and then he said he wouldn't stand for it," Jess told him.

"Can you blame him? We've all gotten a little tired of those ridiculous protests Susie and Mack keep uttering."

Jess sighed. "No, I get what Will was

saying. I was just trying to be straightforward and honest."

"Really?" Connor said doubtfully. "Because I don't even think you're being honest with yourself about your feelings for Will. Oh, it's possible that you didn't have any at one time, but now you do. Why not admit it and see what happens?"

"Because I can't," she said in frustration.

"Why?"

"When I'm with him, I feel like he knows more about me than I know about myself. It's annoying."

"Do you have any idea how many women would give anything to find a man who actually understands them?"

"This is different," Jess insisted.

"How so?"

She couldn't really explain it, so she retorted, "It just is."

"Now, there's the rational side of you I know and love," Connor said lightly.

"Oh, go suck an egg," she snapped. "I never said it was rational. It's just the way I feel."

Connor draped an arm across her

shoulders and hugged her. "You'll work it out," he said confidently.

"You seem to have a whole lot more faith in me than I do," she replied despondently.

"Just about everyone in the family does," Connor said. "Maybe you should think about why that is, Jess. Until you figure out that you're a terrific person who deserves to be happy, you're going to keep getting in your own way." He pressed a kiss to her forehead. "Love you. I've got to get to the office."

She watched her brother leave, then sighed. Something told her that Connor, who—bless his heart—was not known as the most insightful person in the universe, had hit the nail on the head this time. If he could see what was going on with her, then maybe it was time she took a harder look at herself.

Will went to the bar at Brady's after work. It was something he rarely did on his own, especially on a Monday night, but he was still stewing over his encounter with Jess earlier in the day and the whole fiasco on Sunday night.

To his surprise, he found Mack and Jake already there.

"What are the two of you doing here tonight?" he asked.

"We agreed that you weren't yourself at lunch today and something told us you'd be turning up here tonight," Jake said. "Besides, I needed an entire hour to relax without the baby screaming. For a very little girl, she can make quite a racket."

"And yet you expect Bree to deal with her all day," Will commented, ignoring the references to his mood.

"Bree has help, believe me. Her grandmother stops by and takes over for an hour or so. She drops the baby off with Megan every afternoon. And whenever she takes her over to the theater, the girls in her upcoming production take turns fussing over her. This child has more unofficial nannies than any kid on earth."

Will grinned. "In other words, the only time you get to spend with her is in the evening when she's exhausted and crying," he guessed.

Jake nodded. "And I don't have the one thing she wants, food. Only Bree can provide that."

"Are you actually jealous that your wife can breast-feed your baby and you can't?" Mack asked incredulously.

Jake looked startled by the assessment. "That would be crazy," he said, then shrugged. "But maybe." He flushed. "Don't you dare repeat this, but before she was born, I used to sing to her at night. Now the minute she eats, she's down for the count, and Bree's not much better."

"You didn't ask for advice," Will said, "but you and Bree need to talk about this and carve out some time for yourselves. There are a lot of adjustments with a new baby, and the two of you don't want your relationship to get lost in the commotion."

"I suppose," Jake said, sipping his beer. He slid off the bar stool. "I should get home." He hesitated, looking at Will. "Mack and I came over here for you. Is everything okay? Should I stick around?"

"I've got it covered," Mack said.

"Yes, go home to your family," Will told him.

Once Jake had gone, Mack stared after him worriedly. "Do you think they're going to be okay?"

"Of course," Will said.

"I mean, if those two can't make it, after all they went through to get back together, who can?" Mack said.

"They're going to be fine," Will said emphatically.

Mack looked relieved by Will's certainty. "Okay, then, let's focus on you. Want to talk about whatever has you in such a lousy mood?"

"No," Will said, sipping his beer, then looking at Mack. "How about you? Anything you need to talk about?"

Mack shook his head.

They drank their beers in companionable silence, glancing up at the TV over the bar occasionally to watch the sports channel.

"Susie's ticked at me," Mack said eventually.

"I don't think so."

Mack studied him with surprise. "What do you know?"

"Nothing you wouldn't know if the two of you would just sit down and have an honest conversation for once." He sighed heavily. "I spend my entire professional life trying to help people learn to communicate effectively, and not one of the people around me has the first clue about how to do that."

Mack looked justifiably confused. "Are we still talking about me and Susie?"

"Yes, and Jake and Bree, and me and Jess. We're all pitiful."

Mack seized on his words. "Is there a you and Jess?"

"No, of course not," Will said.

"But you just said—"

"Oh, don't listen to me. I'm just frustrated and annoyed and irritable."

"Women will do that to you," Mack said, nodding wisely.

"Amen, brother."

Mick was walking around the attic at the inn making notes and mumbling under his breath. Jess had taken a seat on top of a trunk, out of the way, and was watching him with barely contained excitement.

"Well?" she prodded eventually. "What do you think, Dad? Can it be done?"

"Of course it can be done," he said. "When it comes to construction, I can pretty much turn this room into anything you want."

"At what cost?"

He grinned at her. "That's the question, isn't it? You have a budget in mind?"

Jess shook her head. "Abby said to bring her the estimate and she'd see if we could find the money to do it."

"Tearing out that wall over there, putting in the kind of windows you're talking about, it could be expensive," he cautioned. "How badly do you want that?"

"Really badly," she admitted.

"I can do the job for you at cost, do most of the work myself, in fact. That'll save you some more, but it'll take longer. You in a rush?"

She shook her head. "We'd have all winter," she said. "It would be nice to have it ready when the season kicks back in next spring, though."

Mick nodded. "That shouldn't be a problem."

"Can you open up a fireplace?"

"I can," he said. "You sure you want to break this into two separate rooms, though? It might be nicer if it were one big open space with a cozy seating area in front of the fireplace and a king-size bed facing the windows and that view of the bay and the town. What do you think?

Otherwise it could start feeling cramped. Here, I'll show you."

He sketched out what he had in mind as Jess looked over his shoulder. "Of course, if you want the bedroom to have privacy, we could put the wall in."

"No, you're right," Jess said, studying his drawing. "I should have figured you'd know exactly what to do. Everyone knows these houses in town were designed by the best architect in the world."

"Maybe not the best," Mick said, winking at her. "But I do have a feel for what people want in a place at the beach."

"What you did for Connor and Heather at Driftwood Cottage was amazing," Jess told him. "I couldn't believe it was the same house."

"Give Heather some of the credit for that," Mick said. "I worked with her ideas. Same thing here. You gave me your ideas. I'm just refining them a bit."

"Some of the ideas were Will's," she conceded.

Mick's eyes lit up. "Is that so? He was over here?"

Jess nodded, aware that she'd opened an unfortunate can of worms. "The other day. He helped me clear a lot of the junk out of here." Determined to change the subject, she asked, "Now what about the bathroom? Can you fit in a truly decadent soaker tub and a shower, maybe a double vanity?"

Mick looked momentarily disappointed by her deliberate evasiveness, then shrugged. "Is this a honeymoon suite? Or are you thinking of something more permanent, maybe a living space for you?"

"I'm not a hundred percent sure," she admitted. "Initially I thought it ought to be a honeymoon suite, but Will mentioned it would be a great living space for me. I can't help thinking about that. It would be wonderful to have a real space of my own and not just one of the rooms downstairs."

Mick gave her a sly look. "You need that big tub and shower and two sinks just for you, or do you have someone in mind to share it with you?"

"Don't go there," she ordered. "If I'm doing it, it doesn't hurt to think ahead. Who knows what will happen in the future? Hopefully, I won't be alone for the rest of my life."

"Of course you won't," her father said

immediately. "This place won't be big enough for a family, though."

"Will suggested . . ."

"For a man who doesn't mean anything to you, you sure do seem to be taking his ideas to heart," Mick said.

"It was a good idea," Jess said defensively. "It hardly matters whose it was. He thought I could build another house on the property sometime in the future. I'm thinking maybe in that grove of trees at the top of the hill out back."

"Definitely something to think about," Mick agreed. "Did Will have any other ideas I should know about?"

"None," she said flatly. "When can you get that estimate for me so Abby and I can discuss it?"

"I'll pull something together by this weekend. The three of us can talk about it after dinner on Sunday. How's that?"

Jess threw her arms around him. "Thanks, Dad."

He held her tight and pressed a kiss to the top of her head. "I think maybe I'll doodle around a little and see what I can come up with for that separate house, while I'm at it."

Jess gave him a dismayed look. "You don't need to do that. It'll be years before I'll get around to needing that."

"You never know," he insisted. "It never hurts to think ahead."

"Not that far ahead," she told him.

"Sometimes the future's closer than you think, if you keep an open mind. Won't hurt to see what Will thinks of my sketches, either. He seems to have some excellent ideas. I'll make sure he's invited to dinner, too."

Jess stood perfectly still as Mick walked off. Heaven help her, but she'd obviously just kicked her father's matchmaking tendencies into high gear. Just as clearly, Sunday dinner was going to be a tense few hours.

8

Jess opened her email on Thursday morning and found a contact from a Lunch by the Bay client, who was interested in asking her out for Friday night. Rather than stirring even mild curiosity or anticipation, the invitation sent a chill down her spine. She stared at the words on the screen and saw them for what they were, proof positive that Will was moving on. Why else would he suddenly set her up on a date with someone else? Apparently he'd lost patience with her hesitancy and her refusal to acknowledge even an impromptu picnic as a date.

She was so annoyed by that, she barely noticed a single thing about her prospective date. Instead, she wrote a reply indicating that she was very sorry, but a date was out of the question. Nothing personal, of course.

She winced as she imagined being on the receiving end of such an email. She modified her words to express more sincere regret, though she didn't so much as hint that he should try again.

Of course, as soon as she hit the button to send the email, she was swamped by misgivings. She should have accepted, if only to prove to Will that he meant nothing to her, that she was still open to dating other men. Which she was, she told herself adamantly. Just not one who'd been handpicked by Will and his stupid computer game.

She sighed at her logic. Even she recognized she wasn't making a lot of sense. If Laila or even Connie, who understood having conflicted feelings for someone, knew about this, they'd be all over her for rejecting someone without a single meeting.

"Oh, well, it's done now," she said,

shutting down the computer and heading to the kitchen to discuss menus with Gail.

To her surprise, she found flaky Ronnie in there wearing an apron and following Gail's directions for making a mango-papaya chutney to be served with tonight's grilled fish. He looked up guiltily when Jess walked in.

"I had the front desk calls forwarded in here," he told her hurriedly. "And I've taken three reservations. I swear I'm not blowing off my job."

"He's not," Gail confirmed. "And he's been a huge help to me in here." She gave Jess a look that pleaded with her to give Ronnie a chance. "Actually," she added, "I've been trying to convince him he ought to take a few courses at one of the culinary schools in the area."

Jess regarded Ronnie with surprise. "Seriously? Are you interested?"

He nodded, his expression sheepish. "I've always liked to cook, but my dad had a cow every time I mentioned it. I think I'd like to give it a try, if we can work out my hours here. What can he say if I pay for it myself, right?"

Jess was so impressed by his enthusiasm, she said, "You should definitely look into it, Ronnie." She, of all people, knew how important it was to discover a passion for something. Maybe this would be the same kind of turning point for him that the inn had been for her. How could she not encourage that?

Impulsively, she added, "Find out what the classes cost. I'm not making any promises, but if you're as good as Gail thinks you are, maybe I can find some way for the inn to help foot the bill for at least some of the tuition."

Gail looked as startled as Ronnie by the offer. "Abby?" Gail protested quietly.

"Abby will understand," Jess insisted, but added a clarification to be sure Ronnie understood the limitations. "We may not be able to cover all of the expenses, okay?"

"Anything would be a help," Ronnie replied eagerly.

Jess tried to think of what might convince Abby to find some money in the budget. Only one thought came to mind. She held Ronnie's gaze. "If I can pull this off, you'll have to guarantee us that you'll work here for a year or so as Gail's sous-chef or what-ever she needs once you've graduated."

For the first time since he'd come to work at the inn, Ronnie demonstrated genuine enthusiasm. "Awesome! I know I haven't been the best employee up until now, but I promise that's changed. What-ever you need me to do around here, I'm on it."

Jess smiled at his unexpected display of eagerness. "I'll have to see how it fits into the budget," she cautioned again. "Bring me some information when you have it."

"Will do," he promised. "Thanks, Jess. I mean Ms. O'Brien. You're amazing. I'd better go out there and put these reserva-tions I wrote down into the system before I get food all over the paper."

He practically bounced out of the kitchen. Jess stared after him, then shook her head.

"Who knew?" she murmured. "I didn't think he was ever going to find his niche in the world. You're a miracle worker."

Gail grinned. "Not really. He just needed someone to pay attention to what he wants to do with his life. I started seeing it the first time he helped me out in here," Gail said. "He's good, Jess. With a little training, I think he'll be special. And thanks to the deal you mentioned to him, he'll belong to us, at least for a little while."

"It must feel good knowing that you discovered someone's hidden talent," Jess said, wishing she'd been the one to see beyond Ronnie's screwups.

"You can't discover what someone won't let you see," Gail said. "Ronnie was too afraid of losing this job, which seemed like his last chance, to tell you what he really wanted to try. If you hadn't insisted he help me that day, he might still be out there making a mess of the reservations. Or worse, you might have fired him."

Gail looked up from the bread dough she was kneading and studied Jess more intently. "What's going on with you? You look depressed."

"I'm not depressed. I'm annoyed," Jess replied.

"At Will, I assume. What's he done now?"

"He found me a date, or rather Lunch by the Bay found me one. It's pretty much the same thing."

Gail looked justifiably puzzled. "Weren't you complaining before because he *hadn't* found you any dates?"

Jess nodded. "I am nothing if not incon-sistent, at least where Will's concerned. No wonder he's had enough of me."

"What makes you think he's had enough of you?" Gail asked, then immediately said, "Oh, of course, the date."

Jess nodded. "Let's not waste time on this," she said. "Are you ready to go over the menus for the week?"

Gail looked as if she might argue, but then she pulled a set of laminated pages from a drawer in her desk. Somewhere along the way, she'd developed the kind of organizational skills that Jess envied. All of her most prized recipes had been printed out and laminated, so she could shuffle them around for a variety of menu combi-nations. She occasionally shook things up with new experiments. The ones that proved popular with their guests were printed, laminated and added to the rota-tions.

"Here you go," she said, handing them to Jess. "See what you think. I've been working on some ideas for the Parker wed-ding at the end of the month, too. We're supposed to be pitching that tomorrow."

Jess spent the next hour going over

Gail's menus and the accompanying cost projections, then sat back with a sigh. "I don't know why I don't just give you free rein with this," she said. "You haven't blown the budget to smithereens yet. You have a far better grasp of the costs than I do."

Gail grinned. "I know you hate dealing with numbers. I even know that Abby trusts me. I still feel a lot more comfortable when you've signed off on everything." She poured them each a glass of tea, then sat back and studied Jess.

"Okay, let's get back to Will."

"I'd rather not."

"Just tell me why you've been so determined not to admit you're interested in him."

"It's possible that I've overreacted to some stuff in the past," Jess told her. "It's kind of creeped me out to think he's sitting there analyzing every word I say, but people keep telling me that having a man actually understand where you're coming from is a good thing."

Gail smiled. "I'd say so. With my husband and me, the fact that we're both chefs is fantastic. Whenever one of us has a bad day, the other one really gets it. And we can bounce a lot of ideas off each other. Plus, on Sundays, when we're both off, we love to spend the day in the kitchen experimenting with recipes. It's fun having that love of food in common. All those fabulous aromas . . ." Her voice trailed off as she sighed. "It's an amazing aphrodisiac."

Despite Gail's sigh of rapture, Jess had to ask, "How's it a day off if you're in the kitchen cooking?"

"Because it's something we both enjoy and we don't get to do it together that often." Gail grinned. "Of course, when something turns out really well, then we fight over which one of us gets to use it. Those discussions used to get pretty heated, till we decided we'd just alternate. And, of course, some things work better in a big fancy restaurant like the one where he works than they would here."

"So we get his castoffs?" Jess said with feigned indignation.

Gail laughed. "Hardly. When I think something is perfect for us, I have my ways of winning first dibs on it."

Jess loved the picture Gail was painting of the give and take between her and her husband. In a way, that's what she'd experienced all too briefly that day in the attic with Will. It had been a revelation to see how well their ideas for the renovations had meshed.

In fact, though she refused to admit it to a living, breathing soul, she could hardly wait till Sunday when they'd both see how her father had translated them into concrete designs. Seeing Will on a non-date, much as he would hate the designation, seemed like the smartest way to test whether her feelings for him had really changed.

Will was finishing up his lunch with Mack and Jake when Mick O'Brien walked in and joined them.

"How's Bree?" Mick asked his son-in-law.

"She's great," Jake said, then beamed with the proud papa look unique to a new parent. "And the baby's amazing. I have pictures on my cell phone. Want to see them?"

Mick's eyes brightened. "Of course."

As Jake pulled his cell phone out of his pocket, Will started to stand. Moments like this reminded him of just how far he was away from marriage and a family. "I should be getting back to work."

"Hold on a minute," Mick commanded, then took the cell phone from Jake and studied his granddaughter's latest pictures. "I'm not saying my girls weren't the most beautiful babies on earth back in the day, but this little one is something special."

"Don't say that in front of Abby," Will cautioned. "I'm sure she thinks Caitlyn and Carrie were pretty special as babies, too."

"Well, of course they were," Mick said. "And when Abby gets around to having another baby, I'm sure he or she will be the cutest baby on earth, as well. Right now, this is the baby I get to dote on."

Will chuckled at his logic.

Mick returned the cell phone, then turned to Will. "I just wanted to be sure you'll be at Sunday dinner this week."

There was something in Mick's expression that made Will very nervous. He knew that look. It was born in meddling. "I hadn't planned on it," he said candidly. And if he hadn't already decided against it, Mick's pointed invitation would have convinced him to stay far away from the O'Briens' house. Things between him and Jess were tense enough with Mick getting in the middle of whatever was going on—or, more precisely, *not* going on—between them.

"Then you need to change your mind," Mick said flatly. "I have some sketches ready for Jess. I know she'd like it if you'd take a look, too."

"What sketches?" Will asked suspiciously.

"The redesigned attic for the inn and a house for the property," Mick said. "She told me you'd had some thoughts about both. We'd appreciate your input."

Jake and Mack were listening, their expressions amused. Clearly they both knew precisely what Mick was up to, and architectural sketches had nothing to do with it. These were just a convenient excuse.

"The inn is Jess's baby," Will said. "It has nothing to do with me."

Mick's gaze narrowed. "Is there some reason you don't want to come by?"

"I have other plans this week," Will told him.

"What plans?" Jake inquired innocently.

"A date," Will said, giving his friend a sour look. He might not have one right this second, but he would the minute he got back to his office and called one of the matches on his Lunch by the Bay list.

Mick didn't look as if he believed him. Either that, or he was just unhappy to hear that Will was seeing someone other than his daughter. Giving him a disgruntled look, Mick stood up.

"I'll tell Jess you couldn't make it," he said. "I imagine she'll be disappointed."

"Another time," Will said, relieved to watch Mick walk away.

"Oh, boy," Jake murmured.

Will scowled at him. "What?"

"You lied to Mick," Mack said, his expression as dire as Jake's.

"I did not lie," Will said.

"You really do have a date?" Jake asked skeptically.

"I will within the hour," Will said.

"Doesn't matter," Mack said. "The point is you blew off a chance to spend time with Jess. Mick won't forget that. It'll be a black mark against you from now till eternity."

"What's he going to do?" Will asked. "Forbid me to ever see Jess again? I'm not seeing her now. That's Jess's choice, not mine, by the way."

"Do you suppose Mick understands that she's the problem?" Mack wondered thoughtfully.

"Of course he does," Jake said. "That's why he was here issuing the invitation, instead of leaving it to Jess."

"How twisted is that?" Mack muttered. "I'm so glad that Susie . . . Well, that Mick isn't her father."

Jake chuckled. "Yeah, Mick would have insisted the two of you get off the dime a long time ago."

Will listened and shook his head. It wasn't that they were saying anything he didn't already know, but it was a reminder that it might be wise to continue steering clear of Jess. He gave Jake a sympathetic look. "I feel for you, my friend. Hard to believe you willingly married into this family."

Jake laughed. "After jumping over about a million hurdles, yes, I did. Bree's worth it. And don't try to kid us, my friend. You'd do it too, in a heartbeat, in fact, if you could get Jess to come around."

Will sighed. "You're probably right." It wasn't something he especially liked about himself.

* * *

Jess found herself taking extra care with her appearance on Sunday. She tried on half a dozen outfits before settling on a pair of linen slacks and a sleeveless linen blouse. Both were impossible to keep pressed, so she rarely wore them. When she actually took her makeup kit out of the back of a drawer, she frowned and put it right back.

"You're being absurd," she told her reflection in the mirror.

"Up here talking to yourself?" Abby inquired, walking into her room without waiting for a response to her knock.

"Sadly, yes," Jess admitted.

"You look lovely," Abby said, surveying her. "That peach color in your blouse suits you. It brings out the color in your cheeks."

"Thanks."

"What's the special occasion?"

"No occasion," Jess said, flushing.

Abby regarded her with disbelief. "Then it doesn't have anything to do with those sketches Dad's been working on, the ones he was going to show you, me and Will today?"

"Why would I get dressed up to look at

Dad's sketches?" Jess asked, feigning innocence.

Naturally Abby saw right through the pretense. She hadn't practically raised Jess without learning a thing or two about her younger sister's moods.

"I was thinking it might have more to do with Will," Abby said. "And I came over here to alert you that he's not going to be at dinner. I didn't want you to be disappointed and let Dad catch wind of your reaction when you found out."

Jess couldn't hide how deflated she felt by Abby's announcement. "How do you know Will won't be there?"

"When I arrived earlier, Dad was grumbling to Mom about it. He said something about Will having another date."

Jess sat down hard on the edge of her bed. "I see," she said softly.

"You okay?" Abby asked.

"Sure," she lied. "Why wouldn't I be?"

"Maybe because you're finally figuring out that you ought to be giving Will a chance."

"It doesn't matter," Jess insisted. "Don't make too big a deal out of it. I don't intend to."

"It's probably just one of those computerized matchups, anyway," Abby consoled her.

"More than likely," Jess agreed. "It's just as well he won't be there. All we do is argue lately, anyway." She forced a smile. "We'd probably better head over to the house. Gram likes to get dinner on the table promptly at one on Sundays."

Abby hesitated, a worried frown puckering her brow. "You're sure you're okay?"

"Absolutely." She plastered a smile on her face, more to practice for the rest of the family than out of any belief that Abby would buy it. "I can't wait to see Dad's designs."

"Me, too," Abby admitted, following her down the stairs. "He swears to me his cost projections are very reasonable, at least for the attic renovation. Did you know he was designing a house, too? What's that about?"

Jess nodded. "I mentioned something about maybe building one on the property if I ever have a family, and Dad ran with it. I told him it wasn't anything I'd need in the immediate future, but you know Dad."

"He's put two and two together where

you and Will are concerned and is ready to reserve the church," Abby said, giving her a sympathetic look. "Of course, if you and Will stop playing games and get your signals straight—"

Jess's scowl effectively silenced her sister, at least for the moment. Now all she had to do was suffer through dinner and look over those sketches without letting on that she was bothered by Will's absence. If she passed this test, maybe she ought to try out for Bree's theater company.

Will's date was rapidly turning into a disaster. He'd been so distracted that the woman, a lawyer from Annapolis who'd once worked with Connor in Baltimore, lost patience.

"Why did you ask me out?" Anna Lofton asked eventually.

Will forced himself to meet her gaze. She had dark brown eyes that seemed to see right through him. He imagined that worked well for her in a courtroom interrogation.

"It seemed as if we had several things in common," he said.

"I thought the same thing," she said,

leaning forward. "But you haven't really been here since we sat down. Are you already involved with someone else?"

"Absolutely not," he said hurriedly, startled by her perceptiveness, but unwilling to acknowledge the accuracy of her assessment.

She laughed. "That answer came way too fast. Who is she? The girl who got away?"

Will sighed. "I never had her in the first place," he admitted. "And I'm truly sorry about the way this date has gone. I never should have asked you out for today. It was a knee-jerk reaction."

She studied him curiously. "To what?"

"Believe me, if I told you, it would only make me look like a worse jerk than you must think I am now."

She actually laughed at that. "Now I'm seeing that self-deprecating sense of humor I liked in your emails."

Will grinned. "Should we try this again another day?" he asked. "It might go better."

Anna shook her head. "Not until you get this other woman out of your system," she said. "If that happens, call me. I like you,

Will Lincoln, but I don't want to waste my time. Thanks for lunch, though." She looked around. "If nothing else, I should thank you for introducing me to Chesapeake Shores. I like this town. I have no idea why I've never been down here before. I'll have to come for the weekend next time."

"There's a great inn," Will said, then winced.

"Why do you look as if you regret telling me that?" she asked.

"The woman who owns it . . ." he began.

Anna's eyes lit up as she caught on. "Ah, she's the one. Now I really will have to come back. What's the name of this inn?"

"The Inn at Eagle Point," he said reluctantly. "You'll love it there. It has terrific views of the water and a great chef."

"Is this woman of yours the chef, too?"

"No, just the owner."

Anna stood up. "Well, maybe I'll see you around before too long," she told him.

Will dropped cash on the table for the bill, then walked her to her car. "Again, I really am sorry about how this went. It's certainly not a very good reflection on Lunch by the Bay's matchmaking skills."

"Oh, I don't know. I think the match was

great. Unfortunately, you just happen to have unresolved feelings for someone else. I'll bet you didn't tell the computer that."

Will chuckled. "Hardly. I try not to tell anyone that. Unfortunately, in this town almost everyone already knows."

"Sounds like the curse of small-town living," Anna said. "Tell Connor hello for me if you run into him."

"I will," he promised. "Drive safely."

He watched her put her sexy little sports car into gear and then drive off. Only when she was out of sight did he sigh. Under any other circumstances, maybe even on another day, Anna would have intrigued him.

Instead, he knew she'd just been a substitute for Jess, a way to prove to Jess and everyone else that she wouldn't always have him tied into knots. Ironically, though, what this afternoon had proved was exactly the opposite.

9

Jess tried to work up some enthusiasm for her father's sketches on Sunday afternoon. Mick regarded her curiously when she merely nodded from time to time and occasionally muttered, "Nice."

"Okay, that's it," he said finally, clearly losing patience. "I did these for you, Jess. Have you lost interest already?"

Jess bristled at the accusation, which sounded all too familiar. Her father had had a very hard time accepting her ADD. More than once in the early days before her diagnosis, he'd suggested she simply wasn't applying herself in school. After four children who'd all been overachievers, Jess had been a frustration to him. It was that old annoyance that she heard in his voice now.

Before she could snap out a response, Abby stepped in to smooth things over, as always.

"Of course she hasn't," Abby said, rushing to her defense. "The designs are amazing, Dad. I'm sure Jess loves them."

Jess forced herself to smile. "I do, Dad. And I really appreciate the time you spent doing them."

"Then what's the problem?" he demanded, clearly not pacified. He regarded her curiously. "Does your mood have something to do with Will not showing up today?"

"Leave Will out of it," Jess commanded irritably. "The attic renovations have nothing to do with him. It's my project." She turned to Abby, determined to end any discussion of Will. "What do you think about the costs? Can we pull this off?"

Her sister didn't hesitate. "If Dad does the majority of the work and he can stick to the budget he's given us, I think we can."

Jess finally mustered some genuine enthusiasm. Up until now—Will aside—she simply hadn't wanted to get her hopes up. Abby had rightly kept a tight rein on the inn's finances ever since she'd saved Jess from foreclosure. Though turning to her sister to bail her out had been humiliating, at least she had her inn today because of it. She'd vowed never to mess up financially again, even if she chafed at some of the restrictions. To have Abby loosen the purse strings for this was a huge vote of confidence.

"Seriously?" she asked her sister. "I can move forward?"

Abby nodded, a smile spreading across her face. "I think the expenses are totally justified. You've been in the black for a while now. I'll talk to Trace's dad at the bank about financing."

"Let me go to Laila," Jess pleaded. "I need to handle things like this on my own. I swear I won't sign anything until you've looked it over."

Abby's faint hesitation grated, but eventually she nodded. "That seems reasonable. If you need backup, just let me know."

Mick stepped in. "Jess, let me finance

this and leave the bank out of it," he said. "The renovations aren't that expensive. I don't want you putting the inn at risk again."

Jess shook her head. "I appreciate the offer, Dad, but this is my business."

"Did I say it wasn't?" he grumbled. "Why make a fuss over such a little thing?"

"Because I want everyone, especially Lawrence Riley at the bank, to acknowledge that I've turned the inn into a success. Me, Jess O'Brien. Not my sister. Not my dad. Mr. Riley was so darn sure I couldn't do it. I want to rub it in his face that I have."

Mick relented. "Now, that I can understand. Just don't be too proud to ask for my backing if you need it. Understood?"

Jess threw her arms around her father. "Thanks, Dad." She turned to her sister. "You, too, Abby. If you hadn't had faith in me even after I screwed everything up a few years ago, the inn wouldn't even exist, much less be profitable."

"It was all your vision and your execution," Abby reminded her. "I just got you back on track with the finances."

Jess thought of her promise to Ronnie. "Speaking of that, I need to talk to you about adding a small line item to the budget." She hurriedly explained about Ronnie's enthusiasm for cooking and Gail's conviction that he had talent. To her surprise, it was her father who spoke up.

"I knew you'd do something to get that young man on the right track," he said. "Abby, surely there's a way to help the boy out. That father of his is an idiot not to encourage him to do what he wants with his life. I've half a mind to tell him so myself."

Jess chuckled. "Dad, I doubt that yelling at Ronnie's father will accomplish much." She gave Abby a pleading look. "Can we find a few hundred dollars a term to help with his tuition?"

"He's agreed to stay on to work at the inn once he graduates?" Abby asked.

"Absolutely. I'm sure he'll put that in writing if we want him to," Jess assured her.

"Then I suppose it's a solid enough investment in the inn's future," Abby said. "Let me play with the numbers and I'll get back to you with an answer."

Delighted for Ronnie and totally enthused about the renovation project now that it had a green light, Jess faced her father. "How soon can you get started?"

"How about next week?" he suggested.

Jess appreciated his willingness to plunge right in, but she shook her head. "I need to get the bank's okay first."

"Then as soon as that's in place," Mick said. "I need to remind you again that it will be slower going than usual because I have to keep overseeing the Habitat for Humanity work, but we'll get this done, Jess. It's going to be everything you want it to be." He met her gaze. "You want to take a look at the house plans, as long as we're here?"

She shook her head. In her mind, those plans were all tied up with Will, which was ridiculous, but there it was. "Save them for me, okay? One of these days I'll need them."

Mick nodded and, for once, didn't press the point. "Whenever you're ready to take a look, just say the word."

"I think I'll get back over to the inn and finish cleaning the rest of that junk out of the attic," Jess said. Even such an odious task appealed more now that she knew it was going to lead to the renovations she'd been dreaming about since she'd opened the inn.

"How about some help?" Mick offered.

"That's okay. I've got it." She hugged him tightly. "Thanks again, Dad."

"Anytime, baby girl. Anytime."

Jess tried to sneak out of the house without bumping into anyone else in the family, but just outside, she ran into Gram who was walking back to her own cottage. Jess fell into step beside her.

"It was a great dinner, Gram. I know you made that potato soup. No one does it like you do, and it was perfect for a cool fall day."

Gram gave her a penetrating look, her blue eyes sharp. "Then why didn't you eat more than a mouthful?"

"I did," Jess protested. "It was delicious."

"You might be able to feed someone else that story, young lady, but I know better. I have eyes in my head, don't I? Now tell me what had you looking so glum earlier."

Jess had learned years ago when Gram had taken over the household after Megan had left that there was very little she could hide from her grandmother. At seven, when her mother had first gone, Gram had understood the depth of her sorrow. More important, she had been able to convince Jess that her childish belief that her mother's going had somehow been her fault was nonsense. Gram had made her accept that Megan hadn't gone because Jess was too much trouble. During those awful first months without her mom, Abby had tried her best to step in and make things better, but it was Gram who'd offered the comfort and reassurance she'd really needed.

Moreover, Jess knew she could trust Gram not to spill her confidences to the rest of the family.

"I've been thinking lately that maybe I've made a mistake about Will," Jess admitted.

"In what way?"

Jess gave her an amused look. "You know exactly what way. You've been among the many who've believed for a while now that there was something going on between us."

"Doesn't matter what I think," Gram told her. "So, you're saying that you've realized you might have feelings for him?"

Jess nodded. "But I think it's too late."

"Has he gone off and married someone else?" Gram asked dryly.

"Of course not."

"Then it's not too late. You just have to be willing to put your heart on the line, if you truly want to change things."

"What if it doesn't work out?" Jess asked. "I've lost so many people over the years. Mom went away. Dad was gone most of my childhood, or that's how it felt. Abby, Bree, Kevin and Connor, they all left."

"And they're all back here now," Gram reminded her. "You never lost them, sweetheart."

"It felt as if I did," Jess said, thinking of how often she'd felt left behind. "If I take this chance with Will and it doesn't work out . . ." Her voice trailed off.

Gram smiled. "What if it does work out exactly as you're hoping?" she asked. "That's what I think is far more likely."

"You really think Will and I are right for each other?"

"If you're looking for guarantees, dear heart, I can't give them to you. Love comes with risks. So does life." She squeezed Jess's hand. "But if I were a betting woman—"

"Which we all know you are," Jess

teased. "Your bingo winnings are family legend."

Gram gave her a scolding look. "If I were a betting woman, I'd say the two of you have better odds than most."

"Why?" Jess asked.

"Because I've seen the way that man looks at you. He's been crazy for you since back in high school, maybe even earlier, and he's never let you push him away for long. He just shores up his battered ego and keeps coming back."

"Not this time," Jess said. "It's because of me that he stayed away from dinner today."

"Then maybe you should apologize for whatever you did," Gram said.

"But I didn't do anything wrong," Jess protested. "I just told him how I felt."

"Did you consider his feelings with all that honesty?"

"No," Jess admitted. "I was just trying to be clear. It was silly, really. We'd raided the fridge at the inn, then gone outside to have dinner and watch the sunset. We hadn't even taken our first sip of wine, and all I did was tell him that we weren't on a date."

"And he immediately saw the pattern that Susie and Mack have fallen into," Gram guessed at once.

Jess regarded her with amazement. "How did you see that so clearly when it never even occurred to me, at least not as the words were coming out of my mouth?"

"Never mind me. Is that how Will saw it?"

"Unfortunately, yes."

"Then can you blame him for walking away?" Gram shook her head. "I swear I have no idea what goes on in your cousin Susie's head or why Mack's catered to her whims for all this time. But I can certainly see why another man would refuse to get caught up in the same situation, especially a man who's been in the grandstands watching that foolish standoff play itself out. Sometimes I'd like to shake the two of them myself."

Jess laughed, unable to deny what her grandmother was saying. "I think we all would."

"Then, whatever you do, don't follow their lead," Gram said. "If you want Will, reach out to him. I think it's time a move came from you. I'm pretty sure if you take a chance, you'll find that Will's open to it."

She held Jess's gaze. "Remember this, life is short. I may be in my eighties and I may have lived a rich, full life, but there are no such things as guarantees that anyone will be as blessed as I have been. Don't let love slip away from you just because you're scared."

They'd reached Gram's cottage now, with its climbing roses on the picket fence and a birdbath sitting in the middle of a wild-flower garden in the yard. The cozy little house was like something from a story-book. At least that's how Jess had always thought of it. She'd sometimes wondered how Gram had been able to bear walking away from it when she'd come to take care of them.

"Thanks, Gram," she said, wrapping her grandmother in a hug and noticing how frail she was. There was such strength of purpose and character in Nell that it was sometimes easy to forget that she was no longer young. "I'll think about what you said. You always make things so much clearer for me."

"That's because I've lived a long time. Even with my cataracts, there's plenty that I still see clearly. Love you, sweetheart."

"I love you," Jess said, then watched her go inside before heading off to the inn to think about everything they'd discussed. Maybe Gram was right. Maybe all of her uncertainties and insecurities didn't matter in the end. Maybe reaching out and losing would still be better than never having taken a chance on love at all.

Connie had been called over to the nursery on Sunday afternoon to help Jake load an order of plants for a job that had been postponed twice because of rain.

"I don't see why you didn't call one of the men in to help you," she grumbled as she carried the plants from the green-house to the truck. The answer, of course, was that her brother knew he wouldn't have to pay her, or at least the cynical side of her assumed that was the reason.

Jake gave her the kind of grin that had always won over any woman in the vicinity. It had certainly worked on Bree, but it had lost its power over Connie.

"Because I wanted to see for myself that you weren't sitting at home moping because Jenny's away at school," he said, surprising her. "I don't know why you refused to come to the O'Briens for dinner today. It made me worry about you."

"I just wanted a day to myself," she claimed, unwilling to admit that she'd been half-afraid that Thomas would show up, and she'd be unable to hide her growing feelings for him.

"Thomas was asking about you," Jake said casually.

Connie's pulse skipped a beat. "Really? He was there?"

Jake paused in front of her and leveled a look straight into her eyes. "I got the feeling he was disappointed that you weren't coming. What's that about?"

"Don't be silly," she said, praying that the heat she felt wasn't turning her cheeks a blinding shade of red. "We've just seen a lot of each other because of my volunteer work for the foundation. He probably had some questions for me or something."

Jake looked doubtful, but he didn't press her, thank heaven.

Just then, her cell phone rang. "I need to grab this," she told her brother. "It could be Jenny."

But it wasn't.

"Connie, it's Thomas."

To her surprise, he sounded charmingly nervous. "Hi," she said softly, then moved away for some privacy. "I heard you came to town for Sunday dinner with your family."

"Truthfully, I was hoping you'd be there," he admitted.

"Was there something you needed? Did you want to go over the plans for the fundraiser on Saturday?"

He chuckled. "No, I'm confident that you and Shanna have that totally under control. Besides, Shanna was at lunch with Kevin, so if there had been any questions, I'm sure she could have answered them."

"Oh, of course," Connie said, flustered.

"What are you up to now?" he asked. "Are you busy? Do you feel like grabbing a cup of coffee or something before I head back to Annapolis?"

Connie looked at her filthy hands, the streaks of dirt on her clothes, the old sneakers she'd crammed her feet into when Jake had called. She'd barely combed her hair, and she didn't have on so much as a dab of lipstick. If Thomas saw her now, she'd terrify him.

"Oh, Thomas, I'm a mess. I've been over here at the nursery helping Jake load some plants for a job."

"How close are you to finishing?" he asked, clearly not intimidated by the image she'd painted of herself.

"Fifteen, twenty minutes at least," she said.

"Then another pair of hands will make it go that much more quickly," he said decisively. "See you shortly."

He disconnected the call before she could protest. She wasn't sure which was worse—having Thomas see her in such a sorry state or letting her brother get a glimpse of her swooning over the man.

She spent a full minute debating whether she could get into her office, clean up and change into the spare outfit she kept on hand for days when she wound up helping out in the nursery, rather than the office. Unfortunately, if she greeted Thomas wearing pristine clothes, he was bound to know she'd changed just for him. Never mind what Jake would have to say about it. She decided Thomas would just have to deal. This was who she was, at least some of the time.

"Who was that?" Jake called as he passed with two large plants.

She steadied her voice, then said in what she hoped was a casual tone, "Thomas. He's on his way over."

The five-gallon buckets landed in the truck with a thud. Jake walked back over, his gaze narrowed. "You want to tell me why he's coming here?"

"To lend us a hand," she said brightly.

"Really? We're almost finished. Did you invite him to come?"

"No, I just told him what I was doing, and he offered to help. No big deal."

Jake continued to look doubtful. When Thomas's hybrid car turned into the parking lot, he frowned. "I'm missing something, aren't I?"

"Not a thing," she insisted. "Stop looking so suspicious and be grateful for the help. I'm sure he'd even pitch in on the job this afternoon, if you asked him to."

"Will and Mack promised to meet me over there," Jake said automatically. "You were awfully generous to be offering Thomas's services, though. Is that because you're nervous being around him?"

"Now you're just being crazy," she said,

turning away so he wouldn't see her cheeks burning. "Please hush, before you embarrass me."

When Thomas emerged from his car, he was wearing shorts and a T-shirt, a far more casual outfit than he'd likely had on for Sunday dinner. The T-shirt emphasized his broad shoulders and his muscular arms. His was the kind of tanned, rugged fitness that men who worked out solely in a gym could never attain.

Though he glanced at Connie with a smile, he wisely focused on her brother. "Jake, tell me what you still need to load."

"I'll show you," Connie said, leading him to the remaining plants for the job. "Just these. I told you we were almost through."

"Then there will be time for that coffee," Thomas assessed, picking up the large containers as if they weighed next to nothing.

The minute the truck was loaded, he asked Jake if he'd need a hand unloading at the job site.

"No, I'm good," Jake said, though he couldn't seem to stop frowning. "Thanks for the help."

"No problem," Thomas said.

"You should get going," Connie told her brother. "You only have a few more hours of daylight to get started. You know Mr. Carlson will have a fit if he doesn't see at least some progress today after all these delays for the weather."

"Right," Jake said, though he still appeared reluctant to leave.

When he'd finally driven off, Thomas turned to her. "Well, that went well, don't you think?"

Connie laughed, despite her nervousness. "In what universe? My brother senses that there's something going on with us. He's not going to be happy until he figures out what it is."

Thomas caught her gaze and held it. "Is there something going on with us?" he asked quietly. "Or am I the only one who feels anything?"

She wanted to deny it, to buy herself more time before committing to exploring these feelings that washed over her every time he was nearby.

She eventually drew in a deep breath, then said, "You're not the only one." She met his gaze. "You have to admit, though, that this is scary. Or is it just terrifying for me, because I haven't dated anyone for years?"

"Oh, it's terrifying," he said with total sincerity. "Because I know even better than you the dangers of messing this up. The wrath of the entire family will come down on my head."

"Not on mine?" she asked with a smile.

"I'm older. I'm a man. And everyone knows I'm a terrible risk. The blame will definitely be all mine."

"If it's going to be that dire, are you sure you want to risk it?" she asked, then gestured to herself. "Look at me. No makeup. Dirt from head to toe. The fashion sense of a tomboy. Am I worth it?"

Thomas didn't seem to be the slightest bit put off by her description or her appearance. Instead, he took a step closer, tucked a finger under her chin and kissed her.

It wasn't the smoldering kiss of two people wildly in love. It wasn't a prelude to immediate, no-holds-barred sex. It was the gentle, tentative, exploratory kiss of a man trying to prove that his feelings were real, a man willing to wait for more.

When he stepped back, there was a

smile on his lips and in his eyes. "Let's go have that coffee, okay?"

"You have to at least give me fifteen minutes to clean up," she pleaded. "I refuse to be seen with you in public looking like this. I'll meet you at Sally's or wherever you'd like to go."

He seemed hesitant. "You won't chicken out?"

"My knees may be knocking together and I may be second-guessing myself, but I'm no coward. I'll be there," she promised.

Thomas nodded. "That's good enough for me. Don't take too long, okay? I think you look great just the way you are."

She peered at him intently. "Are you going blind or something?"

He laughed. "Nope. I swear to you I'm seeing more clearly than I have in years."

After he'd gone, Connie raced back to her house instead of to the office. It took a bit longer than the fifteen minutes she'd promised, but the way Thomas's eyes lit up when she walked into Sally's told her the extra time had been worth it.

"Your coffee's cold," he said. "I'll order another cup."

Connie doubted she'd have noticed if it

was colder than ice because suddenly the temperature in Sally's felt like a hundred and ten. She tried to recall one single date in her forty-plus years that had rattled her this badly. Maybe her first one with Sam years and years ago, but she doubted it.

Thomas was gazing at her intently. He leaned forward and confided, "I know we had dinner just a couple of weeks ago, but this feels more like a first date to me. I don't think I was this nervous when I asked Mindy Jefferson to the eighth grade dance."

Connie breathed a sigh of relief. "Thank goodness. I thought it was just me."

"It's going to get easier," he promised her.

"You think so?"

His gaze held hers. "We'll just have to keep practicing until it does."

A smile spread across her face. "I like the way you think, Thomas O'Brien."

He reached across the table and clasped her hand. "Ditto, Connie Collins."

She found the warm, work-roughened texture of his hand comforting. His grasp felt like a man's. There was strength and reassurance and confidence in his grip, all traits that had been in short supply in her life with Sam, a man so selfish he'd left because he'd hated sharing her time with his own daughter.

"Tell me about your ex-husband," Thomas said, still holding her hand in his. "What happened?"

"He's hardly worth talking about," she said.

"Is he still around?"

"No, he moved away not long after the divorce. He and Jenny barely have any relationship at all. My brother's been more of a dad to her than Sam ever was."

"I'm sorry."

"So am I. I don't think I realized it was possible for anyone to not care about their own child. I probably should have paid more attention when he talked about not wanting kids, but I figured he was just scared."

Thomas nodded. "I imagine most people are terrified before they take that step."

"Would you be?"

Thomas looked startled by the question. "I used to think I wanted kids. Anybody being around my brothers and their families would envy them those connections. When I got divorced, though, I was glad there weren't any children to be affected by it. I saw how awful it was for Mick's kids when Megan left."

"Jenny was too young to be affected that much by Sam taking off, but I know over the years she had questions and that she resented me for somehow allowing her dad to get away."

"Did you ever fill her in on what a jerk he was?"

Connie smiled. "Of course not. On the off chance that he ever came back into her life, I didn't want her to hate him."

"That's a pretty generous attitude under the circumstances," Thomas said, his gaze warm. "It just proves what a remarkable woman you are."

Connie felt herself blush. "I'm not re-markable."

"Hey, I get to be the judge of that. You need to learn to take a compliment."

"Usually the most personal compliments I get are customers at the nursery telling me I have a nice phone voice or that I've been very helpful."

Thomas shook his head. "I have to tell you, you have just painted a very dark pic-ture of the intelligence level of the men in Chesapeake Shores."

She laughed, unable to disagree. "I think that's a discussion best left for another time."

He laughed with her. "I hate to do it, but I should probably get back to Annapolis," he said. "I'll see you next weekend at the fall festival?"

"Absolutely."

They walked to her car. He held the door while she got in, then smiled down at her. "It was a good first date."

"It was."

He winked at her. "The next one will be even better."

That wink set off a frisson of anticipation that rattled her even more than his earlier kiss. She had a feeling if this attraction got any more powerful, she was going to throw herself into his arms and cause a scene likely to be talked about in Chesapeake Shores for years. She wondered what her daughter, who thought she was a stuffy prude, would think about that.

10

Jess spent an hour cleaning out the attic at the inn, then lost interest. What she needed, she decided, was to do something even more physical, something that would burn some real energy, maybe help her to stop thinking about Will, about her pitiful lack of a social life.

Never much of an athlete, she wasn't at all like her brothers. Almost the only sport that had ever appealed to her was kayaking. There was something soothing about paddling around on the water, and, from time to time, when the whitecaps kicked up

on the bay, it could be strenuous and challenging, as well.

The inn kept a couple of kayaks on hand
for use by the guests. Both were in their
rack at the foot of the steps, their paddles
locked in place beside them. Using her
key, Jess took the more lightweight of the
kayaks off the rack and lowered it into
the calm water. It was a perfect afternoon,
she thought, noting that quite a few people
had had the same idea. Kayaks dotted the
waterfront, along with way too many
speedboats for her comfort.

Staying close to the shoreline to avoid
the wake of the larger, more aggressive
boaters, she paddled hurriedly along, then
took a turn to the left when she reached the
narrow inlet leading to the more tranquil
Moonlight Cove. There were fewer people
on the water here and no powerboats. It
was a small cove loved by locals because
tourists hadn't discovered it. It was also an
ideal place to spot the occasional eagle or
osprey sitting high atop the branches of the
old oaks, cedars and weeping willows that
shaded much of the shoreline.

And its tiny beach, not that far from

Connor and Heather's Driftwood Cottage, remained inaccessible by road. It had always been especially popular with teenagers looking for a secluded place to be alone.

She thought of the times she'd come here with one boyfriend or another, only to have Connor or Kevin come after her in their small motorboat to chase her back home before she did something utterly foolish. Though she'd protested their protectiveness vehemently at the time, claiming total humiliation, she now appreciated that they'd kept her from an impulsive mistake that could have ruined her life.

Today, though, the beach was deserted. She paddled close to shore, pulled the kayak up onto the sand, then went for a swim before tossing her towel on a tiny patch of warm sand and lying down to dry off in the last rays of the day's sun.

Exhausted, she fell asleep almost immediately. When she awoke, darkness was falling rapidly as it seemed to do especially quickly on fall afternoons.

Muttering an expletive, she grabbed her towel, but when she turned toward where she'd left the kayak, she realized that it was gone, pulled back out to sea on the tide. In the dusk, she could actually see it bobbing on the waves, which set off a few more curses.

Now what? She could probably swim out to retrieve it, but in the gathering darkness, she recognized that wasn't smart. She had her cell phone, though, so she could call for help. Connor or even Kevin would probably come and rescue her. But they'd also lecture her from now till next Sunday about being irresponsible. She could probably even hike through the woods and get to Connor's place, but the same issue would confront her if she appeared on his doorstep and explained what had happened. Besides, as close as Driftwood Cottage probably was if she walked directly there, it would be way too easy to get turned around in the woods after dark.

Almost without realizing she was doing it, she found Will's number on her phone. His lectures would probably be only a shade more bearable than her brothers', but she made the call before she could talk herself out of it.

"Jess?"

"Hi," she said, relaxing at the sound of his voice.

"Where are you? I can barely hear you."

"I'm on my cell. I'm at Moonlight Cove."

"What on earth are you doing there at this hour? It'll be dark any minute."

"Believe me, I know that. I hate to bother you, but there's a problem."

"What kind of problem?" he asked, his tone suddenly crisp and efficient. "Tell me."

"It seems my kayak has drifted away."

"How the devil did that happen?" he asked, and she could practically see his perplexed expression.

"Is that really important right now?" she asked.

"No, I suppose it's not. Give me a half hour."

"Thanks, Will."

"Where exactly are you? Do you have any kind of light you can flash, so I'll be able to spot you?"

"I think if I turn on my cell phone and hold it up, you'll be able to see that. And there's a full moon rising, so that should help, too."

"That'll work. Don't turn on the cell phone right away or the battery could die. Wait a half hour, okay? Give me time to get to your parents' place and grab your brothers' old fishing boat. It doesn't have much of a motor, but it'll get me there faster than my kayak would."

"Thanks."

He hesitated. "You okay, otherwise?"

"Other than feeling foolish, I'm fine."

He laughed. "Foolish passes, trust me. I'll see you soon."

Even after she'd disconnected the call, Jess clutched the cell phone tightly. It made her feel less isolated.

No, she corrected herself. What had made her feel less isolated was hearing Will's calm, reassuring voice, his immediate offer to come after her with no recriminations.

Of course, as nice as he'd been on the phone just now, she knew perfectly well he was likely to have quite a lot to say once he got here.

Will hadn't panicked, at least not for Jess, when he'd heard her predicament. She was perfectly safe at Moonlight Cove.

No, what had flat-out terrified him was the thought of being there, alone, with her. He'd only gone there a handful of times as a teen and never with Jess. He knew, though, that Connor and Kevin had dragged her home from more than a few romantic trysts, always in the nick of time, to hear them tell it. Will hadn't really wanted the details. Just knowing she'd been off with some other boy had been enough to make a knot form in his stomach.

At least that hadn't been the case today. She'd apparently gone there alone. He'd find her on the beach, in some skimpy bathing suit, no doubt, maybe even cold and shivering now that the sun had gone down. With that full moon she'd mentioned already rising, this rescue had danger written all over it. How much could one man be expected to handle before he lost control of himself?

Forcing himself not to dwell on what he might find when he got to Jess, he went to the O'Briens, stepped onto the dock and borrowed the small fishing boat that Connor and Kevin kept there. It was always gassed up and ready to go, and over the years he'd taken it out on plenty of occasions. Though he usually asked first, he figured tonight was one of those times when discretion was called for.

As he stepped into the boat, he wondered why it was Jess hadn't called either of her brothers, but he could guess. A rescue by either of them would have come with a lecture she obviously didn't want to hear.

Ten minutes later, he found the inlet to Moonlight Cove and made his way toward the beach, the boat's little engine chugging along nicely. He figured the sound on the still, quiet night would alert her. Sure enough, he saw a flicker of light on the shore.

"Jess?" he called out.

"I'm here," she said.

"I'd probably better not bring the boat too close to shore. Think you can swim out a bit?"

"Of course," she said. "The moon's plenty bright enough to light the way. I can see you from here. I guess it doesn't matter if I leave the kayak paddles and my towel behind."

"Hardly," he said wryly.

"Thank goodness I thought to put my cell phone into a waterproof pouch," she added. "At least I won't ruin that swimming out to the boat."

He could hear her splash into the water,

then the quieter splash as she swam toward him. He kept talking to guide her, his gaze following her sure, steady progress.

When she reached the boat, he pulled her up, then wrapped her in the thick towel he'd brought along. "Here, take my shirt," he said, when she was dry but shivering.

Even then, though, he could hear her teeth chatter, so he sighed, muttered a silent curse and pulled her into his arms. She stilled at the unexpected contact, then snuggled close.

"You're so warm," she murmured, her breath soft against his chest.

Warm? He felt like he was in the blasted desert. And his body was starting to react to having this almost naked woman—a woman he'd loved for an eternity—plastered against him. This was bad, he told himself. It was hell. He swallowed hard and amended, no, it was heaven.

"Um, Jess, not a good idea," he said, setting her away from him and securing the thick towel more tightly around her. "Take a seat. I'll have you back at the inn in a few minutes."

Thankfully, she didn't cling or argue, because he wasn't sure he could have maintained that noble stance for more than another heartbeat or two.

He steered the little fishing boat back out into the bay and along the shore until he spotted the inn's dock. He pulled alongside it, secured the boat, then scrambled up on the dock and held out his hand for Jess.

She looked up at him, her eyes sparkling in the moonlight. "Thanks, Will. Do you want to come in for coffee or something? Maybe a glass of wine?"

He hesitated. "You should probably take a shower and get into something warm," he said.

"That won't take more than a minute," she told him, her gaze still on his. "I really owe you for coming to my rescue. Maybe we could have that dinner we never got to have the other night. I think there's more of Gail's roasted chicken."

He smiled. "You don't have to bribe me with food and drink, you know."

"I know. Actually I was hoping we could talk."

He stilled. "Oh? About what?"

She looked away, clearly flustered. "You know, just this and that."

"You're going to have to give me more

than that," he said. "If this is going to be another of those conversations where you explain that we're not dating, I'll pass."

Her laugh sounded forced. "Oh, I think I've learned my lesson on that one. I just miss talking to you about stuff."

"Stuff?" he echoed. "When did we ever talk about stuff?"

"A long time ago, before things got so complicated."

"You mean before I fell for you and you didn't fall for me?"

Her chin jutted up stubbornly. "Okay, yes, back then."

"Okay, one more question. Why did you call me tonight? I understand why you didn't call one of your brothers, but why me?"

She looked vaguely rattled by the question. "You were the first person I thought of."

"Any idea why?"

"Because I trust you," she said simply. "And I wanted to make up for what happened the last time I saw you. I felt as if we lost something. I want it back."

Intrigued despite himself by her sudden nostalgia for the old days, he decided to take a chance. Who knew what was going on in that unpredictable head of hers?

"Let's go, then, before you catch pneumonia."

When they entered the inn through the kitchen, Jess pointed him toward the refrigerator. "Help yourself. Make me a sandwich or something if you don't mind. I'm starved. And feel free to raid the wine supply. I'll be back in a few minutes."

Will found a loaf of freshly baked whole grain bread, cut thick slices, lathered them with mustard and mayonnaise, then added thin slices of cheddar cheese, ham and tomato. He found a stash of homemade sweet potato chips, one of the inn's specialties, and put them into a bowl. He'd just poured two glasses of wine when Jess returned.

Her cheeks were flushed, her damp hair tousled, but she looked terrific in a pair of faded jeans and some kind of fuzzy sweater that practically begged to be touched. She was barefoot, her nails painted an unexpectedly sexy shade of dare-me red. It contradicted her otherwise wholesome image. He thought that was one of the things that appealed to him most about her. She was such a mass of unpredictability and contradictions. No man could ever possibly be bored by her.

Of course, what he saw as charming unpredictability, too many others over the years had convinced her was a flaw caused by her attention deficit disorder. She'd become extraordinarily self-conscious and testy about what she viewed as a negative that she couldn't overcome.

"You look about a thousand times better," he said approvingly.

"And this sandwich looks amazing. Thank you. Want to take them into the lounge? We can build a fire, if you want. There's no one around tonight, so we have the place to ourselves again. I love Sunday nights for just that reason. I have the run of the place."

She met his gaze. "Remember when we were kids, how much we loved Sundays because all the tourists would leave by suppertime and the town would be ours again? There were no lines waiting for ice cream or snow cones and our favorite booths at Sally's weren't occupied by strangers."

Will smiled. "I remember." He tore his gaze away. "Why don't you grab the sandwiches and I'll bring the wine, the glasses and the chips? Should I bring dessert, too? There's a decadent-looking cake in the fridge."

"Bring the whole cake," she said, grinning. "I did mention I'm starved, didn't I?"

He laughed. "I'll grab a couple of plates and forks, then."

"Forget the plates. If it's Gail's double fudge cake, we'll just finish it off. Or I will."

Shaking his head, he looked her over. "For a skinny little thing, where do you put all this food?"

"Nervous energy," she said, leading the way into the lounge with its overstuffed chairs arranged to face the fireplace.

"Thank goodness there's wood," she noted, heading toward it after she'd set down the sandwiches.

"Sit. I'll get it," Will said.

She regarded him skeptically. "Do you know how to build a fire? I thought you were the intellectual type."

"I was also a Boy Scout, just like every other male kid in town." He grinned. "Of course, I did flunk quite a few of the tests, so my collection of merit badges is pretty limited. I think it's safe to let me light the fire, though."

He made quick work of getting it started, then saw that instead of sitting in a chair, she'd settled on the floor. She patted the spot next to her. Will sat, but he studied her with a narrowed gaze.

"What's going on, Jess?"

She gave him an innocent look. "I don't know what you mean."

"Maybe I'm reading too much into this, but this scene has seduction written all over it. It seems out of character, at least when it comes to you and me. You've been keeping me at arm's length for a long time."

Bright patches of pink climbed into her cheeks, even as she mustered up a heavy dose of indignation. "You're imagining things," she insisted.

"Am I really?" he asked doubtfully. "Something's changed tonight. I'm trying to put a finger on what."

"Can't I just be grateful to you for coming to my rescue?"

"And that's all this is?"

She shrugged. "Sure. What else?"

Will sighed, more disconcerted than he'd been in years. What else, indeed? For a couple of minutes there, he'd wondered if perhaps his dreams were about to come true.

* * *

Jess hadn't expected Will to call her on her intentions, especially since she wasn't even certain herself why she was suddenly considering breaking her hard-and-fast rule about not dating him. She had to admit, though, that he was right about one thing: something had changed between them tonight. There was a sizzle in the air she couldn't remember ever being there before. Oh, there'd always been the heat of anger or a quick spark of indignation, but never this powerful pull, nor this simmering attraction. At least not until that kiss at Brady's. Since then, she'd felt it more frequently.

Maybe Gram's advice had simply sunk in. Maybe she was finally at a point when she was ready to put her fears aside and embrace whatever there might be between the two of them. How ironic it would be if she was ready now, and Will was the one who held back.

"How often do you go to Moonlight Cove?" Will asked, watching her intently, an odd wariness still in his eyes.

"Not so much anymore. Why?"

"I just heard a few stories," he said.

"From my brothers, I'm sure. To hear them tell it, I was putting my virginity at risk over there at least once a week throughout my teens."

"Were you?"

"Realistically, I suppose I did take a lot of chances," she admitted. "It's funny. Now that I think about it, I'm pretty sure I always counted on Kevin or Connor to rescue me in the nick of time."

"A pretty risky game, don't you think?"

"I do now, of course," she admitted, then shrugged. "But back then, I just wanted to connect with somebody. I was too young and stupid to realize that sex wasn't the answer."

Will looked genuinely surprised by her response. "You were lonely?"

Jess thought about the question. "Not exactly. I mean, our house was always crawling with people, you know what I mean?"

"I do," he said. "I was one of them."

"Did you ever happen to notice that none of them were my friends? Oh, I was tolerated because I was Connor's kid sister or Kevin's or Bree's, but kids my own age steered clear. I got a reputation early as the kid who stirred up trouble in school, the kid who was always disrupting the classroom.

No parent wanted their children around me, as if the ADD might be contagious."

Will's expression filled with sympathy, which Jess found annoying.

"Don't you dare pity me," she told him. "That's just the way it was. By the time I hit my teens, I figured out how to compensate, at least with boys."

"Sex," he said, sounding unbearably sad. "Oh, Jess, didn't you know that all of us hanging out at your folks' place adored you?"

"Maybe *you* did," she said. "The others, not so much. I think my brothers just put the fear of God into them so they'd tolerate me."

Will's expression changed, as if something had suddenly clicked for him. "And that's why you don't trust me when I say I care about you," he said. "On some level, you're still that little kid who's wanting to belong but doesn't think she ever will."

Jess was uncomfortable, as always, when Will started analyzing her. She didn't like it that he could see her so clearly, especially the insecurities she'd worked so hard to hide from the world.

She forced a smile. "How'd we get off

on this tangent, anyway? It's all old news. This sandwich is amazing. Thanks for fixing it."

Will gave her a knowing look. "There you go, scurrying back into your shell. Why do you do that, especially with me?"

"You're the shrink. You tell me."

"Okay," he said, clearly accepting her words as a challenge. "Here's the way I see it. You're scared to death to let anyone get too close. It goes back to your parents' divorce. If the two adults who were supposed to love you could all but abandon you, then how could you possibly be lovable?"

The analysis, which so closely mirrored what she herself had said to Gram recently, gave her pause. It should have annoyed her to have Will hit the mark so accurately, but amazingly it felt oddly comforting. He actually got her . . . and, it seemed, liked her anyway.

Still, she wasn't prepared to give him credit for it too easily.

"I'm not scared of letting anyone get close," she insisted, mostly to be contrary. "I signed up for your dating service, didn't I? Doesn't that prove that I want to find someone to spend my life with?"

"All it proves is that Connie and Laila caught you at a weak moment," he retorted.

She hated that he'd figured that out, too, but she couldn't deny it.

"How many dates have you been on?" he asked.

"You only matched me up with one guy," she reminded him.

"Have you gone out with him?" he pressed.

She sighed. "No."

"Why not?"

"It didn't feel right."

"Tell me why."

She stared at the fire, stubbornly silent.

"Come on, Jess," Will said impatiently. "How about the truth? How am I supposed to make adjustments in my system's criteria if you won't be honest with me? What about this guy didn't feel right?"

"So it's all about you and your precious computer program?" she said, miffed and not really sure why. She didn't want Will digging around in her psyche, did she? So why wasn't she more relieved that all he cared about was how he could fix a Lunch by the Bay computer glitch?

Will's gaze was unflinching. "You're avoiding my questions."

Jess sighed. "It was nothing specific," she insisted. "Maybe it was just the timing. Maybe I was having an off day or something. Don't make a big deal about it. I'll go out with the next guy or the one after that. How many dates have you gone on?"

"Three," he said.

"Including Laila," she said, unable to keep a testy note out of her voice. "What was that about?"

"The computer program said we had a lot in common. We do, too," he added, a surprisingly defiant tone in his voice.

"Then why didn't you ask her out again?"

"No chemistry," he conceded. "I haven't figured out how to factor that into the program. I don't even think it can be done."

Jess chuckled. "Yep, those old pheromones can be a killer, can't they? No telling when they'll kick in."

"Some would say that any two people who are well-suited on other fronts can develop a sexual attraction in time," he said.

"But you're obviously not one of the so-called experts who believes that," she said.

Will frowned. "Why would you say that?"

"The Laila experience. If you believed that attraction can grow over the course of a relationship, why didn't you ask her out again?" she pressed.

"Because, if you must know, you were sitting right there between us on the whole date," he said irritably.

"Me? I was nowhere near Panini Bistro that day."

"You might as well have been," Will grumbled. "Laila referred to you as the elephant in the room."

"How incredibly flattering!" Jess said wryly.

"Oh, you know what she meant," Will said. "She and I both knew I'd have preferred to be on a date with you."

"And yet when you were doing the matches for her, Connie and me, you left yourself out of the running when it came to me. Laila told me."

"Because you'd made it plain that you didn't want to date me. Whatever your reasons for that, I had to take you at your word."

"I see," Jess said, then fell silent. She picked up a fork and took a huge bite of Gail's moist double fudge chocolate cake, then closed her eyes as the rich, dark chocolate flavor burst on her tongue. "Oh, sweet heaven!" she murmured.

She opened her eyes to see Will staring at her intently. "You have to try this," she told him, cutting into the cake and holding a bite-size piece in front of his mouth. He accepted the offering, then sighed.

"It is pretty amazing," he said, though his gaze still seemed to be locked on her mouth. "You have chocolate right here." He touched the corner of her lips with his finger. "And here." His finger skimmed across her lower lip.

To her astonishment, Jess trembled. There it was again, that incredible sizzle. It was even more alluring than the cake, which was saying quite a lot. The unexpected feeling rattled her.

"Um, Will?"

"Yes," he said, still holding her gaze.

"Would you do something for me?"

"Just about anything. You know that."

"Run my data through your computer again," she requested. "But this time, leave yourself in the mix."

"No," he said so quickly it left her head spinning.

"No?" she asked incredulously. "Why not?"

"Because the computer's not infallible. Even I accept that. If it comes back without a match, I don't want you using that as an excuse to justify never going out with me."

"Don't you trust your program?"

"Of course I do, for what it is. It's a way to match up strangers who might be compatible on a variety of fronts."

"Okay, then why not put it to the test with us?" she pressed.

"We're not strangers." He leveled a look into her eyes. "And I already know we're well-suited. I think you do, too."

"But—"

"No, Jess," he said, cutting her off. "Don't even try to deny it. The truth is that you know we could be great together, but you're too terrified to admit it. What I can't figure out is why."

Jess looked away. She had her suspicions about that, but she wasn't ready to own up to them. Ironically, though, it was a relief to know that for once, Will didn't have her totally pegged. Somehow it made him seem less like a shrink and more like a guy she could fall for.

11

As Saturday approached, Connie grew increasingly nervous about seeing Thomas at the fall festival in a neighboring community. Something had changed between them on Sunday. They'd taken their blinders off, admitted to a mutual attraction, but for the life of her, she couldn't imagine what came next.

At her age, did two people just jump into bed together or did they dance around that for weeks on end until one night they found themselves tearing each other's clothes off? The thought of having sex with Thomas—or any man, for that matter—terrified her.

She'd been so young when she'd fallen for Sam. He'd been the only one for her. And after the divorce, there had been Jenny to consider. She didn't want to confuse her daughter by bringing an endless parade of men into the house. Not that there had been any kind of parade lined up, anyway. Even the most casual dates had been few and far between.

Now, out of the blue, there was Thomas O'Brien, an intelligent, sexy man who'd lived a far more sophisticated life than she had. She had no idea how to handle whatever was happening between them.

Pacing around the home she'd lived in almost her entire life, she punched in the numbers for Connor's wife on the portable phone. Heather had been the first to witness the growing attraction between Connie and Thomas and had reserved judgment. Maybe she'd be able to help without laughing her head off.

"Tonight, my place," Connie commanded when her friend answered. "I'm calling Jess, too. I need pizza, a lot of ice cream and a complete makeover."

Heather laughed. "You sound nervous. What's going on? Does this have something to do with the fact that you're seeing Thomas tomorrow?"

Connie stilled. "How on earth did you know about that? This whole festival appearance was fairly last-minute."

"Shanna asked me if I could help you out since I'm taking some quilts to the festival to show," Heather explained patiently. "I called and asked the organizers to make sure our booths are next to each other. Shanna didn't tell you?"

"No, but that's fantastic," Connie said, already feeling better. "Now if I can just talk Jess into coming along, I'll feel . . ."

"What?" Heather teased. "Safe?"

"Okay, yes, at least marginally."

"You do know that you are over forty, the mother of a college student and a beautiful, intelligent woman, don't you?"

"Blah, blah, blah," Connie said. "You try being in my shoes. I haven't dated in what feels like a million years."

"I know for a fact you've had lunch with Thomas, you've had coffee with Thomas, you've even had dinner with Thomas. Call those occasions whatever you want to, I'm thinking they were dates. Were they that scary?"

"No," she admitted. "He's extraordinarily easy to talk to."

"Well, there you go."

"But those were all before," Connie said, trying to explain.

"Before what? Before you knew sex was an option?" Heather chuckled even as she spoke.

"It is not funny!" Connie told her. "I shaved my legs the other day for the first time in ages, and now I have all these little nicks. I am so not ready for dating. I'm pretty sure my last tube of mascara has hardened into some kind of fossil that future generations will examine with awe."

This time Heather didn't even try to hide her laughter. "You are so cute. Please say I can tell Connor about this."

"Not if you value your life," Connie said direly. "If Thomas wants his nephew to be privy to our private life, he'll have to tell him himself."

"Not fair," Heather protested, then added in a noble tone, "Besides, I shouldn't keep secrets from my husband. It's very hard on a marriage."

"You were happy enough to keep a few when you didn't want him to know you were living in Chesapeake Shores," Connie reminded her.

"We weren't married then. Now we have this total honesty pact."

Connie sighed. She understood what Heather was saying. She really did. "Am I going to regret calling you?" she asked plaintively.

Heather hesitated for just a fraction of a second, then said, "No, absolutely not. There are a very few occasions when being a friend trumps everything else. This is one of them."

"Thank you."

"You do remember that Connor already knows about this whole thing between you and Thomas, right? He picked up on it ages ago."

"And then blabbed to Jess and who knows who else," Connie said. "I don't trust him to keep anything to himself anymore, so the less he knows, the better. At some point he might feel he's duty-bound to spill the beans to my brother. I do not want Jake jumping all over me about this."

"You might have a point about that," Heather agreed. "O'Briens do love trumping each other with the latest family gossip.

Are you sure Jess is an exception to that? She's joining us tonight, right?"

"You see, the thing about Jess is that I know a few of her secrets, too," Connie explained. "We sort of neutralize each other. She'll keep mine or I'll spread hers far and wide."

Heather laughed. "Is it any wonder I love this town and this family? See you tonight. Seven-thirty okay? I'll come as soon as I put little Mick down for the night. Connor can take over then. I'd let him do the whole bath and bedtime thing, but I'd come home to a bathroom that looks as if a pipe has burst."

"Seven-thirty's great, thanks. If you own any makeup, you might want to bring it along. I haven't used anything more than lipstick in so long, I've forgotten how to put it on. I flatly refuse to go out and spend a fortune on new stuff till I know whether I can put it on without looking like a clown."

"Maybe you shouldn't bother at all," Heather said. "You have that lovely, wholesome look that is obviously very attractive to a man who loves the outdoors as much as Thomas does. He seems awfully taken with the way you look now."

Connie was startled by the observation, but then a smile curved her lips. "He is, isn't he? I'll be darned."

She wondered how many more surprises were in store while she figured out this whole dating thing.

Will hadn't gone to a fall festival in years. He wasn't especially fond of the crowds or the junk food or the country music that seemed to be a staple of these events. He was, however, way too fond of Jess, and rumor had it that she was going this year. Connor asked if he wanted to tag along.

"Heather's going to have a booth and I've been drafted to help her sell quilts, and she's been drafted to help Connie at the foundation booth. The way I hear it, Jess is going along as moral support for Connie." He shook his head. "It all sounds ridiculously complicated, if you ask me, but I'm a mere man."

Will regarded him blankly. "Why does Connie need moral support?"

Connor's eyes sparkled with mischief. "Haven't you heard that she and my uncle have a thing going?"

"Connie and Thomas?" Will stared at

him, flabbergasted. "Since when? Does Jake know?"

"I sure as heck haven't told him," Connor said. "And I doubt that Connie has. The jury's out on how Jake will react. You know how protective he's been of his big sister ever since she and Sam split up." He grinned. "So, you interested in coming along tomorrow?"

"Count me in," Will said.

Connor gave him what passed for an innocent look from a man who didn't have an innocent bone in his body. "So, how are things between you and my sister these days?"

"Awkward," Will said. "I thought maybe we were making a little progress last Sunday, but then I said the wrong thing, she tensed up, and we were right back where we started."

Connor looked puzzled. "You weren't at dinner last Sunday."

"No, I wasn't," Will agreed, amused as he watched Connor trying mentally to fit the pieces together.

"Then when did you see her?" Connor asked eventually.

"She called and asked me to rescue her

from Moonlight Cove," Will admitted, knowing he was opening a can of worms.

Connor instantly looked incensed. "Who was she with this time? What is wrong with her? Hasn't she learned anything after all the times either Kevin or I had to go save her before she did something idiotic?"

"She wasn't there with a man," Will said, not surprised that Connor had leaped to that conclusion. "She'd kayaked over there, and then her kayak drifted off while she was taking a nap or something."

Connor's annoyance faded for barely an instant, before he got worked up all over again. "I'm not sure that isn't just as bad. What if she'd been stuck there all night? What if she hadn't had her cell phone? I swear, when I see her—"

"When you see her, you're going to keep your opinions to yourself," Will said flatly. "Those opinions are precisely why she called me, rather than you or Kevin. If she'd wanted to hear from you, in fact, she could have hiked through the woods and been at your place in fifteen or twenty minutes."

"Well, somebody has to tell her like it is," Connor grumbled. "She can't behave irresponsibly without someone calling her on it. I don't suppose you did that?"

"No, I didn't. She did have her cell phone. She did call me. She got home safe and sound. All in all, she behaved perfectly logically and responsibly."

"You mean other than letting the stupid kayak drift off in the first place," Connor said, still not pacified.

"It could have happened to anyone," Will insisted. "Do I need to remind you of the time we got stranded over at Jessup's Point because your boat got stuck on a sand bar? I believe it was the Coast Guard that finally tracked us down."

"We were fifteen," Connor retorted.

"And had been out on these waters a hundred times and we still screwed up," Will said. "Stuff happens. It won't help anyone if you make Jess feel bad for making a mistake. She's sensitive enough to everyone's opinion as it is."

Connor sighed heavily. "I know you're right. I just worry about her, you know? She doesn't always think before she acts."

Will understood Connor's concern, but he also thought he knew Jess in some ways better than Connor did. "I worry about her, too," he said. "But here's the difference between you and me. I trust her to handle whatever problems crop up. You still think she's that kid who needs her big brothers to bail her out. Jess is an adult."

"But—"

Will gave him a warning look that silenced whatever he'd been about to say. "Sure, she's an adult with ADD, but she's not some basket case who can't be trusted. Look at all she's accomplished, Connor. She's amazing. It's time the rest of you started seeing her that way and stopped making judgments and rushing to her rescue before she says anything about needing help."

Connor studied him long and hard. "You really do have it bad, don't you?"

Will shrugged. "Nothing new about that."

Connor shook his head. "What is wrong with my sister? Why can't she see what's right in front of her face?"

"She will," Will said. He was increasingly confident of that. The only thing he couldn't pinpoint with any certainty was the timetable. He just hoped they both lived long enough for it to happen.

* * *

Saturday morning had dawned with bright sunshine, a crisp fall breeze and promised to be the kind of day that energized people. Jess helped Connie set up the foundation's booth displaying books about the Chesapeake Bay and providing information on memberships and donations. There was a large jar for cash donations as well.

Right next door, Connor was helping Heather set up the Cottage Quilts booth with its selection of colorful quilts hanging on three sides and additional quilts showcased on tables. Little Mick was scampering between the booths, hoping someone would read to him or take him to one of the food booths set up across the park.

"Come on, kiddo, I'll take you," Jess offered. "Let's go see what kind of sticky food we can find that'll make Mommy crazy."

Heather scowled at her. "Please do not indulge my son with a bunch of junk food."

Jess grinned. "How about a caramel apple? They're a little on the gooey side, but there is fruit inside."

"An interesting spin, but you'll need to cut it for him, then make sure he washes his hands before he comes back here,"

Heather said, then turned to Connor. "Maybe you should go with them."

Jess feigned a scowl at her sister-in-law. "Did you just insult me? I am perfectly capable of taking care of a toddler for a few minutes."

Heather laughed. "Not the issue. My kid has you wound around his little finger. There's no telling what he's liable to talk you into buying him."

"That's an aunt's privilege," Jess told her.

"Then you get him when he starts throwing up," Heather warned. "That's the rule I apply to Connor, isn't it?" She gave her husband an affectionate poke in the ribs.

"Sadly, she's telling the truth," Connor said. "The kid's all yours, sis. Just be prepared. Unlike us, he apparently wasn't blessed with a cast-iron stomach."

"He's three," Jess said. "Give him time."

She held out her hand and little Mick grabbed it. "Over there, Aunt Jess," he said, dragging her toward the funnel cake.

"Looks good," she said at once. "Nothing like a little grease and powdered sugar to start the day."

They were waiting in line when she

looked up and spotted Will heading her way, weaving through the crowd and head and shoulders above many of them. Sometimes she forgot how tall he was, and how petite he'd always made her feel.

"What brings you to the festival?" she called out to him. "I thought you hated this kind of thing."

"It's a nice day. I felt like being outdoors, and Connor told me you all were going to be helping out down here. I figured I could lend a hand."

Little Mick held out his arms, and Will immediately scooped him up. "Hey, buddy, how you doing?"

"Me getting cake," he said excitedly, gesturing toward the sign over the booth. "And ca'mel apple and ice cream, too."

Will laughed. "Is that so?" He looked at Jess. "You're a brave woman."

"So they tell me. Can I get you anything when I get to the front of the line?"

"Not me. I'll stick to coffee for now. I think I saw some a couple of booths down."

Normally Jess avoided caffeine, but she loved coffee. "I don't suppose they have decaf?" she said wistfully.

"I'll check," Will offered at once. "If they

don't, I'll run across the street. There's a little café over there that's open. Why don't you bring the funnel cake back to the foundation booth and I'll meet you there."

"Sounds great," she said at once.

"Go with Will," Mick demanded.

Jess looked at Will.

"It's fine with me," he said.

"You can carry him and hot coffee?"

"Mick doesn't need to be carried all the time, do you, buddy? You can hold my hand and walk back like a big boy."

Mick nodded enthusiastically. "Me a big boy, Aunt Jess."

Jess watched as the two of them left. Something about the way Will had interacted with her nephew warmed her heart. Mick obviously adored Will, and she hadn't sensed even a hint of judgment in Will's tone when it came to the boy. It made her wonder what kind of father Will would be, a thought that gave her pause.

Because thinking of Will in that way was so disconcerting, she focused on the task at hand. She bought the funnel cake, still warm from the grease, and headed back to the booth. As she walked, she broke off a piece and munched it thoughtfully. It might not be healthy, but it sure did taste good. Took her right back to her childhood.

As she approached the booth, Connor caught sight of her and an expression of utter panic crossed his face. He left the booth and sprinted toward her.

"Mind telling me what the devil you've done with my son?" he asked, his voice obviously hushed so Heather wouldn't overhear.

Stunned that her brother could think her so irresponsible that she'd lose track of his son, she scowled right back at him. "Do you honestly think I just walked off and forgot about him?"

"I don't know what to think. He left with you. He's nowhere in sight now. It would be just like you to get to talking to somebody or get distracted and lose track of him."

"Thanks for the vote of confidence," she said, barely containing her anger. The anger was welcome. Otherwise she might have burst into tears. "Mick is with Will. I assume you trust one of your best friends to look out for your son? Oh, look, here they come now, all safe and sound. Be sure Mick gets the funnel cake." She tossed it at her brother, not caring if he instinctively grabbed it in midair or let it drop to the ground, then whirled around and walked off.

"Jess!"

She ignored Connor and kept walking, not sure where she was going until she found herself by the water, the sounds of the festival fading behind her. She walked along the water's edge, trying to still the pounding of her heart, waiting for her tears to dry.

Over the years she'd grown used to the way people, including those in her own family, reacted to some of the decisions she made. If she made a mistake of any kind, it was all too easy to blame it on the ADD.

"Sometimes a screwup is just a screwup," she muttered, swiping at her tears.

Not that letting Will take little Mick was a screwup. Her nephew was probably safer with him than he would be with her, especially in Connor's view. Her older brother clearly wasn't ready to give her any credit for common sense or being responsible, and, dammit, she didn't deserve his lack of faith.

"You busy beating yourself up for letting

me take little Mick?" Will inquired, falling into step beside her.

She frowned up at him. "No, actually I'm berating my brother for having so little confidence in me."

Will seemed surprised by her response. "Good for you." He slanted a sideways glance at her. "You didn't do anything wrong."

"I know that."

"And Connor feels awful for questioning you the way he did," he added.

"I seriously doubt that. He's always been very big on jumping to conclusions where I'm concerned. He doesn't think I have the sense God gave a duck."

Will chuckled. "But you've let him get away with that. You do the same with everyone in your family. You've gotten way too comfortable in the niche they've put you in, the O'Brien who can't do anything right. You use the ADD as an excuse as much as they do."

She whirled on him. "I most certainly do not."

Will didn't back down. "Sure you do. It's easier to fall back on that than to really examine what went wrong in any given situation. I heard you just now, and you're right. Sometimes a screwup is just that. We all make them, even those of us without attention deficit disorders. After all these years, with all you've accomplished, you know that you've been able to manage most of the symptoms. Yet you're very quick to judge yourself when the slightest thing goes wrong."

Jess sighed. "Okay, sometimes, yes. I guess when you grow up with people not expecting you to get anything right, you stop expecting much of yourself."

Careful to avoid his intelligent gaze, she said, "But then I do something right, I turn the inn into a real success, and I forget for a while that I even have ADD. You're right. I manage it. I think that's why it hurts so much when Connor looks at me the way he did just now, as if I haven't changed at all."

Though Will's expression was sympathetic, he tried to reason with her. "He was just scared, Jess. You can't blame him for that."

"He was scared that I'd lost his son," she said. "Like little Mick was some loaf of bread I'd wander off and leave behind."

"It was one second of panic," Will said. "Give him a break. You know Connor loves you. Nobody is prouder of you and your accomplishments than he is."

She closed her eyes. That's what made it worse in some ways. She counted on Connor as more than a brother. He was, in many ways, her best friend. His doubts cut right through her.

"I know," she said softly.

"You ready to go back now?"

"Sure."

"Good, because we're missing all the excitement."

"What excitement?"

"Thomas and Connie dancing around each other like two shy teenagers with their first crushes."

Jess laughed at the image. "They are a little bit like that, aren't they?" Then worry kicked in. "You don't think anyone in the family is going to give them grief over this, do you?"

Will regarded her incredulously. "Of course they will. It's what O'Briens do. It's like some rite of passage."

Jess thought about that and knew it was true. And yet Will, even knowing that, still wanted to be with her. That told her quite a lot about the depth of his feelings.

Back at the foundation booth, Jess spotted her uncle standing next to Connie, his gaze on her as she made a book sale and chatted with a customer. There was a warmth in his eyes that had been absent since the end of his second marriage.

"Look at him," she said, nudging Will in the side. "He's really taken with her, isn't he?"

Will studied the duo, then smiled. "It's nice to see. Connie deserves to have someone special in her life. She's been on her own way too long."

"My uncle doesn't have the world's best track record when it comes to women," Jess fretted. "What if he hurts her?"

Will glanced down at her. "You're worried about the two of them?"

"A little. I love Uncle Thomas, and Connie's one of my best friends. I want to see them both happy, but with each other?" She shook her head. "I just don't know. It's a little scary."

Will laughed. "You think all relationships are scary."

"Don't you?" she challenged.

"Okay, you have a point, but the only way to have love in your life is to take a leap of faith. Otherwise you're just sitting on the sidelines while your life passes you by."

"Don't you owe it to yourself to at least improve the odds? Isn't that what Lunch by the Bay is all about? Looking for compatibility is smart, right?"

"Think about it for a minute," Will said. "Thomas and Connie have a lot of things in common. They're not a couple of young kids rushing into this impulsively. I'm sure they've weighed the pros and cons."

Jess gave him an incredulous look. "Have you weighed the pros and cons about me?"

He grinned. "Of course."

She studied him with a narrowed gaze. "And how'd it turn out?"

"You already know the answer to that."

"So, more pros than cons?"

"Yes, Jess," he said patiently, his eyes lit with amusement. "You only have one thing going against you—in my eyes, anyway."

Curious despite her reservations about

even having this conversation with him, she asked, "What's that?"

"You don't have half as much faith in yourself as I do."

Surprisingly touched by his words, she looked away.

Will tucked a finger under her chin and forced her to face him. "You have a lot to offer a man, Jess. Any man. I hope it's me, but if things don't work out, please don't forget that."

"You really mean that, don't you?" she said.

"I never say anything I don't mean," he assured her.

"But I'm such a terrible bet, Will," she said. "Okay, I know this flies right in the face of what you were just saying, but I don't stick with things. That's the truth, and I might as well admit it. My dating history sucks."

Will didn't seem impressed by her warning. "Don't you think I know that? They were just the wrong guys."

"Abby's told me the same thing, but what if you're both wrong? What if it's me?"

He leveled a look into her eyes that

melted something inside she hadn't even realized was frozen: her heart.

"It's not you," he said quietly. "I *know* that, Jess. I know it."

He sounded so sure, so reassuring, that she was almost convinced that maybe the time had come to finally take that leap of faith.

But then Connor headed their way, and she was reminded that not even her big brother, her best friend, had that much faith in her. How could she possibly risk hurting Will when she knew deep in her heart that the odds of them making it were slim to none?

12

Will stood off to the side with Connor keeping an eye on little Mick, as the women handled the brisk business at their respective booths. Even Jess had been drafted into action, taking donations for her uncle's foundation. He noticed Connor watching her, his expression filled with regret.

"Jess will be okay," Will said, trying to reassure him.

"She wouldn't even look at me when the two of you came back," Connor said.

"She's hurt that you thought for even a second that she'd lose track of little Mick, that's all. She trusts you to be in her corner, and for a minute there, you were just like everyone else, jumping to the conclusion that she'd failed you."

"I was scared for my son," Connor said defensively.

"She knows that. It doesn't make it hurt any less."

"What do I do? I tried to apologize."

"Give it time. You two have had spats before."

Connor shook his head. "This one feels different. It's as if I took something away from her, and she can't forgive me for that."

Will knew Connor was serious, but he nudged him in the ribs anyway. "No need to be dramatic. This will pass, Connor. I guarantee it."

"I didn't know you shrinks were in the business of giving out guarantees."

"Well, it's true that when we're dealing with particularly stubborn, impossible, hard-to-reach clients, we don't like to promise much, but since you O'Briens are all so reasonable, I think it's safe," he said, his expression wry.

"Bite me," Connor responded cheerfully.

"I'm serious, though. Should I apologize again? I hate it that when she looks my way at all, she stares right through me."

"Hey, there's nothing wrong with a sincere apology or a lot of groveling. If you feel so inclined, go for it. Just remember that you wounded her, no question about it. I'm just not sure Jess is in a forgiving mood quite yet."

"Well, I have to do something. That blank look I get when she sees me is killing me," Connor said. "Keep an eye on little Mick, okay?"

"Got it," Will promised. "He may move fast, but my legs are longer. He won't get away from me."

He watched as Connor approached Jess, said something to catch her attention, then faltered when she gave him a look filled with accusation, pain and betrayal. He couldn't hear what Connor was saying, but eventually, Jess's lips curved up just a little. She gave her brother a shove that had him stumbling back a step, then laughed.

"Stop it, you two!" Heather commanded in the tone she usually used to get little

Mick's attention. "If you're going to start a brawl, do not do it in my booth."

"Sorry," Connor murmured, kissing his wife's cheek as Will strolled over to join them, little Mick running alongside him. "I had to make things right with Jess. I told her she could beat me up, if she wanted to."

Heather shook her head, regarding them indulgently. Then she turned to Jess. "And all you managed was that pitiful little shove? I'm ashamed of you. You should have clipped him a good one in the jaw for making you feel bad."

Connor frowned at his wife. "Hey, whose side are you on?"

"In this instance, your sister's."

"Thank you," Jess said solemnly, though her eyes were twinkling. She turned to Will. "I assume you were behind the groveling."

"I might have mentioned that groveling is always an option," Will said. "I assure you, though, that the invitation to beat him up was his. I usually don't approve of physical violence, however much it's called for." He looked from one to the other. "Everything resolved now?"

Connor glanced at his sister. "Are we okay?"

"Yes," she said, throwing her arms around him. "I don't know why what you say matters so much to me, since you're obviously such a big loser."

"But you love me," Connor taunted right back.

Jess grinned. "Yeah, I guess I do."

Connor glanced in Will's direction, then regarded her intently. "Then maybe you'd consider listening to a little brotherly advice from me."

"No," Jess said, her chin tilting stubbornly.

"Stop while you're ahead," Will advised.

"I was just going to tell her she ought to take a serious look at you," Connor protested.

Heather heaved a sigh. "Connor, I love you, but Will's right. You really don't know when to quit."

"I'm just saying—"

"I don't want to hear it," Jess said emphatically.

"And I don't need you interceding on my behalf," Will added. He turned to Jess. "Want to get something to eat?"

"Yes, please," she said at once.

Only as they were walking away together did Will notice the smug expression on Connor's face. He had a feeling his sneaky friend had just played his hand very, very well.

Jess recognized that she'd just been manipulated by a master—her brother. "I just let Connor get away with practically throwing me into your arms, didn't I?"

Will chuckled. "Yep. I fell for it, too."

"Want to go back and beat him up? I think I could take him down with your help."

Will's brow rose. "Are you that unhappy to be spending time with me?"

She thought about it for a split second, then admitted, "Not really."

"That's progress, then," he said with satisfaction.

"Don't be smug. I liked having you on my side earlier, and I liked watching you with little Mick. You seem comfortable with both of us."

He looked amused by the assessment. "Why wouldn't I be comfortable with you?"

"I haven't been very nice to you recently."

"You're wary. I get that."

Jess thought of what Gail had said about having a man truly understand his partner. For the first time she was able to view Will's understanding of her and his apparently boundless patience as a plus.

"What about little Mick? Are you comfortable with all kids?"

"I'd better be if I'm going to continue hanging around you O'Briens. Grandchildren are popping up right and left."

She laughed. "They are, aren't they? What about you? Do you want kids?"

"Absolutely," he said.

She regarded him with amazement. "You said that without even the tiniest hesitation."

"Because having a family has always been my dream." He studied her curiously. "How about you?"

Jess didn't have an immediate answer. She was afraid if she said what came to mind, it would be far too revealing and would give him something to analyze till the cows came home.

Unfortunately, Will was too perceptive. "Jess, are you worried you won't be able to handle kids? Did what happened earlier with Connor reinforce that?"

She hated that he'd nailed it so easily . . . and loved that he knew her so well. Her reactions to Will were getting more and more confusing.

"Yes," she admitted eventually. "I love all the kids in this family. A part of me has daydreamed about being a mom, but I'm not sure I have the slightest idea of how a mom is supposed to act. All I know is that she doesn't run off the way mine did."

"It's true that for a time Megan wasn't the best example. Her leaving was hardest for you because you were so young, but look at the examples Nell and Abby set for you. You couldn't do any better than learning from them."

"I suppose," she said, though she still harbored a lot of doubts. "And then there's the ADD. I know I was furious with Connor for suggesting I'd run off and leave little Mick behind, but it could happen, Will."

"It won't," Will said with confidence.

"How can you possibly be so sure of that?"

"Because I know the kind of deeply caring woman you are. The fact that you're aware that you're easily distracted will make you even more attentive. Your kids will be lucky, Jess."

She was surprised by the comment. "Lucky? Why?"

"Because you're impulsive and unpredictable."

"I thought those were negatives."

"Not to a kid. You'll be the fun mom."

"But kids need reliability. They need stability."

"Which is why you need a steady, reliable man," he teased.

"Like you," she said.

"Of course," he said, his eyes twinkling. "Exactly like me."

She shook her head. "What am I going to do with you?" she murmured.

His smile spread. "Seems to me the possibilities are endless."

For the first time since they'd started this cautious game, Jess let herself relax and remember that she and Will had a long history of friendship that would serve them well. How on earth had she let herself forget that?

There was something different about Connie today. Thomas couldn't put his finger on it. Her eyes were brighter, her cheeks pinker. It finally dawned on him that she was wearing makeup for the first time since he'd known her. Something told him she'd worn it for his benefit, and that made him smile.

"You're looking especially lovely today," he whispered in her ear. The pink in her cheeks deepened to a fiery shade of red that no makeup in the world could match or conceal.

"Stop that!" she said, her voice hushed, her tone indignant.

He laughed. "Stop what? Complimenting you?"

"Yes."

"The only way that'll happen is if you stop looking so beautiful. You take my breath away."

She regarded him with exasperation, hands on her slender hips. "You know, for years now, I've been hearing about the O'Brien talent for blarney, but this is the very first time I've been on the receiving end."

"It's not blarney if it's the gospel truth," he insisted.

"Well, truth or fiction, your timing needs

some work. You do realize that we're surrounded by members of your family?"

"So?"

"They're known for carrying tales," she
reminded him.

Thomas chuckled, unimpressed by her
warning. "There's no one in the family
whose opinion worries me," he said truthfully. "How about you?"

She seemed surprised by his attitude.
"Are you really so confident that people
aren't going to be shocked or appalled if
they find out we're seeing each other?"

"I'll have you know I consider you to be
a perfectly respectable woman," he said,
enjoying the quick rise of color that stained
her cheeks again. She was so wonderfully
easy to tease.

"It's not me they'll be questioning," she
said, practically sputtering with indignation.
"You're the one with the wicked reputation."

"Wicked, is it?"

"Two wives. That could be considered
quite scandalous in some circles. In fact, I
imagine your own mother has had quite a
bit to say about it."

"I didn't have them at the same time,"
he countered. "It was all in a perfectly re-

spectable sequence. As for Ma and me, we've made peace over my decisions. She learned years ago it was a waste of her breath to try to control me."

Her lips twitched at his response, and a sparkle lit her eyes. "Do you not take anything seriously?"

Thomas sobered at once. "I do," he said. "My work and, lately, you."

She blinked as his words sank in, then shook her head. "What am I going to do with you?"

"Quite a lot, I hope. Shall we start with dinner tonight?"

She hesitated for so long, he thought he might have overplayed his hand.

"I'm not at all sure I'm ready to handle a man like you," she told him, though her expression was oddly wistful when she said it.

"Connie, my love, I think you can handle anything life throws your way," he said with total sincerity. "I'll be putty in your hands."

"Somehow I doubt that," she said tartly. "But I suppose dinner's not too big a risk."

"Good for you," he said. "And tonight we're going to Brady's. No more hiding in out-of-the-way places."

"Are you sure about that?" she asked doubtfully.

"I've never been more certain of anything," he said. He studied her intently. "How about you? Are you worried about Jake's opinion? Or your daughter's?"

"I'll admit they're going to be surprised, but they'd probably be stunned if I got involved with any man after all these years."

"Then there's no one standing in our way, is there?"

"I suppose not," she conceded.

"Good for you," he said. Because if there was one thing he knew with absolute certainty, it was that if the two of them were to have half a chance, their relationship had to be open and aboveboard from the start. There was no shame in what they were doing. And whatever doubts his meddling family—or her protective one—might throw at them, it was better to get them out of the way sooner, rather than later.

When Jess got back to the inn late on Saturday afternoon, the kitchen was empty except for an obviously panic-stricken Ronnie.

"Thank goodness," Ronnie said to her

when she walked in. "I've been calling your cell phone for over an hour."

She reached into her purse, then muttered a curse. "Sorry. I guess I left it in the office." She mentally berated herself even as she admitted the oversight. Forgetting the phone broke one of her cardinal rules on the weekend: never to be out of touch with the inn. What was wrong with her? This was the kind of slipup that drove her crazy.

"You're here now," Ronnie said. "We've got a problem."

"What?"

"Gail got sick and had to leave. She told me to take charge, but I don't know what I'm supposed to do, and the restaurant's going to be packed tonight. I took half a dozen reservations myself before I knew she was going to take off." He gave Jess a pleading look. "Maybe we should close."

Jess wondered for an instant if he wasn't right about that. Then again, even if she were dying, Gail wouldn't have gone off and left Ronnie to take over if she didn't think he could handle it.

"Let's take a look at the menu," she suggested, trying to approach the problem methodically to minimize her own increasing panic. "Tell me which of the dishes you think you can handle."

He glanced over the three main courses, then shrugged. "I've helped her with all of them. I guess I could manage as long as there's some help in here."

"I'll get you help," Jess said.

She picked up the phone and called Kevin. "I have a crisis."

Fifteen minutes later, her brother arrived with Abby and Gram in tow. Jess regarded her grandmother with dismay.

"Gram, I can't ask you to pitch in around here."

Her grandmother gave her a withering look. "I don't see why not. I've cooked for a crowd many a time. And, truth be told, I'm far better at it than your sister is. If Abby stays, I stay."

Jess recognized the determined lift of her chin and nodded. "Okay, then, thank you."

She turned to see that Kevin and Ronnie were already huddled over the menus and Gail's laminated pages of recipes. Her brother glanced up.

"Abby, you're on salads," he said. "You

can't screw those up. Gram, Ronnie says the desserts are made, but they need to be cut into proper portions, put onto serving plates. He says Gail usually adds a swirl of raspberry sauce or chocolate for decoration, but you can skip that."

"No problem," Gram said. "I know how to jazz up the presentation of a dessert."

Jess watched the four of them go into action. "Thank you, you guys. You're amazing. You, too, Ronnie. Gail obviously has a lot of faith in you for good reason."

He beamed at her. "Thanks. I guess this is going to be my indoctrination by fire, huh?"

"I guess so. I'll be out front seating people, so let me know if you need anything at all. I can probably shift one of the waitresses in here if you need more help."

"We'll be fine," Kevin assured her.

Feeling confident as she walked out of the kitchen, she placed one more call, this one to her father. "Ronnie's running the show in the kitchen tonight. Do you think you could get his father over here to see what a natural he is as a chef?" She knew it was a risk, but she also knew how much his father's approval meant to the young man. It was something to which she could relate.

"I'll get him there," Mick promised. "I think I'll avoid mentioning Ronnie, though, just in case something goes awry. How about that?"

"Perfect. Thanks, Dad."

To Jess's astonishment and relief, the evening passed without a hitch. No one seemed to have a clue that the kitchen was being managed by an inexperienced kid, an ex-paramedic, an investment adviser and a woman in her eighties. Jess was in awe of them.

When she strolled by to chat with her parents and the Forrests, she looked Ronnie's father in the eye. "How was your meal?"

"Excellent. That chef of yours gets better each time I come here."

Jess beamed at him. "Then you should tell him that."

He blinked for a moment. "I thought your chef was a woman."

"It is, but tonight we've had her assistant filling in. I'll bring him by."

She emerged from the kitchen a moment later with a reluctant Ronnie trailing along behind. "Mr. Forrest, I'd like you to meet the man who ran our kitchen tonight."

The man did a double take. "You cooked this meal?"

Ronnie nodded. "Gail's been training me and I've signed up for some classes."

"Gail thinks he's going to be an extraordinary chef," Jess told Mr. Forrest.

"Well, he's obviously off to an amazing start," Megan chimed in. "Ronnie, the food tonight was superb."

"It was," his father agreed, looking at him with new respect. "I suppose I should have taken you seriously when you said this was something you wanted to do."

"Well, thankfully, Ms. O'Brien and Gail did," Ronnie said, standing straighter. "And to be honest, I can't take all of the credit for tonight. I had a lot of O'Brien help in the kitchen."

Now it was Mick's turn to look startled.

Jess grinned at him. "Long story, but Kevin, Gram and Abby pitched in, too. They were awesome."

"Nell must have been in her glory," Megan said with a laugh. "I have to run into the kitchen to compliment her."

"I'll go with you," Ronnie said, clearly eager to escape.

Mr. Forrest looked at Jess. "You've been good for that boy."

She shook her head. "No, it was Gail who first saw his potential."

"Well, I owe you for giving him a chance in the first place."

"I'm just glad it worked out," Jess said, then went off to speak to the other remaining diners.

By eleven, when the last of the customers had left, she was not only exhausted, she was exhilarated. She looked up from closing out the register just in time to see Will approaching.

"You're too late. The kitchen's closed."

"I was hoping you might have time for a nightcap," he said, just as the kitchen door swung open and her makeshift staff came into the dining room. Will stared at them, openmouthed. "What the devil's going on here?"

Kevin laughed. "We got called into emergency service."

"Did a darn good job of it, too," Gram said, her eyes sparkling despite the weariness evident on her face.

"Yes, we did," Abby agreed. "But I need to get home to my husband and kids. They were laughing their fool heads off about this when I told them where I was going. Gram, you coming with me?"

"I most certainly am," Nell said, though she seemed oddly reluctant to go. She gave Jess a fierce hug. "Thanks for letting me be a part of this. I loved pitching in."

"Letting you? We couldn't have done it without you," Jess told her. "I'm the one who's grateful."

Kevin sank down onto a chair. "What's a man have to do to get a drink in this place?"

Will regarded him with amusement. "Wine okay? I know where that is."

"Get a bottle of red," Jess called after him. She glanced at Ronnie. "Are you sticking around?"

He nodded eagerly. "If it's okay. I'm too wound up to go home."

"Of course it's okay. You're a vital part of this team. You did well tonight." She called after Will. "Bring four glasses, okay?"

Kevin's gaze followed Will. "Seems awfully comfortable around here," he commented.

Jess shrugged. "He's been by a few times."

Kevin's gaze narrowed. "Is that so?"

She frowned at him. "We are not having this conversation. Just because you helped to save my butt tonight doesn't give you interrogation privileges."

"Being the big brother does," Kevin countered.

"You might want to ask Connor how that worked out for him today before you head down that path," she retorted, relieved when Will returned. At least she trusted her brother not to say anything to embarrass Will in front of Ronnie, a relative stranger to the family dynamics.

Unwinding from the frantic night, Jess realized she was glad that Will was here to be a part of it. It felt natural, just the way it had back in the old days when they'd all hung out together. For the second time today she wondered if maybe she'd been making too much of the step from friendship to dating. Maybe it would only mean more comfortable nights like this.

She glanced over and saw the way Will was looking at her, the barely banked desire in his eyes. Her pulse kicked up several notches. She revised her thinking. Maybe it was a little scary after all, the impact he had on her senses. One of these days very soon, she was going to have to decide. Until then, perhaps she could get away with acting like a very young teenager and restricting their dates to things they could do with a crowd. Just imagining Will's reaction to her self-protective strategy made her smile.

The demand for Lunch by the Bay superseded anything Will had anticipated. Even if he'd wanted to go on a date himself— with Jess or anyone else—he was too busy to schedule one. At least that's the excuse he'd given himself for not asking anyone out after the disastrous date with Anna Lofton a few weeks ago.

Okay, that and the fact that things actually seemed to have taken a turn for the better with Jess. He knew she couldn't be rushed, so he was trying to wait for her to reach the same conclusion he had, that they deserved a chance.

Occasions like the chance encounter at the festival and the relaxed evening they'd spent that same day at the inn seemed to be easing her defenses. He just needed to be patient. Of course, years of being patient should have been sufficient practice, but it was getting harder.

A few days after his late-night stop at the inn, he was hunched over his computer keyboard at the office when the door opened and Jess walked in. He stared at her in surprise. It was the first time she'd ever crossed the threshold into his professional domain. Come to think of it, it might be the first time she'd ever sought him out, period.

She stood looking around the room, her gaze filled with curiosity. "No couch," she noted.

"Not all shrinks have them," he replied, diving into the conversation cautiously as he tried to figure out what had brought her into enemy territory. "Most people prefer sitting in a comfortable chair."

"Did you try the whole sofa thing?"

"For a while. Then I redecorated." He grinned. "Did you really come here to discuss my decor?"

"Honestly, I don't know why I'm here."

"Did you want a session?" he asked, enjoying the quick flush of color the question brought to her cheeks.

"You're the last person I'd want poking around in my psyche," she claimed. "You do that enough when we bump into each other."

"Jess, contrary to whatever goes on in that head of yours, your psyche is the last thing on my mind when we run into each other."

She perked up visibly. "Oh?"

Since he didn't intend to lay his heart at her feet only to have her trample on it, he asked again more pointedly, "Why are you here?"

She moved around the office, picking up a magazine here, a piece of sculpture there. When she retrieved a seashell from a shelf behind his desk, she held on to it, studying it curiously.

"Did you find this around here?" she asked.

"On the beach by your house, as a matter of fact." He met her gaze. "Don't you remember?"

"There are probably thousands of seashells, Will. Why would I remember this one?"

"You cut your foot on it when you were about fourteen. You were bleeding all over and trying not to cry. I carried you back up to the house so Nell could bandage your foot."

"And you saved the shell?" she said incredulously.

He shrugged, feeling ridiculous. "At the time I thought I was taking it away so it couldn't pose a danger to you or anyone else again. Then it just sort of stayed with me."

"To remind you of playing Sir Galahad?"

"Something like that."

"Can I ask you something?"

"I wish you would."

"Had you ever thought about kissing me, I mean, before that night at Brady's?"

He smiled at her solemn tone. "All the time."

"Why didn't you?"

He laughed at that. "You never seemed to want me to. In fact, you've been nothing but prickly around me practically from the day we met. And after I became a shrink, forget it. Just like earlier, you act as if you're terrified I'll see something inside you that you don't want anyone to know."

"I don't really have any secrets," she said.

"I think everyone in town has always known all my business."

"Then I shouldn't scare you, should I?"

"Probably not," she said, then met his gaze. "But you do."

Will felt as if the earth had suddenly shifted under him. "Why?"

"I don't know."

Sensing that he was teetering on the edge of a precipice that could forever alter their relationship, he asked casually, "Want to go to dinner tonight and see if we can figure it out?"

"That sounds an awful lot like a session to me," she said warily.

"I don't take my clients out to dinner," he said. "It's unethical."

She regarded him with a penetrating gaze. "So if you ask me a question, it'll just be because you want to know. You, Will."

He nodded solemnly. "Just me."

"Okay," she agreed at last.

Will mentally shouted a few choruses of hallelujah, then stood slowly, feigning nonchalance. "I'll get my jacket."

As they walked outside, Jess slanted a sideways look at him. "So, when you know me better, will you fix me up with another one of those Lunch by the Bay clients of yours?"

Will stopped dead still and stared at her incredulously. Thankfully, before he uttered the first indignant thought that came to him, he saw the definite twinkle in her eyes. He deliberately held her gaze until she shifted uneasily, then licked her lips nervously.

"Well?" she prodded.

He smiled. "Not if tonight goes the way I'm counting on it going."

She swallowed hard. "Then that kiss a few weeks ago, it wasn't just a fluke?" she said as if not quite sure she could trust her own impressions or his actions, as if she needed to clarify before she risked anything. "That's what you want, Will? Us together, as a couple?"

He regarded her solemnly. "I'm not sure how many different ways I need to say it, but to be perfectly clear one more time, yes. I think it's way past time for us to try," he told her, his expression solemn. "Don't you think so? Isn't that really why you came to my office tonight?"

"I think it's terrifying to be changing what we already have," she admitted candidly.

"Have you really thought about what will happen if we start sleeping together?"

"All the time," he said, amused.

"What if we're no good at it?"

He laughed. "Oh, I think we're going to be great at it."

"How can you sound so sure? Maybe we should just test it, see how it goes, before we get emotionally involved."

"Jess O'Brien, are you suggesting we have uncomplicated, no-strings sex right now? Sort of get it out of the way, then decide what comes next?"

Her gaze met his. "I think I am."

Despite the almost overwhelming temptation to let her have her way, Will forced himself to give her a chiding look. "I do not put out on the first date," he teased. "Besides, we're right out here in public. I guarantee you that our first time together is not going to be on the grass in the middle of the town green. What kind of guy would I be if I didn't make our first time romantic?"

"I honestly don't know," she said. "But I think I'm ready to find out."

That was the absolute best news Will had heard in years. He knew that changing their relationship wasn't without its share of risks, but it was time. Past time, according to the way his blood was suddenly racing.

"Then we'll have dinner as planned," he said. "Brady's or somewhere more discreet?"

She gave him a wry look. "Given that my family seems to have spies everywhere, we might as well go to Brady's."

"Start as you intend to finish, then, right out there in plain view," he said approvingly. He noticed the sudden hint of panic in her eyes. "It's going to be okay, you know. It's a date, Jess. One simple meal. Some conversation. Nothing we haven't done before a thousand times."

Despite his reassurance, though, they both knew it was a whole lot more. Tonight's dinner was going to be served with hopes and expectations, *and* with the very distinct possibility of sex for dessert.

13

Jess was on edge all during dinner. Not that the conversation lagged for even a minute. Will was the perfect gentleman, too. He didn't even try to hold her hand across the candlelit table. Still, the intimacy between them seemed to have hit a new level. And yet it hadn't. It was confusing.

"You're overthinking this, aren't you?" he said, regarding her with amusement.

Jess sighed. She should have known he'd be able to read her mind. "Don't you think it's kind of weird, being here like this?"

"Like what? Two old friends having dinner together?"

She scowled at the description. "But we're not just two old friends having dinner, are we? We're two people who've introduced the prospect of having sex into their relationship."

Will frowned. "Maybe I was wrong earlier," he murmured.

"About what?"

"Not having sex right away," he explained. "It seems to be the only thing on your mind, like this giant hurdle you need to get over so you can relax."

"Please do not try to tell me you aren't thinking about it," she said.

"I'm content to live in the moment," he insisted.

She didn't believe him for a minute. Men were always thinking about sex or having sex. Wasn't it the driving force of their lives? She shook her head. "Sorry. I'm not buying it."

"Why not?"

She told him her theory.

Will chuckled. "You really don't think much of men, do you?"

She shrugged. "Well, my experience has been somewhat limited."

Will stared at her with surprise. "How limited?"

His stunned expression put her on the defensive. "Well, I'm not a virgin, if that's what you're thinking. Not that it's really any of your business, but Kevin and Connor didn't always make it to Moonlight Cove in time to rescue me from my reckless self."

His expression turned wry. "Good to know, but just so you also know, I really, really do not want to hear any details."

"As if I'd share them with you," she said testily, then sighed. "But what I'm really trying to explain is that I'm not very experienced at the whole relationship thing. Surely you figured that out a long time ago. You've been around. When have I ever dated anyone for longer than a few weeks or a couple of months? I obviously have a short attention span. I guess it must come with the ADD territory."

Will shook his head. "There you go blaming your ADD for something that's much more easily explained by the fact that those other men have been wrong for you and you've been wise enough to figure it out sooner, rather than later."

"Okay, you've said that before, but why are you so sure of it? Maybe I'm just flighty."

"How long have you been friends with Laila and Connie?"

"They're older, so it's fairly recently that we've become friends, but I've known them all my life."

"So those could be described as long-term relationships in some ways," he persisted.

"I suppose."

"And you've been working with Gail since you opened the inn, right?"

"Sure. What's your point?"

"That relationship seems to be holding up okay."

"Come on, Will. It's not the same," she protested.

"The same character traits it takes to have a healthy friendship or a solid employer-employee relationship are needed to have a long-term relationship with a man," he said.

Jess didn't entirely believe him, but he was the expert in human dynamics. "Seriously?"

He nodded. "Seriously. All of those relationships involve give-and-take, loyalty, forgiveness and, on occasion, a bit of work."

Jess saw what he was trying to say. "But Laila and Connie know about the ADD, so they're pretty tolerant when I mess up. The same thing goes for Gail. She pitches in to make sure I don't let things fall through the cracks at the inn."

"Don't you imagine someone who loves you would do the same?" he asked.

"I guess I never thought about it that way," she admitted.

"So, let's get back to us. Are you scared about us jumping into bed or about us having a relationship? Because I've been waiting for you for a very long time, Jess, so we can move this whole thing along at whatever pace makes you comfortable." He gave her a hard look. "Or are you already trying to create roadblocks to moving forward at all?"

Was that what she was doing? It was entirely possible. She'd gone to Will's office tonight because she hadn't been able to convince herself to stay away. She'd wanted something from him when she'd walked through that door. Had it been uncomplicated sex? Or had she already known deep down that nothing about her relationship with Will would ever be uncomplicated? There were so darn many unexplored feelings between them.

The fact that he sat patiently while she argued with herself was extremely annoying, but that was Will. He'd obviously built his career on waiting out reluctant clients.

She frowned, but finally admitted, "I don't know. This is so much more complicated than I thought it was going to be." She looked into his eyes. "Did you know it would be this hard?"

He smiled. "I knew. You're a complicated woman. There's no surprise for me there."

"Then why bother with me?" she asked him. When he laughed, she scowled, "No, I mean it. I really want to know."

"Because I have never met another woman who challenged me the way you do, who's sexy and vulnerable and far stronger than she knows. I guess a part of me wants to be the man who's there when you finally see yourself for the amazing woman you've become."

Jess's eyes misted with tears at his sweet words and the sincerity behind them. "That's really how you see me? As an amazing woman?"

"Of course."

"Why? You have to be aware of all my flaws. Do I need to list them for you?"

His lips curved. "Are you thinking you can scare me away if you do?"

"Maybe."

"How long have we known each other, Jess?"

"Most of our lives."

"Do you think there's much about you I don't know? I've pretty much seen you in every kind of circumstance imaginable, and what I haven't seen, someone's told me about."

She wanted to believe that he'd seen all of her worst flaws, understood all of her most disastrous mistakes, and cared for her anyway, but how was that possible?

"Maybe you're just glossing over my flaws so you can get me in the sack after all this time," she accused lightly. "Some men will do or say anything to score."

He looked oddly hurt by the suggestion. "I'm not most men. Besides, maybe I just see your flaws as an important part of the fabric of who you are," he suggested. "And maybe I think they pale when stacked up against all of your good points."

When she remained silent, distrusting

his words, he sighed heavily. "I really wish you could see yourself through my eyes," he told her. "I wish I knew how to make that possible because until you do, you'll always doubt you're worthy of love."

Jess couldn't deny what he was saying. She'd spent her entire life—from the moment her mother had walked out and left them—focused on what was wrong with her, how much trouble she was. A pattern of belief begun at the tender age of seven and never denied, but rather reinforced, was almost impossible to shake.

It wasn't that she believed no one could love her, because obviously her parents and her siblings did, but it was a love she'd always viewed as laced with a heavy dose of tolerance and even a sense of family obligation. Theirs was a love she'd put to the test too often. One thing she knew for sure was that if she ever did become involved with a man, she wanted more. She wanted affection that was freely given and deeply felt. No good could come of a relationship in which she felt a constant need to be testing the man's love.

Will watched her as if he knew exactly what thoughts she was wrestling with.

"Well?" he asked at last. "Are you going to bail before we even get started, or will you give us the chance we both deserve? All you have to do is take a leap of faith."

"It might be easier to leap over the Washington Monument in a single bound," she said dryly.

"Come on," he coaxed. "You've got what it takes, Jess. I believe that, even if you don't. Trust me just this once."

"I do trust you," she said, knowing that much was true, at least.

"Then you'll go out with me again? Baby steps, if need be. Lunch. Or a movie. No pressure."

"Can I drag along a chaperone?" she asked, only partially in jest.

His lips curved. "If you must. Just please don't make it one of your brothers. I don't think I could take the humiliation."

She laughed, suddenly feeling a thousand times lighter. "Neither could I. I guess we'll play the chaperone thing by ear."

"How about I drop by the inn tomorrow afternoon? We can run out for ice cream or coffee or something. No big deal. Nothing too scary about grabbing a hot fudge sundae or a cappuccino with me, right?"

"Not unless you try whisking me off to a sidewalk café in Paris for them," she said.

Despite the teasing note in her voice, Will studied her somberly. "Is that what you want, Jess? To be whisked away someplace romantic?"

"Isn't that what every woman secretly yearns for?" she said lightly. "To be totally swept off her feet?"

He nodded, his expression thoughtful. "A good lesson. I'll have to keep that in mind."

Sure, Jess thought. No man was less likely to make such an outrageous, extravagant gesture. Though she had no idea how much money he made with his practice or from the newly created Lunch by the Bay, Will had always lived simply in a small apartment decorated with parental hand-me-downs. His car was at least ten years old. His professional wardrobe, while well-made and expensive, probably didn't take up more than half of a closet. On his days off, she was pretty sure he was still wearing the same faded, comfortable jeans he'd had since his teens.

"I should get back to the inn," she said,

though she was oddly reluctant for the evening to end. She was half-afraid once it did, they would fall back into their old awkward pattern despite the promise of a casual date the next day.

Will nodded. "I'll drive you."

"It's okay. I have my car. It's parked by your office."

"Then I'll walk you back there," he said, leaving cash on the table with their bill, then standing up to hold her chair.

Outside, he reached for her hand. For an instant, Jess was so startled, she almost pulled away, but then she realized she liked the sensation of his fingers curved around hers. How had she forgotten just how sweet such a gesture could be, how comforting? And maybe just a little sexy, she realized as she trembled with a newly discovered physical awareness of the man beside her.

At her car, he opened the door, waited for her to get behind the wheel, then leaned down and pressed a chaste kiss to her forehead. "Drive safely."

She looked up into his eyes, saw the unmistakable desire of a man who wanted much more than a good-night kiss. "Want to follow me to the inn?" she asked.

"More than you can possibly imagine," he said candidly. "But not tonight. You're not ready."

"I think I am."

"Not good enough. You have to be sure," he said, then winked at her. "And you will be."

"So arrogant," she murmured, amused despite herself at this unexpected side of him.

"Confident," he corrected. "I've been patient for a long time. It won't hurt you to gain a little experience with that virtue."

"Is this one of those life lessons you shrinks like to impart?"

"Pretty much," he said, then grinned. "Or it could just be payback. I'll see you tomorrow afternoon, and we can discuss it further."

He pulled back, closed the door gently, then waited for her to start the car and drive away. Jess checked her rearview mirror as she pulled away from the curb. Will was still standing there in the middle of the street, staring after her. She liked believing he was regretting that noble stance he'd taken about not coming back to the inn with her. She had a feeling that she surely was going to.

When Jess walked downstairs from her suite at The Inn at Eagle Point on Saturday morning, Abby and Bree were waiting for her in the lobby.

"Breakfast in the dining room now," Abby said, linking an arm through hers. Bree walked beside them, her eyes glinting with amusement.

"What's this about?" Jess asked. "I know I haven't messed up anything around here lately. That accountant you hired is all over me if I even forget to give him a receipt for replacing the pen the guests use to register."

"Good for him. That's what he's paid for," Abby said.

"You haven't done anything wrong," Bree consoled her. "Other than maybe losing your mind."

Jess scowled at her. "What are you talking about?"

"You and Will," Abby said. "First there was the widely reported kiss, and then last night I hear the two of you were having dinner in some cozy corner at Brady's till closing. How come we had to hear about that secondhand? Shouldn't you have been on the phone confiding in us about your hot date?"

"The date, which came up at the last minute, was none of your business," Jess said irritably.

"We're your sisters," Bree countered. "You're supposed to tell us these things."

She frowned at them. "Do you have some objection to my dating Will?"

Abby's eyes lit up. "Then you *are* dating? This wasn't just some spur-of-the-moment night out or something?"

"Last night was spur-of-the-moment, but in general that's not Will's style," Jess said. "It could be a problem."

"You can't mean that," Abby protested. "Will is exactly the kind of man you need. He's steady and reliable." She held up a hand before Jess could respond. "Which does not equate to boring, if that's what you were about to say."

Jess thought back to their dinner. It had been anything but boring. In fact, there'd been so many sparks flying, it was a wonder she hadn't gotten singed. Sadly, the evening had ended with that very sedate peck on her forehead. It had been frustrating.

"I'm not sure why I'm just finding out about all this," Bree said. "Do you really like him? To be honest, when Jake heard about this, he wasn't happy. He thinks you'll break Will's heart."

"I'm not going to break Will's heart," Jess said defensively. "At least not on purpose. We've only been on one even semi-official date, for goodness' sakes. And it doesn't really count as a date because I sort of turned up in his office around dinnertime and he probably asked me out because it seemed like the polite thing to do." That was her story and she intended to stick to it. It was a lot less complicated than the truth. She frowned at Bree. "Why does Jake think this is any of his business, anyway? Tell him for me that his opinion doesn't count."

"He'll disagree," Bree said. "He and Will are best buddies. And he wasn't saying anything that Connor or Kevin didn't say when they heard, although apparently Connor has seen this coming for a very long time and Kevin started suspecting something was up when he helped out at the inn last week."

"Did you all have some kind of family meeting in the middle of the night and forget to tell me about it?" Jess inquired irritably. She'd been the target of more than one family intervention in her life. She didn't like them.

"We're talking about the O'Briens," Abby reminded her. "You know how news travels along the family grapevine. The vine's been buzzing for weeks. It's now reached a fever pitch."

"This dinner was just last night, and it's not even nine o'clock in the morning," Jess said with exasperation. She scowled at her older sister. "And why are you bugging me about this, anyway? I thought you were all for it."

"I am, as long as you proceed with caution," Abby said. "The word I got last night suggested things might be moving at a more rapid pace. Then again, that could have been the source."

"What source?" Jess demanded. "How did the word spread, for goodness' sakes?"

"Pictures were included with text messages," Abby explained, grinning.

Jess regarded her incredulously. "Who the devil spotted us, the FBI?"

Abby chuckled. "Dad, as a matter of fact. He and Mom were having dinner at Brady's when you two arrived. They hung around to keep an eye on things, then sent out an alert to the rest of us. You know Dad. Now that he's reformed, he takes great pride in being up-to-date on the latest family gossip. If he finds out anything first, he considers it a major fatherly triumph. And he definitely loves to share."

"Oh, God," Jess moaned. "That means they should be turning up here—"

"About now," Bree said cheerfully as Mick and Megan crossed the dining room and pulled up chairs to join them.

"Anything new?" Mick asked.

Jess stood up and scowled at the entire lot of them. "Not one single thing," she announced firmly. "Except that I am officially resigning as an O'Brien."

Her mother laughed. "I don't think you can do that, sweetie. Heaven knows, I tried, and look at me now." She slipped her hand into her husband's. "Back in the fold."

"Everyone should be lucky enough to be an O'Brien," Mick scolded Jess. "We care about each other."

"We annoy each other," Jess contradicted.

"I'm going to work. I'll tell the waitress to put your breakfasts on my tab. Have fun dissecting my life. Let me know how it turns out."

She walked out of the dining room, went straight to her office and called Will.

"Prepare yourself. Apparently we're hotter news than anything on *Entertainment Tonight*."

"Don't I know it," he said with a resigned sigh. "I've just been joined at Sally's by Jake and Mack. I'm pretty sure they've forgotten that I'm the one accredited to give advice."

"Want to consider moving to Hawaii?"

"Nah. I like it here. In fact, it's just started to get interesting."

Jess laughed, relaxing at the sound of the humor in his voice. "Yes, it definitely has."

And to think that it was Will who'd made it that way.

"Jess, I assume," Jake said as Will disconnected the call on his cell phone.

Will merely held his gaze and said nothing. He'd been surprised when they'd called and insisted he meet them for breakfast, but once he'd arrived at Sally's, he'd quickly discerned their agenda. His friends might be well-meaning, but he was determined not to encourage them.

"Of course it was Jess," Mack said confidently. "She's probably getting the same kind of interrogation over at the inn, but her family's a whole lot more experienced at it than we are. *They're* probably getting answers."

Will laughed. "Which should be a pretty good indication that it's time for you to give up."

Jake shook his head. "Come on, man. You and Jess? You can't be serious. I know you've had the hots for her for eons, but I thought you were just going to pine from a distance and then move on to someone more appropriate."

"There is nothing inappropriate about Jess," Will said indignantly.

"She hasn't had a steady boyfriend in all the years I've known her," Jake reminded him. "You're Mister Dependability."

Will's expression immediately sobered. "She pointed out the same thing," he told his friend. "Apparently it didn't occur to her, either, that she'd been choosing the wrong men."

"And you're going to rush right in and succeed where others have failed?" Jake scoffed.

"I believe I am," Will retorted. "Now, maybe we should drop this before I get annoyed. You're part of the O'Brien family, Jake, and, Mack, you're probably going to be one of these days if you and Susie ever start being honest with each other. You should be on Jess's side, not tearing her down."

Jake looked offended. "I am not tearing Jess down. I'm just being realistic. The woman has a few problems."

Will stiffened. "If you're referring to her ADD, it's not a communicable disease, Jake. Let's show a little sensitivity here."

Jake winced. "I'm sorry. I didn't mean to be insensitive. I like Jess. I'm just worried about you. You're a steady, stable, one-woman guy. Jess . . . well, she's always tended to play the field."

"Sort of like Mack?" Will said wryly. "If he can change, and we both know he has, then why not Jess?"

Jake shook his head, his expression worried. "I just don't see it."

"Well, fortunately, you're not the one who

has to," Will assured him. "Nobody understands the situation more clearly than I do."

Mack sighed. "He's telling us to butt out,
buddy," he said to Jake. "We should probably listen."

Will smiled at him. "Exactly. Thank you.
Now I need to get some work done before
I pick Jess up for our date this afternoon."

"So, you have no intention of backing
off?" Jake asked.

"None."

"Okay, then, I have a landscaping job I
should get to," Jake said. "Mack, what are
you up to today?"

"Susie wants to go for a drive and poke
around in some of the shops. She says it's
never too early to start Christmas shopping."

Will laughed. "Not that there has ever
been any doubt about this, but taking Susie shopping is a sure sign that you are
down for the count, my man. Just give it
up and ask her to marry you."

Mack frowned at the suggestion. "We've
never even been on a date. You don't ask
a woman you've never dated to get married. She'd laugh her fool head off."

Will regarded him with pity. "How long

are you going to keep trying to sell yourself on that story? None of the rest of us are buying it. I'm pretty sure Susie isn't, either. If you don't make a move, one of these days she's going to find herself a man who will officially date her and marry her and have babies with her. Is that what you want?"

Mack looked sickened by Will's words. "Of course not, but—"

"No more excuses," Will said sternly. "Don't lose her. It'll hurt if you try and lose, but if you never try and lose, you'll regret it the rest of your life."

Mack met his gaze. "Is that why you're finally making a move on Jess? So you won't have regrets?"

"Something like that," Will acknowledged. "To be honest, I came darn close to giving up myself without trying, but circumstances changed."

"He's talking about the infamous kiss in the bar at Brady's a while back," Jake said.

Will smiled at the memory. "I am. That and a few other things since then. I've been encouraged."

Mack looked disconsolate. "If only Susie would give me some kind of sign that she's ready for things to change."

Will rolled his eyes. "Unlike Jess and me, Susie spends every spare second she has with you. Do you need her to issue an engraved invitation to her bed?"

Jake chuckled. "Like that'll ever happen. She's an O'Brien woman. They like their men to court them."

"All women do," Will said. "I have it on recent authority, they like to be swept off their feet. I'm pretty sure it takes more than flowers and candy. If I figure it out, I'll pass along the tips."

"Hurry up," Mack pleaded. "This whole celibacy thing . . ." He shook his head. "I'm not cut out for it. The only thing that's kept me from taking some other woman up on an offer of uncomplicated sex is knowing that I'll be playing right into Susie's hands. She's just waiting for me to mess up and revert to that niche she's stuck me in. I doubt she'll ever believe I'm no longer some irresponsible player who'll trample all over her heart. Sadly, that reputation has been carved in stone, or into her heart or something."

Will gave his shoulder a squeeze. "I think you'd be surprised about that, if you'd just get up the gumption to move forward."

Mack still didn't look convinced. Will had no idea what it was going to take to bring those two together. He just hoped they didn't take so long that one of them got their heart broken before it happened.

14

Connie glanced out the window of her office at her brother's nursery and saw Thomas's hybrid car turn into the parking lot. Her heart picked up its pace, and she couldn't seem to look away as he emerged and headed her way, carrying what looked to be two containers of coffee and a bag from Sally's.

She cast a frantic glance toward Jake's office, deeply regretting that he hadn't yet left for his job site. Having Thomas show up here once had been awkward enough. Having him back again so soon was really going to stir up Jake's suspicions. She wasn't quite ready to deal with all the brotherly concern that was likely to ensue once Jake figured out why Thomas was turning up so frequently.

Maybe she could manage to keep the two men from crossing paths, she thought, getting to her feet and hurrying outside. She caught Thomas just a few feet from the office door.

"Good morning," she said cheerfully, then added loudly enough to be overheard if her brother happened to be paying attention, "I wasn't expecting you today."

"Though I'm a bit out of practice, it occurred to me that women like the occasional surprise," Thomas said. "I brought coffee and croissants. I thought we could have breakfast together, if you have the time to spare."

"I had breakfast hours ago," she told him. "I'm usually here at the crack of dawn." Seeing the flare of disappointment in his eyes, she quickly added, "But I am definitely ready to take a break. Shall we take a walk and try to find someplace we can talk?"

Thomas regarded her with amusement. "You wouldn't be trying to get me away from Jake, would you?"

"I am," she admitted candidly. "Your last visit didn't go unnoticed."

"Do I need to have a talk with him? Explain my intentions?" Though there was a twinkle in his eye, he sounded willing to do exactly that if she thought it necessary.

Connie regarded him with dismay. "Absolutely not. He's my brother, not my father, and my *younger* brother at that. I'm a grown woman, perfectly capable of making my own decisions."

"Well, of course you are," Thomas said, eyes sparkling at her indignation. "But Jake is obviously very protective of you. I can understand why he'd be concerned about the two of us seeing each other. I have no problem trying to put his mind at ease."

"Really? Because I do," she responded. "It may have been a long time since I've dated, but I think we're long past the era when some man in the family either gets to pick out my dates or put a stamp of approval on them."

Thomas grinned. "I wasn't going to give him veto power, Connie. I thought it might be nice, though, to have him on our side, before all the fuss starts with my family."

She sighed. The O'Briens would definitely be an entirely different kettle of fish. "You might have a point about that," she conceded. "Still, there's a picnic table around back. Why don't we go out there and discuss this? We can decide how we want to handle all the likely family interference."

Thomas nodded. "Fair enough."

Of course, what Connie hadn't considered was that the picnic table was in clear view of Jake's office window. They'd barely taken a sip of their coffee or a bite of their croissants before her brother rounded the building, a scowl on his face.

"Back again, I see," he said to Thomas, his tone unfriendly.

"Jake!" Connie warned.

"I'm just wondering why he's suddenly around here so much," Jake said, his combative gaze never leaving Thomas's face.

"You know we're working together on foundation business," she said, determined to keep up the appearance that their meetings were perfectly innocent.

"And I've been dating your sister," Thomas said, ignoring her hint.

"Thomas!" she protested.

Jake sat down, looking stunned by the unexpected admission of the truth. He turned on her. "Is he serious? The two of you have been dating?"

"We've been out a couple of times," she acknowledged.

"But he's Mick's brother," he said as if there were a crime in that.

Thomas chuckled. "I can see why you might find that worrisome."

"Oh, can you now?" Jake said sarcastically. "That makes you way too old for my sister."

Connie frowned at him. "And exactly how old is too old?" she demanded. "Two years? Ten? Twenty? Do you even know how old Thomas is? Do you even care that after Sam, who had the maturity of a gnat, I might want a man in my life who knows who he is and what he wants?"

Jake looked deflated. "I'm just worried about you, sis. I know you've been lonely for a long time, and even more so now that Jenny's gone to college. I don't want anyone taking advantage of your vulnerability."

She scooted closer on the bench and hugged him. "No one on earth could have had a better brother all these years, but it's time for me to start living my life, Jake. I can make my own decisions about who's right for me."

"And you think Thomas is?" he asked skeptically.

"I don't know yet." She looked across the table and into Thomas's clear blue eyes. "But I do want to find out."

"And I assure you, Jake, I'm not playing games here," Thomas said. "I don't know where this is going, but your sister is the first woman in a long time who's made me want something more in my life. Believe me, I thought long and hard before I asked her out. Nobody understands the family complications better than I do. We'll have a few people on our side and a lot more who are as skeptical as you are, but I think we deserve to figure this out for ourselves, don't you?"

Jake continued to look doubtful.

"I assure you that my intentions toward your sister are entirely honorable," Thomas added persuasively. "I will do my very best never to do anything knowingly that will hurt her."

Jake looked torn, but then he gazed directly into Connie's eyes. "You want this?"

She nodded. "I want this."

"Okay, then," Jake said, looking reconciled, if not happy. "I'll reserve judgment." He scowled again at Thomas. "But if you hurt her . . ."

Thomas nodded. "Understood. I'll need to watch my back."

"Not your back," Jake corrected. "You'll see me coming."

Connie noted the look of complete understanding that passed between the two most important men in her life. In some ways it made her want to shake her head in exasperation. In others, it made her feel cherished.

All in all, though, this potentially disastrous confrontation had gone a whole lot better than she'd anticipated. If they could get past the O'Brien gauntlet half as easily, they might actually have a shot at making this thing—whatever it was—last long enough to see if it could work out.

Will arrived at the inn around two o'clock to find Jess pacing around looking annoyed.

"Bad time?" he inquired.

"You're late," she accused.

"How could I be late? We didn't set a time," he reminded her. "I told you I'd stop by sometime this afternoon and we'd go for coffee or ice cream." A probably inappropriate smile tugged at his lips. "Did you miss me?"

"No, I thought you'd stood me up after all," she admitted. "I figured Jake and Mack had gotten through to you and convinced you I'm a bad bet."

"No one could convince me of that," he assured her.

"But they tried, didn't they?"

"Do you really want me to say something that will encourage hard feelings among the three of you?" he asked.

She uttered a sigh of resignation. "I knew it. They wanted you to back off."

"Wasn't that the message Abby and your family were sending, as well?" he inquired reasonably.

"It's different when it's coming from Jake and Mack," she said. "I don't know how, but it is."

Will resisted the desire to chuckle. "Is anyone else's opinion really important? I'm here. Unless you've changed your mind, we're going out." He studied her intently.

"Or did *your* family convince you that it's a bad idea to date me? Is this really about you having second thoughts?"

She gave him an obviously exasperated look. "Oh, they're not worried about *me.* It's you they're worried about. How's that for ironic? I think everyone's united on that front. It's a little annoying, to be perfectly honest."

"I can totally understand why you'd be annoyed. Let's prove 'em all wrong."

"Until we've run off and gotten married and celebrated our fiftieth anniversary, I think that's going to be all but impossible," she said wryly.

"Then that's what we'll do," he said, holding her gaze.

She grinned. "How do you have so much faith in this when I'm scared to death?"

"I've had longer to get used to the idea," he reminded her. "I was fourteen when I fell for you. You'll catch up. Now, I vote we go for ice cream, but the decision is yours. Coffee or drinks are on the table, too, if you'd prefer."

She looked intrigued. "My vote counts more?"

"On this date, it does." He grinned, then

warned, "It won't always. We're going to be very good at give-and-take."

"Frankly, I've never enjoyed compromise," she told him.

"You'll learn," he said, taking her hand in his. "It's the basis of any successful relationship."

"I'm an O'Brien. We like to win."

"But there can be great rewards that come with compromise," he assured her.

"Such as?"

"The first time you do it, I'll show you," he said with a wink.

She blinked, then laughed. "I'll look forward to it."

Jess wasn't sure about the whole compromise thing, but she had to admit that spending the afternoon with Will had been more fun than she'd anticipated. Not once did she catch herself worrying about whether he was analyzing every word she said.

Eventually, when she said she needed to get back to the inn, he surprised her by asking if she could use an extra pair of hands.

"To do what?" she asked.

He shrugged. "Whatever you need. I'm not bad in the kitchen, if they need help in there, or I could wait tables or seat people."

She regarded him with puzzlement. "Why would you do that?"

"Do you really need to ask? I want to spend more time with you. The inn matters to you, so it makes sense to me that I understand what goes on there." He held her gaze. "And I like raiding that big old refrigerator with you. I thought maybe we could do it again when the restaurant closes down for the night."

"You're after a free meal?" she teased. "Is that what this is about? I thought you were making money hand-over-fist with your practice and Lunch by the Bay."

"Even without the promise of more of Gail's incredible food, I'd want to stick around. You're the draw, Jess. Just you."

She blinked at the heartfelt sincerity in his voice. "Then, by all means, come back with me and hang out for as long as you want. I'll find something for you to do."

What intrigued her more than anything,

though, was the unexpected image she had of what the rest of the night might hold.

Mick wasn't entirely satisfied with the way they'd left things with Jess that morning. She'd gotten her knickers into a knot just because the family had shown a little interest in her relationship with Will. They probably should have known better than to gang up on her, but they'd only done it because they all cared. Why hadn't she been able to see that?

After dinner, he and Megan were settled down for the evening when he stood up and announced, "I'm feeling a little restless. I think I'll go for a walk. I won't be long."

Megan looked up from her book, her gaze instantly filled with suspicion. "You surely aren't thinking of walking over to the inn, are you?"

"And what's wrong with dropping in on our daughter, making sure things are running smoothly over there?" he inquired testily.

His wife laughed. "As if the efficiency of the inn's operation is on your mind!"

He frowned at her. "That's my story and I'm sticking to it."

"You do realize that will tick Jess off just as much as if you walk in there with more questions about Will on the tip of your tongue? I think she's had her fill of family concern today."

"I can handle Jess," he claimed, knowing it was far from true. She was the most sensitive and defensive of all of his kids. If he'd had problems understanding Bree's uncharacteristically shy, reticent nature, he'd been even more uneasy dealing with Jess's difficulties. He'd lost patience far too many times when he should have been sympathetic and supportive.

He'd thought for a time that the diagnosis of mild attention deficit disorder had been nothing more than psychological mumbo jumbo, an attempt to explain away the fact that she'd been a crummy student. It had taken too long for him to accept that it was a real disorder that could affect the way she focused and handled things for the rest of her life. He hated himself for all the pressure he'd put on her to buckle down and fix something over which she had no control.

Now, he thought, was his chance to make up for some of that. He wanted her to know she had his support in whatever she did. If that meant stepping in and making sure this thing with Will turned out the way she wanted it to, he'd do that, though he doubted she'd appreciate the interference.

He realized that Megan was watching him with an exasperated expression.

"You're going over there no matter what I say, aren't you?" she said.

"I am. The only question is whether you want to come along with me."

She sighed heavily. "Well, somebody has to keep you from making things worse," she muttered as she put aside the book she'd been reading. "Let's go."

He grinned. "You can stay in the background if you want to. You don't have to say a word."

"I'll do just that," she said, then grinned. "At least until I have to save you from yourself."

Will's admiration for Jess had increased a thousandfold over the course of the evening. She seemed to thrive on the minicrises that crept up in the kitchen, on dealing with the sometimes outrageous demands of difficult guests. She appeared to be everywhere at once, chatting with a customer, filling a water glass, even clearing the occasional table. He wondered if it was the fact that she dealt with things in the moment that made it so much easier for her to stay focused.

He'd been pitching in wherever she asked him to, amused to find himself taking directions from Ronnie Forrest in the kitchen, a kid who, a few short weeks ago, had been within seconds of being fired. He knew Ronnie's history of job failures and wondered if perhaps he had an undiagnosed case of ADD. Like Jess, now that he'd found his niche in the kitchen, he seemed to be thriving. Will had heard somewhere that quite a few chefs seemed to have attention deficit issues, but worked well in the chaos of a restaurant kitchen.

Now that the last of the customers had been served dessert, Gail and Ronnie were cleaning up in the kitchen, the tables in the dining room were being cleared and Jess was behind the front desk counting the night's receipts. Will joined her.

"You're good at this," he said.

She glanced up and grinned. "I know.

It's pretty amazing when things go without a hitch."

"What are you talking about? There were plenty of hitches tonight. There was that one woman who was dissatisfied with every meal the waitress brought her. I'd have dumped the last one on her head. I don't know what you said to her, though, but she actually walked out of here smiling."

"Oh, that's Mrs. Timmons. She's a widow living on a small pension. She really can't afford to eat out much. It's been a big adjustment for her. I don't know if you noticed, but she ate a few bites of each of the two meals we took to her before she complained. Then I went over and offered to comp her dinner, since she wasn't happy with it, and gave her a free dessert, as well. We both know what's going on, but she salvages her pride and has a night out."

Will regarded her with amazement. "Wouldn't it just be cheaper to give her a gift certificate for a free meal, so she's not running through two or three and sending them back?"

"That would be charity," Jess said. "She'd never accept it. She needs to believe this is something we do to make things right because we've screwed up." She shrugged. "It's no big deal. I feel bad for her, especially since her husband died. Before that, he was always very generous with his tips, so in a way this is payback for his kindness to my staff. And I know how much she looks forward to coming here. The waitstaff knows what she's up to, and they try to be kind to her."

Will shook his head. "I hope word doesn't get out about this little scam of hers. Everybody will be trying it."

"I think all of us with restaurants in town understand her circumstances. We've all found ways to handle it so she's not embarrassed."

Will was about to say something more about her kindness when he glanced toward the front door and saw Mick and Megan entering. "Uh-oh," he murmured, nodding in their direction.

Jess groaned. "Run," she encouraged him. "There's still time for a clean getaway."

"And leave you here, defenseless? Not a chance." He stood up straight and held out his hand as Mick approached. "Good evening, sir. How are you? Megan?" He kissed her cheek.

Megan chuckled. "What a surprise to find you here," she said, her expression innocent.

"I'm sure," Jess said wryly. "The real surprise is having the two of you drop in at this hour on a Saturday night. I thought newlyweds would have better things to do."

"We're just out for a stroll," Mick claimed. "Thought maybe we could join you for a glass of wine."

"Why don't I give you a bottle to take home?" Jess suggested, her expression hopeful.

Mick frowned, clearly unamused. "Will, how about it? Can you stick around and join us?"

"I was planning to," Will responded. "Jess, why don't I get the wine? We can meet in the lounge. Last time I checked, it was empty."

Mick studied him intently. "You seem to be making yourself right at home. You here a lot?"

"I have been recently," Will said. "I'll just go and get that wine. Excuse me."

Mick followed right along behind him. "You'll need help with the glasses, I'm sure."

Will knew he'd be wasting his breath to

argue. "Sure. An extra pair of hands is always helpful." At the wine cooler he asked, "Do you all prefer red or white?"

"White's good," Mick said. "So, Megan and I were at Brady's last night when you and Jess were there."

"Is that so?" Will said, as if it were news to him.

"Seemed like the two of you were on a date."

"Not exactly."

Mick frowned. "What does that mean— not exactly? You don't know if it was a date? Seems to me a thing like that is usually pretty clear."

"Jess dropped by my office earlier in the evening. We were talking and decided to have dinner. Does that qualify as a date?"

"It does in my book," Mick said. "What exactly are your intentions toward my daughter?"

Will laughed. "Didn't take you long to get to the point. I thought for sure you'd try to trick me into telling you what you want to know."

Mick waved off the comment. "Megan's the one who's all about finesse and subtlety. I figure if I want to know something, the best way to find out is to ask. So, what's going on between you and my daughter?"

Will knew Mick's tactics well enough not to be offended by the direct approach. "With all due respect, I think that's between Jess and me," he said quietly. "However, I will say that I've been in love with your daughter for most of my life. I want a future with her. This is all a little new for Jess, though, so there's no telling how it will turn out. I'd appreciate it if you'd let the two of us figure it out for ourselves."

Mick looked momentarily taken aback by Will's bluntness, but then he grinned. "You'll be good for her, son. I just hope she doesn't twist you up in knots along the way. Jess can be unpredictable."

"It's one of her greatest charms," Will said.

"Now I know you're a man in love," Mick said, chuckling. "You need any help moving things along, you let me know. She'll listen to me."

Will gave him a bland look. "Really, sir?"

Again, Mick looked startled, but then he laughed. "Seems as if you have the whole family pegged."

"I've had years to watch you all in action,"

Will said. "And in case I haven't mentioned it enough, I'm grateful for that. You've always made me feel welcome."

"Well, you can expect that to continue, just as long as you don't hurt my girl."

"There's not a chance of that, sir, at least not intentionally."

"Sometimes it's the things we didn't mean to do that can hurt the most," Mick reminded him. "Take that from a man who made a lot of mistakes over the years and lost the woman he loved because of it. I've been blessed with a second chance, and this time I'm not going to blow it."

The door to the kitchen opened and Megan stepped in, a worried expression on her face.

"You two have been gone a long time. Everything okay?"

Mick slapped a hand on Will's shoulder. "Everything's fine. Isn't that right?"

"Perfect," Will agreed. "We've reached an understanding."

Megan's gaze narrowed. "Isn't it Jess with whom you should be reaching any understandings?"

Will nodded. "Exactly the point to which we've just agreed."

She gave him an approving look. "Smart man." She tucked her arm through Mick's. "You're not going to let this one bully you."

"Since when do I bully people?" Mick asked indignantly.

"You've been known to from time to time," she said. "It's your forceful personality, to say nothing of your determination to get your own way. Now let's have one glass of wine with these young people and be on our way, so they can enjoy the rest of their evening."

Mick leaned down and kissed her, then nabbed the bottle of wine from Will's hand. "I think I liked Jess's earlier idea. Why don't you and I take this home and snuggle up in front of our fire? We are still on our honeymoon, after all."

Megan blushed. "Mick, our honeymoon in Paris was months ago."

"That doesn't mean the honeymoon's over. I'm thinking we can make it last a few more months at least. I have some ideas about that. We'll talk about 'em at home."

Will was oddly touched by this evidence that they were still so much in love. Sure, they'd had a rough patch and years of divorce, but they were back together now and, from the looks of it, happier than ever.

"Enjoy the rest of your evening," he called after them, but he doubted they heard.

When he walked into the lounge, minus the wine and without Mick or Megan, Jess regarded him with amusement. "Lose something?"

"Our company. I sent them on their way with our wine, too."

"That's more than okay with me. Wine right now would just make me sleepy." She slanted a curious look at him. "What did you say to get rid of them?"

"I just told your father what he wanted to know."

She scowled. "Do I even want to hear this? How embarrassing is it?"

"He was just being a good father," Will said. "I told him my intentions were honorable." He winked at her. "And that I wasn't so sure about yours."

"Oh, great," Jess said with mock indignation. "So now I'm the one who's trying to lure you into a life of sin?"

Will held her gaze. "Aren't you?"

"Maybe I am. Are you game yet?"

Temptation swirled through him at her serious expression, the heat in her eyes. He leaned closer, tucked a strand of hair behind her ear, then lingered to caress her cheek. He could feel her skin warm, hear the catch in her breath. It would be so easy to close the gap between them, seal his mouth over hers and take what he wanted. What she wanted.

But it wasn't time. Not yet. He wanted more than sex. He wanted a lifetime. And Jess simply wasn't there yet. There was still no telling if she ever would be.

When he kissed her, it was on the cheek. He saw the disappointment in her eyes, and it gave him hope. "'Night, Jess."

"You're actually going to walk out of here, even though I've practically thrown myself at you?" she asked.

"Yes, I am," he said solemnly. "But so you know, it's just about going to kill me to do it."

He was pretty sure he saw a surprised smile light her face as he walked away.

15

On Sunday Jess stewed all day about Will's abrupt departure the night before. She was even more annoyed when he didn't show up for Sunday dinner at the house. Not that she'd specifically invited him. She'd thought it was a given that he'd be there. She'd taken him for granted.

Of course, it was entirely possible that despite what he'd said to her, he was avoiding Mick. Looking for someone else to blame for Will's absence, she found her father in his office after the meal and confronted him.

"Did you say something last night to scare Will off?" she asked.

Mick bristled. "Did he say I did?"

"No, actually he said things were fine, but he's not here today, is he? Something must have happened."

"The two of you were still there together when your mother and I left. Maybe you should think about what you said to him," Mick advised.

Frustrated, Jess sat down in a chair opposite her father. "I didn't say anything. We didn't argue. I thought we were okay."

"Then you probably are," Mick said. "Did he say he was coming today?"

She flinched. "I didn't ask."

"Well, there you go."

"But he's almost always here," she protested. "I've never once asked him to come." She paused, then amended, "It only started changing recently. What's that about?"

Mick regarded her with amusement. "Look, my darling girl, when men and women start seeing each other in a different way, it changes things. You can't take anything for granted."

Once again Jess felt guilty. That was

exactly what she'd done. "Well, it shouldn't be like that," she complained.

Mick laughed. "I agree, but that's just the way it is. From here on out, if you want Will to join us, it's probably going to be up to you to invite him." He gave her a hopeful look. "Unless you want me to do it."

"Absolutely not. Something tells me the less time you spend with Will, the better."

"I didn't pressure him, if that's what you're thinking," Mick said indignantly. "I just asked him what's what. He told me. That was the end of it."

Jess doubted it had been quite that simple, even though both men claimed it had been. "Then make sure it stays that way, Dad. This is between Will and me."

"Then what are you doing in here talking to me about it? Go talk to him."

She stood up. "Maybe I will."

But when she left the house, the thought of trying to track Will down to see why he hadn't come to dinner struck her as pathetic. It shouldn't matter that he hadn't been there. He'd missed other dinners and she hadn't been rattled by it. Why now? Why was she taking his absence today personally?

Of course, it was precisely as her father had said—when men and women started dating, everything changed, took on new meaning. Maturity and self-confidence flew out the window. It was ridiculous.

Instead of going looking for Will, she called Laila.

"What are you doing?" she asked her friend.

"Trying to come up with an excuse to leave my family before they start badgering me about why I'm dating a different man every few days instead of settling down," Laila said.

"Meet me," Jess suggested. "You can explain it to me, instead. I'm calling Connie, too. She was suspiciously absent from Sunday dinner today. She *and* my Uncle Thomas. Either they're avoiding each other or they're off somewhere together. I want to know which it is."

Laila laughed. "Oh, goody. Potential gossip. Where shall we meet? It's too early to go to the bar at Brady's."

"How about the inn? We can go for a walk on the beach and then order pizza later."

"Perfect. I'll be there in twenty minutes.

It'll take me that long to extricate myself from the inquisition that's brewing over here."

Jess disconnected that call, then hit speed dial for Connie's cell phone. "You weren't at dinner today," she said when her friend answered. "Where are you?"

"Home."

"Alone?"

"Why would you ask that?" Connie asked, instantly on the defensive.

"Because Uncle Thomas was missing in action today, too. Is he with you?"

Connie laughed, though it sounded a little forced. "No, he had a foundation board luncheon in Annapolis."

"How nice that you're keeping track of his schedule," Jess commented. "What's he doing for dinner?"

A guilty silence that spoke volumes greeted the question.

"Oh, my gosh, he's coming to your place, isn't he?" Jess said, gloating. "That's why you stayed home, to get ready for his visit. Is tonight the night?"

"The night for what?" Connie inquired testily.

"You know, when the two of you will get down and dirty."

"What a lovely description!" Connie said. "He's coming here for dinner. That's the plan."

"And beyond that?" Jess pressed.

Connie gave a nervous laugh. "I wish I knew. I'm actually scared to death about what might come next."

She sounded so genuinely terrified, Jess took pity on her. "Nothing else has to happen if you don't want it to."

"I know that. It's not as if he's pressuring me. We haven't even been on that many dates. I just know that sooner or later, sleeping together is going to be the next step. What if I've forgotten how?"

"I'm pretty sure you don't forget how to do sex," Jess consoled her. "You're just out of practice. And word is that my uncle has some pretty smooth moves."

"Do you actually discuss stuff like that in your family?" She sighed. "Of course you do. Nothing is off-limits for the O'Briens, which is yet another reason why your uncle dating me is probably a bad idea."

"Not to worry. We'd never openly discuss something that intimate," Jess insisted. "But Uncle Thomas does have quite the dating history. There has to be some reason women flock around him."

"Oh, God," Connie murmured in despair. "I did not need to be reminded that I'm competing with half the single women in Annapolis, who're probably far more sophisticated than I am."

"Stop that!" Jess ordered. "It's going to be fine. He likes you. You like him. After that, it all comes naturally, or so they tell me."

"I hope you're right," Connie said, but she didn't sound convinced.

"Look, Laila's coming over to the inn and we're going to hang out. I was going to invite you, but you're obviously tied up. Call if you need either one of us. We'll talk you down or race over there to run interference. Whatever you need, okay?"

"Thanks. I wish I were going to be there with you."

"No, you don't," Jess said. "Or if you do, you're crazy. Relax and have fun. Despite my teasing, my uncle's a good guy and he would be very, very lucky to have you in his life."

She was smiling when she hung up. It seemed love was in the air, at least for one of them. As for her, well, that remained to be seen.

Thomas arrived at Connie's with flowers, candy and a new book about the bay that he'd been telling her about. He was more nervous than he had been when he'd had to speak before the board earlier. Though he was used to public speaking and it came naturally enough, he was always on edge when he had to explain to the foundation's biggest donors why more progress hadn't been made on restoring the bay's waters. The last thing the foundation could afford was having their donors decide they were wasting their money.

Right now, though, that seemed like a piece of cake compared to facing Connie over a dinner table in her home. There was something about the privacy and the expectations that seemed to go with it that made him feel like a kid again . . . and not in a good way. He was not one of those men who was interested in reliving his youth. Those days had been damn awkward, if he recalled correctly.

When he rang the doorbell, pleased with himself for being right on time, Connie opened it with her cheeks flushed, her hair mussed and her expression clearly flustered.

"I have to grab the chicken before it burns up," she announced and took off without so much as a welcome.

Thomas shook his head and followed her into the kitchen, where he found her already bent over an open oven door.

"Anything I can do to help?" he asked, just as she backed up and straight into him, the slightly-past-golden-brown chicken wobbling dangerously in its roasting pan.

He was about to reach out to steady it, when she yelped, "No, it's hot!" She practically dropped it on the counter, then heaved a sigh before turning to look at him. "Sorry. I'd planned to be more on top of things by the time you got here."

He set down the gifts he'd brought and put his hands on her shoulders to steady her. "It's fine. We're fine. There's nothing to be nervous about." It was amazing, but her obvious attack of nerves had steadied his.

"But I almost ruined the chicken," she protested. "I must have baked a hundred chickens in my time, and I've never practically burned one to a crisp."

"The chicken's not burned," he assured her.

"Maybe not, but it's going to be dry as a bone."

"We'll just smother it with gravy," he consoled her, only to see panic cross her face.

"I forgot all about the gravy. What is wrong with me? Nobody serves mashed potatoes without gravy."

Thomas resisted the desire to laugh. Instead, he met her gaze and held it, then slowly lowered his mouth and covered hers. He felt her sigh against his lips, then relax in his arms. When he pulled away, she looked a little dazed, but a whole lot happier. And so sweetly vulnerable, it made his heart ache.

"Better?" he asked.

"Much. Thank you."

"Kissing you was hardly a sacrifice," he assured her. "In fact, I think I might do it again."

This time a full-fledged genuine smile broke across her face. "I wish you would."

And so, he did.

A couple of hours later, with not one bit of dinner salvageable, they ordered pizza. Thomas assured her it was the best meal he'd had in recent memory. The appetizer had been pretty darn incredible, as well.

Bolstered by her talk with Laila and calmed by their long walk on the beach and a couple of glasses of wine, Jess picked up the phone and called Will on Sunday night.

"I missed you at dinner today," she said when he answered.

"Is that so?" he said.

She could almost see the smile on his face. "It is. Where were you?"

"Trying to catch up on Lunch by the Bay paperwork. It's gotten a little overwhelming."

"Maybe you need to hire someone to help you keep up with it," she suggested.

"I can manage."

"Not if you're skipping meals and not if you intend to court me the way I deserve to be courted."

Her comment apparently stunned him into silence.

"Will?"

"I'm here."

"Maybe where you should be is here," she suggested.

"Jess, what has gotten into you?"

"Not a thing," she claimed. "Well, a couple of glasses of wine, but that's not what's made me daring."

"Oh? Then what has?"

"I've decided to go after what I want."

"And you want me? You're sure of that?"

"Tonight I do," she declared.

"What about tomorrow?" he asked warily. "Or the day after that?"

"Sorry. I can't see that far into the future."

"And I can't live just for the moment," he said with unmistakable regret. "I want it all, Jess. Not a couple of hours or a night, because you've got an itch you want scratched."

She sighed heavily. "I guess I knew it was a long shot. You're very hard to seduce."

"Not really," he assured her. "You just have to figure out the magic words."

Jess considered what he was telling her. She knew the words he wanted to hear, the same words most women wanted to hear—a simple "I love you." She wasn't there yet. She didn't know if she ever would be. How could she guarantee forever, when she couldn't even stick to something for a couple of hours?

"I know the words, Will. I just can't say them."

"I know that, sweetheart. You'll say them when the time is right."

"What if it never is?" she asked plaintively.

"There you go, selling yourself short again."

"I'm being realistic," she contradicted. "I don't have a good track record with follow-through."

"You have a business that says otherwise," he reminded her. "Stop pressuring yourself, Jess. I'm a patient man. And I like what's happening between us."

"It's too darn slow," she said in frustration.

Will laughed. "You should see it from my side. Glacier-slow doesn't begin to describe it. It's going to be worth it, though. I'm counting on that."

"You're either the most amazing man I've ever known or the craziest," she said.

"Let's go with amazing," he said. "Sweet dreams. I'll see you tomorrow."

"When?"

"I think I'll surprise you."

She murmured a curse under her breath

that had him laughing again. "I think I'll move annoying to the top of the list," she stated in exasperation.

"What list is that?"

"The one I'm keeping of your traits," she told him.

"At least you've finally noticed I'm alive. I'll take that as progress."

He hung up before she could snap another curse that would blister his ears. Then she thought about the conversation and found herself grinning, after all. The man did know how to keep her on her toes. Maybe that was exactly what she'd needed all her life.

Will's day fell apart on Monday. He had a patient in crisis and everything else had to be put on a back burner. He canceled his afternoon appointments and headed for the hospital, where the woman had checked herself in but now wanted to get back out again. She was creating such a fuss the staff had pleaded with him to calm her down.

En route, he placed a call to Bree at Flowers on Main. "I need you to bail me out of a jam," he told her, explaining how his day had been going. "Jess is expecting me to turn up at the inn, and if I don't, she's going to be convinced I've gone back on my word."

"Why are you calling me, rather than her?" Bree asked.

"Because you have flowers," he said. "Lots and lots of flowers. I want something that will knock her socks off."

"Ah, that would be the apology special," she said. "No problem."

"Do you get this kind of call a lot?" Will asked, taken aback.

"More than you can imagine," she said. "I have something for the occasions when a dozen roses won't quite do the trick."

"Maybe that would be overkill for these circumstances," he said. "How about classy and romantic, instead?"

"I can definitely do classy and romantic."

"Something uniquely for Jess?" he asked.

"So, this thing between you two is getting pretty serious," Bree said.

"I hope so. Any objections?"

"None from me. I adore my sister. Jake's a little concerned, though."

"So he's mentioned," Will said. "I've told him to butt out."

"Apparently there's a lot of that going

around lately. He's beginning to feel use-less."

Will was lost. "Who besides me has told him to stay out of their business?"

"Connie. It seems she's dating Thomas. Jake nearly went into cardiac arrest when he found out."

"I can imagine," Will said. "Thomas has to be, what, ten years older at least?"

"Something like that," Bree said.

"No wonder she stopped accepting the dates I was setting up for her," Will mur-mured. He pictured Connie and Thomas O'Brien together, and surprisingly, they fit. He'd seen evidence of it firsthand at the fall festival. He wondered if his computer system would see it the same way. "They could work. Connie needs a man who knows exactly who he is, who's accom-plished and settled and can offer her ev-erything she deserves."

"That's the way I see it, too," Bree said. "I'm just worried about what will happen when Dad gets wind of this. He lumps Con-nie in with all the rest of us kids because she's Jake's sister, even though she's quite a bit older. He's liable to accuse Thomas of robbing the cradle and then those two will be back to not speaking again."

"They enjoy their battles," Will said. "I wouldn't worry too much about it."

"I just don't want Dad to make Connie or Thomas feel uncomfortable."

"Right now I think he has his hands full trying to manage me and Jess," Will said wryly.

"Oh, believe me, he can juggle all of us. He was over here earlier today grumbling that the baby's portable playpen should be up here in front where it would get more light. And he thought she needed a warmer sweater and that she should probably start on solid food. She looked too skinny to him."

Will chuckled. "It may be exasperating, but at least Mick's an involved parent and grandparent these days. I remember a time when you all complained about how often he was gone and how little he knew about your lives."

Bree sighed heavily. "Yeah, I think this falls into the 'be careful what you wish for' category."

"Look, I've got to run. I want to get to

the hospital before my patient manages to check herself out. You'll take care of the flowers?"

"Done," Bree said. "And I'll write a sappy note for you, too."

"Maybe you should leave the sappy notes to me," Will suggested. "Stick with 'Love, Will.'"

"Trust me. You're going to need more than that to keep Jess from getting ticked off because you're missing a date."

"We didn't have a date. We had tentative plans." He recalled how Jess had turned a similar situation into a rock-solid commitment just days ago. "Never mind. Go with sappy. Thanks, Bree."

"Anytime."

Will hoped there wouldn't be all that many times when he needed to be bailed out of a jam, but given the sometimes unpredictable nature of his work, it was probably likely. He wondered if Jess would be able to accept that, and, if she couldn't, what would happen to the future he wanted with her.

Tired of waiting around for a man who'd clearly forgotten that he'd promised to come by, Jess dragged herself up to the attic to take another stab at clearing out the last of the debris. Laila had promised to deal with the paperwork on the construction loan by the end of this week. After that, Mick could get started with the renovations.

Annoyed with Will, even though she knew she was probably being ridiculous, she tossed things into garbage bags with a vengeance, barely noticing whether they were worth keeping or not.

When she finally heard footsteps on the stairs, she scowled in the direction of the door, fully expecting it to be Will. Instead, it was her sister, carrying a small arrangement of lilies of the valley in an obviously expensive crystal vase.

"Why are you making such a racket up here?" Bree asked, then grinned. "Or need I ask? You're upset because Will hasn't stopped by."

"What makes you think that?" Jess demanded irritably. "I don't give two hoots about Will."

"Really? Then what are you upset about?"

"Life. Men. I don't know," she said with a heavy sigh. She glanced again at the flowers. She'd always loved lilies of the valley. Her mother had lined a flagstone walkway at the house with them. After she'd gone, Jess had waited each spring for them to bloom, hoping that maybe they'd bring her mother back again since she'd loved them so much. "Where'd the flowers come from? It's hard to get lilies of the valley this time of year."

"But they're your favorites," Bree said. "And I happen to own a flower shop. So when a customer calls and requests something special for my little sister, I knew just what she'd like."

Jess held her breath, then asked, "Who called?"

"Will, of course. Apparently he had a patient with some kind of crisis and he had to get to the hospital. He didn't want you to think he'd forgotten he'd told you he'd see you today." Bree studied her intently. "But, of course, that's exactly what you thought, isn't it?"

Jess nodded, reaching for the delicate flowers and burying her nose in them. When she looked up, there were tears in her eyes.

"Hey, are you okay?" Bree asked worriedly. "Do you suddenly hate lilies of the valley for some reason?"

"No, it's just that they always remind me of Mom. I used to pick them in the spring and bring them inside in case she came home."

"Oh, sweetie, I didn't realize they made you so sad. I'm sorry."

"No, they don't always make me sad. They brought me joy, too, made me feel more in touch with her, I guess, because I knew how much she'd loved them. It was sweet of you to think of them and of Will to send them. Is there a card?"

Bree pulled a card from her pocket and handed it over.

Roses are red, violets are blue, I really wish, I were there with you.

She looked up from the card, laughing. "You wrote this, didn't you? Will would never write such lousy poetry."

"How do you know?" Bree demanded indignantly. "Maybe he would."

Jess stood up and hugged her sister. "Thank you for trying to make me feel better. Why didn't he just call me and tell me what was going on?"

"I think he thought a gesture like flowers

would say more. The guy's obviously crazy about you. More important, I think he gets how you think. You were up here thinking he'd abandoned you, weren't you?"

Jess nodded sheepishly. "It's nuts, I know. It's not as if we had specific plans."

"Don't you suppose that reaction can be traced straight back to Mom leaving? If our own mother could go off and leave us, what's to stop anyone else from going?"

Jess nodded. "Exactly. And for so long I blamed myself. I thought I was too much trouble and that's why she'd gone."

Bree regarded her with surprise. "I didn't realize that. I should have, I guess."

"Why? You're not that much older than me. You weren't much more than a kid yourself. Abby knew, and Gram."

"Did Dad?"

Jess shook her head. "Not unless Gram told him. He was in so much pain himself, he was pretty much oblivious to the way the rest of us felt."

Bree pulled her back down to the floor and sat beside her, shoulder to shoulder. "You do know that not everyone leaves, right? I trust Jake with all my heart. He won't take off. Ditto with Trace. Abby's stuck with him for the rest of her life." She faced Jess squarely. "I think Will falls into the same category. I think he's one of those men who will mate for life."

Jess smiled at her phrasing. "I think so, too," she admitted, then met her sister's gaze with a troubled expression. "What if I'm not one of those women? I know Jake, Mack, half the people who know us are worried about that. Even Connor and Kevin, who know me best, have their doubts I can stick it out."

"They're all worrying about nothing," Bree assured her. "You'll take your time, fret over this from every angle, but once you decide, whether it's on Will or someone else, you'll stick with him. Personally, I think it is Will. I saw something in your eyes when you talked about him the other day. It's the same look Abby gets when she talks about Trace, or Kevin when he sees Shanna, or Connor spots Heather, or even when Mom and Dad see each other. Will's the one, sweetie, but don't take my word for it. Wait until you're sure, but don't walk away because you're scared."

Jess sighed. "It's too late," she admitted. "I don't think I could, even if I wanted to."

16

After Bree left, Jess put Will's flowers on the night table beside her bed where she'd see them first thing in the morning. The lovely scent filled her room and stirred her senses. They also stirred some kind of sentimental reaction she'd never experienced before.

In the time she'd been working in the attic, the weather had turned from a crisp, sunny fall afternoon to a cold, dreary rain. Though she had no idea when Will was likely to get home after dealing with his patient, she felt an unexpected need to be there waiting for him when he returned.

Acting on impulse, she grabbed her purse, a rain jacket, and went down to the kitchen.

"Gail, is there any soup on hand?" she asked, already poking around in the refrigerator.

"I froze some of the last batch of vegetable soup I made," Gail said. "Want me to defrost that?"

Jess shook her head. What a day like today called for was Gram's potato soup and maybe a loaf of crusty bread.

"There's bread, though, right?"

Gail pointed to the counter. "Whole grain, still warm from the oven. I made a couple of extra loaves. I thought you might like it tonight. It seems like that kind of day. Anything that's left will be good for toast for breakfast."

"You're fabulous. Thank you," she said sincerely. "Wrap a loaf up for me, would you?" Then she called her grandmother. "Hi, Gram."

"Well, hello," Gram said. "I'm guessing you have a hankering for some of my soup."

Once again, Jess was taken aback by her grandmother's intuition. "How on earth did you know that? Have you turned into a mind reader now?"

Gram laughed. "Hardly, though some said my mother had what they called the second sight. In my case, it's just knowing each of my grandchildren. Whenever the weather takes a turn like it did today, you were always the first one in the kitchen sniffing around to see if I'd made potato soup."

"And have you?"

"Of course. I wouldn't let you down, would I? Stop by and we'll eat together. I'd love the company."

Jess flushed guiltily. "Would you mind terribly if I took it to go? I thought I'd take some over to Will's, but I will stay and visit with you while you eat."

"That'll do," Gram said without even a hint of resentment in her voice. Somehow she always managed to sound eager to see her grandchildren for whatever time they could spare. She never tried to inflict guilt over the timing or infrequency of their visits. "I'll see you when you get here. Drive carefully."

"I will. See you soon," Jess said, then grabbed another loaf of bread and a few of Gail's cookies for her grandmother before heading out.

"I'm not your personal chef, you know," Gail called after her, feigning exasperation.

"Next best thing," Jess retorted, laughing. "Thanks. You're an angel. No wonder our guests rave about you!"

When she reached Gram's cottage, she pulled her parka hood over her head and made a dash for the front door. It was standing ajar and Gram was already nearby with a towel.

"Here," she said. "Dry yourself off and have a seat in front of the fire. I'm eating in here. It's much cozier than the kitchen."

"I brought a loaf of Gail's bread and some of her cookies," Jess said, handing over the fresh baked goods.

"Wonderful. That bread of hers is just the thing to go with a bowl of soup. Are you sure you won't eat a bite before you go to Will's?"

"No, I'll wait," Jess said, then settled onto the sofa and pulled a handmade afghan over her legs. "This feels wonderful. It's turning into a nasty night out there."

"I hear we could have snow by morning," Gram said. "Be sure you're careful on the roads. Even if there's no snow, you could be dealing with some of that dangerous black ice."

"I will be," Jess promised, studying her grandmother closely. Since leaving Mick's house, after he and Megan had rewed, and returning to her own cottage, her color seemed better. Her social life had certainly picked up in terms of the commitments she'd made at the church. Now that she was free of the demands of looking after a huge house and her grandchildren, she seemed to have been reenergized.

"How've you been? You're not overdoing it, are you?" Jess asked.

"I'm fit as a fiddle, now that I don't have the five of you running me ragged anymore," Nell said. "I've left all those worries to your father and Megan."

Jess grinned. "You can't break an old habit that quickly, Gram. You'll always worry about us."

Her eyes sparkled with merriment. "Oh, I suppose I might give a thought to each of you now and then," she admitted. "Here's *my* news, though. I won fifty dollars at bingo the other night. Should have had the big jackpot—I was only one number away—

but Heather's mother snatched it right out from under me."

"I'd forgotten Bridget had come back from Ohio for another visit," Jess said.

"She was missing that grandson of hers. She got real attached to him while she was staying with Heather. I have a feeling once her husband finally retires, they'll move over here."

Jess was surprised. "From everything Heather told me, I thought they were going to divorce."

"Funny thing about weddings," Gram said. "They make people take another look at what and who matters in their lives. I think when Heather and Connor got married, it did that for the Donovans. Bridget seems much happier now. Seems like she and her husband made some long-needed adjustments." She met Heather's gaze. "Now tell me about you and Will. I gather you've decided to test the waters finally."

"There's nothing much to tell," Jess said with a shrug, not entirely comfortable with discussing this with her grandmother, even though she'd asked for her advice only a couple of weeks earlier. Then the topic had been more theoretical. Now she was about to throw herself into the man's arms, if he'd have her.

"We're spending more time together," she told Gram. "But I think it's going to take some time before we get our signals straight. I'm still a little too quick to jump to conclusions about things and misjudge him."

"An old habit," Gram said. "You learned to protect your feelings at a young age."

"And I still have trouble believing in anyone, Will included."

"And yet you're running over there tonight with soup. That sounds to me like a woman who's allowed herself to care," Gram said perceptively.

"I do care," Jess admitted. "I just don't know how much. I mean, I think I'm starting to care a lot, but I don't entirely trust myself, either. I've jumped into things with men before and then abandoned them the minute I lost interest. With most of them, it didn't matter that much, but I don't want to hurt Will like that."

"He's a grown man, who knows his own mind," Gram reminded her. "More important, he's a man who knows *you*."

"I think I'm figuring out the advantages of that," Jess said, then glanced at her watch.

"Run along," Gram said, smiling at her impatience. "I've put the soup into a container for you. It's in a tote bag on the kitchen table. You can return them whenever you have a chance. Give Will my love."

"I wonder if I should call to see if he's even home yet?" Jess wondered aloud. "I'd really wanted to surprise him, though."

"A surprise would be a nice gesture. I'm sure he'd appreciate it. Take a chance. That's what living is all about, taking a risk now and again."

Jess grinned as she hugged her grandmother. "You're an old romantic, aren't you?"

"I've had a few moments in my time," Gram said with a wink. "Who knows? One of these days, I may have a few more. I keep threatening to take up with a gentleman caller. Drives your father nuts when I mention it."

"Oh, boy," Jess said. "Poor Dad."

Gram chuckled. "Just seeing how he handles me going out on dates will be worth it, don't you think?"

"It will, indeed. Maybe if you do it soon,

it would get him to focus on something besides me and Will."

"You're a dreamer, child."

Jess chuckled. "More than likely. Love you. See you Sunday, if not before."

"I love you, too, darling girl. Enjoy your evening."

"I hope to," Jess said. In fact, her hopes were higher than they'd been in quite a while.

Will wasn't sure which was worse, the struggle to convince his patient to stay in the hospital for further evaluation and treatment or the drive back to Chesapeake Shores in the pouring rain. All he knew was how relieved he felt when he finally pulled into a parking space behind his building, opened the front door and stepped into the heat of the building's small foyer, then got his mail and started up the stairs to his condo.

As he turned toward the top landing, he spotted Jess sitting on the steps with a tote bag beside her. She was leaning against the wall and looked to be half-asleep. No surprise, since it was after eleven.

"Well now, aren't you a sight for sore eyes," he said wearily.

She blinked, and a slow smile spread across her face. "It's about time you came home. I was about to give up hope. I thought maybe you were going to spend the night at the hospital."

"It was a very long and crappy day," he said. "Come on in. What's in the bag?"

"Gram's potato soup and a loaf of Gail's freshly baked bread."

He smiled. "You are a goddess!" he declared.

"I think maybe Gram and Gail are the ones who deserve the credit, but thanks. The soup will need to be heated. I've been out here quite a while. I wanted to surprise you."

"You succeeded. Come on inside. If you've been waiting for me to eat, you must be starved."

"Are you sure you're not too tired for company?"

"I will never be too tired to spend time with you," he insisted, ushering her into his apartment.

He tossed his briefcase and jacket onto

a chair, then took Jess's coat. "Would you mind terribly if I took a quick shower?"

"Go ahead," she said. "I'll heat up the soup and the bread."

He pressed a kiss to her cheek. "Like I said, a goddess! See you in a couple of minutes."

"Take your time."

As he stood under the hard spray of his shower, he thought about finding Jess on his doorstep at the end of an exhausting day. He had no idea what had really brought her there, but just the unexpected sight of her had rejuvenated him. The shower finished the job.

When he walked into the kitchen wearing clean jeans and a sweater, the aroma of the soup and the bread had him stopping in his tracks to sniff the air appreciatively.

When he opened his eyes, Jess was smiling. "Careful, or I'm going to think you're more interested in this food than you are in me."

He slipped an arm around her waist as she stirred the soup. "Right this second, I have to say it's a toss-up," he admitted.

"Now that's a fine thing to say when

you're trying to win my heart," she accused, but there was a twinkle in her eyes. "So, you didn't mind the surprise?"

"Of course not. It was the best part of my day so far."

Her eyes widened. "So far?"

"Well, finding you on my doorstep late at night has raised some interesting possibilities, especially since there's no way I'm letting you go back out on those slick roads tonight. The rain was turning to sleet just as I got back to town."

She swallowed hard. "I see. How comfortable is that couch of yours?"

"I'd never let a guest sleep on the couch," he protested, grinning at her.

"I was asking for you," she said. "I'd hate for you to wake up with a kink in your neck."

Will laughed. "I guess we still have some heavy-duty negotiating to do before the night is over. You'd better feed me first."

He found a bottle of wine and poured two glasses, while Jess put big bowls of steaming soup on the kitchen table, along with slices of the crusty bread and plenty of butter. He pulled out a chair for her, then sat down across from her. He lifted his glass.

"To you. Thanks for being just what I needed tonight."

Jess smiled, her cheeks turning pink. "And to you," she said. "The lilies of the valley you sent couldn't have been more perfect."

"I guess we know each other pretty well, don't we?" he said. "Of course, I can't really take credit for the type of flowers. That was all Bree."

"But you knew what I'd be thinking and that you needed to send something to remind me you hadn't forgotten about me," she said. "It was a sweet gesture, Will. You have no idea how much I appreciated that."

Will looked into her eyes. "Tell me what you were thinking before they came."

She made a wry grimace. "Exactly what you thought I'd be thinking, that you'd abandoned me."

"How am I supposed to prove to you that will never happen?" he asked.

Jess's expression turned thoughtful. "It's going to take time, I suppose," she said. "And practice. All my life, people have gone away. My mother did and, for all intents and purposes, so did my Dad. Even Abby, Bree, Kevin and Connor, they all left me behind."

Will heard the unmistakable hurt in her voice and said gently, "Have you ever considered the fact that, at least in the cases of your brothers and sisters, it's not so much that they left you, but that you were the one who chose to stay?"

She frowned at the question. "Doesn't it add up to the same thing? They were gone, and I was here."

"By choice, Jess. If you'd wanted to leave Chesapeake Shores, you could have. Instead, you chose a local college. You had your heart set on owning the inn long before you bought it. This town was always a part of you. I wonder if you weren't determined to create the home here that you'd longed for as a child." He gave her a knowing look. "I also think you stayed because of your father. You knew how much building this community meant to him. In a way, I think you thought staying would show him how much you loved him."

She regarded him with a thoughtful expression. "I never thought of that, but you could be right." Her expression turned quiz-zical. "By the way, how did you know I'd wanted to own the inn for so long?"

"That didn't even require guesswork on my part. I spent a lot of time with you, re-member? You, Connor and I would walk along the beach, and you'd look up there almost every single time with this yearning expression on your face and declare that someday it was going to be yours."

She seemed stunned that he'd remem-bered that. He grinned at her reaction.

"There's not a lot that you did or said that I can't remember," he told her.

"How was I so oblivious to your feelings for all those years?" she asked, shaking her head. "I must have been so careless with you. I'm sorry."

"Don't be. I wasn't about to say anything about how I felt back then. I knew you had a lot of things to do, and even more things to figure out, before you'd be ready for me. I was just terrified all that thinking and do-ing would happen while I was off getting my own degrees."

"Then I guess it's a good thing I took my time growing up," she said, a smile playing on her lips. She looked up from her soup and captured his gaze. "I have it all together now, Will. At least I think I do."

"Meaning what?"

She kept her gaze steady. "I want you to make love to me tonight," she said softly. "It's not just about the sex and getting it out of the way. I want to take this next step. I think we need to. I mean, it would be crazy if we fell in love and then found out we were totally incompatible in bed, right?"

Will laughed. "So this would be a purely practical test?"

"Something like that." She kept her gaze on his. "Please."

Will had about a thousand reservations, but he also had the same driving need to hold her in his arms that he'd lived with for years. He didn't think he could deny it yet again, not with her looking at him the way she was.

"You're sure, Jess? Really sure? I don't want this to be nothing more than an experiment to you."

"It won't be," she assured him, her expression solemn. "And I am a hundred percent sure."

"You do know that after this, there is no way in hell I will ever let you go," he warned.

"I kind of figured that," she said, looking surprisingly content with that.

He reached across the table and touched a finger to her lips. "I'm not kidding, Jess. This is it for me. There won't be any turning back. I'll still give you all the time you need, but you will be mine."

For just an instant, she looked a little shaken by the vehemence of his claim, but then she sighed. "Okay, then." She held out her hand. "I'm ready. More than ready, in fact. Lately this is all I've been able to think about, you and me together. What it would be like."

Will ignored her hand. He stood slowly and scooped her into his arms, then headed for his room, grateful that he'd had the foresight to straighten the bed and toss his dirty clothes into the closet earlier. He'd left a low light glowing on his dresser.

Jess curled against his chest as if they'd done this a thousand times. He felt her smile against the curve of his neck when she saw the king-size bed.

"I should have known," she murmured.

"I was planning ahead," he told her. "But just so you know, this bed is awfully big and lonely when there's no one to share it."

Tonight, though, he intended to make use of every square inch of it.

On some level Jess had known when she came over to Will's tonight that there was a chance they would wind up here, in his bed. Of course, he'd been so adamantly opposed to it in the past she hadn't been certain she could persuade him it was time. The man had an astonishing ability to resist temptation.

He stripped back the covers, settled her gently onto soft-as-silk cream-colored sheets, then lowered himself beside her, his face level with hers. His fingers skimmed her cheek as he moved a wayward curl off her face.

"Have I mentioned how beautiful you are?" he asked, a breathless quality to his voice.

She smiled. "Actually you haven't."

"Then let me rectify that at once," he said with a grin. "You have the most amazingly expressive face, eyes as blue as the bay on a summer day, and hair that's been lit by the sun."

"Not bad for a guy who writes terrible poetry," she murmured.

He blinked at that. "Poetry?"

"It came with the flowers."

He laughed. "Ah, the sappy, romantic poem Bree insisted was necessary. She messed it up, huh? Some writer she is."

"She tried, but believe me, this was proof positive she should concentrate on writing plays. She is no Elizabeth Barrett Browning. Still, it was sweet that you let her try."

"Anything to put a smile on your face."

A tremor washed through her, along with a hunger that was startling in its intensity. "Um, Will, are we going to get on with this anytime soon? I'm getting a little anxious here."

He laughed. "I was taking my time, wooing you."

"I don't need wooing right now," she assured him. "I need your lips on mine, your body."

She sighed with pleasure as he covered her mouth with his, then slipped a hand under her shirt to find her breasts and tease the nipples into sensitive little buds.

"Better," she murmured against his lips, then moaned as his hands went roving over hips and thighs before sliding down the zipper of her jeans and dipping inside. "Oh, sweet heaven!"

He took such care of her, amazingly attentive care, making her body hum like the strings of a well-loved guitar.

"I had no idea," she whispered against his neck, bucking as he finally touched the most intimate core of her, his fingers wickedly talented. It might be true that she wasn't a virgin, but she'd never been treated with such tenderness.

She started to reach for him, but he held her hands away from him. "This is all about you," he told her, continuing to find ways to pleasure her until she gasped and lost control, clinging to his shoulders as she rode out the remarkable sensations.

He was smiling when she finally caught her breath and opened her eyes.

"Now let's see what happens when we take this ride together," he teased, pulling his sweater over his head and leaving it to her to loosen his belt and slowly lower the zipper of his pants.

He kicked off his shoes and then his pants, then gently pulled her under him. His eyes held hers as he entered her, taking her someplace she'd never gone before with someone she'd never dreamed capable of magic.

It was yet one more thing about which Will had been right, one more instance in which he'd known her better than she knew herself. This night had made her his.

Morning came much too early for Will. If he'd had his way, he wouldn't have left this bed for a week, maybe a month, though given the near-empty state of his bachelor refrigerator, he doubted either he or Jess would have lasted that long.

He rolled over and contented himself with studying the woman next to him. She slept on her back with her arms thrown wide, the covers down to her waist. Resisting the desire to touch her, to awaken her and take her yet again with sunlight just starting to spill into the bedroom, was tougher than anything he'd ever done.

Instead, though, he dropped a light kiss on her brow, then slipped out of bed and took a shower. He'd dressed and started a pot of decaf in the kitchen before he heard her stirring.

He poured them each a cup, then carried them into the bedroom.

"I wondered where you'd gone," she said sleepily, then spotted the cups. "Is that coffee?" She wiggled her fingers. "Gimme, please."

Will laughed. "Nice to know where your morning priorities are. I made decaf especially for you, but if you want breakfast, I'm afraid we'll have to go to Sally's."

Jess studied him over the rim of her cup. "Why did that sound like some kind of challenge?"

Will shrugged. "It probably was. I guess I'm wondering how much you're willing to let people figure out about us. Are you ready to stir up all that speculation?"

She frowned at him. "You say that as if it's some kind of flaw to worry about it. Are you really prepared to face all the gossip?"

"It won't bother me," he insisted.

"But what do we tell people?"

"I don't think we have to tell them anything," he said. "They'll draw their own conclusions from seeing us together. We don't have to confirm or deny."

"I guess it's not really everyone else I'm worried about," she confessed, looking thoughtful. "It's my family, plus Jake and Mack. None of them know how to keep their opinions to themselves, and they've already been pretty vocal with their doubts about the two of us as a couple. At least some of them have been."

"So, you don't want to go to Sally's," he concluded, trying to keep his expression blank, even as his heart took a dive. "Fine. It's up to you."

Jess reached for his hand. "Please don't look like that. I'm not ashamed of what happened here last night. I hope it's the start of something, Will, I really do. But until we're sure, maybe it would be best . . ."

"To keep it a secret," he said. "I get it."

And he did. That didn't mean it didn't hurt like hell, though.

17

Will didn't know why he'd been so surprised by Jess's reticence to go with him to Sally's. Even though she'd initiated what had happened between them the night before, it was evident that she still had serious reservations about them as a couple. He probably should have slept on the stupid sofa, after all. He didn't want just one incredible night with her in his bed. He wanted a whole future. He'd made that clear enough, and still she'd taken off.

"You look grim," Connor said when he settled into a booth opposite Will at Sally's. "Problems?"

"Nothing I want to talk about," Will said. Of all the people in town who might turn up here this morning, why did it have to be Jess's brother? No way was he discussing this with Connor.

Connor leveled a knowing look at him. "What's my sister done now?"

"Who said this has anything to do with Jess?" Will replied testily.

"According to Gram, Jess was headed to your place last night to surprise you with a meal. Since I tried to call her at home off and on all evening to see if she'd gotten home okay, and never got an answer, I'm guessing she stayed with you."

Will groaned. "Is nothing a secret in this town?" No wonder Jess hadn't wanted to show up here with him this morning and give the town more fodder to chew on.

Connor laughed at his apparent frustration. "Not in my family, that's for sure." His expression turned sympathetic. "You two have a fight?"

"No."

"Don't tell me last night was a disaster," Connor said, looking shaken. "You know . . ."

"I know," Will said, then added indignantly, "and it wasn't a disaster. Far from it. And that is absolutely the last thing I will ever say about that."

"Fair enough," Connor agreed. "I'm not all that anxious to be privy to my sister's sex life, to tell you the truth."

"Then why the devil would you ask?"

Connor shrugged. "Felt I had to. So, if everything was okay in that department, why do you look as if you've lost your best friend?"

"I can't control how I look or your interpretation of it," Will said, losing patience with the whole uncomfortable conversation. "Can we please drop this?"

The plea obviously fell on deaf ears.

"Let me guess," Connor began. "The two of you spent the night together, and Jess bailed on you first thing this morning."

Will avoided his gaze. "I really do not want to discuss this with you, Connor. How many ways do I have to say that before you get it?"

"Who better to talk to?" Connor said, not the least bit put off. "Nobody understands Jess the way I do. That's her pattern, pal. She dips a toe in the pool, then scampers away before she risks drowning."

"Nice metaphor," Will said. He'd pretty

much figured out the same thing. "Any thoughts on what I should do to fix this?"

"Be patient with her. Keep coming at her. Let her know you're not going anywhere. You'll have to keep doing that till she believes you. Given her history, she's going to be a tough sell."

Will nodded. "Yeah, leaving seems to be a real theme with her. And, to be honest, I get exactly where it's coming from. I'm just not sure there's enough time or patience to convince her I'm not going to abandon her."

"I hope you're wrong about that," Connor said. "I want Jess to be happy. You're my friend. I want you to be happy, too. I'll admit I was skeptical when I first figured out you were interested in her in that way, but I figure if anybody can work with Jess's issues, it would be you. You have all sorts of insights most of us poor mortal males can't begin to figure out."

"Only if she'll let me in," Will said, allowing his discouragement to show. "I don't know, Connor. Maybe I'm out of my depth here, after all."

Connor frowned at him. "If you're willing to give up after one night—"

"It's not one night. I've been in love with her for years."

"But you've only taken her to bed for the first time last night, unless I miss my guess. Come on. You have to know this is just starting. It'll only end if you walk away."

Will sighed. "And if I do that, I'll only be proving her point," he concluded.

"Looks that way to me," Connor said. "Send her flowers."

"Did that." And it had bought him a night with Jess in his bed. He supposed there was a message there. "But I get what you're saying."

"Then you're still in?"

Will grinned, resigned. "Of course. Your job here is done."

Connor chuckled. "What kind of fee do you usually charge for this advice? Should I send you a bill?"

"I'll buy your breakfast," Will said. "If the advice pays off, maybe there will be champagne down the road."

Connor nodded. "I can live with that."

After he'd gone, Will glanced at his watch. He had less than an hour before his first patient of the day. That was just enough time to run down to Ethel's Emporium.

Most women, under these circumstances, could be wooed with fancy chocolates. He happened to know that Jess's sweet tooth could be satisfied with old-fashioned penny candy, the kind she'd been denied as a kid for fear it would contribute to her hyperactivity. As a result, she'd craved it even more, sneaking off to Ethel's the second she received her allowance.

He picked out a colorful metal sand pail, had Ethel fill it with a variety of the candy, dress it up with a big bow, then asked her if she could have it delivered to the inn. Ethel's brows shot up.

"You and Jess?"

Will nodded. "Me and Jess," he confirmed.

"Well, I'll be."

"Keep that to yourself, okay?"

She frowned at the request. "Best gossip I've had in weeks, and you want me to keep quiet about it?"

"I do."

"Well, seeing that it's you, I'll do it," she finally conceded. "You want to send a note with this?"

Will took out his card and scribbled on

the back of it: "No crummy poem this time, just love."

Of course Ethel read it. She laughed. "That'll do."

"I'm so glad you approve," he said wryly.

"Somebody has to give you their blessing. I'm guessing there will be plenty of doubters."

Will sighed. There certainly were, including the woman in question.

Jess sat in the inn's kitchen, a mug of decaf in front of her along with a cheese danish she'd managed to reduce to a mound of crumbs. She was still annoyed with herself for letting Will down earlier. She'd almost chased after him and shown up at Sally's, but at the last minute she'd spotted Connor's car parked on the street right outside and chickened out. She'd been stewing over her cowardice ever since.

Gail walked in, shrugged off her winter coat and hung it on a peg, then caught sight of Jess. Her gaze narrowed.

"Don't you look chipper," she commented. "What's wrong?"

"Not a thing," Jess claimed.

Gail poured herself a cup of decaf, then grimaced when she took a sip. "If you're going to make coffee in my kitchen, could you try not to ruin it? What if a guest got a taste of this?"

"There are no guests up and about yet," Jess said. She waved toward the much larger espresso machine they used for the guests. "Your toy is untouched. Feel free to work your magic. And, by the way, if you hate my coffee so much, you don't have to drink it."

"I'm caffeine-deprived. I took a chance you'd slipped up and made the real thing," Gail said.

Though she began bustling around the kitchen in preparation for pulling together the breakfast menu, she kept casting sideways glances in Jess's direction. Eventually, with the espresso machine filled and sending out a tantalizing aroma, a mountain of eggs at the ready beside the stove, and bacon and sausage on the grill, she fixed herself a second cup of coffee and sat down across from Jess.

"Okay, I'm about to get slammed with

breakfast orders, so make it quick," Gail said. "What happened between you and Will last night to put that glum expression on your face? Did he send you back into the night without giving you what you went over there for?"

Jess scowled at her. "You have such a charming way with words."

"I like to cut to the heart of things. It's one of the qualities you appreciate in me," Gail said, a grin tugging at her lips.

"This morning, not so much," Jess declared.

"You're wasting time, sweet pea. The bacon's sizzling. I need to get back over there and give it my full attention. Talk."

"Okay, here it is in a nutshell. Last night was great. This morning I blew it."

"How so?"

"I wouldn't go with him to Sally's."

Gail chuckled. "Who could blame you?"

"I'm fairly certain Will does. He looked so disappointed in me, Gail. I felt awful. I practically told him I was too ashamed of our relationship to let anyone find out about it. And do you know what's worse? I drove over there, thinking I should just march right in there and make things right with him, but I got scared off because I spotted my brother's car."

This time Gail didn't laugh or even smile. "I have to ask this," she said solemnly. "Are you really that worried about what people, or more specifically your family, will think? Or is this just what you do? You start to get involved, get scared when the emotions are too much, and then dream up any excuse you can to run? Or to invite the other person to dump you?"

Jess hated the characterization, but she had to admit that Gail might be exactly right. Was that what she'd done this morning? Had she intentionally avoided Sally's, knowing it would hurt Will's feelings and, therefore, practically dare him to give up on her?

She moaned and buried her face in her arms. "I am such a mess when it comes to this kind of thing," she muttered. "You'd think I was fifteen, not thirty. It's pathetic."

"It kind of is," Gail agreed, though her tone was gentle. "Maybe it's time you started thinking seriously about making a change."

"Ironically, the person best qualified to

tell me how to do that is Will," Jess said. "Wouldn't that be the icing on the cake? Um, hey, Will, could you help me find a way to stop screwing up my life?"

Gail didn't laugh. "I know you're joking, but maybe that's not such a terrible idea."

Jess frowned. "I am not going to Will for counseling. Wouldn't that make it unethical for him to date me? It would sort of defeat the purpose, don't you think?"

"Interesting that losing Will as a date is the first thing that occurred to you," Gail noted. "But you need to do something before you keep making the same mistake over and over."

"I know you're right," Jess conceded miserably. "I really do."

Just then Ronnie stuck his head into the kitchen. "Is the girl talk over? There are people in the dining room wanting breakfast."

Gail looked at Jess. "You going to be okay?"

"Of course," she said, injecting a cheery note into her voice. "I'm going to be just fine."

Apparently relieved by their responses, Ronnie stepped inside. "This came a few minutes ago. Maybe it will cheer you up," he said, pulling a sand pail with a mountain of penny candy in it from behind his back. He handed it to Jess.

She started smiling even before she looked at the card. Only one person could have found such a perfect gift for her.

"Will?" Gail guessed.

Jess nodded, then laughed when she read the card.

"Seems like you didn't blow it so badly this morning after all," Gail commented. "Second chances don't come along every day, sweet pea. Make the most of this one."

Jess intended to do just that, even if she had to scramble out of her comfort zone to pull it off.

Thomas had managed to get through an entire twenty-four hours without speaking to Connie, but he had to admit he hadn't liked it. He'd turned it into some kind of test for himself, to see if maybe his feelings for her would cool down with even a tiny bit of distance between them. It had been an exercise in futility. She'd stayed front and center in his thoughts anyway.

He couldn't pinpoint why she got to him

the way she did. She was nothing like either of his wives. She was a strong, independent single mom, who was far from the sophisticated kind of women he'd been involved with in the past.

Even though he'd never had kids of his own, he'd been a close observer of the families of both of his brothers. Jeff seemed to have the whole parenting thing down to a calm, easygoing science. Mick's children had been put through the wringer, but thanks in some measure to their grandmother, they'd grown into fine young people.

Bottom line, Thomas knew the kind of work it took to be a rock-solid parent, even if he'd never experienced it himself. He admired Connie's dedication to raising her daughter on her own. Of course, she'd had Jake around to pitch in, but no question, she was the one responsible for the fine young woman Jenny had become.

Connie was a nurturer. Her home was a testament to that. It was the house in which she'd been raised, filled with the warm touches that made it a home. She'd probably never ordered takeout in her life, at least not beyond pizza. He even wondered about that since it had taken her a while the other day to come up with the phone number for the pizza shop in Chesapeake Shores. Thomas had the closest one to his place on speed dial.

"I hate to interrupt the daydreaming," his secretary said when she stepped into his office. "Your brother's here. Should I send him in? You have a half hour before your next appointment."

"Mick's here?" he asked, surprised.

"He said he had something important to discuss with you."

"Then send him in," Thomas said, leaning back in his chair. Mick had only paid one other visit to his office, when he'd been looking for advice about Megan. That had been startling enough. Thomas could hardly wait to hear what had brought him by today.

Mick came in with a scowl etched into the deep lines on his face. Thomas sat up straighter.

"Is there a problem?" he asked at once. "Is anything wrong with Ma?"

Mick waved off the question. "Ma's fine, though I think she's intent on driving me to drink. She keeps making comments about looking for gentlemen callers."

Thomas blinked. "Ma wants to start dating?"

"So she says," Mick reported. "Frankly, I think she does it just to make my blood pressure rise."

"It would probably be good for her," Thomas said thoughtfully, once the initial shock had passed. "She was used to having her days filled with your family. She's probably bored to tears now."

Mick's scowl only deepened. "I didn't come here to talk about Ma's dating plans. I have something to say about yours."

Now it was Thomas's turn to scowl. "Tread carefully, big brother," he warned. "You're heading onto dangerous turf. My social life is none of your concern."

"It is when I hear you're about to make a fool of yourself with some girl who's young enough to be your daughter, a girl who's like part of the family."

Thomas sighed. "So you've heard about Connie and me."

"I have," Mick confirmed. "What do you have to say for yourself?"

"I'm not going to defend myself to you, if that's what you're hoping for. Connie is hardly young enough to be my daughter.

Not even I was that precocious. She's certainly old enough to know her own mind. We've both gone into this with our eyes wide open."

"'This'?" Mick said. "Exactly what is '*this*'?"

"A relationship," Thomas said readily.

"Then it's true. You're having an affair?" he said, his expression incredulous. "What the hell are you thinking?"

"That she makes me happy," Thomas said, refusing to let Mick's attitude rattle him. "And, thanks be to God, I seem to make her happy, too."

"And what about Jake? How's he supposed to feel about you taking advantage of his older sister?"

Thomas frowned at him. "Nobody's taking advantage of anybody. I can assure you of that. As for Jake, he and I have looked each other in the eye and reached an understanding, so I'm guessing the problem is you, not Jake."

"Okay, what if it is? It's wrong. How can you not see that?"

"What I can see is that this is none of your business," Thomas said. "Connie and I aren't flaunting this in anyone's face. We've been discreet."

"And why is that?" Mick demanded. "I'll tell you why. Because even you know you ought to be ashamed of yourself. You're scared Ma will get wind of this and have a stroke."

Thomas stood up, slamming a fist on his desk as he rose. "That's enough, Mick. You may be my older brother, but I won't have you or anyone else trying to turn this into some sleazy, back-alley affair. Nobody respects and admires that woman more than I do. I won't let you insult Connie or me by suggesting what we've found is something tawdry. And leave Ma out of it, too. The only thing she's ever wanted for any of us is that we find happiness."

Mick didn't look appeased. "If you're so all-fired sure that there's nothing wrong with what you're doing, then why haven't you brought it out in the open? You haven't escorted Connie to Sunday dinner, have you?"

"Because this is exactly the kind of re-action I was hoping to avoid," Thomas declared. "I won't have Connie embarrassed, Mick, and apparently that's the only kind of behavior I can expect from you."

For just a moment, Mick looked taken

aback by his vehemence. His gaze narrowed. "You really care about her? Seriously?"

"It's getting to be damned serious," Thomas said, even surprising himself.

Mick nodded slowly, as if absorbing the information. "I see."

"Do you?" Thomas challenged. "I hope so, because I thought you and I were finally starting to make some progress in mending our relationship. I'd hate to see it go off track again, if only for Ma's sake. How'd you find out about this, anyway? It seems clear to me that Jake didn't tell you."

"I overheard Connor and Kevin talking," Mick admitted. "I couldn't believe what I was hearing, so I decided to come straight to the horse's mouth."

"Well, I suppose I should be grateful you came directly to me, instead of talking about it to everyone else in the family," Thomas said grudgingly. "Once all the O'Briens start dissecting the news, it could put so much pressure on Connie it'll scare her off."

"I don't imagine she'd be scared off if you put a ring on her finger," Mick said slyly.

Thomas froze. "An engagement ring?"

The out-of-the-blue thought didn't make him half as nervous as it should have.

"Or you could skip straight to a wedding ring," Mick said. "You're not getting any younger. The two of you could probably still have a kid together, if you got busy in a hurry."

Thomas gave him a wry look. "Thanks for the suggestion."

"I'm just saying—"

"I know what you're saying," Thomas said impatiently. "But I think Connie and I will have to decide the pace of this relationship ourselves."

"Up to you," Mick said agreeably. "You'll bring her to dinner this Sunday." He said it as if it were a foregone conclusion. "Get this out in the open. Connie deserves that kind of openness, especially when it comes to your family."

Thomas couldn't disagree. He was just afraid she'd listen to the invitation, then turn around and run the other way. He could hardly blame her. He wasn't much looking forward to the occasion himself.

"Maybe," he began, hoping to put it off.

"This Sunday," his older brother said. "Or I'll speak to Ma. I imagine she'll give you an earful about showing some respect for a woman we all care about."

That was the last thing Thomas wanted. "We'll be there," he promised.

Or they'd both head to Tahiti for a few months, where there wouldn't be an O'Brien in sight.

"You have to be kidding me," Connie said when Thomas called to tell her there was a command performance scheduled for Sunday.

"I was going to break it to you when I came over on Friday, but I had a feeling you might need a little time to adjust to the idea. Or maybe to flee the country."

"You just didn't want to tell me when there was a cast iron skillet within reach," she retorted.

He laughed. "That, too."

"Thomas, is this what you really want? Are we ready to go public? We're still finding our way."

"I don't think we really have a choice. Half the family already knows. And now that Mick knows, it won't be long before the others do. I don't want anyone to get the idea that we have anything to be ashamed of. I love what's happening between us."

"So do I, but we haven't even defined what it is," she said. "Maybe it's just a fling."

Even as she said it, she held her breath, praying for a denial.

"Connie Collins, is that what you're really thinking?" he demanded, his voice thick with indignation. "You're not the kind of woman to have flings. Surely you know I'm more respectful of you than that."

Relieved by his vehemence, she allowed herself to smile. "I was hoping that's how you felt, but you never know."

"Because of my wild and reckless reputation, you mean?"

"You've been a bachelor for a while now. Maybe that's the lifestyle you want. For all I know, I'm just a convenient dalliance because you've been bored."

"Absolutely not," he said flatly. "Besides, I'm lousy at being a bachelor. I liked being settled down and married, even if I wasn't very good at it."

"Wrong women," she said succinctly.

"Maybe. Or it could have been me. The jury's still out on that."

"I know," she said. "We've only been to-gether, I mean officially together, a couple of weeks now, and I've already seen the kind of man you are. You've been treating me the way any woman wants to be treated."

"Like a queen?" he teased.

"No, like a real partner. I don't just like sleeping with you, Thomas. I like the way you talk with me, the way you share what's going on in your life, the way you ask for my opinion and seem to genuinely care about what I say. That is such a refreshing change for me. I mean, Jake listens to me from time to time, but my ex-husband never did. Jenny's a teenager. She hardly listens to anyone."

"Well, I will always listen because you're smart. I value your insights," he said at once. "I think we make a good team."

Connie sighed. "So do I," she said softly.

"So you'll put on a brave face and go to Sunday dinner with me?"

"I could just meet you there," she suggested, not sure why the thought of walking in the door with him in front of all those ex-pectant looks terrified her so. "Maybe ride over with Jake, Bree and the baby. Then, if things go okay, I could leave with you."

"No way. We do this together, hand-in-hand. Otherwise I might chicken out," he joked.

She laughed. "As if. I think you're anxious to throw this in their faces."

"Not at all," he said, his tone sobering. "I'm anxious to show them that I'm the luckiest guy around."

Connie blinked back unexpected tears. "Sometimes you say the sweetest things."

"Did I make you cry?" he asked worriedly.

"Only for the best possible reason," she said. "You made me feel like the luckiest woman, not just in town, but on the entire East Coast."

And no one had ever, ever done that before. Forget the daunting O'Briens. She could face down an entire firing squad for a man like that.

18

When Will walked out of his office after seeing his last patient, he saw Jess leaning against the fender of his car in the parking lot. She lifted her hand in a tentative wave, then let it drop back to her side.

Will approached slowly, trying not to leap to any conclusions about her presence. "What brings you by?"

"I've come to thank you and to make amends," she said at once.

He didn't pretend not to understand. Instead, he nodded. "Feel like going to dinner? It'll give you time to grovel."

Her wary expression gave way to a grin. "Who said anything about groveling?"

"I think it's the only thing to do under the circumstances," he replied solemnly.

"I guess that's one more thing we can discuss over dinner," she said. "I'm no good at the whole groveling thing. Saying I'm sorry is tough enough. It goes against my nature to admit I was wrong."

"Do you have any idea what you're sorry for?" he asked, curious to find out exactly how she'd explained her actions to herself.

"Absolutely."

"Okay, then, you can tell me that, too. Where would you like to go? Brady's?"

"I think we should reserve Brady's for celebrations. Since this is all about penance, let's go to the French café on Shore Road."

"Seriously?" Will said, surprised. "Why there?"

"Have you ever sat on those chairs?" Jess demanded. "An hour of that is sufficient punishment for just about any crime short of murder. You should hear my dad on the subject. He's quite vocal, since it's apparently Mom's favorite restaurant ever since their honeymoon in Paris. The fact that he goes there because she likes it tells me a lot about how happy he is these days."

Will laughed. "You're crazy."

"Please don't say that," she pleaded. "You're an expert, and I'd have to take you seriously."

He draped an arm over her shoulders and guided her around to the passenger side of his car, then held the door for her. Before closing it, he met her gaze. "I'm glad you came by, Jess."

"Me, too."

"I'd like to kiss you, but it might not be wise, considering we haven't gotten to the groveling yet. It might send a mixed message."

She chuckled. "Now who's the crazy one?"

Ten minutes later, they'd been seated on the café's uncomfortable wooden and metal chairs that were too small for normal human beings, much less a man more than six feet tall. Will had ordered two glasses of wine, then gave the menu a cursory glance. He didn't recognize half of the dishes and so settled on salad and quiche, wincing at Jess's amused look. "Hey, I'm a real man. Eating quiche doesn't scare me," he told her.

"Good to know," she said, then ordered the same thing.

He stretched out his legs in a futile attempt to get comfortable, then looked at Jess. "Okay, anytime you're ready."

"You're not going to make this easy for me, are you?"

"Any reason I should?"

"No," she admitted. "But if you're so mad at me, why'd you send the candy?"

"To make you smile," he said. "And maybe to pile on the guilt."

She gave him a startled look. "Really?"

"I knew you probably started feeling bad about running off five minutes after you did it."

"I did," she said. "And I really am sorry. Mornings after, at least the kind that matter, are new to me. I panicked."

"Of course you did," he said. "The step we took last night was a big one. It probably didn't help that I'd told you there would be no turning back. Asking you to make a public announcement about it by going to Sally's was probably insensitive on my part."

She waved that off. "What you'd said did throw me for a minute, but by this morning I'd convinced myself you didn't really mean it. Men say a lot of things in the heat of the moment."

"I don't." He leveled a look into her eyes. "I meant it, Jess. I'm in this for the long haul. Of course, if you make me sit on these chairs very often, I may not be able to move well enough to ever make love to you again."

"I suppose that just because I deserved to be tortured for treating you the way I did, I shouldn't have subjected you to it," she conceded with what almost sounded like genuine regret. The twinkle in her eye, however, said otherwise. She might have been forced into groveling, but she was making him pay in her own clever way.

She hesitated, then said, "I don't know if that's enough groveling or not, but I need to thank you for the candy, too. Not only did it make me smile, but Ethel's penny candy is the best. It takes me straight back to being a kid, when I had to hide all that sugary junk from Gram. At least now I don't have to sneak them." She opened her purse and pulled out a fistful of individually wrapped candies. "See. I brought my stash with me. If you're good, I'll even consider letting you have one for dessert."

Will chuckled. "I wouldn't dream of taking even one away from you."

Their meals came, and for a moment, they fell silent. Then Will felt compelled to ask, "Are you feeling better now about where we are?"

She paused, her fork in midair. "I'm still scared to death, if that's what you mean. I've never gone all-in with a guy before."

"Just loved 'em and left 'em?" he said.

She nodded. "I don't want to do that with you, Will. I don't want to hurt you."

"You'll only hurt me if you're not honest with me or if you run without giving us a real chance. It's okay to be scared. This is new territory for me, too."

She seemed surprised by that. "Really?"

"I've dated plenty over the years, even had a couple of relationships that could have gone somewhere, but they always ended."

"Why?"

"Because I knew my heart belonged to you," he said candidly. She needed to hear the truth, not some spin designed to protect his ego or to keep her fear at bay. "Up until a few weeks ago, I kept trying to find someone who could make me forget about you, but it was useless. Now I'm going for broke, Jess. I'm going after the woman I want, no-holds-barred."

She looked troubled by his words. "But what if I can't live up to your expectations?"

"The only expectation I have is that you'll give us a fair shot at something that could last. No more running off or hiding because you're scared."

She nodded slowly. "Fair enough." She glanced over at him. "I almost came after you this morning. I got as far as Sally's."

"Why didn't you come in?"

"Connor," she said succinctly.

"You saw your brother with me?"

She shook her head. "I saw his car. That was enough. I wasn't ready to face him, to have him start piecing together what had happened."

"He knows," Will said, then added hurriedly, "I didn't tell him. He figured it out all on his own."

"But you confirmed it?"

"Pretty much. He's the one who told me not to give up."

She regarded him with dismay. "You were going to give up just because I wouldn't go with you this morning? What happened to being all-in?"

"My ego," he conceded. "Or maybe fear that you'd never be ready for a real relationship. Then Connor made me see that turning my back on you now would only prove what you believed all along, that nothing lasts, that everyone walks away and promises mean nothing."

"I see. I guess I owe my brother, after all. Who knew Connor would be the one to come up with really helpful advice?"

"I would have come to the same conclusion on my own," Will assured her. "It was just a momentary lapse of faith." He reached for her hand, enfolded it in his. "Then I reminded myself that anything worth having is worth fighting for, Jess. A future with you? It's worth just about anything."

"No matter how much trouble I am?" she asked, the wistful note in her voice telling him that she'd gone back in time to Megan's departure.

He brought her hand to his lips. "You could never be too much trouble. Not for me."

"There's a good chance I'm going to test that," she warned him. "Probably over and over again."

He smiled. "I'm ready for that."

And he was. Today was the last time he was going to let doubts overrule his heart, even for a minute.

Though Jess was relieved to have cleared the air with Will, she knew that every day was likely to present a new challenge. She'd spent too many years doubting herself to suddenly believe that she was totally one hundred percent lovable. She also recognized that she was going to have to continue to make some overtures herself, prove to Will and herself that she was truly ready for whatever the future might hold between them.

Though she hadn't seen Will since earlier in the week, she'd spoken to him several times. She knew he'd been spending a lot of time at the hospital with a troubled patient and playing catch-up with the Lunch by the Bay business. She'd suggested he hire someone to do some of the matchmaking work, but he insisted he needed to be hands-on with the process, at least until he was satisfied that his system was valid.

On Saturday, frustrated at not having snagged even a few minutes with him, she called his cell phone.

"Where are you?"

"In my office."

"Obviously not with a patient, right?"

"No, I'm busy playing matchmaker."

"Maybe you should be worrying more about your own love life," she teased.

"For a woman who wasn't sure she even wanted to date me, you sure are getting to be demanding," he replied, his voice laced with humor.

"I've never had a real boyfriend before, at least not the kind who's declared himself, not one I could take home to my parents. I'm thinking maybe it's time for you and me to make this official, in front of all the O'Briens at once."

Will fell silent at the suggestion. "Official?" he said eventually.

Jess laughed at the startled note in his voice. "I'm not suggesting we hit them with an engagement, Will. Just that we show up together for dinner tomorrow. Most of them have guessed about us, anyway. Let's just get this public announcement thing over with."

"You know that's likely to unleash even more pressure," he said.

"I've thought about that. Meddling is just what they do. I can take it. The only thing that really matters is how we feel, right?"

"Right," he agreed readily. "And if you're feeling that comfortable with the way things are, then tomorrow works for me."

"Really?" Now she was the one surprised. She'd half expected more resistance, more caution.

"Of course. If you're ready for the questions, I certainly am."

She laughed. "Actually, there's a reason I picked tomorrow for our debut. Fewer questions."

"Why's that?"

"Connie and Thomas are making their first appearance as a couple. I figure we'll just be a background footnote."

"You're a far more devious woman than I'd realized. I like your plan. Shall I pick you up at noon?"

"How about eleven-thirty? I don't want to miss their arrival, just in case people faint."

"Do you really think anyone's going to be that shocked?" he asked. "I've heard the word on the street. Of course, maybe that's just because Jake came to lunch reeling when he found out. And Kevin and Connor have known for a while. Who do you think hasn't figured it out?"

"Well, the way I hear it, Dad knows. That means Mom knows. Shanna and Heather are in on it and have been almost from the beginning, even before Thomas and Connie were admitting it to each other. I'm not sure about Abby and Trace. I doubt they're in on the secret. And Uncle Jeff's family's probably in the dark, unless Mack said something to Susie. I suppose the real question mark is Gram."

"Seems to me she's used to having surprises thrown her way," Will said.

"But she's always had strong opinions about divorce. Not only has Thomas divorced twice, but Connie's divorced, too. Gram's liable to head straight off to church to pray for their souls. It's going to upset her, Will." She hesitated. "Maybe I should warn her, so she's not caught off guard."

"Sweetie, it's not your secret to share," Will reminded her. "I've watched your grandmother take a lot of hits over the years and bounce right back. I think she'll surprise us all and give them her blessing."

"What makes you say that?" she asked, curious to understand his rationale.

"Your grandmother's lived a long time. She's seen just about everything, and she's far more tolerant than judgmental, even when it comes to the things she believes in deeply, like her religion."

"You could be right," Jess conceded. "But bring some smelling salts, just in case."

Will chuckled. "Will do. And if I dig my way out from under all these Lunch by the Bay applications, I'll give you a call later tonight or stop by. Otherwise, I'll see you tomorrow at eleven-thirty."

"I'm counting on it," she said.

And as she hung up the phone, she realized it was one of the few times she'd counted on anything without holding back a part of herself in anticipation of someone letting her down.

Mick's gaze narrowed when he saw Will walking up the path with Jess, her hand held securely in his.

"You two are getting mighty brave," Mick said.

Jess gave him a surprisingly contented look. "We're working on things. Stay out of it."

Mick laughed. "I got that message the other night, and if it hadn't sunk in then, your mother's been repeating it just about daily."

"I guess Mom is a better influence on you than I realized. I'll have to thank her."

Mick held out his hand to Will. "Good to see you again."

Will chuckled. "You, too, sir. Since you're waiting out here on the porch, I gather the main attraction hasn't arrived yet."

"If you're talking about my brother, you're right," Mick said. "Wouldn't put it past him to take the coward's way out and stay away, or try to sneak past me and go in the kitchen door."

Jess frowned. "He'll be here, Dad, with Connie. And I don't think they're going to be sneaking around. I hope you're not going to create problems for them."

"Hey, I'm the one who pushed him to get things out in the open. No reason to make that girl feel they need to hide their relationship."

"Does Gram know what's going on?" Jess asked worriedly.

Mick shook his head. "I thought about saying something, but your mother told me to stay out of that, too. Dang woman won't let me meddle anymore, leastways not half as much as I'd like to."

Jess's expression brightened. "Now I really do have to thank her. Where is she?"

"In the kitchen trying to help your grandmother. As usual, though, Ma has her own way of doing things. I don't know what happened to that plan they had for the rest of you to pitch in with bringing things for Sunday dinner, but as near as I can tell, Ma's taken over again. I said something about it the other day, and she nearly snapped my head off."

"I'm sure she did," Jess said. "Gram needed a bit of a break, but she wasn't really ready to give up the reins of being matriarch of this family. Either that, or maybe she realized that most of the rest of us are absolutely hopeless in the kitchen. I'll go in and see if she'll let me do anything."

"Go at your own risk," Mick said. "Will, you want to join me out here on the porch? Feels like we're having a bit of Indian summer today. Who knows how long we'll be able to enjoy the outdoors before winter sets in for good."

He noticed that Jess cast a worried look at Will and was about to step in to rescue him, but Will gave a slight shake of his head. "I'll stay with your dad. Since he's sworn off meddling with the family, maybe I can convince him to help me by becoming a matchmaker at Lunch by the Bay."

Mick frowned at him. "What the devil is that?"

"It's my computerized dating service," Will explained. "I'll tell you all about it. You might have some ideas for things that can be added to the compatibility test."

Jess laughed outright at that, but Mick had to admit he was intrigued. He waved off his daughter. "Go on. I want to hear about this. I am the expert in this family, after all. I'm sure Will can benefit from what I've learned over the years."

"Dad, you're a meddler, not an expert," Jess corrected.

"Look around you, young lady. Your brothers and your sisters are all happily married, aren't they?"

"And you're taking credit for that?"

"Of course I am!" Mick said indignantly.

Jess shook her head, her expression filled with barely concealed amusement. Then she stood on tiptoe and kissed Will's cheek. "Call if you need rescuing."

"I won't," Will assured her.

After she'd gone, Mick sat down in his favorite rocker. "Things seem to be good between you two," he commented, not even trying to hide how pleased he was by that. He'd been worried about Jess for a long time, but Will was exactly the kind of solid, no-nonsense guy he would have chosen for her.

"Like Jess said, we're working things out," Will replied. "She has a lot of baggage to overcome."

"Her mother leaving," Mick said. "And me being gone so much."

Will looked surprised. "That's it, exactly."

"I regret that I wasn't more tuned in to her back then, to any of the kids, for that matter. I made a bad situation worse for all of them. Believe me, I know what a blessing it is that most of them have forgiven me."

"You've been making strides with Jess, too. I see how she's more relaxed with you now than she used to be. She's not on edge every second, expecting you to judge her."

"You're right, but it hasn't happened with Megan," Mick said ruefully. "Those two are still dancing around each other like boxers waiting to see who's going to throw the first punch. I thought when Megan and I gave Jess that fancy stove for the kitchen at the inn before it opened, she'd start to make peace with her mother, but it's been slow going. One minute they're okay, the next Jess gets her back up over the littlest things."

"That'll change," Will said confidently. "Especially with Megan trying to keep you out of our business. Jess will appreciate that."

Mick chuckled. "Why do you think I told her? She needs to see that her mother's on her side, always has been, even when she was gone. It just about killed Megan to leave all the kids behind, but especially Jess. She had so many problems then, and none of us knew why. Took us way too long to get a proper diagnosis, partly because I didn't want to hear that there was anything wrong with one of my kids. Made me feel like even more of a failure as a parent."

"It's in the past, Mick, and nothing you did created the problem. Stop beating yourself up over it. In the end, you got her help. And Jess has learned to compensate for her ADD. She's made all sorts of adjustments to manage it, even without resorting to medication. Personally, I think you were wise to try other things first. She had a mild case and doctors are sometimes too quick to give kids pills, rather than trying alternative therapies. She'll always have the occasional slip, I'm sure, but look at everything she's accomplished. It's even more impressive, because of what she had to overcome to get there."

"I couldn't be prouder," Mick acknowledged. "And before you ask, I have told her that. I tell her all the time. One of these days, I pray she'll start to believe me."

Will gave him a nod of understanding. "I'm hoping for the same thing when it comes to my feelings for her. She doesn't trust them yet, but I plan to stick around until she does."

Mick liked the young man's openness. He always had. "You need any help, you'll let me know?"

Will smiled. "You'll be the first."

Mick fell silent for a minute, then turned to Will. "Enough about Jess for now. Tell me about this matchmaking thing. You actually have a way to see if people are compatible on a computer?"

"I think I do," Will said readily, his expression animated. "I've only been offering the service for a couple of months now. We've had one marriage already, which frankly I thought came way too fast, but a few other couples have hit it off as well."

Mick thought about the potential of such a thing. "You signed Susie up yet? I think it's time she left Mack in the dust. The man should have made his move by now."

"Susie hasn't asked for my help. As for Mack, I know he's crazy about her."

"He has a strange way of showing it," Mick said, then glanced up just in time to see Connie and Thomas walking toward them. His brother leaned down to whisper something in her ear that wiped the panicky expression from her face. Connie beamed up at him, her eyes shining.

"Well, will you look at that?" Mick murmured. "I had my doubts, but it looks as if there's something special going on there, after all."

"Seems that way to me, too, sir," Will said.

Mick stood up, shook his brother's hand, then kissed Connie's cheek. "Glad you could make it."

Connie looked him square in the eye. "I was under the impression it was a command performance."

Mick chuckled. "I suppose it was, at that. I figured you turning up here with this brother of mine would show what the two of you are made of. Come on inside. You're here before most of the others, so there's only the hurdle of telling Ma what's going on."

"I think I'll do that on my own and out of the earshot of the rest of the family," Thomas said. "Especially you."

Connie looked up at him, her jaw set determinedly. "Hold on, Thomas. I thought we were in this together."

"We are," Thomas said, regarding her with concern. "I thought it would be easier on you if I paved the way."

"The day I fell for you, I gave up on easy," she said wryly.

Mick regarded her with delight, then slapped his brother on the back. "I'm beginning to get why this works. You've found a woman who doesn't pull any punches."

"Indeed, she doesn't," Thomas said, smiling down at her. "Let's go, then."

"I brought smelling salts," Will said, then shrugged at Thomas's startled expression. "Jess's idea. She's in the kitchen, too. Tell her to come get me if you need 'em."

Thomas frowned at him. "Just what this family needs, another wiseass. I thought Mick had a lock on that territory."

Mick laughed heartily. "I might have once, but it seems the next generation is following in my footsteps nicely!"

19

Despite the brave show she'd put on for Mick, Connie's knees were knocking together as she and Thomas approached Nell O'Brien's domain. Though she'd been in the kitchen dozens of times before, she had a feeling this time was going to decide whether she really belonged.

Thomas gave her a sympathetic look and squeezed her hand. "Ready?"

She gave him a shaky smile. "As I'll ever be."

She was about to push the door open, when he held her back. "Maybe I should make one thing clear before we go in there."

"What's that?" she asked tremulously.

"No matter what my mother says, no matter how she reacts or what objections she raises, nothing changes between us. We're solid."

"Don't say that, Thomas. We're talking about your mother. You may be a grown man who's lived his own life for years now, but I know Nell's opinion still matters to you. You wouldn't be the person you are if it didn't."

"That may be so," he agreed. "But you matter, too. What we have is new, and we still have things to work out, but this isn't some passing fling. I'm not going to bolt if there's the least sign of disapproval. I just want you to believe that."

She touched his cheek, then withdrew her hand. "I want to," she said wistfully, then forced a smile. "Now let's do this, before I turn tail and run."

Thomas laughed. "You've never run from a challenge in your life. I'd stake my bank account on that."

"Don't be so sure it couldn't happen now. I've never faced anything quite like this. Nell's a formidable woman."

He smiled. "We're talking about Ma. She

barely comes up to your shoulder. You can take her."

She gave him a horrified look. "As if I'd try."

He laughed. "I'm just saying, there's nothing to be scared of here."

Then, before she could drag in a deep enough breath to steady her nerves, he pushed open the kitchen door and strode inside, her hand still securely in his. If he noticed she was lagging a bit behind, safely in his shadow, he didn't turn to protest. Across the kitchen, Jess offered a supportive smile.

"Hi, everyone," Thomas boomed in his heartiest voice. He went straight to his mother and kissed her cheek. "Ma." He looked her over. "You look well."

Nell gave him a suspicious look, then caught sight of Connie hovering behind him. "I imagine you've come to tell me that the two of you are getting serious about each other," she said, her expression giving nothing away about what she thought of that.

"We have," Thomas said, drawing Connie up to stand beside him. "Though how you've figured that out is beyond me."

"I learned to read my sons a very long time ago. This handwriting has been on the wall for some time now." She turned toward Megan. "And if it hadn't been, Megan and Mick would have given it away with all their whispering when they thought I wasn't paying attention."

Megan cast an apologetic look toward Connie and Thomas. "Sorry. For once, we actually thought we were being discreet."

Thomas just chuckled. "Mick should have known better. He, Jeff and I all knew Ma had supernatural hearing and eyesight. When we were boys, we never got away with a blessed thing." His gaze returned to his mother. "So, how do you feel about this? I know it might seem complicated or unorthodox since I'm a few years older and have some baggage, but Connie doesn't seem to mind that."

"I have plenty of baggage of my own," Connie was quick to add, then held her breath to await Nell's verdict.

Nell looked from her son to Connie and back again. "You know my beliefs about divorce," she said, her tone stern. "That said, I've never believed I could or should try to impose my beliefs on you, Thomas. I raised you and your brothers to think for yourselves and to follow your hearts. Connie's a fine woman. If she makes you happy and you do the same for her, it's not for me to object."

She opened her arms to Connie, then kissed her cheek. "You've been like a daughter around here for a long time now. I hope this son of mine makes that legal one of these days." Then she took Connie's hand in hers, gave it a reassuring squeeze. "If he gives you one bit of trouble, you come to me. He may be too big for me to throttle, but I have my ways of bringing him into line."

Connie felt relief wash through her. Tears stung her eyes. This was far more support than she'd expected. "Thank you so much, Mrs. O'Brien. I'll be sure to do that."

"It's to be Nell now," his mother stated emphatically.

Thomas listened to the exchange and feigned a scowl. "You are not to be teaming up with my mother against me," he told Connie indignantly.

She laughed. "I won't," she assured him. "As long as you don't give me any reason to."

Nell joined in her laughter, as did Megan and Jess, the tension in the room a thing of the past.

"You'll definitely do, girl," Nell said approvingly. "I knew you were a wonderful sister and a strong mother, but it seems you're more than capable of taking on a man like my son."

"She is," Thomas confirmed, his gaze on her warm. "Now, if you don't mind, I need to go have the last laugh on Mick. He thought this wasn't going to go half so well."

Nell scowled. "You're not going to start another one of those wars with your brother, are you?" she demanded.

"Nope, just a little gloating, I promise," he told her, giving her a hug that lifted her off the floor. "Connie, you coming with me?"

"I think I'll stay here," she said, once again feeling at home in this kitchen with these women who'd always felt like family to her and now, just maybe, were going to be. At least if things with Thomas kept on progressing the way they seemed to be.

Something about the whole exchange between Connie, Thomas and her grandmother had made Jess yearn for the kind of approval that had just been doled out so readily to her friend. She knew it was crazy, but she suddenly wanted her mother's blessing for her relationship with Will, something she'd never expected to yearn for. After all, she'd lived a lot of years without Megan's approval. Ever since her mother's return, she'd taken pride in keeping her at arm's length most of the time. Why would she suddenly want to change that now?

As Nell took Connie under her wing and talked her through the ingredients in one of Thomas's favorite dishes, Jess turned impulsively to Megan. "Could we talk?"

Since it was one of the few conversations between them that Jess had initiated, her mother looked surprised by the request.

"Of course we can. Let's take a walk outside and enjoy this wonderful weather." She turned to her mother-in-law. "Nell, can you spare us for a bit?"

"Sure. Connie's here to help with anything I need, and the others will be here soon."

After they'd left through the kitchen door and were walking across the lawn toward the bay, Jess nodded in the direction of the house. "Did you expect things to turn out that way?"

"Not really," Megan admitted. "But Nell's always been full of surprises."

"She seems happy that I've been seeing more of Will lately," Jess said, broaching the topic tentatively.

Megan smiled. "We all are. He's good for you, I think. How about you? What do you think?"

"For a long time I thought it was really annoying that he could read me so well. I accused him of trying to analyze me all the time."

"And now?"

"It's actually kind of nice to be with a man who really gets me," Jess admitted.

Megan nodded. "It is, isn't it?"

"Is that how it is with you and Dad?"

Her mother chuckled. "Oh, sweetie, it's taken us years to get to that place. We certainly weren't in tune when you kids were younger. You know that's the main reason I left, so believe me, I know exactly how important it is to be able to communicate with a spouse, to have them understand what makes you tick."

"And Dad does that now?" Jess asked skeptically.

Her mother's expression turned thoughtful. "He tries, and I can't ask more than that. And I've learned to speak up, something I never did back then. I think we both learned a lot while I was gone. I think we matured, probably in ways we wouldn't have if I'd just stuck it out and stayed miserable."

She faced Jess, tucked a windblown curl behind her ear in a tender, motherly gesture that almost brought tears to Jess's eyes. That mother's touch was something she'd longed for so deeply as a child. More than once, she'd thought she'd never experience it again. Abby's attempts to fill in, well-meant as they had been, had fallen short. Gram's had come closer, but she still hadn't been Megan.

"Why so introspective today?" Megan asked gently. "Are things moving along too quickly with Will?"

Jess surprised herself by nodding. "We're together, physically," she said. "And that's great, but emotionally I feel like I'm still trying to catch up. He's made it clear that he's in love with me, and has been for years. I'm not sure what to do with that."

Megan looked troubled. "You don't have to do anything you're not ready for. Is he pressuring you in some way?"

"No," Jess admitted. "He's being amazingly patient, but I feel guilty that I don't trust my own emotions yet. I have all these new and totally unexpected feelings, and I don't know how to handle them."

"You're scared," Megan concluded. "Of what? Of being hurt? Being left?"

Jess nodded. "It's not as if it hasn't happened before," she said, unable to keep a bitter note from her voice.

"Me," Megan said. "Oh, sweetie, you have to know how deeply I regret what happened, and the impact it had on you. There are so many things I wish I'd done differently back then. I wish I'd taken you with me on the day I left, instead of waiting. By the time I was ready to bring all of you to New York, you wouldn't even speak to me on the phone. I let your father convince me you were better off here, in familiar surroundings."

"I guess I understand why you did it, but back then I hated you," Jess admitted. "I felt betrayed. I was only seven, and you didn't even say goodbye. You left Abby to break it to all of us that you'd gone."

"That was unfair to you and to her," Megan admitted candidly. "I've done everything I can think of to make it up to each of you. I will tell you how sorry I am forever, if that's what it takes." She looked into Jess's eyes. "Will that ever be enough?"

"I don't know," Jess said. "I want it to be. I want it to be behind me, so I can move forward, not just with Will, but with anyone. I'm not sure it's possible for a kid to seal off her heart, but I think that's exactly what I did. I'm terrified to feel that way again."

"So you don't trust anyone," Megan said sorrowfully.

"Not a hundred percent, no. I've even been cautious with Abby, Bree, Kevin and Connor. They left, too. Oh, the circumstances were obviously different, but I still felt left behind. I resented them for a time, too, though I know they didn't deserve it. They had their own lives to live, just like you did."

"Oh, sweetie, you have no idea how awful that makes me feel," Megan said, her eyes brimming with tears.

Jess thought she'd come out here to get her mother's approval of her relationship with Will, but she realized now it was to air all of this old anger and bitterness. She and her mother had been tiptoeing around each other ever since Megan had come back to Chesapeake Shores a few years back. There had been peace, but not reconciliation.

Jess recognized that it was time either to let go of the past, or accept that they would never share the bond of mother and daughter again. She realized how desperately she wanted that bond, and the only way to have it was to forgive.

Swallowing hard, she stared into her mother's tear-filled eyes, saw the genuine pain, and somehow her heart released the last of the anger she'd felt for so many years.

"I want things between us to get better," Jess whispered. "I want my mom back."

Megan opened her arms and Jess walked into them. "I'm right here, sweetie. I'm right here."

They were both openly crying when Mick found them to announce that Sunday dinner was on the table.

"Everything okay here?" he asked worriedly.

"Everything's good," Megan assured him, a catch in her voice.

He looked toward Jess, awaiting her answer.

She couldn't seem to squeeze a word past the lump in her throat, but she nodded.

Mick gave a nod of satisfaction, then left them to make their way back to the house on their own.

Jess knew the reconciliation, so long in coming, would be bumpy, but today had been a good start. Linking arms with her mother, she slanted a look at her.

"Quite a day, huh?"

Megan smiled, her cheeks still damp. "The very best," she agreed. "I finally feel as if I have my family whole again."

Ever since they'd sat down at dinner, Will had been watching Jess, lines of worry etched on his face. Jess had tried smiling to reassure him, but he didn't seem to buy the smiles or her upbeat chitchat with the rest of the family. As soon as dinner and the cleanup had been completed, he snagged her hand.

"How about heading back to the inn?" he suggested. "You can show me the progress your dad has made on the attic."

"You're going to be amazed," she told

him, as eager to be alone with him as he seemed to be with her. "The windows are in and the views are fantastic. Let's go."

"Sneaking out?" Abby inquired, looking amused when she caught them leaving through the kitchen door.

"Nobody's sneaking," Jess said indignantly. "Everybody's busy. They won't even notice we've left."

"Only reason I know to slip out without saying goodbye is because you don't want anybody asking what you're off to do," Abby teased. "As your big sister, it's my duty to ask."

"And as your very independent sister, I'll tell you it's none of your business," Jess retorted. "You have plenty of other siblings to watch over like the mother hen you've always been. Go interfere in their lives."

Abby laughed. "What am I going to do now that even you are too grown up for me to boss around?"

"Believe me, Caitlyn and Carrie will be teenagers soon enough," Jess reminded her. "You'll have your hands full with those two."

"Don't remind me," Abby said. "Thank goodness for Trace. They actually listen to him. Their father and I are considered the enemies already."

"Maybe it's time for you to think about adding to your family," Jess said, broaching a subject that almost no one else had dared. "I know Trace would love to have a baby or two of his own. Have you considered it?"

Abby's expression froze. "Now it's my turn to tell you to butt out," she retorted.

The unexpectedly sharp tone of voice told Jess that she'd stumbled into something very touchy. "Will, why don't you wait for me outside?" she suggested, determined not to drop the topic now that it had been raised.

When he'd gone without comment, she turned a penetrating look on her sister. "Okay, what's going on?"

Abby frowned. "Didn't I just tell you to leave it alone?"

"You know I never do what I'm told. Sit down and talk to me. Is there a problem?"

Abby sat, but she avoided Jess's gaze. "Not with me getting pregnant, if that's what you mean. We haven't been trying."

Now Jess knew she was treading on tricky turf. It might be easier to back down, but she thought about what Abby would do if the situations were reversed. She'd push until the other person got a troubling subject out into the open.

"Why not?" she asked her sister.

"You know what happened when I had the twins," Abby said. "Wes immediately wanted me to quit work and stay home."

"And you're scared Trace will do the same thing?"

Abby nodded, looking miserable. "No matter how many times he swears to me it will never happen, I'm scared to death he's kidding himself. I'm afraid that once a new baby's here, he's going to balk at me going off to work in Baltimore every day. And then what? We start fighting all the time? Wind up divorced the way Wes and I did? I love my career. I've worked hard to get where I am."

Jess gave her sister's hand a squeeze. "Of course you have. I don't think you're giving Trace half enough credit, though. He actually likes being a stay-at-home dad to the girls. He can do his work at home. There's no reason for him to insist that you be there, too. He's not Wes, and the situations just aren't the same."

Abby sniffed, found one of the ever-present tissues in her pocket and blew her nose. "That's what he says," she conceded.

"Oh, sweetie, I certainly have a mountain of trust issues of my own, but even I can see that Trace has never given you a single reason to doubt him."

"I do know that," Abby said.

"Then keep talking. Don't let this drag on until it's too late and all the options are gone."

"Yeah, the ticking of my biological clock is pretty loud these days." When she met Jess's gaze, her expression remained troubled. "I can't help wondering if it's more than the whole Wes thing."

Jess regarded her with surprise. "Such as?"

"I was just seventeen when Mom left. I took over with all of you. In some ways, I feel as if I've had not just the twins, but four other kids. Maybe that's enough for me."

Jess had never considered the toll Abby's sense of responsibility toward all of them might have taken on her. "Then you need to talk that out with Trace, too. Here's what I see, though. You're a great mom despite your career. Trace is a fantastic stepfather, but the two of you should have at least one kid together." She grinned. "But, hey, my opinion isn't the one that counts."

"Actually, your perspective is helping. Trace and I have been over this so many times, I feel as if we're talking in circles."

"Then I'll add one more thing. Maybe once you have one baby and see how smoothly it goes, you'll even have a couple more. That big old house he bought for you should be filled up with kids." She touched her sister's cheek. "I know from experience how blessed they'd be."

Abby gave her a watery smile. "Thanks for the pep talk. You're pretty smart."

"I'll bet I'm not telling you anything your husband hasn't already said. Listen to him, big sis. Trace loves you, and he would never, ever do anything to take your work away from you. He understands that it's a big part of who you are. Better yet, he's going to be right there with diaper duty and all the other demands of raising a family. You'll have a partner."

"I know you're right," Abby said. "*He's* right. I just get these flashbacks, you know?"

"Believe me, I know," Jess said.

Abby sighed heavily. "Okay, your work

here is done," she said, waving Jess off. "Go with Will and do whatever it is the two of you are going to do."

"Not that we need your permission," Jess said wryly, "but thanks."

Jess found Will waiting patiently for her just outside the kitchen door. "How much did you overhear?" she asked.

He didn't bother trying to deny that he'd heard most of it. "It's a complex situation," he said carefully. "But you gave her good advice."

"The same thing you would have told her?"

He smiled. "Pretty much. Not that she asked me. You have good instincts when it comes to other people, Jess. You should start listening to some of your own advice, especially when it comes to choosing the people you can trust."

She lifted her eyes to meet his. "Intellectually I know I can trust you, Will. It's just this gut of mine. It hasn't quite made the leap."

"But you did make some kind of progress today with your mother, didn't you? I saw it on both of your faces when you came inside to dinner. You looked lighter, and whenever Megan glanced your way, she looked happier than I've seen her in a while."

Jess nodded. "It was kind of huge, actually. I had this big argument with myself about letting go of the anger, or holding on to it and never having the kind of mother-daughter relationship I've been missing all these years. I decided I'd been punishing not just her, but me, by withholding my affection and forgiveness."

He smiled at her. "So you let it go."

"I did. It was pretty amazing, actually. I made the decision, and it was like it all just vanished in a puff of smoke. I'm sure it's not really going to be that easy, but it was a start, Will."

"A great one," he agreed. "One of these days I hope you'll be able to do that with me, just decide I'm one of the good guys and open up your heart to me."

"Maybe I'll try having another one of those stern talks with myself and see what happens," she said, not entirely in jest. "In the meantime, I like where we are."

"Which is?" he asked.

She frowned at the question. "You don't know?"

"I want to hear your interpretation."

"Together. A couple. Friends finding our way toward something more," she said. "I don't know how else to put it."

He leaned down and pressed a kiss to her lips. "That'll do for a start."

The kiss, chaste though it was, stirred something inside her. It went way beyond friendly.

As they got closer to the inn, she slanted a look toward him. "This friendship thing," she said casually. "I'm thinking it still needs to have benefits."

Will regarded her with amusement. "Is that so?"

"What do you think?"

"Since you've lured me over here and I haven't objected, I think the benefit package is definitely open for discussion."

"Then isn't it a good thing that my room is even closer than the attic?" she said. "Better yet, it has a very comfortable bed."

"All an important part of the negotiations," Will agreed. "One question, is the bed an antique?"

"No, why?"

"Squeaky springs."

Jess laughed. "It doesn't matter. The last of the guests checked out hours ago. If we change our minds and decide to make love on the staircase, there's nobody left to be shocked by our behavior."

Will looked a little too intrigued by the idea. "The staircase, huh? And the foyer? What about the kitchen?"

"All to ourselves," she said, laughing. She met his gaze. "What on earth do you have in mind?"

"You'll see," he promised, a wicked glint in his eyes.

"It's going to be quite an afternoon, isn't it?" she asked, her breath catching in her throat and her pulse kicking up a notch or two . . . or five.

"I most definitely hope so," he agreed, grabbing her hand and leading her inside, then locking the front door behind them. "No point in taking chances on the arrival of unexpected guests."

Jess laughed. "Who knows? It could draw in an entirely different clientele."

"The door stays locked," he said firmly, but that was the very last cautious thing he did.

From that point on, he showed a reck-less abandon that matched anything Jess had ever aspired to, proving yet again that they were an astonishing match, even without a Lunch by the Bay computerized stamp of approval to back it up.

20

Jess was in her office Monday morning, daydreaming about her incredible night with Will, when Gail came in, her expression tense. Since Gail was the kind of woman who rarely let anything rattle her, Jess immediately sat up straighter.

"Something's wrong," Jess said at once. "What is it?"

"Apparently our order for this week slipped through the cracks," Gail said, her tone filled with annoyance. "What happened?"

Jess felt her stomach sink. "What are you talking about? I know I called it in. I always call it in on Friday."

"Well, you didn't last week," Gail said. "When the truck didn't turn up first thing this morning, I called the food distributor. They had no record of an order being placed on Friday. I know I filled it out for you before I went home on Thursday and left it here on your desk. You were supposed to place it first thing Friday."

"I did," Jess insisted, trying to sort through the papers on her desk to find it. The clutter was so disorganized it was almost impossible to find anything. "I called it in, then put the original back in the kitchen afterward, like always. I'm sure of it."

"It's not there," Gail said, not even trying to hide her increasing impatience. "Keep looking. I'm sure it's buried there somewhere."

Just then Jess found the order, without her usual checkmark and initials to indicate the task had been completed. She uttered a curse. "I'm so sorry, Gail. I'll call it in right now. Maybe they can still get it here this afternoon."

"They can and they will. I always keep my own copy, so I gave it to them when I called." The tension in her shoulders finally eased and she sat down opposite Jess.

"I'm sorry for coming in here so angry, but I was just so darn frustrated when I had to scramble to figure out what I could put on today's lunch menu with what we had in stock."

"You shouldn't have to do that," Jess told her apologetically. "This was my fault, Gail. It won't happen again."

"Yes, it will," Gail said more gently. "Look, Jess, I know we decided a while back it would be best if you actually placed the orders, but maybe that's not such a good idea. Maybe we should go back to the way it was in the beginning, with me handling it, then giving you a weekly report for the accountant."

Jess hated retreating to the system Abby had initiated after the threatened foreclosure disaster, but how could she argue? "That would probably be best," she conceded. "I thought I'd developed my own system for keeping track of things. I thought it was working."

"It has been until lately," Gail agreed. "I don't know if it's this thing with Will that has you distracted or if you're getting bored with all the details around here or what. But this isn't the first time you've slipped up."

"It's the first time I've forgotten to place an order," Jess protested.

"True," Gail said. "But the maid had to scramble a couple of weeks back because the laundry service hadn't been notified we needed extra linens because of a heavy guest turnover. And Ronnie had to pacify a guest who'd asked for a room on the first floor, only to find he'd been put upstairs. You'd taken the reservation, but hadn't made a note of it. Remember those incidents?"

Years of hearing a litany of her mistakes didn't make it one bit easier for Jess to hear these. The same acid churned in her stomach. "I'm sorry," she apologized yet again.

"I know that," Gail said. "And we've all tried to make allowances—"

Jess cut her off heatedly, "Because of the ADD. I don't want anybody making excuses for me, Gail. I should have a handle on this. It's not rocket science, for heaven's sake, and I'm the one in charge."

Gail immediately looked alarmed by her frustrated outburst. "We're not judging you."

"Of course not," Jess said bitterly. "Nobody ever judges poor, messed-up Jess.

They just cover for her or work around her, whatever it takes to get the job done."

"Nobody's judging you, Jess, or covering for you, for that matter. It's not as if Abby's been over here questioning us to see if you're doing everything perfectly. She has confidence in you these days, and so do we."

Though Gail sounded sincere, her words didn't make Jess feel any better.

"I swear to you I'm only bringing this to your attention because you didn't seem to be aware of it," Gail said, clearly trying to smooth her ruffled feathers. "I thought maybe you could fix it, maybe make an adjustment of some kind before something more serious happens."

Jess sighed. "I'm sorry. Again. I shouldn't be taking my frustration out on you. You're only the messenger. I will deal with this, Gail. And, yes, take over placing the orders yourself again. I have no idea why I've gotten so lax recently. It's not Will. I am sure of that."

"May I ask you something then?" Gail asked hesitantly.

"Sure."

"Are you still happy running the inn? Do you think you've lost focus because there aren't any new challenges to tackle?"

Jess regarded her with surprise. "What makes you ask that?"

"When I took the job here and you and Abby told me about the ADD, I read up about it on the internet. Sometimes when things get to be too routine, boredom sets in. Has that happened for you?"

Instead of taking offense that Gail had been studying her disorder, Jess thought about what she was suggesting. Was it true? Was she more distracted lately because she was tired of the same routine now that things were running relatively smoothly? It was certainly true that there weren't the kind of daily challenges she'd faced when she was trying to get the place up and running. Back then, there'd been something new every day to keep her on her toes. Of course, then her crime, according to Abby, had been making too many expensive, impulsive purchases without regard for any sort of budget.

"You could be right," she admitted slowly. "I took on fixing up the attic for that very reason, but then Dad took over all the work, so I haven't even had that to occupy my time."

"Do you want to sell this place?" Gail asked. "Move on to something new?"

"Absolutely not," Jess said, as sure of that as she was of anything. "The Inn at Eagle Point was always my dream. Will reminded me of that just recently. And I do love this place. Running it, seeing everything I envisioned fall into place . . . Gail, it's the happiest I've ever been."

"Then how are you going to keep it new and exciting for yourself?" Gail asked.

Jess sighed. "I honestly have no idea. I didn't realize until just now that I was slipping back into my old ways, ignoring stuff that didn't interest me, losing track of things."

"I have a thought about that," Gail said. "If I'm not overstepping."

Jess had to swallow her pride, but she said, "Of course not. Tell me."

"We could sit down sometime and brainstorm some ideas, if you want to," Gail began cautiously, then warmed to the subject. "Maybe we could come up with some new promotions, a few events, like wine tastings, that kind of thing. I've been jotting down notes for a while now."

Hearing the excitement in Gail's voice, Jess caught her enthusiasm. She nodded eagerly. "Let's do that. How about first thing tomorrow?"

"I'll meet you in the kitchen at six," Gail said. "We'll brainstorm over scones and coffee. How's that? I think I can make those orange-cranberry scones you love almost as well as your grandmother now."

"Don't let her hear you say that," Jess warned. "But that sounds perfect. And thank you for being understanding about all this."

"I love this place as much as if it were my own," Gail said. "It's the perfect job in the perfect location. And I love working with you."

"When I'm not making your work a hundred times harder," Jess replied ruefully.

"Hey, I live for challenges, same as you," Gail said. "Lunch, by the way, is going to be amazing. Apparently I do my best work when I have to be inventive."

"Then I'll call the family and get them over here," Jess told her. "I know a jam-packed dining room, full of people singing your praises, will make up for a lot."

Gail laughed. "Indeed, it will. I live for an appreciative audience."

Jess managed to keep smiling until Gail had left, but then she put her head down on her desk and let the tears flow. Somehow she'd convinced herself that the inn was going to be her personal savior, that these episodes of slipups and distractions were under control. History should have taught her otherwise.

She allowed herself five full minutes of despair and self-recriminations, then sat up. Even though the promise of brainstorming new ideas tomorrow sounded great, she had a feeling it was going to take more than that to get herself back on track. Whatever she and Gail came up with would be fun, but she needed a more absorbing challenge. Maybe what she needed was to expand her business, to find another small inn that needed to be refurbished and brought back to life.

She turned on her computer and, ignoring the piles of paperwork on her desk, started looking for real estate in nearby bayside communities, even a couple of available properties by the ocean suitable for bed and breakfast locations.

When she finally glanced at her watch and realized the entire morning had sped by and she'd never called her sisters, her sisters-in-law or her mother to join her for lunch, she railed against herself all over again. If she didn't get on this, it was going to be one more thing for Gail to hold over her head.

"What the devil is wrong with me?" she muttered under her breath as she dialed her mother's art gallery. Hadn't this morning been a wake-up call, after all?

"Mom, Gail just told me our lunch menu today is going to be spectacular. I know it's last-minute, but can you come over?"

Megan seemed taken aback by the invitation, but there was a pleased note in her voice when she responded. "Give me twenty minutes, okay?"

"Perfect. See if Heather can get away, too," she suggested, since Heather's quilt shop was right next door to the gallery. "Maybe she can ride over with you."

"Will do," Megan promised.

She called Bree and Shanna next. Shanna said she couldn't leave the bookstore on such short notice, but Bree sounded ecstatic about having an excuse to get away from Flowers on Main.

"It's been a zoo in here this morning," she complained. "Half the town's apparently sick and the other half is sending flowers. I've been desperate for a reason to escape. My employee's pretty new, but she can handle it for an hour. I'll have to bring the baby, though."

"No problem," Jess assured her. Cuddling her new niece might be just what she needed.

The more the merrier, in fact. Hopefully in all the commotion, she'd be able to forget about the disastrous, frustrating way her own day had started.

Will knew there was something going on with Jess. She'd been unusually quiet all evening. The mere fact that she'd shown up at his office with dinner was proof that she wasn't herself. After that one visit weeks ago, she hadn't willingly come inside the place.

Once they'd finished the excellent beef stew and biscuits she'd brought and had a good start on a bottle of excellent red wine, he set his glass down on a corner of his desk, leaned forward, and looked into her eyes.

"What's going on, Jess?"

She gave him a startled look. "I don't know what you mean."

He gestured around. "You came to my office."

"I figured you'd be working late. I brought you dinner. What's the big deal?" she asked defensively.

That defensive note in her voice only confirmed his suspicions. Of course, calling her on it might not have been his smartest move. It might fall into that category she despised, evidence he was analyzing her. Still, he hated seeing her like this. Whatever was going on, she needed to get it out.

"Something happened today, and you're trying very hard not to talk about it," he guessed.

"True," she conceded, though she didn't look especially pleased that he'd hit the mark. "And I'm still not a hundred percent sure I want to talk about it with you."

"Why is that?"

"Because I'm not sure if you can separate being my boyfriend from being a shrink."

"Are you worried about me not being able to differentiate, or are you the one with that problem?"

She looked vaguely startled by his suggestion, but then to his surprise, she nodded. "Me," she admitted.

"Okay, let's attack this from a different direction," he suggested. "If I were just your boyfriend, what would you expect from me if you brought me a problem? Sympathy? Understanding? Advice?"

Her expression turned thoughtful. "Sympathy and understanding, for sure."

"No advice?" he asked, trying not to smile.

"I think that sneaks over the line into the whole shrink thing."

"Well, to be honest with you, I don't give a lot of advice in my business. I just help people to work through their problems. They do all the hard work. I pretty much keep my opinions to myself."

She regarded him with surprise. "Really?"

"Most of the time," he confirmed. "Does that help?"

"Yes, I think it does."

"So, what happened today?"

She launched into a description of all

the mistakes she'd made, the litany filled with the kind of self-loathing that made him want to gather her in his arms, but she didn't need consolation. She needed to find a way to restore her faith in herself.

"Why did this hit you so hard?" he asked when she'd finally wound down. "You've handled much tougher slipups. Look at the whole foreclosure episode when you had to get Abby to bail you out. This was nothing by comparison."

"I guess I'd gotten used to thinking that my system for managing things was perfect," she admitted. "When Gail came to me about the order, then reminded me of all the other things I'd let fall through the cracks recently, it shook me up."

She met his gaze. "More than that, it made me start to think that I need a new challenge, that I'm never going to be satisfied just to have the inn open and running smoothly. I'm always going to need something else to tackle."

Will had some idea where she was headed with this. "By extension, are you thinking that applies to your relationships, as well? Do you think I won't be enough for you once we get into some kind of a routine?"

She looked startled by the comparison. "After yesterday, how can you ask that? I think you'll be able to keep things fresh and exciting for a very long time."

He smiled. "Good to know," he said, though he doubted it would be that easy. He imagined that making love, even spectacularly, could drift into a familiar pattern after a while unless a couple really worked to keep the sparks alive. He'd never been with anyone long enough to test that theory, though. Neither had Jess.

He looked into her troubled eyes. "Jess, what's really going on in that head of yours? This isn't just because you forgot to place a couple of orders or messed up a reservation."

"Probably not," she admitted. "I guess it made me realize that I'm never going to grow out of the ADD. It's always going to be with me."

"More than likely," he agreed.

"How can you put up with that?" she asked plaintively.

"Because it's just one piece of who you

are. You have to stop defining yourself by your ADD. You're Jess O'Brien, owner of a successful inn. You're beautiful, smart, funny, impulsive, just a little crazy and quite possibly the most exciting woman on the planet."

She finally allowed herself to smile. "You're just saying that because you want to get lucky again tonight."

"I got lucky enough yesterday for a week, though I certainly wouldn't say no to a repeat performance," he told her. "My point is that I love *you,* Jess. The whole package."

"But I'm so flawed," she said.

Will knew she was serious, but he laughed. "Aren't we all? Your flaw just happens to have a name. I have a whole list of my own. Stick with me long enough and you'll have to deal with all of them."

She regarded him with amazement. "Do you have any idea how good you are for my battered ego?"

He grinned then and beckoned to her. "Come over here and show me."

She laughed. "Seriously?"

"Seriously."

She glanced around his office. "You know, Will, this is one of those times this place could benefit from a couch," she said as she settled onto his lap.

"I'll get right on that first thing in the morning," he promised, then lowered his lips to hers. "Until then, we'll just have to do the best we can."

It was amazing to discover just how clever they could be.

Thomas had suddenly vanished, or so it seemed to Connie. She hadn't seen him since the Sunday dinner at the O'Briens, and she'd heard from him only once. She had no idea what to make of it, and she was almost afraid to call and ask him what was going on.

Now that they had Nell's blessing and the fear of family conflict had abated, was he bored with her? She hated that so many doubts had surfaced, and hated even more her unwillingness to make the call that could resolve them. What was she? Sixteen?

Unfortunately, as she sat staring at her phone, willing it to ring, or maybe trying to convince herself to pick it up herself and use it, Jake walked in.

"You look gloomy," her brother declared. "What's wrong?"

"Nothing."

"Connie, you've never been the kind of woman to sit around and sulk with no reason."

"I am not sulking," she retorted indignantly. "I'm just thinking about a few things."

"Such as?"

She frowned at him. "Since when do you want to have deep, philosophical discussions about the state of my life?"

"Since you started dating a man I'm not convinced is right for you," he said. "Is that it? Are you having second thoughts about Thomas?"

"Not at all," she said at once, then drew in a deep breath. "But he may be having them about me."

"No way!" Jake said at once.

Connie smiled. "Thanks for the vote of confidence."

"Come on, sis. What's not to love about you? You're beautiful, you've always had your head on straight, you're the ultimate nurturer, you're a terrific cook, and you handle things around here for me as if the job were next to nothing, when I know otherwise."

"Gee, if I were looking for a new job,

that would be great on my resume," she said wryly. "Are you so sure any of that is what keeps a man interested?"

"Of course it is. Well, except for the part about how smoothly you run this place." He grinned. "That probably matters more to me than it would to Thomas."

"Unless I decided to take a job with his foundation," she said idly.

Jake immediately looked alarmed. "You can't be serious."

"No, not really," she admitted. "Though I do love working with him. It's probably best, though, if I continue to do that as a volunteer. I'd hate to go to work for the foundation, then have our relationship blow up. How awkward would that be?"

"Has he asked you to consider a job there?" Jake persisted, still looking concerned.

"No, I was just thinking out loud," she said. She patted his hand. "Not to worry. I'll still be slaving away here when I'm in my dotage."

"I know this might not be the most fulfilling job you could ever have, but your being here handling the day-to-day stuff has been a godsend for me. I know everything is under control so I can concentrate on the landscaping part, which is what I love the most. We've been a good team, don't you think?"

She smiled. "I told you, you can stop fretting. I'm not leaving."

"But I don't want you to hate your job. How about a raise?"

She laughed. "I'm not about to turn down a raise, but I wasn't angling for one."

"I could make you a partner," Jake said, his expression turning thoughtful. "Then you'd have a real stake in the company."

Though the conversation hadn't started about her career path, Connie couldn't help being intrigued by the idea. "I certainly don't have any money to invest," she reminded him. "Not with Jenny in college."

"I'd say you've earned plenty of sweat equity in the place."

"Not enough to have controlling interest, I'm sure," she said, grinning.

"Heaven save me," Jake said fervently. "No, you don't get to take over. Let me think about this some more, see what I can work out that's fair. You interested?"

"Will it mean more work?"

Now he grinned. "No."

"Just more money," she said.

"Yes."

"And a bigger say than I have now."

"You have plenty of say right now," he said. "You just don't have control, and you still won't. My vote will always count more than yours."

She rolled her eyes. "It's been that way since you were a baby. You had Mom and Dad wrapped around your finger the day you were born. When you got a little older, you started working on me."

"Stop complaining. Have I not been the best brother in the entire world?" he taunted. "Was I not there for you when Sam left? Was I not the best uncle ever for Jenny? I even kept her groping boyfriend's hands off of her."

"At least as far as we know," Connie said wryly. "I try not to think about what's going on now that she's away from home."

Jake winced. "Yeah, let's not go there." He studied her. "So, are you feeling better about things?"

He looked so hopeful, she could only nod. "I'm feeling a whole lot better about work," she said truthfully.

Fortunately, Jake was a typical guy. He missed the subtext completely.

"That's great," he said. "We'll talk more in a day or two."

She shook her head as he left the office whistling, obviously pleased with himself. Then she scowled at the phone on her desk. "Ring, darn it!"

But the other man in her life remained stubbornly silent.

21

Will was having lunch with Mack and Jake when Laila approached, her expression troubled.

"Do you have a minute?" she asked him, after greeting the other men.

"Sure," Will said. He turned to Mack. "Order a grilled ham and cheese for me, would you?"

"As if you needed to say it," Jake taunted. "That's what you have every Thursday."

Will frowned. "Are you suggesting I'm predictable?"

"Disgustingly so," Mack agreed, laughing. "There have been bets placed on how long it will be before you actually shake things up and order something different."

"My money's on never," Jake added.

If Laila hadn't been standing there, Will might have said something more pointed, but he settled for a scowl, then muttered, "I'll be back, and we'll finish this conversation then."

Laila led the way outside and headed toward one of the benches on the town green, still looking grim. Even after they were seated, she couldn't seem to summon up a way to get into whatever was bothering her. In a woman he'd always found to be direct and forthcoming, her behavior was uncharacteristically reticent.

"Do you need counseling about something?" Will prodded carefully. "Would you be more comfortable in my office?"

She shook her head. "Truthfully, I don't know quite how to get into this," she began, then took a deep breath and added more bluntly, "I think there may be a problem with your dating service. A serious one."

Alarm bells immediately went off for Will. "What sort of problem?" he asked, dread settling in his stomach.

"Once a match is made, you pass along contact information, right?"

"Only with each party's permission," he said. "Why? What's happened?"

"I've been getting some calls in the past week. First, it was just a couple of odd hang-ups, but twice now there have been obscene messages left on my answering machine. I brought the tape." She reached into her purse and handed it to him.

"Why not take it to the sheriff? And what makes you think it has anything to do with Lunch by the Bay? I'm not questioning you, just asking how you came to that conclusion."

She nodded, not looking the least bit offended. "The timing, I guess. It could be some random jerk, I suppose, but it started right after I turned down a second date with this one guy I'd met through your company."

Will winced. "Are you sure it's the same man leaving the messages?"

"Not a hundred percent, no," Laila said. "I tried to check the number for the incoming calls, but it's blocked. I've listened to the tape maybe four times now, hoping I could tell for sure if it's his voice, but I can't swear to it. I'd had a prior message from the guy before we went out, but I'd erased it as soon as I'd called him back."

"No reason not to," Will agreed.

"I came directly to you because I thought maybe you'd want to check it out before the police get involved," she told him. "If it turns out I'm right and this goes public, it could ruin your company's reputation. I certainly didn't want to take a chance on that without proof."

"Damn the company!" Will said heatedly. "I don't want my clients harassed like this. It's wrong. Why don't we go back to my office right now and call this guy? I'll put him on speaker phone, and we can compare his voice to the tape. Maybe if we do it together, we'll know for certain. Then, one way or the other, we'll go straight to the police."

Laila nodded. "Thanks. I thought I was a pretty tough woman, but I have to admit these messages shook me up. You'll see what I mean once you've listened to them."

"I can see how much they've disturbed you, and you're not the kind of woman who gets rattled without good reason," Will said grimly. "Let's go and see what we can find out."

"What about your lunch?"

He gave her a wry look. "Haven't you heard? It's the same old boring thing."

She laughed. "I'll take you out for something more exciting as soon as we get this resolved," she offered.

"Sounds like a deal to me." He studied her as they walked. "You okay?"

She forced a smile. "I will be, as soon as this guy's off the streets."

"Until that happens, why don't you stay with your folks or Trace and Abby?"

"I don't want them to know about any of this. They'll just worry. Plus, you know Trace. He'll never let me hear the end of the fact that I used a dating service in the first place, even yours."

"Then stay over at the inn with Jess."

She gave him an amused look. "You going to stand guard over both of us?"

"Absolutely."

"Then I'll think about it. It makes sense, actually, though I hate giving in to fear."

"Sometimes fear can be a healthy thing. In this case, I think it's justified."

After he'd heard the tape, then placed the call to the man they suspected, Will felt even more strongly about that. When he spoke to

Vince, he was careful not to suggest he was aware of the calls to Laila. He acted as if he were only inquiring about how Vince liked the Lunch by the Bay service.

"It's been great, man!" Vince said enthusiastically. "Thanks to you, I've found quite a few women I otherwise wouldn't have met. I've been staying in close contact with a couple of them."

"Which ones?" Will asked innocently. "I like to know which matches seem to be working out."

"That Laila from the bank? She's a real hottie." He named another client, as well.

Will shuddered as he listened. Though the comment could have been made in all innocence by any man, there was an unmistakable undertone that set off alarm bells.

Will wondered if the other woman had been receiving the same kind of calls. Rather than saying something that might give away the true reason for his call, Will forced his voice to remain neutral.

"Thanks for the feedback, Vince. I really appreciate it."

When he'd hung up, he glanced at Laila, who looked as if she'd been sickened by the call.

"He's done this to someone else, hasn't he?"

"Possibly," Will said. "I'll call her to find out, then I'm turning everything we have over to the police. Okay with you if I have them come here right now?"

She nodded, but her complexion was ashen.

"Want me to call Jess and have her come over here?"

She looked relieved by the suggestion. "Would you? I don't know why this has shaken me so badly, but I have to admit knowing I was right has turned my stomach."

"No problem." He made the call, then explained the situation to Jess. "I think Laila could use your support right now."

"Give me five minutes," she said at once.

"Thanks."

"I'd like five minutes alone with that son of a bitch," Jess said furiously. "I'd teach him a thing or two about being a real man."

Though the situation wasn't even re-motely amusing, Will smiled. "That's one of those things I love about you. You're always willing to jump right into the fray for your family and friends."

"Of course," she said. "It goes without

saying. Tell Laila to hang in there. I'm walking out the door of the inn right now."

Will disconnected the call and relayed the message. He was about to place the call to the other woman but decided to wait until Jess arrived and could sit with Laila. He'd make the call more privately, then notify the police.

Just thinking about how something he'd intended to be a good thing for the lonely singles of Chesapeake Shores could turn out this way made him want to slam his fist into something. Agreeing with Jess, he thought the most obvious choice would be Vince's face, or perhaps some other more appropriate part of his anatomy.

Jess was still boiling mad that anyone could have done this to her friend. She'd been tempted to call Connie but had stopped herself, uncertain if Laila would want anyone else to know about the obscene calls.

When she stormed into Will's office, she found Laila looking pale and shaken, but her usual spirit was sparkling in her eyes.

"Oh, sweetie, this just sucks," Jess said, pulling her into a hug, then dragging a chair closer, so she could sit right next to Laila.

"How are you doing?" she asked, as Will left the room to make phone calls.

"Better, now that Will's handling things and you're here," Laila said. "On one level, I'm scared to death. I didn't realize I was until we pretty much confirmed it was the man I thought it was. It put a face to it, you know?"

"I know," Jess said.

Laila tried to smile, but it never reached her eyes. "On another level, I'm spitting mad. I'd like to take this guy apart with my bare hands."

"You wouldn't have to do it alone," Jess assured her. "I'm ticked, and I can only imagine how infuriated Will must be."

"I don't want something like this to ruin this company of his," Laila said.

"I'm sure he doesn't care about that."

Laila nodded. "That's what he said. He suggested maybe I should stay with you at the inn until this is settled. Would that work?"

"Absolutely. You can have the room next to mine at no charge, or I can bring a roll-away bed into my room if you'd be more comfortable that way."

"Will said he'd stand guard."

Jess chuckled. "I don't doubt that for a

second. I can't seem to shake him loose these days."

"Do you want to?"

"No, which surprises the dickens out of me," she admitted. "Scares me a little, too."

"I'm glad things are finally working out," Laila said. "You two wasted a lot of time."

"More than I'd realized," Jess said, looking up as Will returned. "How'd it go?"

"The other woman had the same problem but hadn't told anyone. She's on her way over. So are the police."

Laila's expression brightened. "Then this could be over today?"

Jess worried about her assumption. "Don't get ahead of yourself, Laila. The police might have to do their own investigating."

"She's right," Will said. "I made a quick call to Connor to ask him how the police were likely to proceed. He thinks this will be enough to get things started, but even if both of you press charges and Vince is taken into custody, he could be right back out on bail."

When he arrived, the sheriff's deputy told them the same thing. He regarded both Laila and the other woman somberly. "If you've got someplace else to stay for a while, it might be a good idea to do it. Let's get this guy behind bars for good before you let down your guard. The reason people like this leave their messages on answering machines is that they're basically sick cowards. He's not going to be happy about being identified."

Will turned to his other client. "You have a place to stay?"

She nodded. "I have an older brother here in town. I can stay with him. I'll probably need to be there to keep him from killing the guy, anyway."

The deputy winced. "I did not just hear that."

Laila smiled at her. "Ditto with mine, which is why I'm not saying a word to him just yet." She looked pointedly at Jess when she said it. Jess nodded her agreement.

"Okay, then, we'll go pick this guy up," the deputy promised. "I'll stay in touch with you, let you know what's going on."

"Thanks," Will said.

He turned to Laila and the other woman. "Any expenses you have because you're out of your homes, I'll cover," he assured them.

"That won't be a problem," the other woman said.

"And Laila's staying with me," Jess told him.

Will didn't look appeased. "I'm just saying, if you need it, the help's there, and I'm not just saying that because I'm worried about repercussions. I feel a deep sense of responsibility to both of you."

Laila regarded him with concern. "Will, you're not to blame yourself for this."

"I agree," the other client said. "It could have happened with any other service or in some online chat room. There are sleazy people in the world."

"I know that," Will said. "I should have figured out some way to weed them out."

Jess could see from the deeply troubled expression on his face that he'd taken this incident to heart and placed all the blame squarely on his own shoulders.

Having Laila close by was more fun than Jess had anticipated when she'd made the offer. And, though she didn't want to admit it, Laila also made a nice buffer between herself and Will. The intensity of their relationship needed to cool down, though she had to admit she missed some of their more impulsive escapades.

"You're using Laila as an excuse not to spend time alone with me," Will accused a week into the arrangement. "Why is that?"

"I'm not," Jess denied automatically, then winced at his penetrating look. "Okay, maybe I am."

"Why? Were the feelings getting too scary?"

Though she hated to admit to being afraid of anything, she nodded. "I hate that you can read me so darn well."

He laughed. "I know. It's a curse, isn't it?"

"You're joking, but it's not that funny," she retorted. "I wonder sometimes if it wouldn't be easier to be in a relationship in which I could remain a woman of mystery."

"You'd go ballistic the first time some man didn't know intuitively what was going on in your head."

"Maybe so," she said. "But I doubt it."

"Want to test it?" he asked, regarding her with a challenging look. "You could always date a few guys, then report back."

"I assume you wouldn't be the one fixing me up with them," she said, then realized the implication of her remark. "I'm sorry. I didn't mean that the way it sounded, as some kind of knock on Lunch by the Bay."

Though he'd stiffened, Will said, "I knew what you meant, and no, I was most certainly not going to fix you up. I was just offering you a time-out, if that's what you really want. Go, test the waters."

Jess was more shaken by the offer than she'd thought she would be. "Do you want to get rid of me? Is that what you're saying?"

Will's tense expression immediately fled. He reached out and pulled her close. "God, no," he murmured in her ear. "It's the last thing I want."

She relaxed into his embrace, feeling secure once more. "Good, because it's the last thing I want, too. As for all this time with Laila, she needs our company right now, and maybe it is good for us to let things simmer for a bit, instead of turning the heat up so high we burn out."

Will laughed. "Our relationship is not going to burn out, Jess. I don't see it happening."

"It could," she said, wishing she could be as certain as he was. She was close. It sometimes felt as if forever was within her grasp, but then panic set in.

One of these days, though, if Will remained steadfast long enough, she hoped to be exactly where he was, knowing that their future was as inevitable as breathing.

Even though his relationship with Jess seemed to be progressing nicely, Will still found himself walking on eggshells when they were together, especially lately with Laila as an almost constant companion. Much as he liked Laila and understood the reason for her presence, it occasionally grated. He and Jess were almost on the cusp of having it all. Adding a bystander to the mix was slowing things down too much for his taste.

Still, he did feel good about the progress he and Jess had made. And ever since their conversation about losing their privacy, she'd made an effort to ensure that they had at least a few stolen moments of alone time every evening. Or maybe that was Laila's doing. She seemed to sense Will's frustration in ways Jess did not.

Despite the ups and downs of the past ten days or so, Will was still stunned when he arrived at the inn to pick Jess up for a scheduled date and discovered that she'd apparently gone off on an overnight trip for the inn without bothering to mention it to him. His heart sank.

"Did she leave a message for me?" he asked Laila, who was on her way out to spend the evening with Trace, Abby and the twins.

"Sorry, no," she said. "I thought for sure she'd called you."

"Any idea where she went?"

"She got a call earlier, something about some real estate or something, and took off right after she made sure I'd be with Trace and Abby tonight."

"Okay, thanks. Enjoy your evening. If she happens to call you, tell her I stopped by." He had to wonder, though, if even that would trigger her memory and remind her that she'd blown off a date. Was this her ADD, or was she sending him a message about how truly unimportant he was in her life? With Jess, especially recently, it was impossible to say.

An hour later, he was reluctantly matching couples on the Lunch by the Bay website and debating whether he shouldn't be calling it quits and shutting down the site for good, when his cell phone rang: Jess, according to the caller ID.

"Hey," he said quietly.

"I am so, so sorry," she apologized. "This

trip came up at the last second and I completely forgot to check my calendar. Laila called me to tell me. Why didn't you?"

"I figured something important must have come up," he said. "I understood." And he did. For someone with ADD, keeping track of details was a constant struggle. He was actually surprised something like this hadn't happened sooner. Of course, it had at the inn, but those things hadn't directly affected him.

As if she'd read his mind, she immediately snapped back, "Dammit, Will, this isn't about the ADD. I forgot to check my calendar, period. People do that kind of thing all the time. No one makes excuses for them and no one patronizes them."

"I am not patronizing you," he said, treading carefully. "I thought I was saying that I understood what happened. It's not a big deal."

"Blowing off a date with you *is* a big deal," she contradicted. "And you shouldn't be giving me a free pass just because I happen to have ADD."

"Are we honestly going to fight about the fact that I'm not upset with you for forgetting our date?"

"Yes, because it's symptomatic of exactly what I was afraid of when we started seeing each other. I mess up. You check your psychology text or something and figure it's classic ADD, and all's well."

"Look, I would much rather be with you than home alone working on Lunch by the Bay matches, but this is simply not as big a deal as you're trying to turn it into. We'll see each other when you get back."

"So, now I'm crazy?"

Will sucked in a deep breath and prayed for patience. "Jess, what's really going on here? Is this more of that discussion we started to have the other day? Are you deliberately trying to find a reason to break up? Did you want me to blow a gasket over the date so you'd have some trumped-up excuse to walk away?"

"Oh, stop trying to analyze me," she retorted, then hung up.

Less than a minute later, his phone rang again. "I'm sorry, Will. I really am," she said, sounding genuinely contrite. "I have no idea why I'm being such a pain. I guess it's because I already felt guilty and you letting me off the hook is making me feel even guiltier."

"Where are you?"

She hesitated. "Why?" she asked, sounding puzzled.

"Because if you're not that far away, I could get in my car and we could straighten this out in person."

"You would drive somewhere tonight just to settle a stupid argument?" she asked, sounding stunned.

"I would drive anywhere to be with you," he countered. "As for settling arguments, I hear that making up can be all kinds of fun."

"Actually I'm not that far away," she told him. "I was invited to take a look at an inn that's up for sale just outside of Ocean City. Since I left late, I booked a room for the night."

So that's what this was about, Will thought. No wonder she'd gone dashing off. "You're thinking of buying another inn?" he asked, not entirely surprised.

"I honestly have no idea if I'm interested or not," she admitted. "I loved the process of getting everything ready, but now that The Inn at Eagle Point is a success and I have the right people in place, I don't know, it's not quite the same."

"You're bored?"

"It's not because of the ADD," she said defensively.

"I didn't say it was," he said mildly. "A lot of people like the challenge of opening a new business, then turning it over to a management team."

"Then you don't think I'm nuts for considering this?"

"Absolutely not."

"Will you drive over and take a look? It's a little shabby, but the setting's very romantic."

"Give me directions," he said at once. "And chill a bottle of champagne while you're at it. We have some making up to do."

Unfortunately, he was sure this was going to become a pattern with the two of them. Right now there was an edge of excitement and passion to these unexpected ups and downs, but relationships couldn't go the distance that way. He understood that better than anyone.

Then again, if he'd wanted smooth sailing, his heart should have picked just about anyone except Jess O'Brien.

22

Thomas had been down with the flu for over a week. Not that there was ever a good time for getting sick, but this couldn't have happened at a worse one. He knew Connie was probably wondering what on earth had happened to him, but just the thought of picking up the phone to call her had been too much. He'd been asleep most of the time anyway. Today was the first time in days he'd dragged himself out of bed and actually showered and shaved. He even considered trying to get into the office for an hour or two.

Dressed in clean clothes and feeling

almost human again, he was debating whether or not chicken soup would be a mistake, when his doorbell rang. He crossed the living room and opened the door to find Connie standing there with an armload of groceries and sparks in her eyes.

"You're an idiot!" she declared and swept past him.

So much for sympathy, he thought, though he couldn't help admiring the way she'd gone on the attack first thing. She was a formidable woman when her back was up. In that respect, she reminded him of his mother.

"You seem upset," he said mildly, following her into the kitchen.

"After not hearing from you for days, which we'll discuss in a minute, I finally broke down and called your office and discovered you'd been home with the flu. Sick as a dog, according to your secretary, who's not all that impressed with you at the moment, either. She said something about you snapping at her a few too many times when she called with questions."

"I was sick," he protested.

"Men!" she muttered. "They're the worst

patients in the world. Believe me, Jake was no picnic. Thank heavens, he's Bree's problem now."

Thomas bit back a smile. "Apparently you're not here to cheer me up."

She didn't seem to find the comment amusing. "No, I'm here to assess the situation, see if you're ready for some decent food, and then, as soon as I'm assured that you're on a path to a full recovery, I intend to give you a piece of my mind for not calling to tell me what was going on."

"How long are you planning to stick around?" he inquired. "Looks as if you brought a lot of food. You have a suitcase with you, by any chance?"

She frowned at him. "Soups and stews require a lot of fresh ingredients," she said. "As for how long I'll be here, I'll let you know when I think you're well enough to leave this apartment." She surveyed him from head to toe, her expression suddenly suspicious. "You don't look that sick."

Uh-oh, Thomas thought. "I couldn't stand myself anymore. I took a shower and shaved right before you got here. I actually feel pretty good. I should be able to get back to work tomorrow. In fact, I was thinking I could run over to the office this afternoon until you showed up."

"Have you eaten anything?"

"I was just debating whether to chance it," he told her.

"Okay, then, I'll get busy. I brought some ginger ale. You can drink that while I cook."

"Somehow in the past few weeks I've missed the fact that you are incredibly bossy," he said, taking a couple of steps in her direction until she was backed into the counter.

For the first time, she looked vaguely wary. "Thomas?"

"Yes, Connie."

"What are you doing?"

"I think I know what the best medicine is," he said. "I was planning to test my theory. And, in case you're worried, I'm long past being contagious."

Before she could scoot away, he leaned down and kissed her, lingering over the kiss until he heard her sigh and felt her hands clinging to his shoulders.

When she finally pushed him away, the sparks were back in her eyes. "If you're feeling that frisky, mister, then we can get straight to that conversation about what people in a relationship are supposed to do in a crisis."

He smiled, poured himself a glass of ginger ale and took a seat at the kitchen table, then regarded her attentively. "Do tell."

She frowned at him. "I don't think you're taking this seriously. I was worried about what had happened to you."

"You thought I'd had second thoughts," he guessed.

She nodded. "I hated myself for it, but yes."

He gestured toward the chair next to his. "Sit."

"I need to get that soup started."

"I can eat soup from a can," he said. "This is more important."

Though she looked appalled by the suggestion of canned soup, she did sit down, though it was fairly gingerly and on the edge of the seat.

"What?"

"I've had some time to think the past few days, at least when I wasn't zonked out or praying for death."

She winced at the description. For a moment Thomas thought she might reach for his hand, maybe even give it a sympathetic squeeze. That's what she would have done if she weren't currently so annoyed with him. Instead, she just sat there, waiting.

"Okay, here it is," he said. "I'd planned to take care of a few details first, go out and buy a ring, pick some romantic setting, things like that."

Her eyes widened as the words registered.

"But now seems like the right moment," he added. "I don't want you to ever have these doubts again about where we stand. So, Connie Collins, will you do me the incredible honor of marrying me?"

Since she looked a little shell-shocked, he rushed on, making his case. "I know this is fast, but we've both been on this earth long enough to know when something's right. And we also know how short and capricious life can be. I don't want us to waste a single minute."

He looked into her eyes, which seemed to be shimmering with unshed tears. He wasn't sure what to make of that, so he pressed his point. "Will you marry me?"

The muscles in her throat worked, and

it seemed to him she was struggling to get air. He frowned. "Are you choking or something?"

She shook her head. "I'm just trying to find the right words," she said.

"It only takes one," he reminded her quietly. "Yes . . ." He hesitated, almost afraid to mention the alternative. He sucked in a deep breath finally and added, "Or no."

Once more she opened her mouth, but no sound emerged. Instead, she nodded.

Thomas felt the tension in his shoulders relax. "Was that a yes?"

A smile broke across her face then, even as tears streamed down her cheeks. "It's a yes! I think we may both be a little crazy, but yes, Thomas O'Brien, I will marry you."

"Come here," he said, gathering her into his arms and holding her. "I will do this all over again, if you want the romantic setting and the whole nine yards."

She rested a hand against his cheek. "This will do," she said. "As proposals go, I think it was pretty memorable."

"Do you still want to get into that lecture you had on the tip of your tongue?" he asked.

"Maybe later," she told him. "For now,

you've done a pretty good job of redeeming yourself."

"Pretty good?"

"Okay, an amazing job."

"Did I happen to mention that I love you?" Thomas asked. "It should have been the very first thing I said."

"I'll forgive you," she said with a slow smile, "as long as you keep saying it for the rest of our lives."

"Done," he said, then kissed her again.

Even as she melted in his arms, he asked himself yet again how he'd managed to find such an incredible woman at this stage of his life. Maybe it was some of that luck o' the Irish Ma was always talking about.

Will thought he and Jess had done a fine job of making up once he'd joined her just outside of Ocean City. They'd needed a weekend away together more than either of them had probably realized, but when they got back to Chesapeake Shores on Sunday night and dropped Jess's car off on their way to grab dinner, Will called his answering service and discovered they'd been deluged with calls. The news about the dating service's client had leaked out around town, if not in the media.

"All hell broke loose while you were gone. We have stacks and stacks of messages for you," he was told. "We've separated them into pro, con and certifiably crazy."

"I'll be by to pick them up," Will promised, then turned to Jess. "I'm sorry to end the weekend so abruptly, but I have to deal with this."

"I'm coming with you," she insisted. "What can I do to help? Want me to come to the office and help you field calls? At least I can screen out anything you don't need to be dealing with right now."

Will was tempted, but the weight of responsibility forced him to refuse. "This is my problem. I just wish I knew what to do. I never anticipated anything like this. Maybe Lunch by the Bay needs to be shut down entirely."

"Don't make that decision now, not until you've gotten a better feel for the fallout. You didn't deliberately set some pervert loose on the women of Chesapeake Shores. He did that himself. I think your clients will indicate the best course of action. You don't want to let down the ones who've been happy with having a service that concentrates on making matches locally."

Will's mood brightened. "There have been at least some satisfied customers."

"And even a wedding, right?"

He rolled his eyes. "I'm not convinced that's one I want to brag about. Let's see if it lasts more than fifteen minutes or so."

But after picking up the messages, he found one from that couple. "We're in your corner," it read. "Don't let this get you down."

"There," Jess said, when she saw it. "That's exactly what I was talking about. Take your cues from people like that."

He leaned down and kissed her. "Thanks for being so supportive, but I really need to deal with this. Do you mind if I take you back to the inn, after all?"

Jess looked as if she might argue, but instead, she reached up and pressed a hand to his cheek. "I'll walk back. Call if you change your mind and need my help. Thanks again for coming to Ocean City to look at that property with me."

"My pleasure." He winked at her. "So was making up."

In fact, the memory of that was going to

get him through whatever lay ahead with this Lunch by the Bay mess.

Ever since the night she'd forgotten their date, Jess had tried harder and harder to keep track of every single detail in her life, especially those that concerned Will. It was a daily struggle, and it was wearing on her. Surely a real relationship shouldn't cause such constant anxiety over messing up?

Unfortunately, with Will buried under the weight of handling the dating service fiasco, she'd been left with more and more time to chew over the state of their relationship. Even she recognized the probability that she was creating problems where none existed.

She was sitting in her office staring despondently at the contract for the property near Ocean City and wondering if she dared to make such a huge commitment, when Abby turned up. Her big sister's gaze immediately narrowed.

"You look exhausted," Abby said. "Aren't you sleeping?"

"Not that well," Jess admitted.

"Problems with Will? I heard about the

sicko who exploited Lunch by the Bay. How's he taking it?"

"He's been worrying himself sick, of course, especially about Laila and the other woman this guy harassed. He's not going to rest until the guy's behind bars. Unfortunately, at the moment, he's out on bail, though the judge says he'll revoke it if he makes one single harassing call or goes anywhere near any of the women involved."

"Laila's still here with you?"

Jess nodded.

"She could stay with us," Abby offered. "Trace was livid when he first found out, but he's calmed down now."

"Talk to her, but it's fine if she stays here till this guy goes to court."

"She's not in the way?" Abby asked.

"Of course not."

Abby regarded her perceptively. "Would Will say the same thing?"

"I'm sure he would," Jess said, then sighed. "Or maybe not. He thinks I'm using Laila as a buffer, though lately he's so swamped with work, it hardly matters."

"Are you using Laila as a buffer?"

"Maybe. Sometimes."

"Why, if things are really okay with the two of you?" Abby asked worriedly.

"Will's been a saint. Maybe it comes with being a shrink, but he's so understanding sometimes it makes my teeth hurt," she said wearily. When Abby looked quizzical, she added, "From clenching them." She couldn't seem to stop the tears that welled up. "I think I should break it off with him." It was the first time she'd dared to voice the words aloud.

Abby stared at her incredulously. "Because he's too nice to you?"

"Because it's too hard being the kind of woman he deserves. I know he's doing what he needs to do right now about this dating service crisis, but I'm feeling left out. I know I need to grow up, but when he's not around, I start imagining he won't ever be back. I could list chapter and verse exactly why I react like this, but I can't seem to stop the feelings from just rolling right on in."

"Sweetie, sure he's busy these days, but you're the kind of woman Will wants, and you're certainly everything he deserves and more. He would tell you the same thing. If you're feeling pressure, then you're putting it on yourself. I don't think he expects you to be anyone except the fantastic person you are."

"I know that. I still feel as if one slip-up will ruin everything. I don't need a shrink or you, for that matter, to tell me that it goes back to Mom leaving, but how do I get past that?"

"Time," Abby said. "And Will understands that, probably better than any other man would."

"But I'm being so unfair to expect that much patience from him."

"Has he complained?"

"No."

"Okay, then. Count your blessings, sweetie, and stop looking for a way out."

Jess sighed. "It's only because I'm terrified of losing someone who really matters, you know."

Abby smiled. "I know, and I'm relieved that you do, too. If you remember nothing else, remember this. Will knows your flaws, Jess, and he chose you!"

For the first time in days, Jess let herself relax. "He did, didn't he?"

"Do you think Will is smart?"

"Brilliant, actually."

"Do you think he's the kind of man who knows his own mind?"

"Of course."

"Then why are you questioning his judgment? The only question you really should be asking yourself is whether you love him enough."

"You mean as much as he deserves?"

Abby smiled at her. "No, enough to take the chance that what you two have is strong enough to last forever. Last time I checked, you were a pretty big risk-taker. Don't let fear and caution start ruling your life now."

Relieved by the show of support, Jess jumped up and hugged her. "You're the best big sister in the entire universe."

Abby grinned. "Even though I'm going to tell you that the figures on the contract for that inn you want to buy don't make financial sense?"

Jess laughed. For once she didn't resent Abby's interference. "I think I'd already figured that out. Besides, who needs a new inn, when I can have this one *and* the best man in the world?"

Abby nodded approvingly. "See how smart you are? Will's going to be a very lucky man."

Jess shook her head. She was the lucky

one, not just because of Will, but because she had her family behind her, no matter what.

Despite her resolve to open her heart to Will, the time they spent apart as he dealt with the Lunch by the Bay crisis was starting to take a toll on their relationship. Once again, Jess's insecurities kicked in, because it seemed no matter what she offered in the way of help and support, Will rejected it. He insisted that the entire burden for fixing things rested on his shoulders. He was wearing himself out.

Tired of being pushed aside, Jess went to Sally's at noon one day, determined to get in Will's face. She'd heard that's pretty much what Connie had done with Thomas, and look how that had turned out. They were now officially engaged.

But when Jess arrived at Sally's, she found Jake and Mack in their usual spot, but there was no sign of Will.

"Where's Will?"

"Hiding out in his office, I imagine," Mack said. "He hasn't shown his face in here for a week."

"And you two are just sitting here when

he needs you?" Jess demanded. "What kind of friends are you?"

Both men flushed guiltily.

"She's right," Jake said. "We shouldn't be letting him get away with this."

Mack didn't look entirely convinced, but he asked, "Are you suggesting we stage an intervention?"

Jess thought about the various O'Brien interventions to which she'd been a party. She hadn't much liked them. Still, it was a method Will might appreciate.

"Let's go," she said grimly.

At least if Will was furious, she'd be there with backup.

Will was staring out the window of his office when the door opened, and Jess, Mack and Jake barged in.

"Enough of this!" Jess declared forcefully.

Will stared at her bleakly. "Enough of what?"

"Hiding out," she said.

Mack gave him a commiserating look. "She's right, man. No one's as upset with you as you are with yourself. That guy who made the calls is the criminal, not you."

"I know that," Will said testily. "But it was my company he used to do it."

"Then shut down the company," Jake said. "I imagine a lot of people will be upset at losing a way to connect with other people, but you might as well punish them, too."

Will blinked at Jake's tone. "It's not about punishing anybody. It's about making sure people are safe."

Jess regarded him with understanding. "You can't singlehandedly keep the world safe, Will. There are creeps out there. Even if you shut down Lunch by the Bay, they'll still find some other way to harass women."

"But this happened on my watch," he said stubbornly.

"And you've apologized repeatedly, individually to your clients and publicly," Jess said. "Laila's not blaming you. Neither is anyone else."

Mack draped an arm around his shoulders. "Come on. Have lunch with us. Sally has a tuna on rye with your name on it."

Will frowned. "It's a tuna melt."

Mack shrugged. "Whatever. It's time for you to get your life back." He glanced pointedly toward Jess. "You get what I'm saying?"

Will chuckled despite his sour mood. "You're not a man of great subtlety, Mack. I get what you're saying. You two go on ahead. I need to speak to Jess for a minute."

"But you'll come to lunch?" Jake pressed. "This intervention thing worked?"

Will laughed at the hopeful note in his voice. "It worked."

"Thank goodness," Jake said. "This kind of stuff is way out of my comfort zone."

After they'd gone, Will turned his attention to Jess. "How'd you talk them into coming over here?"

"I didn't have to do that much talking. They care about you."

"And you? Do you care about me?"

She looked into his eyes. "So much it scares the daylights out of me."

Will recognized the genuine fear behind her words and knew they weren't over the hump quite yet, but they were getting there. One of these days Jess would take that final leap of faith. If for that reason only, Jake was exactly right. He needed to be ready to claim the life he'd always wanted and not sitting in his office wasting his time on regrets for things over which he'd had no control.

23

Despite the display of caring evident in the unexpected intervention Jess had staged in his office, Will was still terrified he was going to lose her. He knew that the time he was spending on this business crisis was scaring her, that she felt neglected and abandoned.

Will knew firsthand how dangerous it was to let her go on allowing her insecurities to take over, but up to now he'd felt he had no choice. He was spending every spare minute trying to reassure his clients or debating with himself the merits of simply throwing in the towel on a business that no longer held his interest.

Realistically, he knew that even before the crisis, Jess had been pulling away from him, and it didn't take someone with his advanced degree in psychology to figure out why. She was terrified he'd take off, just as her mother had all those years ago. Mick, though he'd stayed in the lives of his children, had pretty much turned to work after the divorce, so the two people who should have been teaching Jess about lasting, unconditional love and relationships had taught her about loss, instead.

Will knew all too well that love didn't come with guarantees, not of forever, anyway, but perhaps he could persuade Jess that theirs had the potential to withstand the test of time. Maybe all she really needed was the concrete commitment that he intended to try for.

Most important, there wasn't time to waste. He needed to do it now before the situation between them deteriorated even further than it already had. Nothing in his life was more important than Jess, and she needed to know that.

He started by asking Mick's permission to marry her. That didn't go half as smoothly as he'd expected. Apparently Mick had reservations about letting his youngest daughter marry anyone. Megan jumped in to save the day.

"Do you have a ring yet?" she asked Will, shooting a warning look at Mick that kept him silent.

"I was going to look this afternoon," he said.

"Wait here."

An awkward silence reigned while she was gone. "My reservations don't have anything to do with you," Mick said finally. "It's Jess. She doesn't stick with things. You know that, don't you?"

Will bristled on her behalf. "She'll stick with this," he said confidently. "She might have attention issues, but her heart's just fine. She knows how to love."

Mick regarded him with surprise. "I should have figured that you'd understand her better than most."

"Because I'm a psychologist?" Will asked. "It has nothing to do with that. It's because I've been in love with her since we were kids."

Mick seemed to be digesting that when Megan returned and handed a small black velvet jewelry box to Will. "If you like that, you can use it as an engagement ring. It was my mother's and her mother's before that. Jess always admired it. I think she'll appreciate the significance of having something with a long history of love behind it."

He opened the box to find a perfect diamond in an old-fashioned gold setting that was absolutely perfect for Jess. The setting was as delicate in its way as she was, the stone as glittering and as enduring. He met Megan's misty gaze.

"It's perfect," he said. "I don't know how to thank you."

"Just make our girl happy," she said, tucking her hand into Mick's.

"Or else," Mick murmured, but there was a twinkle in his eye.

Since Will intended to do everything in his power to meet that one request, he wasn't worried about consequences. The only thing terrifying him at the moment was that Jess might find some reason to say no.

It wasn't enough to have her parents' blessing, Will decided, or even the perfect engagement ring. He had to do something that would appeal to Jess's need for real romance in her life, a gesture that was a little over the top. He had a pretty good idea of what it should be, but it was going to take some help to pull it off, especially since winter had settled in and the outdoor plan he had in mind could wind up with both of them in the hospital with pneumonia if he didn't handle it just right.

He called Mack, Jake, Connor and Kevin together for beer at his place. When they were all settled and staring at him expectantly, he announced, "I'm planning to ask Jess to marry me."

Rather than whoops of delight, he was greeted by four worried expressions. It was Connor who risked speaking.

"Are you sure she's ready, man? You know how skittish she is about any kind of commitment. I don't want you to put your heart on the line and have her stomp on it."

"My heart's been on the line for years. I think we have a real shot here, and I'm going for it. Will the four of you help me or not?"

Kevin looked puzzled. "Are you talking

about us signing on to be ushers or something like that?"

"The time will come for that, but right
now I need help with proposing."

"And you're asking Mack?" Jake said,
giving Mack a poke in the side. "He can't
even muster up the courage to ask Susie
on a real date."

"Bite me," Mack replied.

"Focus, guys. I'm serious here," Will
said. "I want to propose at Moonlight Cove."

"But it's freezing cold," Kevin said.

"Thus the need for help," Will said impatiently. "I'm going to go over there tomorrow and set the scene, a bonfire, candles,
flowers, all of it. Then I'm going to pick up
Jess. Obviously I can't leave candles and
a bonfire burning, so somebody's got to
work with me, then stick around until we
get back."

"You want us there when you're proposing to our sister?" Kevin asked incredulously. "Bad idea. Nobody wants an
audience for something like that."

"Maybe we should be there," Connor
argued, his expression still dire. "If things
don't work out the way Will wants them to,
Jess might need a shoulder to cry on."

"Or he will," Jake chimed in. "Come on, guys. The man has asked for our help. We can't turn our backs on him."

"Thank you," Will said. "And for the record, I don't want any of you as witnesses to the proposal. As soon as Jess and I get there, you're to take off, not hide in the bushes making rude noises or something. We're not twelve, for goodness' sake."

"We wouldn't do that," Mack said indignantly.

"Speak for yourself," Connor said.

Will stood up and glared at him. "Do not make me regret this," he said grimly.

"You won't," Mack said, standing to give him an awkward hug. "Right, Jake?"

"Absolutely. We've got your back," Jake said, directing his own scowl toward Connor and Kevin.

Kevin glanced toward his brother, then sighed. "Count us in, right, Connor?"

"I'm in," Connor agreed.

Will nodded.

"When's the big night?"

"Sunday," Will said. "It was a Sunday when she called me to rescue her from Moonlight Cove. I figure that was the real start of things changing between us. I'm hoping she'll see the significance of that."

"You do realize you're going to show all of us up with this grand gesture of yours," Kevin said. "Our wives will never let us hear the end of it."

"And you're setting the bar real high for Mack, here," Jake teased. "Susie's going to expect something spectacular."

"I'm pretty sure my cousin would be satisfied with an actual invitation to dinner that includes the option of sex after," Connor said.

"You don't know a blasted thing about what Susie needs," Mack retorted.

"I'm just saying—"

"Well, don't," Mack said, putting an end to the topic. "I'll see you all on Sunday. What time, Will?"

"Two o'clock?" Will suggested. "After Sunday dinner."

"Works for me," Connor said.

With the others in agreement, Mack took off, slamming the door behind him.

Connor winced. "Was it something I said?" he asked dryly.

"Yes," the others replied in unison.

"I think the subject of Susie is a touchy one these days," Will said. "Maybe you should leave it alone."

"He's never gotten all bent out of shape before," Connor protested.

"Well, he did today," Jake said, his expression worried. "Will's right. We need to leave it alone. Whatever's going on with those two, they need to figure it out for themselves."

"Suits me," Kevin said. "Is there some kind of a game on? All this talk about relationships and romance is getting to me. I need a dose of testosterone."

"Done," Will said, flipping on the TV and finding a basketball game.

Not that he was able to concentrate on it. All he could think about was what might—or might not—happen just a few days from now when he asked Jess to marry him.

One by one on Sunday, Jake, Will, Connor and Kevin made their excuses and left the O'Brien house. Jess stared after them.

"Something's up with those guys," she said, looking to her sisters-in-law for confirmation. Bree, Heather and Shanna merely shrugged.

"I have no idea what's going on in Connor's head half the time," Heather said.

"Ditto," Shanna said of Kevin. "The man keeps everything to himself until I pry it out of him."

"Then you really don't know what they're up to?" Jess asked.

"Not a clue," Heather assured her. "Do you have plans with Will later? Maybe he'll fill you in."

"I guess I do," Jess said. "He mentioned he'd stop by the inn around six, but who knows? Sometimes things come up. Especially lately. The few dates he's made, he's broken at the last minute. He says it's because of the Lunch by the Bay situation."

Bree studied her knowingly. "How are you handling that?"

"I panic, of course," Jess admitted. "But I'm getting better. Most of the time Will does exactly what he says he's going to do. And when he can't, he calls at least, so I'm not waiting and wondering."

"Why don't you hang out here with us this afternoon?" Bree suggested. "It's been ages since we've all gotten together for some good, old-fashioned girl talk." She glanced up just then and spotted Megan in the doorway. "Mom, how about it? Want to sit around and gossip?"

Megan's gaze went straight to Jess. "I thought you had things to do at the inn."

"I do, but if I head over there now, I'll just be worrying about whether or not Will's going to show up. I might as well hang out here."

Megan shook her head. "I think you need to be there."

Jess regarded her mother with suspicion. "Mom, do you know something the rest of us don't?"

"Not really," Megan said, but the flush in her cheeks said otherwise.

"Spill it," Jess commanded.

Megan chuckled. "I can't do that. Trust me, though, you need to go home. And don't you dare stay here just to be stubborn."

Jess reluctantly stood. "Nothing like getting kicked out of my own home."

"Your home is at the inn," Megan reminded her. "At least that's what you've always told me whenever I've suggested you move back in here with your father and me."

"Uh-oh, she's got you there," Heather said. "Now run along. Something tells me that once you're out of the room, we can get your mother to blab to us about whatever's going on with the guys."

"I've been known to eavesdrop," Jess threatened.

"Do you really want to spoil the surprise, if there is one?" Bree asked. "Just go home, sweetie."

Jess didn't like it, but she went, muttering all the way back to the inn. She hated being left out of the loop, especially with her own family.

Determined not to dwell on whatever it might be that her mother hadn't told her, she changed into old jeans and a baggy sweater and went up to the attic. Mick had been making good progress. The large, open room that would eventually be here was taking shape. The windows had already been installed, giving her a sweeping view of the bay and the town.

Though she'd planned on cleaning up some of the construction debris just to keep busy, she found herself instead sitting by the window gazing out at the reflection of the sunset. Though the sun set behind the inn, it still turned the water into a shimmering, fiery spectacle.

That's where she was sitting when she saw Kevin's boat, the one he'd donated to Uncle Thomas's foundation, pull up to the dock. To her surprise, it was Will who leapt onto the dock and secured it.

She started down the stairs and heard him call her name as he came through the front door.

"On my way down," she said. As she rounded the landing, she said, "Why do you have Kevin's boat?"

"We're taking it out," he said.

She stared at him. "Are you crazy? It's freezing out there. It's not a night to be on the water."

"Which is why you need to run back upstairs and dress warmly," he said, his expression unrelenting. "I have a surprise for you."

"I'm not sure how I feel about a surprise that requires me to freeze my butt off."

He laughed. "You'll like this one. I promise. Now, scoot."

Though she still had her doubts, she trusted Will enough by now to do as he'd requested. She changed into wool slacks, a long-sleeved shirt and sweater, then added lined boots, her heaviest winter jacket, a hat and a scarf.

"I feel like an overstuffed snowman or something," she grumbled when she joined Will downstairs.

"Stop complaining. You'll be grateful for every layer."

Once they were out on the boat and Will had moved into the bay's open waters, the air seemed to cut right through her clothes. "Will, this is crazy. We should go back."

"We won't be on the boat for long. Look up."

She followed the direction in which he was pointing and caught a glimpse of a full moon above, only partially visible between the dark clouds that seemed to be rolling in.

"It's going to rain," she predicted.

"It is not going to rain. If anything, we'll get some snow. Stop being such a pessimist."

"Snow?" she echoed sarcastically. "Just what everyone wants when they're at sea on a boat with an open deck."

"You can always go below until we get where we're going," he said.

"Which will be when?"

"Ten, maybe fifteen more minutes."

She sucked in a breath and stared at him. "Moonlight Cove? On a night like this?"

"Trust me," Will requested quietly.

Jess looked into his eyes and felt herself relax for the first time since he'd brought her on this whole outrageous excursion. "I do."

She stood beside him at the helm as he guided the boat into the cove.

And then she saw it, some kind of bonfire ahead on the shore. She turned to him in wonder. "That's for us?"

"It is," he said with a smile. "What do you think?"

"I think you're just a little bit crazy. You didn't start it, then take off without someone to keep an eye on it, did you?"

"Have you ever known me to be irresponsible?"

"Never," she conceded. "Who's here?"

"Doesn't matter. If all goes according to plan, they'll be gone as soon as we set foot on shore."

"About that. You can't take this boat all the way into shore."

"I know, which is why I brought along

my double kayak. We'll anchor the boat, then row in. You game?"

She smiled at him, suddenly eager for whatever lay ahead. "I've come this far. I see no reason to stop now."

When the boat was secure, Will lowered his kayak, then helped her down to it before following, himself. As they rowed toward shore, Jess could see that he'd done far more than build a bonfire. Around the perimeter, there were hundreds of big white candles buried in the sand. In among them were baskets of flowers far too delicate to survive long in the cold. For the moment, though, they were beautiful. She could smell the scent of roses as soon as her feet touched shore.

"Will, it's absolutely beautiful. This may be the most romantic setting I've ever seen."

She heard a subtle cough from the direction of the woods and chuckled. "Your helpers, I presume."

"My helpers, who were just leaving," Will said loudly.

There was more rustling from the surrounding woods, then the sound of the motor on Kevin and Connor's little fishing boat. Only when the chugging had faded into the distance did Will lead her to a blanket where there were glasses, wine and a picnic waiting.

"Why did you do all this?" she asked, looking into his eyes. "You should know by now that you don't have to impress me."

"I think I do," he said. "Especially now. I have a lot to make up for. I've been neglecting you."

"I appreciate the gesture, but I really do understand why you've been so busy," she said.

"Doesn't mean that my not being around hasn't worried you," he said, his gaze on hers. "Am I right?"

Jess nodded. "A little. You know me too well."

"I've been trying to tell you that. But that's not entirely why I did all this. I wanted you to have a special memory of Moonlight Cove with me, the kind of memory you'll be able to treasure for a lifetime."

Tears burned in Jess's eyes. "Oh, Will." She reached over and put a hand on his cheek. "I love you."

It was the first time she'd said the words, and she wasn't sure which of them was most surprised, but then Will began to smile.

"It's a good thing," he said softly, "because there's one more thing about tonight."

"What's that?"

He reached in his pocket and drew out two small packages. "This one first," he said.

It was wrapped in midnight-blue paper and tied with silver ribbon, reminding her a bit of the sky, at least on the nights when its scattering of stars were visible. Jess almost hated to open it, but there was nothing she loved more than presents. This one promised to be special.

Inside, she found the most delicate antique gold-and-diamond necklace she'd ever seen. The stones were small, but the perfect size for the gold filigree in which they were set.

"Will, it's lovely," she whispered. "It looks old."

"It was my grandmother's," he said. "She gave it to me before she died and told me to save it for the woman I love. That's you, and I want you to have it now."

"Are you sure?" she asked, almost holding her breath.

"I've never been more sure of anything," he insisted solemnly. "In fact, that's what the second gift is about."

This time the box was smaller, the size of a ring, and like the other one, the velvet was old and somehow familiar. Jess couldn't seem to tear her gaze away, but eventually she did.

"Will?"

Holding her gaze, he slowly flipped open the box.

Jess stared at her great-grandmother's engagement ring, then looked back into his eyes. Her head seemed to be spinning, but maybe that had something to do with the glass of champagne she'd had while sitting up in the attic waiting for him.

"Where'd you get this?" she asked, though the answer was obvious. Her mother must have given it to him, unless he'd taken up jewel thievery in his spare time.

"Your mother thought it might make the perfect engagement ring. She said both your grandmother and your great-grandmother wore it and had long and happy marriages."

"Why would my mother give you an engagement ring?"

He chuckled. "Are you being deliberately difficult? Do you think we could focus on the implication for the two of us? I'm asking you to marry me, Jess O'Brien, and I want you to know that my commitment's for a lifetime, just the way it was for your grandparents and your great-grandparents. The necklace and this ring both represent my faith in what we have, my unwavering belief that it will last a lifetime and be every bit as strong as the marriages that have gone before."

She blinked back tears as she met his gaze. "A ring doesn't guarantee anything," she said stubbornly.

"No, but it can be symbolic. It can stand for my love for you, which has only grown over the years."

"We've just been dating a few months."

"But I fell in love with you when we were fourteen. I'm sure if I'd told anyone that, they'd have dismissed it as puppy love, but I knew better, even then."

She shook her head, trying to understand that kind of certainty. "Will, I do love you, but I'm still trying to catch up."

He gave her a wry look. "I noticed. Now, let's get back to the ring. You know what they say in the wedding ceremony, a ring is a circle, representing something with no end. Now that we've started this, Jess, there's not going to be an ending. I believe that with all my heart. I'm committed to making this work."

"Most people start out believing they can make a marriage last," she said. "If they didn't, they wouldn't bother."

"Ah, but most people don't have someone like me with all these mediating skills to make sure it happens," he said. "Enough excuses, Jess. What's it going to take to convince you that what we have is strong enough to weather anything? Will you ever be any more ready than you are tonight?"

She looked him in the eye. "Kiss me."

Will seemed startled by the command, but he was obviously eager to comply. After a long, searing kiss, he studied her curiously. "Did that help?"

She nodded. "That kiss at Brady's, the one that came out of the blue, was how I first realized I was crazy about you." She grinned. "They've only gotten better."

"Thanks for the vote of confidence. And?"

"If we kiss like that every single day for the rest of our lives, I think we'll have it made," she said, settling into his arms. She wasn't sure which warmed her more, the bonfire or having Will's arms securely around her. She held out her hand and admired the sparkle of the diamond in the firelight. "It's beautiful, isn't it?"

"Beautiful," Will agreed, but when she glanced up, he was staring directly at her, not at the ring. She smiled at him.

"I know I haven't always had a lot of faith in us," she told him. "But I do love you, Will. And I'll promise to do whatever it takes to focus on that and not on all the bumps in the road."

"Now there's a promise I can get behind," he said, breathing a sigh of relief.

The road ahead might not be smooth. Jess recognized that, but she also knew it was going to be the journey of a lifetime.

It was then, as they were warmed by the heat of their kisses, surrounded by the heat from the bonfire, that the snow began to fall.

"I think it's a sign," Will whispered against her lips.

"A sign of what?"

"That our lives are going to be touched by magic."

Jess caught a snowflake on the tip of her tongue, then laughed. "I thought they already were."

* * * * *

Look for *Beach Lane* by Sherryl Woods, the next story in her Chesapeake Shores series, on sale from MIRA Books in June 2011 at your favorite retail outlet.

DISCUSSION GUIDE

1. Jess O'Brien has struggled throughout her life with attention deficit disorder. Do you know anyone who has dealt with ADD or attention deficit hyperactivity disorder (ADHD)? Did medication help? Were there strategies that helped them, especially as adults, cope with daily living and organizational issues?

2. In addition to her ADD, Jess was also deeply affected by the departure of her mother when Jess was only seven. In what ways do you think this affected Jess and her relationships in later years? Have you had to deal with a parent leaving after a divorce? Or have you ever been the parent who left? How did you handle those situations?

3. Jess's relationship with Megan has been cautious at best ever since her mother returned to Chesapeake Shores. Jess eventually realizes that she'll never be truly happy unless she lets go of the

past. Have you ever been deeply hurt by someone and held on to the anger? How did you eventually forgive and reconcile, or did you?

4. Jess, Connie and Laila turn to an online dating service in an attempt to liven up their social lives. Have you ever used a dating service? How was the experience? Do you think it's a good way to meet new people? What are the benefits and risks compared to other ways to meet new people?

5. Will uses his experience as a psychologist to devise the Lunch by the Bay dating questionnaire. Do you think it's possible to design a test that will reveal true compatibility? What about the likely chemistry between two people? Is there some way to measure that? How important is attraction versus compatibility?

6. Will has known Jess for most of her life and is well aware of all of her flaws, as well as her strengths. Initially Jess feels as if he knows her almost too well. Do

you think that's possible? Is his deeper understanding of her a blessing or a curse? Do you have or would you want a partner who truly "gets" you?

7. When Connor thinks momentarily that Jess has lost track of his son at a fall festival, she is obviously hurt by his re-action. Why do you think her brother's attitude affected her so deeply?

8. The romance between Thomas and Connie takes everyone by surprise. Why do you think that is? Is it because of the age difference? Or the compli-cated family dynamics? How much is concern for Nell O'Brien's reaction be-cause of her deeply held religious be-liefs about divorce? Do you think Nell responded appropriately by giving them her blessing despite her own convic-tions?

9. Will deliberately chose Moonlight Cove as the place to propose to Jess. What significance do you think there was in that choice? Or was he simply trying to create a particularly romantic setting?

10. Both the ring and the necklace Will gave to Jess when he proposed had a long family history behind them. Do you think that made them more meaningful for Jess? In what way?